Secret Vendetta

Secret Vendetta

BOOK 1 OF THE VENDETTA DUET

KATHY LOCKHEART

Editor: Susan Staudinger
Proofreader: Jovana Shirley, Unforeseen Editing, www.unforseenediting.com

Cover design:
Model cover design: © By Hang Le
Photographer: Michelle Lancaster (www.michellelancaster.com)
Discreet Cover: Wild Love Designs

ISBN 978-1-955017-22-0 e-book
ISBN 978-1-955017-15-2 Paperback
ISBN 978-1-955017-23-7 Hardcover
ISBN 978-1-955017-24-4 Paperback (alternate cover)

Published by Rosewood Literary Press

Also by Kathy Lockheart

Deadly Illusion

Fatal Cure

Lethal Justice

Grave Deception

To the ones who believe that behind every villain, there's a love story waiting to be told.

Author's note

While The Vendetta Duet is on the lighter end of the dark romance spectrum, it contains violence and other content that may be triggering for some readers. I prefer you go into a story without spoilers, but if you would like **a list of detailed triggers**, you can find it posted on my website at KathyLockheart dot com.

P.S. SECRET VENDETTA is Book One of the Vendetta Duet and ends on a cliffhanger. The story concludes in Book Two, SILENT VENDETTA.

CHAPTER 1

Luna

I n just nine minutes, Dominic's blood would paint my skin and mark me for death.

Not that I sensed the cataclysmic chain of events that would soon unfold. Standing here right now, all I knew was that sweat laced my palms, just like it always did before hearing the jury's verdict.

This anxiousness was honestly a good thing, though, because it reminded me how much my clients meant to me—the underprivileged people who didn't have the means to defend themselves against a powerful and imperfect system. I'd become a public defender to make sure they didn't get railroaded like my father did, who'd been wrongfully convicted for a murder he did not commit.

The day they took him from us, a piece of me was stolen, carved out of my heart with a rusty dagger. A wound that had spread toxins through my blood and never scabbed over.

But at least my dad was still alive. The poor victim my father was accused of killing would never be reunited with loved ones, and I never took for granted that I had a chance to get my father back.

My ultimate goal in life might sometimes seem insurmountable, but so help me, I was going to prove my father was innocent and get him out of prison. It was why I fought against the odds of our financially challenged circumstances to put myself through college and law school to become a criminal defense attorney in Chicago.

Did I meet my share of clients that might be guilty? Of course. And it bothered me, working the cases where people had intentionally broken the law, but defending them didn't mean helping them evade consequences; it meant ensuring their rights were protected and their punishments were in line with their crimes. Plus, I was serving a greater good, upholding the justice system's vital balance, and more frequently than people would assume, I worked cases where I firmly believed my client was innocent.

Like this one.

Dominic was not guilty of this homicide charge. There was no physical evidence tying him to the shooting of the victim, and Dominic's ex-girlfriend—who claimed he did it—was an unreliable ex with a vendetta against him for breaking up with her. As for the victim owing Dominic money—the alleged motive—the victim owed many people money.

Besides, I knew Dominic. After my dad was arrested when I was in elementary school, Dominic stood up for me when other kids picked on me for our family's tragedy—at his own social expense. That takes some serious moral character, if you ask me, and there was no way the boy who used to rescue caterpillars from the sidewalk before they'd be stepped on could have taken a life.

He'd moved away a few years later, and we'd lost touch, but he'd always held a special place in my heart.

So, when Dominic was indicted, I jumped at the chance to defend him. Professionally, I was confident in the case we'd built. Personally, a gnawing fear strangled my chest—what if it wasn't enough?

I watched the eight men and four women of this jury walk to their seats, scanning their faces, searching for any clue which way this was about to go.

Judge Alcon shifted his gaze to the twelve jurors. "Ladies and gentlemen of the jury, have you reached a verdict?"

Papers rustled, wooden seats creaked, and a bead of sweat slid down my back in the oppressive air. The columns that flanked the judge's mahogany bench stood as strong as some of the verdicts handed down to people—the future of many lives changed forever with two powerful decisions: guilty or not guilty.

"We have, Your Honor," the foreman said.

"Would the defendant please rise?" Judge Alcon looked over his wired glasses at our table.

Dominic and I both rose to our feet. I squared my shoulders, memories of sleepless nights and tireless work steadying me, yet I still couldn't stop the tension from trying to squeeze my temples to death.

"We, the jury, in the above-entitled action, find the defendant, Dominic Hopkins…"

Hearing those words brought me back to when I was a little girl, my Mary Janes swinging inches from the courtroom floor, anxious for them to finally let my daddy come home and help me finish the tree house we'd started building together—having no idea that instead, we were about to enter a new hell.

"Not guilty."

I released a breath so deep, that it turned into a shuddering sigh, a heavy weight having lifted from my chest, allowing me to breathe fully and freely.

Dominic's chest sank six inches, too, and he closed his eyes as if allowing the significance of this moment to fully sweep into his heart before eventually looking at me.

"I don't know how I'll ever repay you," Dominic whispered, every word dripping with gratitude.

"Your freedom is the only reward I need."

How wonderful that the grim chapter in his life had finally ended, and ahead lay a blank canvas, ripe with opportunities and hope. As his public defender, what a fantastic victory for me, too. Not many had managed to score a win against the prosecutor, ADA Hunter Lockwood, whose record was nearly as unblemished as an untouched snowfield.

But beneath my joy, an uncomfortable ache stirred within me like an insidious fog at sunrise.

If only Dad had this same outcome.

A good person wouldn't have such a selfish emotion in someone else's victory, but I guess it was only human to have envy creep into such a pivotal moment. During the nineteen years my father had already served, he'd lost monumental parts of his life he could never get back. The joy of raising his only daughter, the intoxicating taste of freedom, and tragically, the ember of hope that life would ever get better.

Hope that he'd ever reclaim a life where he could experience the blades of grass beneath his toes. Or smell the enchanting fragrance of wildflowers on a countryside walk, hear the symphony of crickets serenading the night—a chorus that once accompanied him holding hands with his daughter under a starlit sky.

Now, the vibrant memories of being truly alive had faded, much like whispers lost to a dying breeze, their essence dissipating as time stretched on, until all that remained were haunting reminders of what had been lost.

All because a different courtroom, ruled by the blind eyes of justice, had gotten it catastrophically wrong.

"Thank you." Dominic wrapped his arms around me—his neck slightly damp from perspiration—just as he'd done right after my father went to prison.

The warmth of his embrace transported me back, the weight of that first hug after my father's imprisonment heavy in my chest.

"I'm so sad." Tears stung my eyes, and a choked sob slipped out.

I traced the cold, untouched sheets on my bed where Dad usually sat, reading tales of heroes and far-off lands, his voice lulling me to dreams.

Dominic pulled me into a tight embrace, letting my tears soak into his shirt, which carried the comforting smell of butter cookies—a scent that reminded me of simpler times.

Now, nothing would ever be simple again. I wanted to throw things and scream at how unfair this was, but this heartbreak was so excruciating, all my energy had been sucked from me.

Softly, with a trembling voice, I admitted, "I wish I could close my eyes and never wake up."

"I'm so happy for you." I forced a smile through the searing pain in my ribs.

After the judge dismissed the jury and finished the court's proceeding, Dominic's cousin, Franco, walked up and squeezed Dominic's shoulder.

Which was odd. I'd have expected a bigger reaction than that.

Hunter Lockwood, on the other hand, pinched the bridge of his nose in apparent disbelief that he'd suffered a rare loss.

The guy had a seriously intimidating win rate. I knew that if I had any hope of beating him, I needed to do some recon, so for his last two trials, I'd sat in the back of the courtroom, taking notes of which objections he raised, and which ones he didn't. The types of questions he asked witnesses and the types he didn't. The goal was to study his moves and create kick-ass countermoves, like a stealth ninja he'd never see coming.

My hormones didn't seem to get the memo that I was there for a purely professional reason, though. They started to fixate on non-recon things. Like the sound of his voice—which was seductively deep and seemed to echo off the walls before sliding over my skin like a caress. And how the guy was Greek god–level gorgeous. His black hair was always perfectly cut like a model, and whenever he'd take his suit jacket off, I had to pry my stupid eyes from the muscles pressing against his shirt, or else I risked becoming hypnotized into a sexual haze.

And then there was his distractingly gorgeous face. Dark facial stubble framed his perfectly sculpted jaw and pouty lips, and his cerulean eyes were so captivating that they could make you forget the next point in your argument.

But whatever.

I assured myself I was not attracted to Hunter Lockwood. Refused to be. I mean, the guy was trying to put Dominic in prison, for crying out loud. I could control...whatever this was. Attraction, I think. An F5 version of it, but still. I could do this.

All I had to do was avoid him.

When this trial started, he made it easy. Aside from the judge, jury, and occasional witness on the stand, Hunter Lockwood never looked at anyone. People speculated it was a tactic he used to maintain a competitive advantage—to dehumanize the defendant—but whatever his reasons, he'd walk into court each day staring at his phone, and once seated, he'd look down at his papers, making notes in perfect penmanship.

Never looking at anyone else. Certainly not me.

Until now.

Hunter's eyes shot through the distance between us like an arrow flying through the air, landing on its target: my face.

His stare definitely activated some kind of launch sequence in my lower belly.

Traitorous hormones.

I'd expected him to look hostile, angry, even, since he'd lost, but as his gaze swept over me, his eyebrows relaxed into what appeared to be curiosity.

"Luna Payne," Elizabeth Wood said. This terribly inconvenient heat in me wanted to plead with her to come back another time, but I kept it together. It wasn't easy to drag my attention away from Hunter to smile at her, though. Not easy at all. "Tell me you've reconsidered my boss's offer."

Elizabeth had made a name for herself in Chicago over the past decade at the private firm she worked for.

"You're too good to be a public defender." She raised her sharply drawn eyebrows. "Come work with me. We need you."

"These people need me."

She frowned. "My boss said she'll increase her last offer by fifty percent. That's three times what you make now. Plus better benefits."

The figures swirled tantalizingly in my mind, almost making me reconsider. After all, retrying Dad's case was going to be expensive.

But that was the whole problem with public defenders. The really good ones would get snatched up by pricey law firms, leaving only the inexperienced and inferior ones behind. The vulnerable people who relied on public defenders needed excellent attorneys by their side, or they could face the same nightmare my father had gone through.

Plus, Elizabeth's firm was also known for working their lawyers to the bone, and that bloated salary wouldn't help my father's case if I had zero time to work on it.

"I'm flattered you're interested in me." I offered a gracious nod. "But I'm happy where I'm at."

Hunter Lockwood rose to his feet, packing up his papers.

Elizabeth's eyes darted in the same direction as mine, catching where my attention had drifted.

"You know he made Chicago's most desirable bachelor again this year," she announced.

Of course he did.

"Those blogs should report on more important stories," I said. Like innocent people wasting away in overcrowded prisons for crimes they didn't commit. "I don't get why he's spending his days as a lawyer, anyway." Thanks to his father's estate, Hunter was a billionaire before he even went to law school. "He wears a $9,000 Brioni suit every day and arrives at the courthouse in his charcoal-gray Aston Martin DBS. I googled it. Know how much it's worth? Base price: $330,000."

"Googling him, huh?" Elizabeth's eyes sparked with a mischievous glint, making my neck catch fire.

"The guy just tried to put my friend behind bars," I reminded her.

"You and I both know he was just doing his job," she countered. "Besides, with a jawline and bank account like that, he could collect toenail clippings and put them into alphabetized jars for all I care."

I bit back a smile.

Did she have to look *that* delighted when Hunter started moving?

"Speak of the devil." Elizabeth grinned a little too wide, thank you very much, and walked toward the exit, adding, "Congratulations on your win today, Luna."

And then, God help me, Hunter headed toward me. He kept his eyes locked on mine, buttoning his jacket slowly.

I kept my chin up, hoping to God that my voice box would freaking work if I needed it, because right now, it was suffering from an instant case of severe dehydration.

Hunter stopped in front of me, putting his hands into his pockets while mine began to sweat again—this time from pheromone poisoning.

"We haven't been formally introduced. I'm Hunter."

"I know." *Beginner's guide to humiliating oneself. Step one: light a match. Step two: engulf cheeks. Step three: hold shoulders square and respond how you should have to begin with.* "I'm Luna."

"Luna." He nodded gently. "You're the public defender everyone's been talking about."

Ugh, I figured hearing him this close to me for the first time wouldn't be that different from hearing him in court. Wrong. His dark and sensual voice would absolutely be replaying in my ears all night, no matter how much I fought it.

"The one wreaking havoc on the state's conviction rate."

"That's an exaggeration," I assured. "But thank you."

He held still for a second. Probably sensed I needed a minute to recover from his sensuality.

"Only a sparse few have won against me in court." Hunter's gaze raked over my face so meticulously, he seemed to be cataloging every pigment of my skin and thick, wavy brown hair before navigating to my attire.

A suit I'd snagged off the clearance rack at the outlet store I could afford. One with a tiny red stain on the right sleeve that earned it an additional 75% off. In the store, I'd convinced myself no one would notice—it was only the size of a pencil eraser—but of course, Hunter Lockwood's eyes zeroed in on said stain.

Of course.

I slammed my hand over the unfortunate ink, and dammit if he didn't smirk before dragging his gaze back to mine.

Good Lord.

That smirk of his did all sorts of unwanted things to me, and those eyes bored into me, commanding attention with a magnetic pull. It was as if I stood defenseless in the face of a raging cyclone, his tempestuous storm of a gaze sucking me into his vortex. Where I'd willingly surrender.

Heck, I'd grab a freaking patio umbrella to make it easier to be swept into his whipping winds.

"You're not what I expected." His voice was a low murmur, the corners of his mouth twitching with a hint of playfulness. "You're rather...intriguing."

Intriguing.

Someone who passed the bar on her first try shouldn't have her knees literally weaken at his compliment.

He's your professional adversary, Luna. Do. Not. Encourage. These. Butterflies. For. Hunter. Lockwood.

"There's a sea of reporters out front." His voice dipped with a touch of regret, making me wonder if he'd been looking forward to giving a statement like he usually did whenever he'd win a case. This story had drummed up regional interest because a local politician happened to be at the bar, having a drink when the homicide occurred.

"I'll be taking my client out to give a statement." Hopefully, once I left Hunter's orbit, my IQ would return.

"No, you won't," Franco said.

I turned around to see that both Franco and Dominic had come closer.

"Dominic, the media slaughtered you." Just like they slaughtered my father all those years ago. Always wanting a villain for their story and casting someone in the role, innocence be damned. "You deserve to tell them they got it wrong."

And let's be honest. I'm salivating at the chance, too. Not just because of Dominic, but also because nineteen years ago, I'd been too young to give the press a piece of my mind.

"We don't need the press, Dom," Franco said.

Some unspoken warning passed between them, something that crackled in my bones. I was convinced Dominic was innocent, so why was his cousin giving me the opposite vibe?

Franco glowered at Dominic. "No press."

"They're going to swarm you for a statement."

Please let Dominic prepare *something* for them—having your creepy cousin glare at reporters wouldn't make them see they'd been wrong. Plus...

"If you refuse to give them one, they might just follow you to your car."

"Then I'll pull it around back. I'll meet you behind the courthouse, Dominic."

With one last glare at Hunter, Franco walked out of the room.

"I'm giving a statement." I took a small step closer to Dominic. "I hope you'll join me, but even if you don't, I'll still be addressing the reporters."

Dominic pulled his lips into a smile that didn't quite reach his eyes.

"Thanks again, Luna. I appreciate all you did for me. I'll, uh..." He put his hand on the back of his neck, watching where his cousin had vanished. "I'll call you later, yeah?"

For a man who had just been found not guilty, what was with him walking with his head cast down and his steps slow—dragging his feet as he walked away?

"Well," Hunter said, "maybe you should reconsider your victory speech."

Fat chance. "No. Someone needs to defend Dominic in the public eye." Otherwise, they'd just spin his not-guilty verdict as an injustice, and I was tired of it.

Hunter stood there for a moment—looking like a fallen angel among us mortals, damn it—while his eyes seemed to savor my every detail.

"Well," he finally said, "congratulations, Luna. You certainly kept me on my toes."

He winked at me—while I pretended I didn't have a hot flash over it—and then ambled off, female groupies all rising in their pews, ready to worship their god. But he ignored every one of them calling his name as he left.

Thank goodness that encounter was over. I'd gone my entire life without acting like a seventh-grade girl drawing hearts in my notebook, and I sure as hell wasn't about to start now.

I was allergic to relationships—which was another whole story.

Relationships? Why the hell did *that* word enter my mind? This was nothing more than attraction—unwanted attraction at that, and it would fade.

I would make sure of it.

I quickly packed up my belongings, touched up my lipstick, and started my path to the front of the courthouse, where reporters would be waiting on the steps.

A sudden chime from my cell phone broke my train of thought.

Charlotte: Have you heard?

I stopped cold. Charlotte and I didn't text very often; we had no reason to, outside of the fact our dads were friends. Her father was my dad's only friend, truthfully. They'd been cellmates for five years.

Me: Heard what?

The three dots on my screen pulsated, my throat growing drier with each one.

Charlotte: Your father is hurt.

My feet cemented to the floor as my heart began spasming.

Me: Hurt how? Is he okay?

Charlotte: I don't know. I don't have the authority to call and check up on him, but my dad was visiting another friend at the prison and heard.

Me: What happened?

And why hadn't the prison called me?

Charlotte: A fight broke out, and your dad is in the infirmary.

The prison hospital.

My stomach collapsed in on itself.

Me: Thank you for telling me, Charlotte. Seriously, thank you.

And then I turned and started jogging to the opposite end of the courthouse, where my car was parked.

Instantly, my reasons for hiding it in the back parking lot seemed insignificant. My car was a piece of crap, and I wanted to avoid the possibility of some reporter following me all the way to it. Looking professional was imperative, particularly to my clients who were scared, and I didn't want them to think that their lawyer was so incompetent with finances that she couldn't afford a basic car payment. So, I parked it out of sight.

I jogged down the bustling main corridor, veering right into a quieter hallway. Then I hung a left, another right, and finally, I headed down the last passageway leading to the back parking lot, wondering...

What happened to my father?

Was he going to be okay?

He shouldn't even be in that godforsaken prison!

The exterior door gave way with a forceful push, and the summer's sweltering heat assaulted me. The rhythmic click of my heels echoed on the asphalt, and as I rounded a colossal truck that obscured my vision, preparing to navigate through the sea of vehicles, a sudden snag caught my foot.

I stumbled, my palms scraping against the unforgiving pavement. With wide, horrified eyes and a dread washing over me, I absorbed a scene that would forever be etched into my nightmares.

I had tripped over a lifeless leg, belonging to someone that was bleeding profusely.

No. Not someone.

Dominic.

While a menacing figure, cloaked in dark cloth, stood over Dominic with a knife, its serrated edge dripping with crimson.

I realized with horror that it was Dominic's blood, which was also dripping from a gash in Dominic's neck, his skin filleted gruesomely like a steak. The assailant standing over him wore a split-face mask, one side red, the other side black, with a strange gray mesh covering the eyes from view. Still, I felt those eyes boring into me.

The woman who'd just stumbled onto Dominic's murder.

The comforting warmth of the sun retreated, and every sound faded into a deafening silence as an ominous chill crawled up my spine, weaving icy tendrils around my ribs.

As I stared at a wolf who'd cornered a lamb that had wandered into his den.

CHAPTER 2
Luna

Every movement, every sound, seemed to halt, as if the world held its breath with me.

The sun's heat was merciless as it beat down on the iron-scented blood, which mixed with the faint smell of engine oil leaking onto the ground from a rusted pickup truck I'd fallen next to. A rainbow of colors shimmered off the rows of vehicles, which were flanked by the courthouse on one side, and a grass embankment overgrown with dandelions on the other. Somewhere in the distance, a plane droned on, its sound battling against the loud thud of my heartbeat echoing in my ears.

Among all of it, my gaze was drawn back to the blood dripping from the cruel metal blade.

Poor Dominic had been spared spending the rest of his life in prison, only to be killed. Why?

The assailant, who appeared to be male, remained motionless, his masked gaze pinning me in place.

The air seemed to contract, suffocating, choking the very oxygen from my lungs.

Run, the voice inside my head whispered urgently.

As I scrambled to my feet, a faint, agonized moan from Dominic anchored me to the spot.

Oh my God. He's still alive.

If I fled, it would sentence Dominic to death—be it from bleeding out or suffering another vicious strike from his cold-blooded killer. But if I stayed…

The masked man seemed to assess me.

Was he debating which victim to strike next?

I scanned the ground around me, desperate for a weapon, spotting a shard of glass the size of a dinner knife glistening in the sun. I grabbed it and ignored the biting pain as it cut into my flesh.

"Back away." I held the makeshift knife out in front of me with a shaking hand.

His weapon outmatched mine, but he had a jugular just like the rest of us.

"You come any closer, hand to God, I'll stab you," I warned.

His lips—the only part of his body exposed—curled up slightly.

That's when the haunting recognition hit me.

The long-sleeved black shirt, black pants, black combat boots. Black gloves, dual-colored mask that covered his head, neck, and face, and the unusual mesh concealing his eyes. It was the same attire people had described after witnessing violent attacks. Not many people had seen him—he was usually stealthy when he'd commit his crimes, but every once in a while, he was spotted.

"You're the Windy City Vigilante." My voice trembled.

Echoes of footsteps rippled through the eerie silence, and the Vigilante's head swiveled in that direction before he took off running, vanishing between the sea of vehicles.

Collapsing beside Dominic, I pressed my hands against his neck, desperate to staunch the bleeding. The blood saturated the ground next to him, seeping into the asphalt cracks like gruesome creeks and pooling outward. Its iron scent mixed with the hot rubber and tar of asphalt, which dug its coarse texture into my knees.

My arms trembled as Dominic's warm blood escaped through the gaps between my fingers, hot tears blurring my vision.

"Someone help us!" My voice seemed muffled, swallowed by the sweltering vastness of the empty parking lot, but Dominic's blood was all too loud, my fingers slick as I tried to stop the flow.

"Hold on, Dominic. You're going to be okay," I whispered, but even the light breeze was mocking, bringing no relief. The world was uncomfortably still, the hum of distant cars only emphasizing our isolation, and his skin was already a ghastly white, his lungs making a gurgling sound.

And then, his eyelids fluttered before slowly descending, sealing away the life behind them.

"Don't go," I sobbed. The same two words I'd said to my father all those years ago. He'd had as much choice in being hauled off to prison as Dominic did to losing his life.

"Help!" I cried again, the shimmering screen of my phone on the nearby ground beckoning me. But using it to call 911 meant releasing my pressure from his wound.

Footsteps stomped closer.

Oh God, what if that's not help? What if the Vigilante changed his mind and was coming back to finish us both off?

"Dom!" Franco, Dominic's cousin, ran and knelt at Dominic's side. "What the fuck happened?"

"When I came outside, his throat was cut. Here, put pressure on his neck."

I moved my hand to Dominic's wrist.

His vein isn't throbbing. No!

I placed my palms on his chest.

"He was still *conscious*?" Franco asked.

"He *was*."

Something passed through Franco's eyes, as though a calculation inside a computer was taking place in his mind. Whatever answer the equation spit out, Franco's face hardened, and he glared at me with a look that sent cold shock waves through my core.

I began pumping his chest. *One. Two.*

"What did he tell you?"

I snapped my stare to his. "What?"

Three. Four.

Franco frantically rifled through Dominic's pockets, one after the other.

"What are you doing?" I asked. "Stop it! You need to keep pressure on his neck!"

Five. Six.

Franco bolted to his feet and grabbed my upper arms, making me gasp.

"Where is it?" Franco yelled.

I tried to yank away from him, but he was too strong.

"Let me go!" I shrieked. "Dominic needs CPR!"

"Where is it?" he snapped again.

I tried once more to twist away but failed.

"Where is *what?*" I shot back, looking at Dominic's chest, which desperately needed compressions.

"You play stupid, it ain't going to end well for you."

"I have no clue what you're talking about. Now let me go so I can try to save your cousin!"

Instead, Franco grabbed my throat.

CHAPTER 3
Luna

"And then what happened?" Detective Rinaldi asked.

Her blonde hair was slicked back into a bun so tight, it pulled the skin of her cheekbones up, compensating for the crow's feet around her eyes.

I took a deep, shaky breath. You would think I'd be an expert on how to handle trauma. Turns out, not so much.

"A car drove by, and it scared Franco off. He shoved me down." I'd landed in Dominic's blood. "I resumed CPR but…"

It was too late. I couldn't believe Dominic was dead—it was surreal, like I'd wake up any second and someone would tell me this was all a nightmare. He was still alive when I'd stumbled across him. What if I hadn't wasted so much time walking toward the reporters? If I'd taken a direct route, could I have saved him? Would my presence have been enough to deter the Vigilante's attack, or would I have fallen victim to him, too?

The questions and what-ifs haunted me, lingering in my mind like a ghost, tearing at my soul and leaving me with a sense of emptiness that seemed to swallow me whole.

"And you have no idea what Franco was looking for?"

"No." Why had I been the one to stumble across Dominic, anyway?

Shouldn't Franco have been the one to find him? "Franco *walked* up to us." I shook my head. "But he was supposed to pick Dominic up in his car."

Was that a clue to his strange behavior?

"Deputies found Franco's car with slashed tires," she explained. "We believe the Vigilante did it to give him time to carry out his attack."

I clenched my teeth. The damn Vigilante. It wasn't bad enough that he'd slaughtered Dominic in broad daylight—brazen and arrogant, by the way, to do it in the back of a courthouse. He went through the extra effort to set up his spider's web, slashing tires so no one would come to Dominic's rescue.

What a vile, repulsive excuse of a human. A coward who didn't want his victims to be able to fight back—ambushing them like this and cutting off any chance of hope.

This wasn't just a murder.

It was an execution. And that broke my heart and burned it with white-hot rage in equal parts.

"Is there any evidence on the security cameras?" I asked.

"We're looking into it. Nothing helpful so far," she said.

Of course not. The Vigilante was meticulous in his attacks, never being stupid enough to have his car pop up on street cameras or anything.

"Why would he do this at the courthouse?" I asked. "It's a risky place to kill someone."

"Perhaps he thought this would be his only chance to get to Dominic."

"Or maybe he thinks he's invincible." My voice came out low and biting. "He's gotten away with killing people for two years and counting."

But he wasn't invincible. He would make a mistake someday, and maybe that day was today. Maybe they would finally catch him.

"What the hell happened?" Hunter Lockwood muscled his way past the police officers, their protests falling on deaf ears as he pushed his way through the small crowd gathering—who stood at the far end of the parking lot, gaping at the dead body. Police had already sectioned off the crime scene with two layers. Yellow tape sectioned off the official crime scene while cops manned another layer, to hold people thirty feet away from it.

Only someone with immense influence with law enforcement could get away with breaching that line of cops.

Hunter stared at Dominic, whose skin was ashen after his blood had drained from his body—coating his hair in its sticky death.

A June breeze floated through the air, birds happily singing their melodies, a stark contrast to the clicking of a crime scene camera, documenting the brutality of death.

I had studied crime scene photos before, but there was something different when a man was murdered right in front of you, his blood all over your skin. Something different when the victim was your friend. Something different about pressing your hands to his wound, desperately trying to stop him from dying.

Only to fail.

Hunter's eyes, with laser-sharp intensity, locked on to mine, then trailed down, taking in every blood-smeared detail. I could only imagine what I looked like. Dominic's blood coated parts of my suit, and my right hand was bandaged with gauze, thanks to my pathetic excuse of a weapon.

"You okay?" Shattering the haunting silence, his soft voice was like the calm after a storm, a welcome relief to the ice-cold terror that had gripped me moments ago.

I dared to meet his gaze again, finding refuge in the depths of his warm eyes that reminded me of an ocean wave just before it broke over the sand.

"I'm okay," I managed, trying to convince myself more than him.

His steady stare continued to hold mine, before he seemed to reexamine the blood covering me in more scrutiny. Glaring at my gauzed hand.

"You're bleeding." Notes of anger mingled with concern in his tone.

Among the crimson smeared throughout my body, his eyes

pinpointed the one anomaly, the one discrepancy that was my own blood amid the chaos.

"Luna," he said in a tender murmur. "How badly are you hurt?"

I blinked. "Just my palm." My voice came out in a monotone. "The EMTs are going to take me to the ER to get stitched up when I'm done giving my statement."

Hunter's chest inflated, and his attention shifted to the detective standing next to me.

"Should I be worried the Vigilante might come after me, too?" I asked her.

Hunter looked from me to the detective.

"How tall would you say the Vigilante was?" the detective asked.

I blinked hard, willing the fog clouding my mind to lift, forcing the memories to sharpen against the haze of trauma. My gaze slid over Hunter, trying to superimpose the looming figure of the Vigilante over his frame, gauging the differences inch by inch.

"He was about three inches taller than Hunter and twenty pounds heavier. At least."

"Are you sure?"

I nodded. "The Vigilante wore skintight clothing. And his boots were, like, three or four sizes bigger than Hunter's, too."

Rinaldi wrote that in her notebook. "Good. This is good, Luna. You're doing great. Hunter, you're what, six foot one, two hundred twenty pounds?"

He nodded.

"Size eleven?"

"Ten," he corrected.

"Okay, so we'll go with six foot four, two forty. Size fourteen boot?"

"Yeah." My surroundings blurred once more, each sound becoming distant, as the choking grip of shock tried to pull me under. I'm not sure how long I stood there, but eventually, Hunter's hand on my shoulder snapped me out of my trance.

"You done with her?" he asked Rinaldi.

"For now. We're going to transport her to the precinct to collect her clothes," she said.

Which were now evidence.

"Can you collect them here?" Hunter pressed.

"Don't have another outfit on hand," she said.

"I'll take care of that. Got evidence bags?"

After a moment, Rinaldi snapped her fingers toward one of the officers, who brought clear bags with bright red labels on them.

Good. I wanted to get out of here as fast as possible so I could check on my father at the prison infirmary, and changing here was a lot faster than driving to the station.

"Come on." She motioned for me to follow her through the door, where I was met with a gust of air-conditioning that skated over my skin and made the hairs on my arms stand on end as we walked down the hallway and into the women's restroom.

To my surprise, Hunter followed us into the white-tiled room, which housed three stalls and two sinks—one of them leaking with slow drops that echoed in the space.

With a deliberateness that seemed to contrast the chaos outside, he gently placed his laptop bag on the pristine floor with a muted thud. Carefully, he peeled off his suit jacket, followed by his tie, the silk slipping through his fingers like water, pooling on the top of his leather satchel.

And then he began to unbutton his shirt.

Never taking his eyes off me.

"What are you doing?" I managed.

"You're shorter than me. My shirt will be like a dress on you."

As the last button came undone and he slid the fabric off, the sight of his bare torso caught me off guard. Didn't most men wear undershirts beneath their suits? Maybe when you have high-end fabric, you don't need them.

His muscles were exquisite. He probably hired the best chefs, who cooked food packed with vitamins and antioxidants. Probably had a personal trainer, too, working out each muscle into perfection.

He handed his shirt to the officer, flashing me one last concerned gaze before he turned around and faced the wall.

Giving me privacy, evidently.

"Okay," she said. "Take your jacket off, place it carefully in this bag."

I did as she said and repeated it with my shirt and skirt.

Then slid my arms into the sleeves of Hunter's white button-down, which came to my mid-thighs. The silky fabric was going to get ruined with blood. Even though Hunter was a billionaire, it had to cost a thousand dollars, and that was a lot of money he was sacrificing, simply to help me get out of these bloody clothes faster.

"She's done," Rinaldi said.

Hunter, with the slightest hesitation, turned to face me once again, studying me as the detective had me sign each sealed evidence bag.

"EMTs will take you to the hospital now," she said.

"I can't go to the hospital. I have a...personal emergency to deal with."

She arched a brow. "More urgent than a wound that won't stop bleeding?"

Hunter shifted slightly, a flicker of a question evident in the slight tilt of his head.

"Yes."

Her face fell into concern. "Is everything okay?"

"I...I'm not sure. I need to go to Joliet to find out."

Rinaldi blinked. "Your father?"

Many people in law enforcement knew about my father, and evidently, Rinaldi was one of them.

When I nodded, her eyes softened, and the downturn of her lips conveyed a deep, unspoken sympathy.

"Tell you what." Her eyes cast over the blood still smeared across my skin. "How about you let me call them and see what's going on while you clean up in here?"

"I..." Seeing my father myself would ease the knot of anxiety in my chest, but the Joliet Prison—technically called Stateville Correctional Center and located just *outside* Joliet—was an hour and a half drive from here in good traffic. The allure of uncovering my dad's situation swiftly tugged at me. While I could pick up the phone and dial myself, a call from a Chicago detective carried a weight that commanded immediate attention and answers.

"That would be great," I said.

"I'll see what I can find out."

"I'll take her to the ER while you do that." Hunter casually shoved his hands into his pockets.

"No." The last thing I was going to do was spend more time with Hunter Lockwood. My head was spinning from this traumatic experience, and having it hijacked with his spell would make it impossible for my mind to clear.

"*If* I go, I'll go with the EMTs."

"You want to ride in an ambulance?" Hunter asked.

"I can take an Uber."

"Luna"—Hunter stepped forward—"it's just a ride. And we're neighbors."

He knew that? Had he been as surprised as I had been to discover my little cottage was within walking distance of his mansion?

The Lockwood estate sat on a bluff overlooking Lake Michigan, and surrounding it, on the outskirts of the mainland, a scattering of small cottages remained, once used for the many staff working at the main house. The ones that sat empty, the estate manager evidently rented out—presumably because an occupied cottage was better than a vacant one.

Who knew? The point was, what a shock that had been to find out Hunter Lockwood was not only a neighbor, but also technically my landlord. I knew there was a mansion down the way, of course—you couldn't miss it. But I didn't know that it was occupied by Hunter Lockwood until it was too late. I mean, what were the odds? The Chicagoland area had its fair share of affluent areas, and I happened to stumble onto *his* property.

Yes, Hunter was hot, but the walls between my personal life and work had always been sacred. I was too private of a person to live near a work colleague, let alone a courtroom adversary. Let alone become his tenant—that gave him too much power over my living situation, which could create issues that might carry over into the courtroom.

The night I found out, I'd pored over every line of my rental agreement, the glaring cancellation fee making my stomach churn. Still, I scoured other rentals in the area, but thanks to the economy, the only available rentals were way out of my price range.

I'd reasoned he probably didn't even know we were neighbors—we'd never bumped into each other before, and surely, a billionaire wasn't involved with details like tenant agreements. After a while, I concluded I'd never see Hunter in the wild, outside the courthouse.

But now here he was, very much outside the confines of a trial. And, evidently, aware of our neighbor status.

"I'll make that call while you clean up," the detective said. "If you'd like, I can have a deputy go with you to the hospital and make sure you get home safely, given Franco's threat."

Hunter's eyes snapped to me. "Franco threatened you?"

"When someone grabs your throat, the threat is implied," I said.

Hunter's jaw shifted, his voice a growl. "He put his hands on you?"

What was with the anger radiating from his words? Why would Hunter Lockwood care if Franco tried to suffocate me? I mean, sure. A human caring that another human doesn't die was natural, but this —this level was something different.

He flexed his fingers and snapped his focus to Rinaldi. "You'd better find him quickly."

She cocked her head, appearing as confused by Hunter's anger as I was. "Are you and Luna close?"

Hunter's eyes, now stormy and dark, met mine briefly, then swung back to Rinaldi.

"Where I come from, a man who strangles a woman doesn't deserve to exist outside of a jail cell."

Rinaldi's eyebrows furrowed, and after a moment, she looked back at me, either waiting for a response to her original question or seeking an explanation as to why this shirtless heartthrob had gone all ferociously protective.

Even if I wasn't in shock, I wouldn't have the answer to *that*.

"A deputy isn't necessary," I assured. The Chicago police were severely short-staffed these days, and I was more than capable of getting inside my home and locking the doors. I'd rather they use that manpower to actively search for the Vigilante and Franco.

"You sure?" Rinaldi waited a beat after I nodded, then quietly left the room.

Rolling up the too-long sleeves of Hunter's shirt, I stared at myself in the mirror. Crimson clumped the strands of hair together near my shoulder. The EMTs had already cleaned the sticky blood off my right hand when they'd dressed my wound, but only my hand—blood remained on my forearms and had somehow gotten onto my neck of all places.

Dominic's blood. My childhood protector and friend.

I dashed over to the paper towel dispenser and yanked six sheets from it, walking back to the sink and dousing them in water. Scrubbing away the blood on my skin so hard that the paper shredded into pieces.

I bit my lip to keep myself from crying. I was not going to cry, not in front of Hunter Lockwood. Later, I could sob all the tears that I was swallowing right now.

I tossed the blood-soaked paper towels into the trash can and retrieved fresh ones, wetting them, and began working at the back of my neck, where the haunting stickiness of Dominic's dried blood tugged at strands of my hair.

"Here." Hunter's voice was low, full of compassion now rather than anger. "You're missing some spots."

He walked up behind me and took the paper towels from my hand, his fingers grazing mine. I twisted my hair up into a ball on top of my head and looked down so Hunter would have better access to my neck.

"Get it off," I pleaded through a shaky voice. "All of it."

I didn't realize my hand was trembling until Hunter placed his on top of mine.

"You're safe now." The comforting baritone of his voice calmed my tremors, and when I lifted my gaze to the mirror, we locked eyes—quietly existing in the silent space of the aftermath, where past courtroom drama collapsed in the aftershock of violence.

I inhaled shakily, trying to mask the vulnerability in my voice. "Why are you helping me?"

He stroked the skin that met my hairline as gently as he'd spoken, the paper towels' damp coolness soothing my neck.

"You were part of a violent crime, Luna. If there's something I can do to help, I will." There was an undercurrent to his voice, though, some deeper meaning than simply being a Good Samaritan. "Can I ask what happened?" His tone was velvet, as if crafted from the finest dark chocolate, melted to the perfect temperature to caress my senses.

With every stroke of the napkin, I felt one inch closer to myself.

"It was the Windy City Vigilante. He slashed my client's throat. I tried to save Dominic. I grabbed a piece of glass and was going to stab the Vigilante if it came to it, but it didn't help. Dominic still died."

Hunter stilled.

"You were going to *fight* him?" I couldn't tell if his voice was full of shock that it would have put me in more danger or if it was full of judgment at how stupid that would have been. In our line of work, we knew what often happened when a victim tried to fight back in a robbery, for example.

But as Hunter stared at me in the mirror, something else passed over his face—a profound emotion, based on the tightening of his eyebrows.

"It didn't work." I had to swallow the lump in my throat. "Thanks to the Vigilante, Dominic's cousin thinks I have some sort of... evidence against him."

His eyes sharpened. "Evidence?"

"Maybe not evidence. I don't know. He thought I took something from Dominic, and whatever it was, it mattered more to him than giving Dominic CPR."

The door creaked open, revealing Detective Rinaldi, her phone pressed to her ear. She ended the call, her expression unreadable as she faced us.

"Okay. It sounds like there was a fight at the prison. Your father was hurt, but not critically. They're not transporting him to a hospital. They're just treating him in the infirmary, so that's a good sign it's not serious."

"What are his injuries?"

"They wouldn't release that information to me."

"Did someone attack him?" Or was he collateral damage to another fight that broke out?

"I'm not sure. But they said that you can try to call later and that you may be able to visit him tomorrow."

"Tomorrow?" I choked. "I need to see him today."

"It sounds like they're not allowing any visitors right now. But they assured me he's going to be okay."

It was a relief to hear that he was physically okay, but I needed to see him with my own eyes and find out what was going on.

"I'll call the prison myself, see if they'll give me more details," I decided.

Hunter's voice was unwavering, insistent. "*After* I take you to the ER."

"Before you leave," Rinaldi said, "I need to ask Luna something. In private."

CHAPTER 4

Luna

Rinaldi's face was drawn, a deep crease forming between her brows, and her usually firm posture seemed to droop ever so slightly. It felt like an eternity before we were finally alone in the ladies' room.

"Did you find out something else about my father?" My chest tightened.

The hum of the air conditioner vent drifted its icy air over my exposed skin while the sterile white tiles of the bathroom provided a vivid backdrop to the crimson-stained napkins, hastily discarded into the open trash can. A grisly sight that clashed with the faint scent of floral perfume attempting to mask the lingering violence.

"No," she assured. "Listen, I hate to do this, but I'd like to ask you for a favor."

Rinaldi's brown eyes looked almost amber in this light, casting hues of frustration that settled into the cracks of her nude lipstick.

"This Vigilante has been a plague infecting this city for nearly two years now. He tries to justify his criminal activity as retribution for crimes allegedly perpetrated by his victims, but he's nothing more than a serial killer. And he needs to be stopped. Not many people have seen him, though."

Rinaldi scratched the side of her face so harshly, that it left a red mark.

"And those that have were typically at night, in the dark, making the visual descriptions unreliable. You're the first one who's had a good look at him, and given your exceptional standing as a criminal attorney and the fact that he killed one of your clients—"

"Friend," I corrected.

"Right. I think you'd be the best face to make our fight more public. To turn up the heat on this bastard."

I clenched my fists so hard, fresh blood oozed from the stinging slice on my palm. Why hadn't the heat been a freaking inferno before? If it had been, maybe Dominic would still be alive.

Why was this guy still on the loose?

My father did *nothing* and was locked up within a couple of days of that person's death. This Vigilante had been *murdering* people *repeatedly* for two years and was still on the loose. Free to live his life, free to hunt his next victim.

Maybe the cops hadn't worked as hard as they could because he'd targeted some not-so-nice people, but for God's sake, he had at least two dozen suspected deaths tied to his name.

Or maybe he had been a top priority, but the Vigilante moved through the city like a shadow—always a step ahead, elusive, mocking their best efforts.

"I'd like to do a press conference later today." She cracked her knuckles. "While the news outlets are still circling for blood, I'd like you to give a statement."

Of course police would want a fresh face on this. Having a killer at large for this long was making law enforcement look weak. Escalating frustrations over their lack of progress had been rumbling through the rumor mill—especially when the Vigilante was giving the justice system a black eye in the process.

You would think being the most dangerous and feared man in the city would make everyone hate him. But everywhere I looked, graffiti of the Vigilante's initials, if you will—WCV—was paired with either "Hero" or "Monster," showcasing the city's division. Most sided with

"Monster," but some felt he was righting the wrongs of justice, especially when news outlets included the alleged crimes of the victims in their Vigilante coverage. And so long as public opinion on him was split, we might not have all the eyes open and cooperating to catch him.

"He must think that Dominic was guilty of homicide." I huffed. "Despite the jury's verdict."

How dare the Vigilante do this to him. How dare the Vigilante waltz around the city, deciding who gets to live and who dies.

"Maybe we could use Dominic to finally sway public opinion of him." I stepped forward. "The media focuses on the guilt of the Vigilante's victims, but Dominic was innocent, so you could use his unjust slaying to make them see he's nothing but a cold-blooded killer." Maybe then we'd get more leads.

Rinaldi's eyes softened into pity. "All due respect, I don't believe Dominic was innocent."

My head snapped back. "A jury disagrees with you."

"And if I don't think so," she continued gently, "others won't either."

"You don't know that. This is an opportunity to clear his name *and* catch the Vigilante."

"You know as well as I do that the media will zero in on the murder Dominic was charged with."

"Good. He was found not guilty, so they'll see he didn't do it."

"Have you seen the media declare any Vigilante victim innocent?" she pressed.

I pursed my lips.

"They find something with each victim, and Dominic will be no exception. He can't be the poster child for the hunt against the Vigilante."

I clenched my teeth. It was horrid enough that the Vigilante was slaying people, but it was also terrible that he was dividing the city into two groups: those who agreed murder was never okay and those who believed the victims had it coming.

Each time I heard whispers that the Vigilante was doing society a favor, my gut churned in rage. That man was tearing the city's soul apart, and it infuriated me that any attempt I made to clear Dominic's name would probably just do the opposite in the court of public opinion.

"We need someone that'll rattle cages. We need *you*," she continued. "If we don't catch the Vigilante soon, our funding is going to get cut, and if the funding gets cut, our hope of catching him will all but vanish. I'm sorry to ask you to do this today, after what you've been through, but we need to strike while the iron is hot."

Part of me wanted to say no. Maybe it was unfair to be angry at the police—we were on the same side of justice, after all. But teaming up with the very people who had failed to lock the Vigilante up before he killed my friend left a putrid taste in my mouth.

And yet, if there was anything I could do to stop that psychopath, I needed to try.

"Okay."

Her shoulders, which had been pulled taut like a bowstring, sagged with a visible sigh of relief.

"Thank you, Luna. I'll have someone be in touch with the details. You get your hand stitched up, go home and change, and I'll have them schedule a press conference for this evening. Prime-time news, hopefully."

Rinaldi flashed a sympathetic smile and started to walk away.

I took a steadying breath, the fog of emotions lifting just a bit.

"Detective?"

She turned back around.

"Can you please keep me posted on Franco?" I asked. "Not sure how worried I should be that he thinks I have something of his."

She nodded. "We'll be turning Dominic's residence upside down to see what we find." They'd searched it before his trial, but maybe something new would pop up, and they'd get to it before Franco would. "Also putting alerts out on Franco, too. I'll keep you informed if we find anything."

She paused. "I'm glad you're okay, Luna. Thanks again for agreeing to the press conference."

As soon as she was gone, I took a deep breath to focus my mind back on my father and stepped out of the restroom.

Where Hunter was leaning up against the wall opposite the door. Surely, a busy man such as himself had a million other places he needed to be, but based on his relaxed stance, he was in no rush to leave, holding me in his sapphire gaze.

And based on his stern tone, he wasn't going to take no for an answer when he said, "Come on. I'm taking you to the hospital."

But Hunter Lockwood couldn't take me to the ER.

He didn't know I was about to face one of my biggest fears.

CHAPTER 5
Luna

"I strongly advise you to reconsider having a deputy escort you, too," Hunter said. "At least for the next twenty-four hours or so."

"I'm getting stitched up, going home, and locking my doors." Assuming the prison still wouldn't let me visit today.

As I stepped outside into a different section of the parking lot, rays of sunlight bathed my skin, replacing the chilly confines of the building, and the tangy scent of freshly cut grass replaced the stale iron scent of blood.

Hunter had graciously given me his suit jacket, so I was more covered, but it meant he distractingly had no shirt on. His chiseled lines seemed to glisten in the sunlight. The guy was such a spectacular specimen that he made the rest of us humans look like when it was our turn to be created, the universe was on a coffee break.

"Thank you for the clothes, but I'll drive myself to the ER," I said.

Luckily, my car was *outside* the police tape. No way in hell I'd let Hunter Lockwood see me exposed to one of my greatest fears: needles.

I loathed needles. Whoever the masochistic scientist was that came up with the idea to stab medicine into your body should face the jury of us needle-fearing patrons. The last time I had to get a shot, I almost threw up. Like *gagging to the point of eyes watering* almost throwing up, and that was from one prick. This time, I'd be stabbed repeatedly in my sensitive palm.

The barf forecast was high with a chance of fainting.

I'd rather shove my face into a beehive than have Hunter Lockwood witness the exorcist-level reaction I was probably about to have.

Hunter put his hands into his pockets, as if waiting for me to come to my senses.

Or surrender to his pheromones. One or the other.

"Look, like I said…it was really sweet of you to lend me your clothes and to help wash the blood off of me, but I feel a lot better now, so I'd prefer to drive myself."

"Why's that?" Hunter asked.

"For starters, I can take care of myself."

"Of that I have no doubt. But you're bleeding, Luna. I won't allow you to drive yourself."

Allow me? *Did he hear his word choice there?* "Look. Again. Thank you. But I've got this. So, I'll see you later."

I walked away from him, then wound through the cars of the parking lot until I reached my old clunker.

But the guy was even more stubborn than I'd given him credit for. He followed me and eyed my dilapidated 2007 Kia Spectra. Average retail price: $2,500. My price: $1,700, thanks to the driver's side door being red while the rest of its body was an off-white, the rusted rims, the tears in the seats, and the smoke damage from the chain-smoker who owned it before me. But it got me from point A to point B and didn't siphon my limited funds.

Hunter's eyebrows arched up, a hint of amusement in his eyes as he let out an incredulous, "Wow."

"We can't all drive Aston Martins."

He stood there, watching as I opened the door, pretending it didn't sound like a slow-motion car accident of bent metal. I got inside, shut the door with a crunch, put my seat belt on, and shoved my key into the ignition.

Anxious to get out from under his stare.

When I turned the key, though, my engine groaned in protest.

No. Don't do this to me. Not in front of Hunter.

It was on my to-do list to take it to the dealership to get looked at. It had been making a funny noise lately, but I didn't have time to do it until next week. I tried to crank the engine again. And then again, but the universe had a wicked sense of humor.

I leaned forward and pressed my forehead against my steering wheel in despair.

Hunter knocked on the window with his knuckle. "May I give you a lift, Luna? Or do you prefer to ride to the ER with the tow-truck driver?"

Five minutes later, I was sitting inside Hunter Lockwood's Aston Martin as he drove me to the hospital. I tried to call an Uber, but somehow, he won that argument, and here I was.

But it was fine. I had a new plan. I'd have him drop me off at the front doors, and I'd go inside and have my needle meltdown in private.

I just hoped I wasn't getting blood on his seat. I had never been in a vehicle this fancy before. It looked like the black leather had been stitched by hand, as soft as velvet, and everything was covered in it— even the dashboard, for crying out loud. It was like being inside a leather onesie, coated in Hunter's delicious cologne.

Because it wasn't distracting enough, having him next to me, with his ripped muscles trying to kidnap my gaze.

I'd already completed my call to the prison. Predictably, they wouldn't give me much more information on the phone—just confirmed there was a fight and that my dad would be okay. But the worst part of the phone call was when they said I had to wait until Sunday to see him because after he got out of the infirmary, he'd be spending twenty-four hours in solitary for his part in the altercation.

It made me sick. I knew my dad; he didn't start fights, so if he was involved in one, they were punishing the wrong person.

My fingers drummed against the armrest, each second stretching out longer than the last as I began counting down the agonizing forty-eight hours until I could put my eyes on him. All the while, the discomfort of wearing a man's shirt as a makeshift dress gnawed at me, its length barely reaching my thighs.

I tugged at Hunter's button-down, hoping to coax more coverage, but the motion drew Hunter's gaze to the toned expanse of my upper leg. His eyes lingered there, longer than car driving standards would recommend, before wandering slowly and deliberately back up to my face, making my skin tingle where they passed.

Heat rushed to my cheeks, and his mouth curled up slightly.

Dammit.

It royally sucks when you enjoy being checked out by the one person you do not want to be attracted to, and not only does your body blow your cover, exposing how much you like it, but the panty-melter notices you enjoying it.

When he returned his attention back to the road, my eyes decided to take on a life of their own and drift downward, drawn irresistibly to his chest. It was lean and muscular, a canvas of strength meticulously sculpted by hours of dedication. Each muscle was distinct, the dips and curves throwing tantalizing shadows under the soft light.

It took a serious fight to force my eyeballs away from the exquisite lines of his abs and back up to his face.

Where his eyes were already on me, catching me drooling over him. Based on the pull of his lips, he liked every minute of it.

This was all so infuriating; why did he have to enjoy making me blush, and why did he have to be so...so...irresistible?! It didn't help that everything about him seemed so...intoxicating—like he'd been designed by a team of experts specifically for maximum appeal.

But did I really have to sit here and admire the scrumptious details? The way his lean forearm looked as it dangled on the steering wheel? No matter how hard I tried, it was frustratingly impossible to ignore just how attractive Hunter was.

"I have to say, I can't believe you were going to fight off a knife-wielding vigilante," Hunter's voice was low. "While it was unnecessarily dangerous, I'm impressed."

The hint of admiration in his tone gave my heart an unfamiliar, erratic flutter.

I'd never had someone handle me the way he had before— normally, I was too fiercely independent to need help from anyone. It was as shocking as it was exhilarating, sparking heat that radiated across my skin.

"Anyone would've done the same thing," I said.

Hunter's face fell, and his Adam's apple rolled.

"Not everyone." His tone was deep and sad with a pinch of anger throbbing through it. I wanted to know what he meant by that, but I could tell whatever it was, was something incredibly painful.

"You said you grabbed a shard of glass to fight him?"

I nodded.

"Where did you learn those fighting instincts?"

I pursed my lips and stared at the congested road in front of us.

"Does it have anything to do with being the daughter of a notorious killer?"

I crossed my arms over my chest. "Meaning what, my father taught me how to hurt people?"

"I didn't mean it that way," he said.

"My dad isn't a *notorious* killer. That implies he's up there with Ted Bundy or something. And he's innocent."

His sea-glass-colored eyes seized mine, making my neck heat so much, I had to look away.

I hated that I had no control over these stupid flutters that took flight when he looked at me like that. I'd never gotten them with other guys.

"I lost my dad when I was a kid, too," Hunter said. "He died when I was nine, and nothing was the same after that."

I raised my eyebrows, shocked that Hunter Lockwood had exposed such a private part of his life to me.

"As hard as that was, I can't even imagine what it must've been like for you." His tone was soft and kind, making my guard relax even more.

No one had ever tried to put themselves in my shoes before.

Something about his admission, the revelation of his personal tragedy, filled the air around us with an intimate honesty. It was a truth that echoed with familiarity, a poignant realization of how broken our lives were from an early age. Our experiences, though different, were cut from the same cloth of life's suffering.

I guess I could've continued being evasive about my life, but Hunter was being *win a badge of honor* nice, driving me to the ER, and even humbled himself by confiding that piece of his history.

So, I cleared my throat and answered his original question—where I'd learned my fighting instincts.

"Being the daughter of a convicted killer doesn't make you very popular," I started. "I was bullied in school, so I learned to defend myself."

"Define bullied." The protective flare in his voice took me off guard; it took me a moment to answer.

"A lot of verbal stuff, name-calling, trashing my locker, that kind of thing. But it was also physical at times."

"Give me an example." His jaw tightened.

"I was thrown into a dumpster once. I got jumped five times. I begged my mom to let me homeschool, but she was all righteous about how we had done nothing wrong, and we would not be chased out of our school or our neighborhood, yada yada. She went to the principal and demanded action, but you know how bullying goes. So, eventually, I got good at defending myself."

Hunter clutched the wheel tighter, driving in silence for a minute as if he had to push an emotion aside.

"Can I ask a personal question?" Hunter asked.

"Admitting I had been thrown into a dumpster when I was younger wasn't personal enough for you?"

The side of his lips curled up slightly.

"I know the salary of a public defender."

"Let me guess. My entire salary is probably your coffee budget."

His lips curved higher. Until today, I had never seen Hunter Lockwood smile, and holy hormones, did it do things to my lower belly.

"You should be able to afford a better car than that hunk of metal."

There was not an ounce of condescension in his tone, but rather curiosity.

"Unfortunately, I have this pesky thing called student loan debt. And then on top of it, I'm investigating a case on the side, and as I'm sure you know, investigations can be very expensive."

He seemed to consider this.

"I heard you filed the writ of habeas corpus."

Our eyes briefly met before he returned them to the road. He sat slouched in his seat, his right elbow on the center console.

I was surprised he'd taken enough of an interest in me to learn that tidbit.

"Last resort for your dad's case, isn't it?" he asked.

I hated how much of a long shot this was. Up there with getting Apollo 13 home safe. Normally, any motion for appeal had to happen within a short time after the verdict, which my family filed and lost. And typically, a motion for a new trial had to be filed within three years of the verdict. But there were exceptions. Still, I knew in my bones this was our attempt at a Hail Mary.

"The last resort is when he's home, where he belongs. Where innocent people belong."

He stopped at a red light, the hospital now within view.

"Is that why you're a criminal defense attorney?"

I twisted my hands in my lap. "The justice system failed my father *and* the victim he was accused of killing."

Hunter tilted his head slightly. "So, you want to make sure everyone gets a fair trial."

"If my clients are guilty, I advise them to plead so and then help them through the process. The way I see it," I added, "better nine guilty men walk free than one innocent person goes to prison."

Hunter chewed the inside of his cheek.

"How intriguing," he said. "You fight against injustice, one case at a time, and then you take on an armed assailant twice your size. You're like a little leopard, aren't you?"

I blinked. "A what?"

He looked out at the road in front of him.

"A leopard is gorgeous…" *He finds me gorgeous?* "Yet unassuming on the outside. But it's one of the best fighters in the animal kingdom. It doesn't matter if its opponent is a bigger cat with a stronger jaw or has more physical strength. The leopard is an exceptional fighter with great agility, never backing down from a battle."

His eyebrow quirked, as if he were enchanted by me, making my body warm.

"As a criminal lawyer, do you see the injustice in the legal system?" I asked.

"The justice system isn't perfect," he admitted. "But I've come to believe that some people are capable of doing terrible things."

On both sides of his Aston Martin, some of the tallest buildings in the world flanked the four-lane road, canopied by a cloudy sky. The pedestrians walking along the sidewalk always seemed happier on Fridays, tasting the weekend coming before us.

"Is that why you became a prosecutor?" I asked.

Hunter shifted in his seat, appearing uncomfortable with my question.

Which was odd. In any profession, one was often asked what motivated them to choose it. And he had just asked me the same question.

"When I inherited the money from my father's estate, I started a tech business while I went to Harvard."

Of course he went to Harvard.

"How did you start a business and go to school at the same time?"

"I hired an executive staff to help run the business. When it grew to a billion-dollar market cap, I lost the hunger to spend the rest of my life running it, though. Guess it was the challenge of starting it I'd been after. Maybe I'd wanted to walk a mile in my dad's shoes or something because he'd helped grow my grandfather's business." Hunter put his turn signal on and glided the car through a bend. "I remained the sole equity owner and left the daily operations to my executive team while I went to law school."

Geez. Who has a side hustle that grows to a billion dollars? People who can afford to hire others to run the business for them, I guess.

It didn't go unnoticed that he never answered my question about why he had become a prosecutor. Law school was a grind, and you couldn't get through it without a serious level of passion.

"How long have you been working on the case?" Hunter asked.

My whole life.

"A couple of years." For this particular motion, anyway. But throughout college and law school, I had been studying and researching any possible outlet to get Dad released.

"You truly think he's innocent?"

"I know he is."

"It's a long shot and a lot of work to get a habeas corpus granted," Hunter mused.

Yeah, but what was the alternative?

"What would you do if someone you loved was wrongfully convicted and was sentenced to serve their entire life in prison because of it? How far would you go to save them?"

Hunter stared out the windshield, taking a deep breath, and when he spoke again, his voice had dropped to almost a whisper.

"It's tragic," he said. "How one event can haunt every moment of your life."

A bitter ache twisted in the pit of my stomach, a biting reminder of the shared pain etched deep within our souls. We were both tormented by our fathers' absences. His dad had been snatched away by the cold, indiscriminate hand of death. Mine, ensnared by the unforgiving steel bars of imprisonment. The torment was the same yet uniquely different—a kaleidoscope of despair that shadowed our lives in sorrow.

Yet, as I studied him, I noticed an added depth to his grief. It wasn't just the usual mourning; there was a tinge of something more, an unspoken agony that lurked in the corner of his mournful gaze.

After what we'd already shared, would he tell me what it was?

Before I could ask him, though, he pulled up to the emergency room doors and stopped.

It was jarring to end such an intimate moment so abruptly, but there was another car behind us, waiting for him to move.

"Thanks again for the ride. I'll, uh..." I tugged his shirt down another inch. "I'll get your shirt and jacket back to you next week, if that's okay?"

"Keep them, Luna." His voice was a low rumble, deeper than before, and when he looked at me, it was like an anchor, drawing me in. The ambient noise of the hospital's drive-up entrance faded to a distant hum, every particle of my attention captured by the weight and warmth in his eyes.

A tightness gripped my throat, making me swallow.

"Thanks again for everything." I offered him a tentative smile. "I'll see you around."

I wasn't sure why Hunter furrowed his eyebrows slightly, but he watched me get out of his car and walk into the building.

Shockingly, there was no wait in the emergency room, so I was escorted back immediately. A nurse came in, took my vitals, got all of my information, and now, I was bouncing my knee so harshly, it could probably cause tendon damage, waiting for the skin-stabber to show up.

A soft knock at the door had my eyes darting up, anticipating the sterile white of a lab coat. Instead, the door swung open to reveal a man wearing designer suit pants, now paired with a black workout shirt that he must have stored in his car.

"What are you doing here?" I demanded.

With an unhurried pace and relaxed shoulders, he sauntered into the room, exuding an air of nonchalance.

"They told me which room you're in."

"That's not what I mean. Why are you still at the hospital?"

Hunter sat in a metal chair that made a high-pitched sound against the floor from its movement, looking so out of place, he almost looked like an intruder. His suit pants were tailored to perfection with luxurious fabric that seemed to absorb the harsh fluorescent lighting —quite the contrast to the hospital scrubs I'd seen the nurses wearing. His polished Italian leather shoes gleamed, pristine and alien on the worn linoleum, and the sharp scent of his expensive cologne mingled uneasily with the antiseptic sting of the hospital air. It was like witnessing a lion in a cage, a creature of power and majesty forced into a world that wasn't his own.

"Last time I checked, you don't live at the hospital," Hunter said flatly. "My offer to drive was round trip."

"Okay, are you ready, honey?"

The nurse practitioner—whose name tag read *Jennifer*—walked into the room and glanced at Hunter.

"He was just leaving," I said.

"I wasn't, actually." Hunter grinned at her.

"He was," I countered.

Jennifer put her hand on her hip and opened her mouth to tell Hunter to leave. At least, that's what it looked like she was about to do until recognition bolted through her features.

"Are you…"

"Hunter Lockwood." He winked at me in triumph. Which was so frustrating.

"Oh, Mr. Lockwood," Jennifer cooed. "Your donation has done so much for this hospital! The new cancer wing is making a huge difference in people's lives!"

A wing?

I glared at Hunter.

Figures. Of all the hospitals in the city, I had to land in the one where Hunter's name was probably plastered on a wall or door somewhere.

First of all, it struck me just how different we were. Here I was, going to have a hard time coming up with the money to repair whatever was wrong with my car, while he was funding entire wings of hospitals. But of more importance, I was merely a patient who needed stitches. He was a massive donor to this place.

No one at this hospital would make him leave.

Which was just freaking great. I was about to endure one of my most irrational fears.

And evidently, my landlord and growing crush was about to have a front-row seat to it.

CHAPTER 6

Luna

"Y ou okay, honey?" The nurse practitioner raised her brows.

"You look like Casper," Hunter said.

"Gee, thanks."

I probably did look like a ghost. My heart hammered against my rib cage, every beat drowning out sounds, leaving the world distant, as if I were underwater.

"You a fainter?" She put her hand on her hip.

"Er..."

"I'll have you lie down, hon."

Good idea. That way, if I passed out, I wouldn't fall forward and break my face open. That would require extra stitches.

I lay down and stared up at the ceiling as she unwrapped and disinfected my palm before applying a local numbing cream to the area.

"Need you to stop shaking, hon."

"Sorry."

I was trying—I really was—but every time she touched my hand to see if the numbing cream was working yet, my hand quivered uncontrollably beneath her touch.

"You were brave enough to fight against an armed assailant just fine, but getting stitches does this to you?" Amusement danced through Hunter's words.

I glared at him. "Shut up, Hunter."

He smiled wide enough to show his perfectly white teeth.

"I'd prefer if you left," I reminded him.

But the stubborn billionaire made no move.

Jennifer now tried to poke my hand with an injectable numbing agent, which made me shake harder. Of course.

And as I did, Hunter's lips twitched, the smirk dissolving as a shadow of concern crept into his eyes. He scrubbed his jaw, staring at me, seeming uncertain how to help me through my little crisis.

"Tell you what, hon. I'm going to give you a sedative to stop the shaking, okay?"

I nodded. A sedative. Good. *Make me fall asleep. Then you can shove my hand under a sewing machine, and I'll be too drowsy to give a crap.*

In theory.

Flashes of the last time I'd been under a sedative danced at the edge of my consciousness—the room spinning, voices sounding distorted. But I was not about to tell her it hit me harder than they "preferred." They could hook me up to an anesthesia machine for all I cared.

She vanished from the room for a moment and came back in with a white paper cup.

"This'll relax you," she said as I downed it. "I'll give it time to work and be back shortly."

When she left the room, Hunter pulled his chair closer to the exam table. He looked at my non-injured hand, some sort of debate flickering in his eyes before he looked back at my face.

"Tell me how to get your mind off of this," he said.

I eyed him. "See that paper towel dispenser?"

He looked at the shiny metal thing. "Yeah?"

"Rip it off the wall and knock me unconscious with it."

The playful lines around his eyes smoothed out.

"The sedative should help," I said.

"It'll help with the shaking, but you still need to get your mind off of this." His voice was deep and soothing.

The tight knot in my chest began to loosen, and a comforting warmth spread through me.

Thank you, pharmaceuticals.

"I told you, you could leave," I said.

"Am I making you more anxious by staying?"

The warmth continued to seep through my blood, spreading to the tips of my fingers and toes, my muscles slowly turning into goo.

"No." Oddly, I didn't hate having him here as much as I assumed I would. Maybe it was the drugs. "But I don't want to barf in front of you."

Hunter's lips lifted in the corners. "I don't care if you throw up in front of me, Luna."

"Well, I do. We're adversaries in the courtroom, and we're basically strangers. I don't like puking in front of strangers."

"We're not strangers."

"I know almost nothing about you," I said.

Hunter's gaze locked on to mine, unwavering and intense, as if searching for something beneath the surface.

"Maybe I'd like you to," he said.

He reached out and brushed a strand of hair from my face with his thumb, his touch gentle yet electric, sending sparks up my skin that spread throughout my body.

"I can see the medicine is helping." Jennifer's voice shattered the bubble Hunter and I were in, jolting me back to the sterile room.

It took me a moment to refocus my attention on what she was about to do.

The meds were helping my muscles liquefy, but now that I'd broken free from Hunter's powerful stare, a flutter of unease tickled the pit of my stomach again.

"This'll only take a few minutes," she assured.

Says every madman before he tortures you, I'm sure.

She wheeled her chair to the other side of the exam table and began cleaning off my palm again, the sharp scent of disinfectant invading my nostrils.

I started drumming the fingers of my good hand against the exam bed.

"Need you to hold still for me." Jennifer lined up an injection. "This is lidocaine. It might cause a brief stinging or burning sensation, but it will numb the area very quickly. Small poke."

The sudden prick of the needle sent a sting flaring at the injection site, and when I cringed at the slight burn the nurse had warned me about, Hunter grasped my uninjured hand between both of his.

His touch caught me off guard. As did his eyes—the unexpected security of his grip pulling my focus back to him. His fingers tightened around mine, and a surge of something—concern, understanding—passed between us. What had begun as a simple ride had evolved into something deeper.

"Okay, hon," the nurse said.

The world seemed to gray around the edges, leaving just Hunter's gaze and mine in sharp focus with the sensation of time slipping away.

The nurse pressed her fingertip on my palm, ensuring it was numb.

"I'm going to start the stitches now."

When I bit my lower lip nervously to keep myself from trembling, Hunter seemed to notice this and cleared his throat.

"My dad was murdered," he said.

At this, the nurse practitioner stilled for a moment.

His voice, deliberately casual amid the clinical setting, rocketed my attention away from the impending needles and into the atmosphere of Hunter Lockwood.

Even before he told me about his dad's death during the car ride, I knew his father had passed; it was how the four Lockwood brothers had come into their inheritance. But I always assumed his dad must've died of a heart attack or car accident or something.

"He was murdered?" I asked.

"You want to prove your dad is innocent. And I want to find my dad's killer," Hunter said. "Guess we both have a Moby Dick we're chasing."

"They never caught the killer?"

Hunter shook his head. "Unsolved, to this day."

"I had no idea," I said. "I'm sorry."

Come to think of it, my best friend, Sean, who was a true crime podcaster, mentioned something about a tragedy that befell the Lockwoods. When he'd brought it up, I shut him down because I didn't want to hear it; any sympathy I might gain for Hunter risked me losing my edge against him in court.

"It was a long time ago." Hunter's smile held a fragile edge, his eyes dimming just slightly, a cloud passing over them.

"My dad was accused of killing a kid," I said. Again, the nurse practitioner stilled. "A teenager." Not sure why I said that. To assure him there was no way my dad could've been his father's killer, maybe?

Or to get the most heinous accusation out in the open before he continued to look at me like this—like I was the only being worthy of his coveted attention. Because when he looked at me like this, Hunter Lockwood pulled me higher into his orbit, where I feared I would never come back down to earth.

But he didn't look away. Instead, he tightened his grip on my hand, his eyes deepening with silent empathy, as if trying to fathom how hard that must have been on me, growing up.

Because, yes, it was bad enough to have your father accused of murder. It was a whole new horror level for him to be an accused *child* killer—the victim only seventeen years old.

"All done," Jennifer said.

My focus snapped back, the room and Jennifer's voice suddenly sharp.

"It's over?"

"Until the sedative wears off, you'll be unsteady on your feet. You'll need to be careful."

I sat up.

Holy hell, she's not kidding. The room tilted slightly, my head trying to detach and float away. But my hand...my non-injured hand was steady, still locked in Hunter's grasp, his other hand now on my shoulder, holding me in place when I started to sway.

I never imagined that in my time of need, it would be Hunter Lockwood who would see me through the crisis. Earlier at the court-house, helping me get out of bloodstained clothes, driving me to the emergency room, literally holding my hand throughout the procedure.

But mostly, baring his soul, if only to help my mind escape my fear of needles.

Maybe this was why so many women were desperate for him. Maybe they knew that underneath the model-level looks, sinfully sexy gaze, money, and power was a kind and gentle man.

His features tightened, a mix of fury and worry etching across them.

"I'm going to make some calls, Luna. Find out what we can about Franco."

CHAPTER 7

Hunter

"You can leave her here, sir," the security guard said. "I'll stay with her until you bring the car around."

I ground my teeth, looking out at the sheets of rain washing over the black skyscrapers from a summer storm that had come on suddenly. It smelled like mildew, the asphalt a minefield of puddles.

Most people wouldn't think twice about leaving Luna for a minute to retrieve a vehicle, but until I understood how concerned we should be over Franco, a prickling dread settled in the back of my neck. The guy had choked her, for God's sake.

As a prosecutor, I'd learned to assume the worst of what people were capable of, and I'd also learned through my share of cases that the act of choking was a grave warning. Statistics showed that when someone choked another person, the risk of them eventually murdering that same individual increased tenfold.

Ten.

And that didn't even factor in the risk that this asshole thought Luna had something of his—something worth strangling her over.

I hoped I was wrong, but there was a good chance that encounter wouldn't be the last time Franco came for her.

And next time, what if someone wasn't there to interrupt him?

When someone murdered my father, I was a kid, and it never stopped echoing in the hollow caverns of my heart. The weight of my failure pressed down on my soul, molding it, changing its very fabric into a creature of guilt and regret.

I hadn't shielded him from impending danger, but maybe, just maybe, I could safeguard her.

I'd called the detective before I joined Luna in that hospital treatment room and confirmed the cops hadn't caught Franco yet. Nor did they have any leads on his whereabouts.

Which made me worry he'd gone into hiding.

Luna was leaving this to detectives, but I wasn't. I had the means to help, and I would. I needed to call my PI. Get him on this immediately, and in the meantime, try to behave rationally.

Sixty seconds—surely, she'd be safe with a guard?

"What's your name?" I asked him.

Greg's eyes glinted with a hint of awe, a look I recognized all too well from those hoping to benefit from my family's power.

"Greg," he said.

I motioned for him to step aside with me.

"Greg," I said in a low enough tone that Luna would not overhear. "If anything happens to her while I'm getting my car, there will be no shadow dark enough in this city to hide you. You understand?"

Widening his eyes, he swallowed hard, nodding slowly.

Smart man.

Not the smartest thing I had ever done—a prosecutor threatening a security guard—but this whole damn thing was putting me on edge.

"I'll be right back."

As I jogged to my car, rain smeared all over my face, making it harder to hear as I placed the call.

"Mr. Lockwood."

"Barry. I need you to do a deep dive on someone for me."

"Sir?"

"I need you to look into a man named Franco Hopkins."

A small pause elapsed, the storm bathing the city in rain.

"Is he related to your father's case?"

"No. I'd like to know how dangerous he is." Because hopefully, I was overreacting.

Silence hung on the line for three footsteps before Barry said, "Sir, respectfully, I agreed to work on your case because it's one of the most famous unsolved murders in the country. You can hire any private investigator to chase down small matters like this."

Shouldn't surprise me that Barry was offended. Barry Mansfield wasn't an ordinary private investigator. He was an ex-CIA agent, the most sought-after private investigator in this country, reserved for only those who could afford his services. His last client was the vice president of the United States.

It took me three years to finally land him. All the other private investigators I had hired, no matter how good they were supposed to be, had been unable to solve my father's murder. And tonight, Barry and I were supposed to meet for the first time to get him started on the case.

"This isn't a small matter," I said. "Franco Hopkins threatened a friend of mine, and I'd like to know how concerned we should be." I wouldn't leave Luna unprotected until I knew.

Once I reached my car, I escaped the rain by climbing into the dry interior, shutting the door with a soft click. Starting the engine, I allowed the call to switch over to Bluetooth. The rain was an absolute downpour, like an avalanche of water washing over my car so heavily, the windshield was a torrential blur despite the frantic wipers as I drove through the parking lot toward the front door.

When Barry still hadn't responded, I added, "I'll be more focused at our meeting tonight once I know what the situation is. That's all I need, and I'm relying on you to deliver."

The line filled with the heavy weight of Barry's sigh, the seconds stretching out like hours before he responded.

"Very good, sir. I'll see what I can dig up before we meet at six."

Until then, I wouldn't leave Luna alone.

Whether she liked it or not.

CHAPTER 8
Luna

The deep resonance of Hunter's voice vibrated through me.

"Come on, Little Leopard."

Before I could even process the pet name, Hunter's arm hitched around my waist and pulled me further from my slumber. The leather on my back shifted to the breezy air as Hunter helped me out of his Aston Martin.

I must have fallen asleep on the way home from the hospital, and now, we were in front of the little cottage I called home.

Tucked away on the outskirts of the bustling city of Chicago, this quaint cottage's stone—a mosaic of gray and brown—was twined with flowering ivy, and in the summer, the hum of bumblebees and the soft whispering of the ancient oak trees seemed to wrap it in an almost-mythical aura. The roof's weathered shingles slanted down to meet small, diamond-paned windows that were often half-hidden behind white lace curtains that fluttered in the breeze whenever I'd open them.

The summer rain had passed, but the pea gravel walkway that was lined with yellow flowers had water draining off to the sides, and the aroma of freshly soaked earth wafted from the front lawn.

Hunter secured his arm around my waist as I took my first step.

"The hell?" My friend, Sean, pushed off the wall of my porch, his eyebrows attacking his face with anger when he looked at my bare legs and at the bizarre shirt I was using as a dress. But mostly because I was wobbling. And Hunter Lockwood had to stabilize me.

"Sean?" I asked. "What are you doing here?"

Now that I was looking, his van was parked off to the side.

"What happened to you?" Sean threw my left arm over his shoulders, crouching down to compensate for my height as he pulled me away from Hunter.

Well, tried to, anyway, but Hunter tightened his grip on me and glared at Sean.

"Who the hell are *you*?" Sean asked. But as soon as he did, recognition flickered in his eyes.

"Who the hell are you?" Hunter growled.

"He's my best friend," I said. Technically, if you didn't consider acquaintances as friends, Sean was my only friend. We met when he'd reached out to ask a few questions about my father's case for his podcast, and once I realized he believed in my father's innocence, we started to spend time together.

"What happened to her?" Sean repeated, trying to pull me away from Hunter.

"Long story," Hunter said as he pulled me back to him, my left arm sliding down Sean's back.

Sean wasn't about to take that lying down though. He knew I wasn't friends with Hunter, and I could only imagine what in the world was going through his mind. Why was I half naked? Why was I acting drunk in the middle of the day?

"I've got her, dude." Sean's fingers tightened around me, attempting to tug me back with a determined pull, but Hunter resisted, keeping me anchored.

"Step. Aside," Hunter snapped.

Sean looked like he debated arguing further, but it wasn't like Hunter was trying to hurt me. Maybe Sean thought about how hard he'd worked to grow his podcast into a small business. Maybe he feared an army of lawyers descending onto it if he pissed Hunter off.

Whatever the reason, Sean reluctantly shoved his hands into his pockets and watched me with guarded eyes as Hunter navigated me to my front porch.

He fished my keys out of my purse, which was amusingly dangling from his other shoulder, unlocked the door, and helped me inside.

The interior of the cottage was cozy. The main room contained a charming fireplace made of the same stone as the exterior, crowned by an aged timber mantel. On cold nights, the fire flickered, casting a warm glow that danced on the weathered wooden beams overhead, filling the room with a comforting, golden light.

To one side, a small kitchen—which had a cast-iron stove and vintage copper pots hanging from hooks—sat next to a dining room so small that the four-person table took up most of the space.

Which was the spot I pointed to.

"I want to sit there." Just until the meds wore off. Then I was going to take the longest shower in history.

"You'll be more comfortable on the couch or in your bed," Hunter said.

So bossy.

"There," I repeated.

Something told me that Hunter would never normally budge with getting his way, but after looking at me for a few seconds, his chest swelled, and he frowned.

Begrudgingly, Hunter helped me sit down at one of the dining room chairs, placed my purse on the ground, and scanned my table, which was blanketed in papers. Along the wall, brown cardboard boxes full of other paperwork were stacked on top of each other.

"Jesus."

"This is how regular folks live, Lockwood," I said. "We don't all have moats and dragons guarding our castles."

"Is *this* what you're doing every night?" Hunter picked up a piece of paper, which had my father's name on it. "When your dining room light is on at all hours?"

He noticed my light on?

I yanked the paper from Hunter's hand. "I told you, my father is innocent, and I'm going to prove it."

Hunter glanced at the mountain of paperwork, then eyed Sean again, before looking over at the television in my living room, which I'd accidentally left on this morning.

Currently, a story was airing about the Vigilante and his latest attack.

His gaze shifted, a hint of intrigue narrowing his eyes as they settled on the odd assembly of figures perched on the fireplace mantel. They might seem quirky to others, but for me, those trolls were a link to happier days. When I was a kid, my dad and I had started a collection, and now, the supposed good-luck charms were simply reminders of the precious time I shared with my father that was cut way too short.

"I have to meet my PI," Hunter said. "He's looking into Franco to assess the threat level."

"What threat?" Sean's voice was high-pitched. "And who the hell is Franco?"

"He's the man who choked Luna."

Sean's face paled, his lips parting in shock, clearly unprepared for the gravity of what he'd just heard.

Hunter's voice carried a note of authority as he said, "I'll call someone to tow your car to the shop, get an estimate for the repair."

"What's wrong with your car?" A line appeared between Sean's brows.

"I can do that," I assured Hunter.

But he flexed his selective listening skills, letting my comment dissipate in the air as he nodded toward my best friend.

"You trust him?" Hunter asked me.

Sean looked offended Hunter had the nerve to ask that.

"Yes."

"Good." Hunter walked up to Sean. Looking at the two, you would assume Sean would be the one with all the power, what with how much taller and bigger he was than Hunter, but each step Hunter took resonated with a kind of unyielding dominance, his eyes never wavering from Sean's.

"Don't leave her alone," Hunter said. "I'll be in touch when I know more."

After Hunter glared at him one last time before walking out the door, Sean took a seat opposite of me.

"Okay, you're going to tell me everything. Who Franco is, why he choked you, why you're half naked and blitzed in the middle of the day, why you have a bandage on your hand, and why, all of a sudden, things are hot and heavy between you and Hunter Lockwood."

"Things are not hot and heavy between us."

"That guy is into you. With capital letters. But explanations first— Franco, bandage. Drunk."

I rolled my eyes slightly, but filled Sean in on it all. Every time a new detail emerged, Sean's tongue flicked over his teeth, his fingers raking through his hair, as if trying to process the weight of it.

After a series of follow-ups, he nodded his chin in the direction of Hunter's mansion and asked, "Why was he here?"

"He stumbled across the scene where I'd been hurt and drove me to the emergency room." I left out the part where he held my hand, how he looked at me, and how he made me feel things I didn't want to feel.

"And for the record, I'd never date Hunter Lockwood."

As attracted as I was to him, what happened today didn't change the fact that Hunter and I were too different to be compatible. He was rich; I'd grown up poor. I defended people while he prosecuted them. Plus, I'd undoubtedly go up against him in court again, and dating my adversary wasn't responsible. Not to mention the whole landlord situation.

I shook my head. How could I have let myself get carried away today? He was kind to me, and I could be grateful for that, but that didn't change anything.

"He's a prosecutor," I added. "I know he's just doing his job, but you know how much I loathe prosecutors." An irrational emotion maybe, but a human one, after one of them seemed almost vicious in his efforts to lock up my father.

"There's a fine line between passion and hate. I saw the way you were looking at each other," Sean said. "You really think you can straddle that line without crossing it?"

"I don't want to date *anyone*, let alone Hunter. What I want is to get my dad out of prison."

Sean ran a hand through his hair, his bicep flexing against his T-shirt.

"Why are you here, anyway?" I asked.

Sean took a deep breath, pulling out his phone to show me the blazing headline and rapidly increasing comments.

"It went public today. That you filed the writ of habeas corpus. A true crime reporter posted about it, and now it's all over social media."

"So?"

"So, I wanted to warn you. Sometimes, folks can get a little...dicey toward people trying to get convicted killers out of prison. Especially convicted child killers."

CHAPTER 9
Hunter

I needed to hurry. Traffic had been a bitch, coming home from the hospital, and checking my wristwatch, the second hand ticked on. I was already three minutes late to my meeting with Barry and counting. I had already annoyed him earlier today by asking him to look into Franco Hopkins, so I certainly did not want to show up to our meeting later than I already was.

I needed to run upstairs, get a shirt on, and meet Barry in my home office. Confirm Franco was nothing to worry about so I could get back to the task at hand: finding my father's killer.

"Mr. Lockwood," Maria said when I walked inside from my garage. Wearing a white apron over her plump figure, her hair pinned up in its usual gray bun, she looked at my mismatched outfit—a workout shirt and designer suit pants—with curiosity. "I showed—"

"Barry to my office, who's waiting for me. Yes, thank you, Maria."

I walked toward the main staircase.

"Yes, sir, but I was going to say…"

She didn't need to finish her sentence because when I walked into the next room, I spotted them.

They stood, sipping scotch in the newly decorated great room of my family estate. I had remodeled the entire mansion two years ago, hoping more windows, white trim, and lighter furniture would chase the dark memories that haunted this house since my childhood. Making it look completely different than it had been when I'd been a boy, finding my father reading in this room.

Now, the three-story windows bathed the beige couches, end tables, and glass coffee table in early evening light. An olive tree sat in the far corner, concealing the spot where I'd fallen when I was four and split my chin open. Every time my eyes landed there, I could almost feel the warmth of my father's gentle touch, and hear the soothing tone of his voice as he bandaged my wound. And how it was only five years later that he'd died.

The window light stretched to the other side of the room, which housed the grand staircase and the upper balcony overlooking it all. From that spot, I used to sneak peeks as a child, watching my father's eyes dance over the pages, his sighs echoing up to my hiding place.

My dad's brother—Uncle Alexander—was in his typical polished form today. Wearing a custom-tailored blue suit that accentuated his six-foot frame, he had styled his hair—dark with a few strands of gray —with just enough product to look polished yet sophisticated. I'd admired the elegance he carried himself with since I was a kid—when Uncle Alexander stepped into the role of a father figure, filling the void left in the wake of his brother's death. And I appreciated how he'd always been there for us four boys and my mother, too—up until the day she passed away from a battle with breast cancer.

Uncle Alexander would always pull us into warm embraces, ruffle our hair, or share stories of our father, creating a bridge to memories lost. But I suspected his constant presence was not due solely to love or family obligation. After the death of his only brother, we became more than just nephews to him—we became the closest thing he had to ever seeing his brother again. In us, he'd see his smile, hear his voice, and he'd grasp on to the echoes of my father.

My uncle was wonderful to our family, but he wasn't without his faults. As much as he accused me of being trapped in the past, chasing my father's killer, my uncle was obsessed with his own. Or more specifically with the legacy that my grandfather had built—the legacy of a Fortune 500 company built from the ground up and the name that went with it: Lockwood.

But it wasn't the sight of my uncle Alexander that made my eyebrows hit my hairline; it was who was standing next to him.

"What are you doing here?" I asked.

"Saw the zoo on the news." My brother Grayson was dressed in black slacks and a fitted black shirt, as if he hadn't gotten the memo that it was summer. "Were you there?"

Was a courthouse slaying what it took for him to reappear?

"Yeah. Had trial today."

"You okay?" Uncle Alexander asked.

"I'm fine. But now's not a good time; I'm late for a meeting."

Unfortunate timing. Grayson and I hadn't spoken in weeks.

"With another private investigator," Uncle said.

Even as a grown man, the disapproval in his voice had this way of grinding against my spine.

"Is that the real reason you're here?" I couldn't hide the irritation in my tone. "To try and talk me out of this again?"

"We just wanted to check and see that you're okay," my uncle claimed. "It's not every day you turn on the news and see a murder at the courthouse."

Yet his shoulders were drawn tight, like they always were when he was about to say something he knew I wouldn't like.

"You're both welcome to stay, but I have to get to this meeting." I pivoted toward the back hall.

"I heard you helped Ms. Payne," my uncle said, stopping me in my tracks.

"How do you know that?"

"Doesn't matter."

I loved my uncle, and knew he meant well, but I didn't appreciate the way he butted into my business.

"She was injured during the attack." I flexed my fingers at my side, turning back to him. "I drove her to the hospital."

"I saw you down at the cottage." He narrowed his eyes.

I paused. "I drove her home afterward."

Grayson looked between me and my uncle, taking a sip of his scotch, as if he could swallow the tension now filling the room.

"Women throw themselves at you every chance they get, and you have never driven any of them home."

"Like I said, she was injured, so I gave her a ride."

His gaze lingered a tad too long, his head tilting in silent challenge. "From the looks of it, it seemed like more than just a simple ride home."

"You were watching me?" I scoffed.

"I was waiting for you after seeing the news." His gaze moved to the cottage at the bottom of a slight hill from the main house. "When I looked outside, I saw you with your arm around her." He licked his lip. "I thought you didn't date."

"I've dated lots of women," I retorted.

"That encounter looked like more than a one-night event." Uncle Alexander raised an eyebrow.

First, he gives me a hard time for having only one-night stands, and now he's giving me a hard time because he thinks I'm too interested in a woman? Pick a side.

I didn't appreciate this crap. I tried to bite my tongue; wanting to show respect to the man who'd helped my mother through all those difficult years.

Tried being the imperative word.

"I don't mean to sound crass, but this needs to be said." My uncle looked into the bottom of his glass, where two ice cubes were dying a slow death. "She's not Lockwood material, Hunter."

"So long as you don't mean it to sound crass."

My uncle tightened his lips. "She's the daughter of a killer. A child killer."

A muscle twitched in my jaw. "When will you ever let go of this pedigree bullshit?"

"People look at you, they see billions in the bank."

"Which is it?" I asked. "Is she a gold digger or bad for our Lockwood brand? Pick your issue with her."

"The Lockwood name and fortune are something people try to go after all the time. What kind of an uncle would I be if I didn't warn you to be careful?"

"All due respect, I'm not a child anymore."

My uncle's heart was in the right place, but he'd always been over-protective, overcompensating for us boys being fatherless. Particularly when it came to trusting new people. Like how Alexander always insisted on meeting any new friends of ours, and when he did, he'd basically interrogate them with questions about their background, intentions, and even their family history. It was infuriating enough as a teenager.

And now here he was, doing something similar when I was a grown man.

"I have to go," I snapped. "So, if you don't mind, I think it'd be best if you just leave."

I did not appreciate him bulldozing his way into my life and trying to tell me how to run it.

My uncle's chest swelled as he set his glass of scotch on the coffee table and walked toward the front door—the grand entrance. Where he stopped and turned, his shoulders softening.

"I didn't mean to offend you, Hunter. I'm sorry. I just want what's best for you."

The slight quiver in his voice sent a pang of guilt through me, a stark reminder that behind his prickly demeanor, he was trying to protect me.

As he walked out of the house, I shoved a hand through my hair.

"Is that why you're here?" I turned to my brother. "To team up against me over something that hasn't even happened yet?"

Yet?

Grayson walked over to the windows. "No. Like I said, I heard about the bloodbath on the news and thought I'd pop in to see how you were doing. When I arrived, Uncle Alexander was already here."

I glanced in the direction of my office, then looked at my watch. Before walking over to my brother.

"You vanished for four weeks this time," I said. "Not a word."

Like a walking cliché to my statement, Grayson said nothing.

"All three of us texted you," I challenged. "Alexander did, too."

I wonder if Alexander gave Grayson a piece of his mind before I came in here.

Grayson raised a brow. "You guys are comparing notes now?"

"When you have a brother that mysteriously and repeatedly vanishes for long periods of time, without so much as a word? Yeah. You check in with each other to make sure you're not dead or something."

Grayson looked out the window, at the little cottage of complications.

"Uncle Alexander will come to his senses if you like her," he mused.

"You know every time you vanish like this, I wonder if it's going to be the last time I ever see you."

"Are you dating her?" My brother motioned toward Luna's place.

"You want to vanish, whatever. But what's with the no texting?"

" 'Cause I haven't seen Alexander get that worked up in a bit."

"It takes two seconds to fire off, *Hey, brothers. FYI, I'm not dead.* Is that too much to ask?"

After a long sigh, Grayson looked down at his drink.

I flicked my fingers at my side and glanced at my watch again.

"At least tell me this," I said. "Is it just *our* family? Or do you disappear from everyone?"

Grayson took a slow sip of his scotch, swirling it around in his mouth before clearing his throat.

"It's not our family," was all he said. And I could tell by his eye avoidance, that was all I was going to get from him. Again.

The first time he disappeared like this, he'd made it pretty damn clear that he had no intention of sharing where he was going or why, so I had accepted his boundaries. Because what choice did I have?

What I didn't accept was leaving us hanging to wonder if he had simply vanished or if he died or something.

I pinched the bridge of my nose while Grayson nodded his chin toward the little cottage of complications.

"When he saw you with her, he must've seen something that got him all worked up. What was it?"

Part of me wanted to keep going after him. I'd always tried to respect his privacy and not press him too hard on his secrets, but it was the *no communication* part that got under my skin. But for now, I let it go, and answered his question.

"I don't know."

Grayson side-eyed me.

I scratched my jaw. "She was loopy from a sedative they gave her at the hospital, so I was helping her inside when her friend tried to take her from me. If you were watching from a distance, I suppose it might have looked...possessive."

Grayson considered this. "So, who is she?"

I sighed. "My polar opposite."

"She really the daughter of a killer?"

If only I had a big scotch in *my* hand.

"She believes her father is innocent."

I tried to place the unfamiliar pang in my chest as my mind floated into sad curiosity.

"Imagine what life must've been like in her shoes." I cleared my throat. "Walking around with a scarlet letter on her chest as the child of a convicted killer. She could have let that hold her down. She could have run and hidden in seclusion, but she didn't. She put herself through college and then law school and shows up every day in that courtroom with her head held with so much confidence you would never guess what she's lived through."

Grayson studied me. "You admire her."

I tightened my jaw. "It doesn't change things."

"Screw Uncle Alexander and his legacy bullshit. You've never shown an inkling of interest in any woman beyond one night. You like her? Go for it."

"I can't."

"Why?"

"It's complicated." Dad's murder screwed me up in the head, made it impossible for me to get close to people.

Grayson took a slow sip of his drink, staring out the window.

"You know what she did when someone was in danger?" I asked, the pang growing into an all-out ache. "She ran *toward* it. Put herself in harm's way to protect someone. She was fearless. Most people see danger, and they run the other way, but she lunged in front of it. She jumped into action, tried to save him, unlike..."

My brother turned his body, bringing his entire focus onto me.

"You were a kid, Hunter."

I couldn't look him in the eye.

"A nine-year-old cannot take on a grown man," he said. "Let alone an armed one."

"Easy for you to say." I tried to swallow down the knot of shame in my throat, but it remained lodged there, where it'd set up a home all those years ago. "You weren't the one home alone with him when it happened."

He didn't see and hear Dad choking on blood as he fought for his last breath.

"I can't stand back and allow something to happen to her, too," I added.

"*Allow?*" my brother hissed, his eyes flashing, probably realizing he wasn't extinguishing my guilt. Probably realized he never could. "Look, if you like her and want to help keep her safe, go for it. But don't you think it's possible you're overreacting?"

"I'm not."

"You've convinced yourself you did nothing to save Dad, and then the first flicker of danger that pops up with this girl, you're convinced she's about to die, too. And that it's your responsibility to save her."

"It's not a *flicker* of danger. She was attacked. And now that asshole thinks she has something worth choking her over."

"My point is," Grayson said, "your past might be like a magnifying glass to the present, making every danger seem larger. Amplifying your alarm for her."

Maybe. But it didn't change how I'd proceed.

"Do you think it's possible that you don't want to get close to her because you can't stomach losing another person you care about?"

"That's not it."

"You push everyone away before they have the possibility of getting close to you," he said. "Thus the string of one-night stands. But if this girl made you feel something before you had the chance to squash it? You should embrace it."

I shook my head. "I want to stay focused on finding Dad's killer."

Grayson's nostrils flared, and a sharp exhale escaped him, his jaw clenched in visible frustration.

"You ever stop to wonder why you work so hard to find Dad's killer?"

"To bring him to justice."

"Is that why?" Grayson asked. "Or is it a way of not accepting Dad's death?"

A heavy silence settled between us, the weight of Grayson's words sinking deep. My throat tightened, making any response impossible.

Grayson sighed. Set his drink down.

"Hunter, if you keep living in the past, it'll prevent you from having a future."

"You're one to talk." Grayson was as tortured and screwed in the head as I was. Look at all the fistfights he'd gotten into as a kid and now his vanishing acts.

"I have to go. I'm late for a meeting."

Maybe once I knew Luna was safe, I'd be able to focus.

"Barry, I'm sorry I'm late."

Barry's salt-and-pepper hair and matching beard reflected the early evening light that draped through the oversized window opposite my desk. When he rose to shake my hand, I had to look down at his stocky frame, clad in a dove-gray button-down, fitted black trousers.

His black leather jacket was an interesting touch—unorthodox, compared to the other investigators I'd worked with. Those ones always wore slacks and a tie.

"I appreciate you meeting with me. I'm excited for you to work on my father's case. Please. Sit."

I took a seat in the leather chair behind my mahogany desk. A surge of anticipation raced through me, seeing Barry Mansfield in the flesh, right in my office. He had solved more cases than any cold-case detective had in their entire career. The guy had a knack for uncovering facts, finding the right people to talk to, and actually *persuading* them to divulge pertinent information. Plus, he performed gymnastics with his analytical mind.

None of it was a sure thing, but it was hard to contain my thrill that I might finally get the answers that had eluded me my whole life.

"What did you find out about Franco Hopkins?" I asked.

With meticulous care, Barry placed his phone at a precise angle on my desk. He pressed the green recording button, and he gave it a once-over, ensuring the microphone was positioned equally between us.

"If it's all right, Mr. Lockwood, I'd like to get our prelim meeting about your father's case done first in case we run out of time. The next few days, I have meetings set up with police to go over the case, and I need to be prepared for them."

We wouldn't run out of time. But I held back my frustration because the stakes were too high to risk him getting pissed and walking away.

He was my last hope of ever finding the culprit who had killed my father. And why.

"What do you want to know?"

"I'd like you to recount everything that you remember from that night," Barry said.

"Have you had a chance to review the case files of all the other private investigators?" I asked, tapping my fingers lightly on the table and forcing a neutral expression, though my eyes darted quickly to the clock.

"I prefer to start with a fresh slate. It's been my experience that unconscious biases can weave their way into case files. Other private investigators' theories, for example. Once that happens, you're no longer looking at it with a fresh, completely unbiased set of eyes."

I rubbed my brow bone. "My father was home, working in his office."

"This one?"

"No. The office down the hall. I never go in there anymore. My mom and brothers were out that night, so it was just me and him. Someone broke into our home. Went into my father's office and slit his throat."

"Do you know how they got in?"

"The room next to my father's office is a mudroom. A place where us kids could come in from the backyard with our muddy boots and wash our hands in the utility sink. Police believe that's where the intruder entered. It was the only door that was unlocked in the house."

"So, this person may have had knowledge of your home's layout."

"Yes."

"Or they thought no one was home and were startled when they found your father. Did a lot of people know the layout of your home?"

I shifted. "A lot of people did. Family. Friends. Staff. Business associates. Not to mention strangers and acquaintances that would attend my father's elaborate parties."

"Did the killer take anything that night?"

"No. After my father was murdered, the assailant fled. Presumably out the same door he'd come in."

"*He*. So, they know it was a man?"

I shifted. "Yes, I saw him."

"Was he masked?"

"No."

"They have you work with a sketch artist?"

"Not enough detail to make an ID."

Barry scratched his ear. "The driveway leading up to your home isn't just long; it's secluded, winding." Which should have been gated, I noted. But Dad had never put in a gate around the estate. Mom almost put one in after his death but settled for a state-of-the-art security system and security team instead.

Barry continued to pull more details about my father's case from me, the ones I could remember, at least. I tried to stick to the facts, attempting to avoid any, as he said, unconscious biases that I may have formed throughout the years.

"And there was no evidence, no DNA, no fingerprints left behind?" Barry said.

"None."

"Did your father have any enemies?"

"None that I'm aware of. My father was the kindest person I had ever met. I had never once seen him lose his temper or even yell at my mother. Or us kids."

"What about his business?" Barry asked.

"From what I understand, his employees revered him. I was only a child when he died, so it's possible there's something I'm unaware of, but no other private investigator found anything that would point toward a likely motive for his death."

Not a thing.

When someone takes the life of the person who is the center of your universe, and you have no idea why, it haunts you day and night.

Barry continued to ask me clarification questions before finally winding down the meeting.

"What is your initial gut feeling telling you?" I asked.

Barry frowned. "It's dangerous to form hypotheses this early in the case. My next step is to read everything you provided me, and then go to the police station to read through all the police reports."

Barry stood up, as if he'd forgotten the urgent request I had for him earlier.

"What did you find about Franco Hopkins?"

Barry pressed stop on his phone recording and put his cell phone in his pocket.

"Franco Hopkins is a gangster. He's been running a crew for years, and he has unsavory men on his payroll who are linked to suspicious deaths, but no convictions."

"Hit men." My stomach sank.

Barry nodded in affirmation.

Shit.

I'd suspected the guy was dirty—but having hit men on your payroll took things to a whole new level.

"Until recently," Barry continued, "Franco has been out of the country, building up another organization he planned to put his cousin in charge of. So, there hasn't been a lot of chatter about Franco. Plus, the guy is good. Flying under the radar, never leaving enough evidence behind to get himself arrested."

"So, he's dangerous."

"Very."

I raked a hand through my hair so hard that a sharp pinch yanked a couple strands out as I stared at the unsuspecting cottage down the road.

"I'm sorry, sir. I hope your friend…"

Makes it? Survives? What was the end of that sentence?

Whatever it was, Barry cleared his throat and decided not to finish it.

"I'll be in touch," he said. And then he left me alone in the room to process this information.

What the hell was I going to do about this?

Anxiety churned in my gut as I began pacing, wanting to pull Barry back here, get him to help me more with Franco. But what, exactly, would I ask him to do?

Could someone locate and reach out to Franco? Offer him a payout to leave Luna alone? No. That would never work. Franco was convinced she had something of his, and without providing it to him, he wouldn't be cooperative.

Could I get the word to Franco that Luna had no such evidence? Even if I could find Franco, he would never believe the lawyer who tried to put his cousin behind bars.

I paced faster.

There has to be a solution. This cannot become like it was when I was a kid, having a killer lurking in the shadows. How can I protect her?

Getting a restraining order would be a start, but I had prosecuted several murderers whose victims had an active restraining order in place. That piece of paper didn't keep the likes of Franco Hopkins from killing their targets.

Fuck.

I picked up my phone and made the only call I could.

"I need you to do something for me," I said. "It's urgent."

CHAPTER 10
Luna

The clicking of camera shutters rose in intensity as I stepped up to the microphone positioned in front of television cameras, still photographers, and reporters packed within the media room. I squinted as cameras flashed like fireflies in a summer field and a hush spread through the crowd like an ocean wave, the room seemingly holding its breath.

Waiting to hear what I was about to say.

I should have braced myself better for this angry ache that pulsed through my stomach as I stared at reporters. I remember my mother, eyes red and voice shaky, dialing one news outlet after another, her pleas for them to listen met with cold rejection. They weren't interested in running a single segment telling my dad's side of the story, too busy labeling him a child killer. I had been desperate, naively convinced that if just *one* reporter would give us the opportunity to explain the truth, everyone would see he wasn't a murderer.

But no one gave us the chance. And now here I was, standing in front of people just like them.

My hands clutched the sides of the podium, knuckles whitening as the weight of my decision bore down on me. That microphone before me wasn't just a device; it was a chance to tell them off for their smear campaign against Dominic and to describe my father's plight with injustice. This was live TV, so it wasn't like they could stop me, and for God's sake, Dad deserved someone to defend him not only in court, but also in the public eye.

A restless cough echoed from the back, and hushed whispers filled the gaps between the silences. A woman at the front glanced pointedly at her watch while a guy moved his finger in a circular motion at me, then pointed to the camera.

I set my prewritten speech down on the stand and opened my mouth, prepared to mend some scars of my past, but the words lodged in my throat with the image of Dominic bleeding out in my mind's eye. With the Vigilante standing over him, holding that knife.

If I failed to use this opportunity to help catch an active killer, how would I be able to sleep at night?

Yet the words to clear my father's reputation burned my tongue and threatened to erupt.

"Good evening. My name is Luna Payne. I am a criminal defense attorney in the state of Illinois, and earlier today, I was an eyewitness to the crime committed by the man known as the Windy City Vigilante."

Stay on point, Luna. Your time to clear Dad's name is coming.

"I know some people in this city think this type of vigilante justice is doing society a favor since these perpetrated assaults target alleged violent criminals, but I saw firsthand what the Windy City Vigilante is capable of, and I can tell you, he is nothing more than a cold-blooded murderer."

A chorus of whispers built like a crescendo, and I squinted, momentarily thrown off by a particularly aggressive camera flash.

"Earlier today, he ambushed my client and killed him in broad daylight. This vigilante is growing more brazen and is becoming a danger to our society. Anyone who stumbled onto that scene could have gotten hurt or killed themselves."

"Is it true your client was actually guilty of murder?" a reporter shouted.

A bead of sweat threatened to drip down my back.

"My client was found not guilty," I said tersely. "And even if he wasn't, the so-called Vigilante attempts to veil his crimes beneath the blanket of justice, but he is circumventing thorough investigations and criminal processes for his own agenda. The only thing we know for certain is that he is a violent killer that needs to be stopped."

"If the Vigilante is watching right now, what do you want to say to him?"

I locked eyes with the lens of the central television camera, picturing him on the other side.

"Your reign of violence is coming to an end. We will find out who you are and put you behind bars."

CHAPTER 11

Luna

"Uh, Luna?" A soft knock preceded my bedroom door creaking open wider than it already was. "There are some guys outside your place."

Sean had slept on the couch all night, even though it was completely unnecessary for him to stay and babysit me. But Sean was worried about Franco's threat, not to mention the Vigilante's potential reaction to yesterday's press conference. I did essentially throw down the gauntlet, after all. Nothing like poking the bear to elicit an angry response.

Come to think of it, I was surprised I'd never heard from Hunter last night. Sure, Sean ended up staying the night, and Hunter could probably see his van from his mansion, but still. Hunter seemed genuinely concerned about Franco and my safety.

Franco. Could his guys be outside? Or maybe the Vigilante, here to off the person who'd witnessed his last crime?

My heart trampolined into my throat.

My hands shook slightly as I reached into the closet, gripping the baseball bat, its cold, hard surface providing a small measure of reassurance. Then I grabbed my phone and tiptoed into the living room to glance out the front window to see how many men were out there.

"What the hell?" I tossed the baseball bat onto the floor with a clank and set my cell phone on the kitchen table before storming outside into the early morning air.

The sun had only recently risen, birds chirping away, perched in the various trees surrounding the cottage.

"Excuse me!" I snapped to the man standing on the ladder on my front porch. "What do you think you're doing?"

The guy was holding something black in his hand, something with wires that he was screwing into the roof's overhang.

The bearded man stared down at me. "Installing the security cameras, ma'am."

"I didn't order any security cameras. You have the wrong place."

"This is the right place, ma'am."

"It's not. Take them down. Now."

I glanced out at the other handful of men installing security cameras around the perimeter of my cottage.

"I can't do that, ma'am."

"Take them down, or I will call the police."

"Feel free; I have all the paperwork in order."

I clenched my fists. The morning breeze was gentle, but I wouldn't be in about five seconds.

"If you don't take those down, I will knock them down with a baseball bat!"

The guy rolled his eyes and gave me a dismissive wave.

"Destruction of private property is a crime," he said lazily and continued securing the camera in place.

"This is my private property!"

"This here is part of the Lockwood estate, ma'am."

I blinked.

"Hunter Lockwood ordered these?"

"Yes, ma'am."

Mother. F'er.

Rationally, I knew Hunter meant well and that he was doing this as an act of protection.

But installing cameras around someone's private residence was a *complete* invasion of privacy. I had found solace in the comfort of my yard, doing yoga and going for walks because it was the only place I was free from the suffocating thoughts in my head. Now I couldn't even hide on the side of the cottage out of view from the mansion—someone would be watching my every move, robbing me of my sanctuary.

The sight of the camera triggered a momentary flashback of reporters shoving their intrusive lenses into my face—voyeurs getting footage for their smear campaigns. Also without my consent.

I clenched my fists tighter, my lip quivering.

How dare Hunter install cameras like this? I thought we'd shared a special understanding yesterday, but evidently, he had so little respect for me, that he didn't even think I deserved a choice in the matter, nor a heads-up.

How stupid of me to let my guard down. I had started to trust him a little, and he went and did this.

What an act of betrayal.

I did not pass go. I did not collect $200. I charged up the expansive emerald lawn separating our homes.

Hunter's mansion sat on a hilltop of arrogance, looking down at the people he apparently thought he could control.

It was a longer walk than I preferred, but I was still blood-pumping furious when I reached his ridiculously gigantic front doors. Who had solid mahogany doors with intricate hand-carved designs? Presumably custom-made.

I raised my fists and leaned into them, ready to pound so hard, it might crack one of those designs, but when I swung, the door flew open.

I gasped, flailing my arms to try to regain my balance, but face-planted into the bare chest of Hunter Lockwood. Wearing a pair of casual gray cotton pants and nothing else, he caught me in his firm arms. And had the audacity to hold me for a beat.

I shoved Hunter off me and glared at him.

"How did you know I was here before I knocked?"

He motioned to his own security cameras—notably the ones pointed to the pathway between our homes.

"Saw you marching up here like the big bad wolf getting ready to huff and puff and blow my house down."

I wanted to slap that smirk off his face. His caring behavior yesterday didn't undo the line he'd crossed today.

"Care to explain to me why there's a bunch of men outside my place, setting up cameras, Lockwood?"

He leaned against the door frame as his gaze glided over my appearance with a flare of lust in his eyes.

Damn it. I hadn't even thrown a robe on when Sean woke me up, and then I became so angry, I had stormed outside and all the way over here without giving a second thought to my sleeping attire: a barely there tank top with no bra and a pair of shorts that my ass cheeks were slightly hanging out of. All so tight, it left nothing to the imagination.

"You're angrier than I thought you'd be, Little Leopard."

My nostrils flared. "Don't call me a pet name. Get the cameras down."

"A thank you would be nice."

"Thank you?" Unbelievable. "Let me give you some advice." I stepped into his space until our noses were only inches apart. Super annoying that I had to look *up* at him; *he'd better not misconstrue that in our power dynamic.* "If you think any woman would appreciate being spied on, you're more out of touch with reality than I thought."

"It's a security system."

"And you just installed it. Without any heads-up."

"According to my private investigator, Franco Hopkins is a very dangerous man," Hunter said while I tried to hide the anxiousness that took flight in my stomach. "Franco believes you have something of Dominic's, and if he's desperate enough, he'd do just about anything to get it back. And he has other dangerous men at his disposal more than willing to do his bidding. Not to mention the Vigilante is still out there. After what you witnessed and the press conference that followed, who knows if he's planning to come after you next?"

"It's not *your* decision what protection methods *I* employ. I have door locks, a cell phone capable of dialing 911, and a baseball bat, among other security measures that do not involve you *spying* on me. Those cameras violate my rights."

His eyes narrowed. "I wanted to surround your cottage with armed men but thought this was an acceptable compromise. For now."

"For now." Unreal.

"I'm trying to keep you safe, Luna."

"Good intentions don't relieve you of your responsibility to respect the rights and boundaries of other human beings."

Hunter tightened his jaw, and his piercing gaze hardened as he peered down at me in barely contained restraint.

"I'd venture to say that most people, should their life be threatened, would appreciate the efforts I'm going through to help you."

"I don't need your help, Hunter."

His posture tensed. "I'm not accustomed to people talking to me like this."

"Well, maybe growing up rich and powerful makes people too afraid to speak their mind around you." I put my hands on my hips. "But you don't have to worry about that with me."

His brows, which had been drawn tight in irritation, slowly relaxed as the edges of his mouth curled up, a spark of mischief appearing in his eyes.

"Do you find this entertaining?" I snapped.

Hunter's features softened, and he took a deliberate step closer, lowering his voice to a velvety tone.

"I find you fascinating."

My body betrayed me, warming as his eyes roved up and down my body.

"People probably look at your small frame and assume you would back down from any confrontation, but you lean into it. You *are* the confrontation, aren't you, Little Leopard?"

I clenched my jaw. "Take the cameras down. Immediately."

I turned on my heel and tossed my hair over my shoulder, digging into the ground with each step away from his front door, resisting the reflex to tug at my too-short shorts, where my ass cheeks were currently launching their own escape.

I could imagine the scene before him, a thin, five-foot-four woman with a tangled mess of brown hair storming down the front lawn of his mansion.

"I won't be taking them down."

I turned around, wondering if my face was as red as it felt.

"You cannot put cameras on my private property without my consent."

"Actually, it's *my* private property. I own the cottage. You're the tenant. And as I'm sure you'll read in the rental agreement that you signed, I have the right to install a security system so long as that system doesn't breach the privacy inside the dwelling."

Son of a...

I would absolutely read that rental agreement much closer when I got home. Even if that clause was in the contract, Hunter might think he won here, but I knew exactly what I would do next.

CHAPTER 12
Hunter

"Sir, we have a problem," my lead security officer said as soon as I answered my phone. Located at an off-site location, he kept an eye on my estate, mostly, but also monitored threats that came up from enemies I'd sometimes make as a prosecutor. But last night, I'd given him a new task. "Have you looked at the security footage recently?"

I tightened the towel around my waist, having just finished showering when my phone had gone off. During which I couldn't stop grinning from my earlier interaction with that feisty spitfire Luna. Damn, that woman was fine when she was mad.

"Not for an hour or so. Why?"

The cameras outside Luna's cottage also came with an alarm system that would get triggered if anyone broke into her house. Which had created a complication that we had to work around.

Normally, when a person entered their home armed with a security system, they would have to punch in a code so it would deactivate that alarm within thirty seconds. But having that code meant the person could also *deactivate* said system. Perpetually.

Luna wouldn't be cooperative, so I gave my team the task of handling the logistics. The security system would remain armed at all times, which meant anytime a door or window was opened, my security team had to ensure it wasn't a break-in or actual threat—at which time they'd enter the code to cancel the cavalry.

Rinse. Repeat.

We'd already tested the system earlier today, and it was working great. Giving me a small sense of peace that Luna was protected.

"You might want to take a look, sir. Let us know how you'd like to proceed."

I walked into my bedroom and tossed on a pair of boxer briefs and shorts, checking the security cameras on my flat screen.

But the footage was...

What in the actual hell was I looking at? Was that an *ass crack*? I flipped through the different cameras, but they were all the same—two slightly blurry butt cheeks, each with its own crack.

Son of a bitch.

I rushed out of my house, making a beeline for that little cottage.

Looking up at the security cameras, I clenched my fists.

Little trolls dangled from a string in front of them, their hair taped against the rim so that their little bare asses were pressed against the camera lenses.

I walked up to Luna's front door and swung my fist to pound on it, but she opened the door mid-swing, making me fall forward slightly. Just like she'd done when she'd stomped to my place.

When I pushed myself upright—without knocking her fragile frame over—I nearly forgot what I'd come here to say. She was dressed in a tank top, no bra, with her nipples pressing against the fabric. She probably knew it would distract me from my mission and unleash images of throwing her to the ground and releasing my anger until she screamed my name.

I had to force myself to concentrate, which further aggravated me.

"What the hell?" I pointed to a security camera.

"Good afternoon to you, too, Hunter. Having a nice day?"

"Take them down."

"You know, I saw you storming over here. Huffing and puffing like you were going to come blow my house down," she said slowly, an evil glint in her eye, repeating my words from earlier. Then she took a sip of her water, a smile dancing dangerously on the edge of her lips.

"Take. Them. Down."

"I'm sorry," she said in a much-too-pleasant tone. "If you read my rental agreement, it states that while *you* may have the power to install security cameras, the space in *front* of the security cameras doesn't belong to you. It's occupied by your tenant."

Unbelievable. I wasn't sure if she was right. I was a criminal prosecutor, not a real estate lawyer. Why did my business manager rent out these godforsaken cottages, anyway? Who cared if they were abandoned? We could've hired people to take care of them. I'd rip him a new asshole for putting me in this position, and so help me, I'd have my real estate lawyer look at that contract with a fine-tooth comb.

But in the meantime...

I jumped up and yanked the troll down.

Threw it to the ground.

"Hey!"

Made my way to the next camera.

"Stop!"

Did the same thing.

"Hunter, I swear to God, I'll put them back up."

Closing the gap between us, I captured her gaze, ensuring she couldn't avoid the intensity burning in my eyes.

"You want to get yourself killed? That's up to you. But I'm not going to stand by and allow it to happen."

"*Allow.* There's that word again. Here's a news flash, Hunter: you don't own the world and all the people in it. We have the right to live life as we choose."

"You have no right to be this reckless."

"You have no right to spy on me with your cameras."

As I edged closer, the sweet aroma of strawberries from her breath teased my senses.

"These cameras are here to keep you safe."

She jabbed a finger at me, her voice filled with defiance. "You're used to controlling everyone and everything, and you can't handle the fact that I'm not going along with it. Maybe that's what you're really pissed about."

"Is that really what you think?"

The groan of an engine cut through the tense silence between us.

"Why do you care, anyway?" she barked. "Don't you have better things to do with your time than obsess over a *tenant?*"

Her emphasis on the word *tenant* twisted a sharp blade in my gut. Rage bubbled up inside me, my knuckles whitening. Why *did* I care this much? And why couldn't I stop thinking about her covered in strawberries and whipped cream while I licked it off her body?

"You want a reason? How about this? I own this cottage and have a vested interest in not having a homicide take place on my land."

She faltered, her chest deflating. Even as she attempted to hold her chin high, a tiny tremor betrayed her lips.

Damn, I was an A-hole. I shouldn't have snapped like that. Should have told her the reason I wanted to keep her safe was because it was *her*. Did she honestly think I'd be so callous as to look at her as nothing more than a tenant after what we'd shared?

"You're such a dick," she said.

I pushed a hand through my hair and forced myself to take a calming breath.

"I'm sorry." I pinched the bridge of my nose, and then I searched her eyes, yearning for a hint of understanding, a glimmer that she grasped the depths of my concern—that if something happened to her, it would take me back to a dark place I couldn't endure. "Maybe you think the cameras are an overreach, but this time, I want to do something before it's too late."

She caught her breath before a hint of realization softened her gaze.

A cardinal, perched upon a nearby tree, unleashed a jubilant chirp that sliced through the stillness. A gentle breeze tenderly caressed her gorgeous hair, each strand dancing and intertwining with the whispering wind, which carried a sweet scent of blooming flowers and dew-kissed grass.

A man cleared his throat. "Pardon the interruption, but are you Luna Payne?"

My muscles tightened, and Luna blinked. "I am."

"I need you to sign here, please."

I glared at the black sedan idling in the driveway. What delivery driver used a black Mercedes?

Luna signed for what appeared to be a letter, based on the flat folder.

Signature required, I noted.

The guy climbed back into his Mercedes, the engine humming as he drove away.

"Luna, don't open—" But before I could finish warning her it might be from Franco, she'd already torn the folder open and was reading whatever paper was inside.

At first, her eyes were wide, scanning the top again, as if rereading it to make sure she hadn't misunderstood.

"What?" I growled, unable to shake the irritation from our fight.

She grinned, pointing at the paper. "Someone is threatening to kill me!"

What in the actual hell?

"And you're *smiling*," I said.

"Do you know what this means?"

"That you're certifiable."

"No. They say they want me to back off my father's case. Someone is scared! It went public that I filed the writ of habeas corpus. So, whoever this is knows that I'm trying to get my dad out of jail!"

"Your dad is convicted of killing a *child*. Maybe it's some nut bag who has a problem with that."

Lord knew Luna seemed to be a magnet for threats. Were all the bad men in the city going to come after her now? How in the hell was I going to keep her alive?

"No." Luna smiled wider, holding the paper up. "This is not just anybody. Anybody could post a threat on social media or on the dark web. Whoever this is had this letter sent to me directly and made me *sign* for it."

I'd have to have my PI check into this. See if there was a postmark trail of who'd sent it. Doubtful with a death threat, but sometimes, criminals were morons.

Luna continued, "Made sure I received it. Which means this is a legit threat!"

"And yet you're *still* smiling."

"This means someone is worried!" She began pacing, like she couldn't control the excitement buzzing through her. "God, I hope this isn't why my dad was in the infirmary," she mused.

Finally, she looked worried. Disturbed. Appropriate behavior.

But then she shook her head. "No. When I called yesterday to check on him, they said he wasn't the target of the fight. He was collateral damage."

Her eyes lit up as they scanned the letter once more, and the excitement that must have been waiting to break free for nearly two decades couldn't be contained. Guess she'd get back to her worry later, but for now, her posture straightened, and a heaviness seemed to lift off her shoulders.

"This means they know something about my dad's case. They know my dad is innocent, and they don't want me digging around and getting his conviction overturned. Because if that happens, somebody might actually look into the case again and find the real killer!"

"You know, Luna, when someone receives a death threat, the appropriate response is to go inside, call the police, and be scared."

But she didn't look scared at all. She even hopped—freaking hopped—as she went inside her house.

And that's when a chilling thought settled in: she wasn't just working her ass off to get her father's case overturned. She was letting it blind her, dangerously so. Although Luna was in there, calling the police right now, she wasn't having the appropriate emotional response, the one that sparked self-preservation when faced with danger.

Which meant keeping Luna Payne alive was going to be a lot harder than I thought.

CHAPTER 13

Luna

"Dad." I breathed a sigh of relief to finally see him, but as he plopped down in the seat across from me, a pang of hurt stabbed my heart at the sight of his face. One of his eyes was swollen with an angry shade of purple and blue while his lip was split and puffy. And that was just what I could see through the smudged, fingerprint-streaked glass partition that divided us.

The harsh glare of fluorescent lighting reflected unnaturally off the cold steel tables bolted to the floor, and a faint, acrid scent of industrial cleaning solutions hung heavily in the space, where hushed conversations were interspersed with the authoritative voices of the guards.

"What happened?" I asked.

"It was nothing."

"You're sitting funny."

"I'm fine."

"Your ribs hurt, don't they?"

"They'll heal. Just bruises."

"Did someone attack you?" Because now that I'd had more time to digest that letter, what if the prison was wrong? What if the target of the fight *was* my father?

"No, honey, fights in prisons happen all the time."

"You need to be honest with me."

"I am being honest. My cellmate was the one getting attacked over a territorial dispute. It had nothing to do with me. I was just trying to protect him and took a few hits while doing so. That's all."

I searched the depths of his eyes, looking for any hints of deception, but only found the familiar, sincere gaze I'd always known. But this fight was a grim reminder of just how dangerous prisons could be.

Case in point, the guys at the far end of Joliet Prison's visitor room were staring at me—out of anger or sexual desire, I couldn't be sure. Either way, Sean would be berating himself for agreeing to lend me his van today to visit my dad, unaccompanied.

With my car still awaiting an estimate in the shop, I had to do some serious convincing for Sean to let me come alone, but he had a podcast to record today, and I reminded him that a prison had guards everywhere. It was safer than most places, really. Plus, other than asking to borrow his vehicle, my visiting my dad wasn't his decision. I'd take public transportation if I had to.

I needed to see that Dad was okay.

And he was, as okay as he could be in this godforsaken place.

Prison had aged him—not just the time he had spent physically in there. The emotional and psychological impact of living behind bars in an institution left their marks. Deep lines etched into the pale skin of his face, prematurely sagging near his jawline and above his eyelids. His green eyes had dulled in color, and the whites of his eyes had darkened into an ivory. His hair was almost all silver now. He looked seventy-seven, not fifty-seven years of age.

I hated that he saw very little daylight. I hated that he had no control over his diet or nutrition. When I was a child, my dad had a muscular, tan, athletic frame. He jogged a lot, and he walked everywhere since we didn't have a car. But now, his bones were starting to poke through his emaciated body. Some prisoners spent a lot of time working out, but with how solemn he seemed during our visits, I suspected my dad was too depressed to bother.

"I heard there was a murder at the courthouse," Dad said.

Crap. It always amazed me how quickly intel floated through prison.

"Heard you were there when it happened," he added.

"It was that Vigilante." I swallowed. "He killed Dominic."

Dad's eyebrows furrowed. "Dominic Hopkins?"

I nodded.

"The kid that used to live a few blocks from us?" Another nod. "Why?"

"Because the Vigilante is a psychopathic serial killer."

"Did you get hurt?" Dad's widened eyes combed over my face. I hid my bandaged hand beneath the table.

"I'm fine. The Vigilante ran off a few seconds after I saw him," I assured, leaving out the part where I'd gotten stitches. Also leaving out the part where Franco seemed to think I'd taken something from Dominic as he lay dying.

"But you actually came *face-to-face* with the Windy City Vigilante?"

Uh-oh.

"Only for a few seconds."

Dad's voice rose higher. "What if he's worried you could identify him?"

"He wore a mask."

He leaned forward. "Yeah, but what if he's second-guessing leaving a witness behind that might be able to help police ID him?"

Dad hadn't seen the press conference then, where I publicly put pressure on the city to hunt him down. Guess I'd file that little nugget away for a later time.

"I have no idea who the guy is," I assured. Though I'd been wondering about it ever since.

Surely, he was some stranger I'd never met, but when one comes face-to-face with a masked killer, one can't help but look at the people in her circle and wonder. No matter how statistically unlikely it was.

A guard escorted another prisoner into this visiting room. My mind was spinning...

"How tall would you say Rodney is?"

Rodney—Charlotte's father. My dad's former cellmate and only friend. According to my dad, Rodney was always professing his innocence and spiraled into anger, often griping about guilty men walking free while Rodney was serving time for grand theft auto—a crime he didn't commit.

I'd seen him once, on the other side of the visitor room, but he'd gotten out a couple of years ago. Right around the time the Vigilante started his crimes.

"Rodney isn't the Vigilante." Dad leaned back in his chair. "He's a family man."

Maybe he was before the justice system ruined his life.

"I know, but how tall? Six two?"

My dad looked down, and winced when he moved the wrong way. "How tall was the Vigilante?"

"You first."

Dad's mouth pursed. "Six four. How tall was the Vigilante?"

"Same height."

Plus, Rodney had the same build as the Vigilante, and it would explain the Vigilante's motive—seeing criminals getting off scot-free while Rodney had served time.

Come to think of it, why hadn't Sean ever explored the case of the Vigilante for his podcast? It would make for one heck of a true crime episode. Maybe even a string of them, trying to solve the identity of the masked criminal.

"Rodney isn't the Windy City Vigilante." Dad shook his head.

I was glad Dad was so certain because I wasn't. But maybe that was silly. Chicago had three million people in it. The odds I knew the man behind the mask were slim to none.

"Yeah. Silly thought," I claimed, looking at the big clock and counting down the time we had to discuss one other important topic. "Anyway, change of subject. I officially filed the writ of habeas corpus."

The familiar wave of unease washed over my dad's face. The one that appeared anytime I talked about the work I was doing on his case.

When I was a kid, Dad's public defender did the best he could, filing the necessary motions after his guilty verdict. It included a notice of intent to pursue post-conviction relief and several other appeals. But none of them helped.

The state of Illinois was convinced they'd gotten it right.

But the reason my father was found with the body was because he had been walking home from work that night and happened to stumble upon the boy bleeding in an alley. My dad had blood on him because he had given him CPR and mouth-to-mouth while screaming for someone to call for help. And they seemed to overlook what my father said in his first statement to the police and in every statement since: that he had seen someone else in that alley. A man who'd gotten into a dark vehicle and driven off.

The police didn't believe my dad's version of events because it was too dark to see what this unknown male looked like; thus, he couldn't provide them with a description or an adequate description of the vehicle or plate number. They didn't believe him because there were no other witnesses who could back up his story. They didn't believe him because he was found at the crime scene with the victim's DNA on his shirt.

But mostly, they didn't believe my father because he had a motive. The day before, the kid had come into the convenience store where my dad worked and had stolen twenty-three dollars' worth of stuff. As a result, my dad's job was jeopardized when he got reamed out by his boss.

The theft was caught on camera, so when the kid wound up dead the next day, it was speculated my father had sought revenge.

The lack of any other suspect absolutely had to have weighed in the jury's mind during my father's trial. I mean, when only one suspect appeared before them, and a prominent prosecutor pointed the finger at my father, what else were they to think?

When the medical examiner described the brutal beating that would cause his injuries, my dad was the one at the receiving end of the jury's disgusted and horrified glares.

A revenge kill, the prosecutor claimed, dodging and weaving the facts of the case to string together a plausible story. It didn't matter that my dad had no injuries on his fists that you would expect to find if he'd just been in a violent altercation. My dad had no scratches or marks of any kind.

The kid was an athlete, but he hadn't fought back? Never landed one single punch?

And why didn't the kid have defensive wounds? If he was being beaten, he didn't instinctively throw his arms up to defend himself?

Didn't matter.

Dodge and weave, the prosecutor went, speculating a weapon had likely been used, such as a bat or a pipe. And when they couldn't find that weapon, he dodged and weaved again, saying my dad had somehow miraculously hidden the weapon where no one had ever found it.

You can't have it both ways, I remember thinking. Weaving a narrative that fit with certain evidence and dismissing other evidence that didn't fit with that same narrative. But that was exactly what the prosecutor did.

But my father was innocent, so I was certain the jury would declare him not guilty. Because back then, I was naive in thinking you couldn't be convicted of a crime you didn't commit.

My mom was convinced of that, too, which was why she'd allowed her eight-year-old daughter to hear the verdict.

I remember seeing those jury members filing in, fidgeting with the bow on my dress as I sat in that hard wooden bench.

"We find the defendant," a man in the courtroom started.

My heartbeat was like a butterfly, so excited to finally, finally have the last day of the trial here. I couldn't wait to show Dad the backyard. I'd cleaned all his tools with a scrub brush, so they were nice and shiny, and the wood was waiting there, too. After we went out to dinner to celebrate, we could go home, and finally, he could read me a bedtime story.

Life would go back to normal, only this time, I'd never take him for granted. Ever. I'd hug him every single chance I got, and I'd bake him cookies if Mom let me, and I'd kiss his cheek a hundred times every morning.

I'd made a list of all the fun things we'd do together, too. Like going to the zoo, and he could finally teach me how to ride my bike with no training wheels.

"Guilty."

My heart crashed to the ground. The guy had read it wrong, and he needed to correct it, but instead, he handed the paper off to someone else, who also didn't correct it.

"Mom, what's happening?" My voice was high-pitched.

I searched for reassurance, but instead was met with tears dripping down her cheeks.

I dragged my gaze to my father, and when he looked at me over his shoulder, his eyes were also blurry with tears, and his lip was quivering.

"Mom..." I choked. "What's happening?"

"I'm so sorry, Luna."

No. No, no, no!

This had to be a mistake!

I hopped up and ran toward my dad, dodging the arms of my mom, squirming out of the hold of some security guy, and slammed my chest into my daddy's, wrapping my arms around his neck.

"Daddy, what's happening?"

"I'm sorry, Luna."

No! This couldn't be real!

When hands tried to pry me away from my dad's arms, I swatted them away, my high-pitched cries the only sound in the courtroom.

I'm never letting him go. If they take him, they have to take me. I can't live without him! I can't live without his pancakes in the morning. I can't live without him playing tag with me outside, or barbequing hamburgers on the grill just the way I like it, or hugging me and loving me and being with me every single day. The only thing that got me through this trial was the firm hope that soon, he'd return to us.

But now they were stealing him from us.

"Daddy has to go away for a little while," he said.

"People said if you're found guilty, you'll never get out," I cried.

"I'm so sorry, honey," Daddy whispered. His large hands, callused and

warm, gently cradled my small face, thumbs brushing away the salty tears that dripped over my lip and onto my tongue.

"You'll be okay," he said.

"No. I won't. This hurts too bad, Daddy. I'm scared. I don't want to live without you."

"Your mother will be with you. And we can visit all the time, okay? I'm still here, honey. And I'll always be with you. In there." He tapped the spot over my heart.

No.

"Will they let us hug each other if you go to prison?" My voice trembled harder.

His breath quivered. "I don't know."

There had to be a way out of this!

"Run with me, Daddy," I whispered desperately in his ear. "We can hide somewhere they'll never find us."

We can sprint out of this courthouse and into the woods, and then we can spend the night and make a fire and wait until people aren't looking for him and walk to the next town and get on a bus and go far, far away.

"It doesn't work like that, honey." Dad's eyes overflowed with tears, and he tried to smile the way he did whenever he tried to calm me down.

A security guard grabbed my arm, his hand as cold as his heart.

"No!" I shouted.

But the guy wrenched me away, my fingers stretching out for my father—reaching, grasping for him, my chest ice cold, robbed of his warmth.

"Daddy!" I kicked wildly in the air as the guy held me to his torso, unable to stop them from making my dad stand up and start walking toward the door.

"I love you, honey."

"Daddy, don't go!"

When the heavy door clanged shut behind him, my sobs echoed in the courtroom with the deafening finality that left an excruciating void.

. . .

My father was gone, ripped from my world, and I was cast into an alternate reality, a nightmare I never woke up from.

When I got older, I even wrote to the Innocence Project, but they got flooded with thousands of letters a year. They only had the bandwidth to take on one percent of the cases, which meant ninety-nine percent of the desperate pleas for help went unanswered. Including ours.

Mom had long given up by that point, accepting the injustice. She disapproved of me dedicating all of my time to my father's case, telling me I was being foolish and wasting my life, chasing false hope. Which created a strain in the relationship between my mother and me.

"Are you seeing anyone?" he asked.

"Dad..."

"I worry about you. You dedicate every waking hour to this case, and it's not healthy."

"Sitting in a prison cell isn't healthy."

"No father would ever want to sentence his daughter to this kind of life. You need to make friends, Luna. Date. Go to clubs, whatever it is young people do these days. I don't want you to wind up alone because of this."

He'd been trying to convince me to give up on him for a long time now.

"I'm fine, Dad." How could I move on with my life while my father rotted in prison? I couldn't ever truly be happy unless his wrongful conviction was overturned.

"I know how expensive that private investigator was that you hired."

"Dad..."

"He didn't find anything new."

"That's not true. He made a list of next steps. Like hiring a second medical examiner to review the autopsy."

"And how much will that cost, Luna?"

"You let me worry about that."

My dad frowned. "Please, for my sake, just let this go. It's been almost twenty years."

"Only two of which I've been a lawyer," I reminded him. "I believe we can demonstrate that your original representation was inadequate, Dad. There were some procedural things your public defender should have done differently. Please be patient and trust me."

My cell phone buzzed. I almost didn't look at it, heartbroken by my dad's hopelessness, by his lack of excitement that things had finally been put into motion. But when I did check it, my heart started racing.

"Oh my God." I smiled. "Dad. I need to get you a suit."

I turned my phone to show him the email.

"The judge has set a date for our hearing."

"Does that mean he granted it?" Dad asked.

Did he not listen to any of our prior conversations?

"When you file a writ of habeas corpus, they schedule a hearing. You and I will stand before the judge, and he'll rule on the motion then." If he declined it, it'd be game over. "If he approves it, we begin the process of requesting a new trial." Which was another step. "Point is"—I smiled—"the hearing for the habeas corpus is actually on the calendar."

"Time's up." A guard tapped my dad's shoulder.

Hot tears threatened to spill, the familiar pang of separation clutching at my heart, as it did every time we said goodbye. I wanted so badly to bring him home to a warm bed, and a homemade meal with me. Not let him go back to suffering in a concrete cell with bars.

"I love you, Dad."

"I love you, sweetie."

His smile, tinged with sadness, lingered in the air as he shuffled toward the imposing steel door. Its deafening bang echoed the finality of our parting.

Every departure was a jarring reminder of the reality we'd been thrust into. A reality where a cold, unyielding gate stood between a father and his daughter.

The oppressive walls receded behind me as I walked out of the prison, replaced by the vastness of the outside world, but a loneliness clung to me, suffocating in its grip. Fresh air and the enchanting smell of a coming storm were too light after the suffocating gloom inside. It seemed wrong that a world of liberty existed a mere stone's throw away from where my father wasted away.

As I threaded my way through the labyrinth of parked cars, footsteps, measured and unhurried, echoed behind me. A shiver prickled the back of my neck, creeping its way down as each step became heavier than the last. The rhythmic tap seemed to mock my racing heartbeat, lurking ever closer in the silent space.

Over my shoulder, I threw a hurried glance. Vehicles stood like mute witnesses under the weak lighting of the coming storm, but there was no discernible figure. Yet the steps that had mirrored my own had stopped as suddenly as mine had.

Turning abruptly, I cut a path to the right, weaving between two hulking SUVs. The footsteps swung, matching my change in direction. Heart pounding in my ears, I darted behind three more cars and spun sharply to the left, attempting to throw off whoever might be following me.

The harsh echo of the footsteps skewed left as well, confirming my worst fears.

This time, when I risked a glance over my shoulder, a figure emerged. A hood obscured his face, hands plunged deep into the recesses of his hoodie. He stood with a predatory lean, shoulders slightly hunched, his posture casting an unmistakable shadow of menace merely thirty feet away.

Surely, no one would dare attack someone in a prison parking lot. They had cameras. Guards right inside those doors, maybe even perched at other locations. My eyes darted around, searching for the help I assumed was here, only to be met with emptiness. No guards in sight, and if there were security cameras, were they actively monitored? By people who would come running if they spotted an attack?

My hands shook as I fumbled in my pocket, fingers desperate to grasp the cold metal of my keys. A rising taste of bile burned my throat, the sharp sting of encroaching panic as I threaded the keys between my fingers, transforming the mundane into a makeshift weapon.

My feet shifted into a jog, and the man matched my pace, his footfalls a grim metronome.

I glanced back at the building, but running back to it would take too long—he'd catch me. The van was closer. The smarter option was to get inside it, lock the doors, and speed away.

I was only four rows away now, but he was gaining on me.

My harsh breaths synced with my rapid steps as I sprinted past the first row, then the second, and finally the third.

I was only a few feet away from the van when something dark flashed behind me.

And slammed into my back.

CHAPTER 14
Luna

My shoulder collided with the unforgiving pavement with a sharp jolt, absorbing the brunt of the impact and shielding my face from the blow. Intense pain radiated through my arm a split second before my chest crashed onto the hot, rough surface.

I rolled onto my back with a figure looming above me. His face shrouded in shadows, he stood over me with an unsettling stillness, his piercing gaze fixed on me.

Each heartbeat thudded in my ears, deafening and frantic.

That's the guy who was looking at me in the visitor room.

He had a ghastly scar that marred his face, a sickeningly white line that twisted and contorted into a grotesque lump of flesh, as if the wound had never fully healed, forever frozen in a state of agony and decay. But it was his eyes that truly chilled me to the bone. They were as dark as the void of space, devoid of any flicker of humanity, haunting me with their cold, empty glare.

And in his hand, he clutched a box cutter.

How the heck did he have that? You couldn't get into a prison with a weapon, so he must have hidden it in the parking lot or his vehicle nearby.

Behind him, dark clouds battled the sky in gradients of dark blue and black, swirling together as if priming itself for the coming storm.

While down below, a tornado of danger whipped around me.

"Help!" I jolted to my feet.

As he lunged, I dodged his outstretched hand, pivoting to the right and reaching Sean's van in mere seconds. The chilling presence of my assailant loomed just steps behind, that cold blade threateningly close.

My trembling fingers fumbled on the unlock button, missing it once before managing to push it on the second frantic attempt. Jumping inside the hot, stale air, I locked the doors, slammed my foot on the brake, and raised my finger to push the Engine Start button.

But before I had the chance, a rock crashed into the center of the window, causing me to shriek. Glass shattered into fragments with a symphony of sharp cracks and piercing pops, leaving a mosaic of shards in their wake.

I shoved my finger on the Start button, thrilled to hear the engine rumble to life, but just as I clutched the van's gearshift, my assailant reached through the broken window, unlocked the door, and jerked it open.

He grabbed my hair and yanked my head so hard, that my scalp stung. Fighting against his strength, my body a tug of war between safety and danger, I stretched my fingers toward the gear shift. If I could slam it into reverse, I could break his grip and speed away from him.

Bonus if I ran him over in the process.

My fingertips grazed the slick wood, but with a biting yank to my head, my body jerked to the left and began to slide out the door. My arm flailed for an anchor, something to pull me back, but instead, I grabbed the item in the cup holder.

A steak knife. I didn't want to leave the house without protection, and since I couldn't bring a weapon into the prison, I left it in the van.

My attacker tossed me onto the pavement, this time on my left side.

When he raised his arm, I thrust my knife into the soft flesh just above his knee, and as he howled, I ripped it back out and pushed myself up.

A forceful jolt rocked me as a solid arm snaked around my waist from behind, pulling me taut against a hardened form. With a gasp, I speared the knife into his forearm and yanked it up again, but before I stabbed him a second time, his grip loosened.

My eyes darted around the parking lot for anyone who could help, but the place was desolate and silent. The air held a biting chill that filled my lungs with isolation while a metallic tang of rain on steel lingered in the air, mingling with the earthy scent of dust and gravel.

The distant prison walls loomed, casting an oppressive shadow, an unreachable refuge. My only hope was the sanctuary of the van, where I needed to get back to the driver's seat and speed away.

My gaze darted to the driver's door, but my assailant blocked my path. Could I make it to the side door? Wait...

Is that the rear hatch that's open? Oh my God, it is! Its button must have gotten bumped in the struggle!

My feet slammed against the asphalt so hard, that the bones of my feet cried in pain as I rounded the back and jumped inside.

Pushing the button on the hatch to close it.

Sean had taken the second and third row seats out. He typically traveled alone and used the van's storage space to haul all of his audio equipment and case files, but right now, it was empty. Which would make it easier to navigate to the driver's seat and speed off.

The hatch descended slowly with a soft whine as I heaved myself forward, but suddenly, rough hands grabbed my hips, yanked my weapon away from me, and slammed my back to the warm floor of the van.

Where the guy pinned me down, his knees flanking my hips.

One clammy hand on my shoulder.

The other holding the box cutter to my throat. The edge of the blade pricked my skin as the hatch continued its leisurely descent, preparing to trap me inside with a demon panting the promise of death.

But just before the van's rear hatch shut entirely, a dark flash rolled beneath it.

My assailant jerked, and suddenly, he was off me, disarmed, pinned against the wall of the van.

With a knife to *his* throat.

CHAPTER 15
Luna

My breathing reverberated off the interior walls, their rhythm staggered as the surreal scene before me sank in. Inside the back of the van with me, squatting between me and my hooded attacker, a man dressed in all black with a two-toned mask dominated the space with his size.

The Windy City Vigilante pressed the jagged edge of his knife against my assailant's jugular so tightly, a single drop of blood sprouted beneath it while he turned his masked face toward me.

"Are you all right, Ms. Payne?" His voice slithered into the silence, deep and dripping with malice, making the hairs on the back of my neck prickle.

My mouth forgot how to work, evidently.

"Did he hurt you?" the Vigilante pressed.

Yes. But the words remained lodged there, too stunned to speak to the most dangerous man in the city. A killer, who'd just saved my life.

Glimpsing at the tinted windows, I caught the faint reflections of Sean's podcast advertisement, which wrapped around the entire van, creating a one-way view. No one could see inside this vehicle unless they came around to the windshield or the broken window.

"Get the fuck off me!" the guy snapped, drawing the slow turn of the Vigilante's head back to him.

"Who are you?" the Vigilante asked in a rough, grinding voice that reminded me of sandpaper scraping over gravel.

No answer.

"What were your orders?" the Vigilante pressed.

"Go to hell," he spat in response.

The Vigilante speared the guy's upper thigh with his blade, inches away from his manhood.

His roar bounced off the walls, piercing my eardrums.

Could someone hear that? I glanced at the broken window.

Run, Luna. For God's sake, run away. Move!

But my body was frozen, my mind racing to figure out what was going on here. Was this guy part of Franco's crew? Or the one that had sent me that threatening letter? After all, we were here at the prison.

If it was the latter, this guy might be the only one who knew something about my dad's case—something that could help free my father.

"Do you know about the filing?" I demanded.

The Vigilante kept the blade against the man's jugular as he swiveled his head toward me in a brief but electric moment. As I stared at the gray mesh covering his eyes with that red-and-black mask of his, it was as if time stood still, and in that instant, an unexpected connection between us burned that went beyond the chaos of the situation—likely rooted in dumbfounded gratitude for having just saved my life.

For a heartbeat, maybe two, the Vigilante remained unmoving, an eerie statue, and then with deliberation, his face swung back to the assailant.

"Answer her," the Vigilante demanded.

"Go to hell."

The Vigilante drove his blade into the guy's other thigh, again inches from his manhood, but he must have missed the critical veins and arteries because blood did not pool beneath him. Not yet, anyway.

"I don't know about no filing," the assailant groaned, spit forming near the corner of his mouth. Right by that scar.

Outside the van, distant thunder rumbled through the sky while in here, the only sounds were the assailant's labored breaths, each one a rasping gasp of agony. His face was slick with grease, shimmering in the dim light, a mask of pain and fear.

Trapped in the back of a van with two violent men, I knew I should probably stay quiet, but I couldn't stop myself. The desperation to get information about my dad's case was too strong.

"Do you know something about Richard Payne's case?" My heart swelled with hope.

But the attacker merely glared at me and then spat. If I'd been closer to him than four feet away, it probably would have landed in my eye instead of on my chest.

The Vigilante swiftly slashed the assailant's cheek, filleting him like a piece of meat—skin peeled back and the wound so deep it nearly punctured the inside of his mouth. A blood-curdling shriek was so loud, it vibrated the air itself. He shoved at the Vigilante's chest with a thud, but the Vigilante had a knee on the man's thigh and had a better angle and greater size going for him.

Three more pained breaths escaped the assailant before the Vigilante pressed the tip of his knife against the man's crotch.

"What filing?" The assailant's voice rose an octave. "I don't know anything about Richard Payne, okay? I was told to watch the visitor room. See if she shows." He nodded to me.

"And if she did?"

"Get the USB drive."

"What USB drive?"

"Dominic always had it on him. It was missing when Franco found him dead."

My chest deflated in despair. As this guy's eyes darted around, they revealed nothing but anger and fear, confirming he didn't have any information that could help my father; he was just one of Franco's henchmen.

"Why would Franco think *she* has it?" the Vigilante pressed. "I'm the one that killed his cousin."

"Dominic and Franco were fighting for months before he died, and Franco threatened him. Dom said if anything happened to him, he'd turn evidence into the cops that would put him away for life." The assailant nodded toward me. "Dominic told Franco *she* was the one he'd give it to. She was with Dom when he died, so he figures he gave it to her."

"Even if that were true, why would he think she hasn't turned it over to the police yet?"

Great point.

"If she turned it over, he'd be in jail by now. So, he figures she still has it."

"Why would she sit on the evidence?"

"Because everyone's too scared to go against Franco, man."

"And he sent you here," the Vigilante clarified.

"He'd staked out her place, was going to confront her there, but it's surrounded by cameras or whatever, so he did some digging and found out her dad is an inmate and that she visits him most weekends. Told me to come here and see if she showed."

"He thinks she'll waltz around with a USB drive?"

No answer.

The Vigilante's back straightened. "If she's taken out, she can't give it to anyone, right?"

The assailant's ugly lips curled into a snarl.

"I recognize you," the Vigilante said. "You're Anthony Pike, yeah?"

The assailant's eyes darted to me, then back to the Vigilante.

"You've killed two women. That I know of."

No denial. It seemed to take the Vigilante a few seconds to recalibrate.

"Where the hell is Franco?" he asked.

Anthony licked his lips, grimacing from the pain of his oozing cheek. "He moves around. Contacts us with burners he changes out."

"So, you have no way to reach him."

"No."

"Then how were you going to tell him that you took care of this?"

"He calls *me*, okay? Not the other way around."

The Vigilante twisted the knife in his hand, silent for several seconds before pointing its blade at Anthony's nose. "Then here's what's going to happen. You're going to come with me. And when Franco calls, you tell him you eliminated her."

Anthony's eyes widened slightly. "He'll find out she's alive, and when he does…" He shook his head.

The Vigilante bit his lip. "Then you tell him you need to meet. Let me handle him."

"The hell I will."

"You seem to be under the impression you have any options here. You do as I say, or I slit your throat."

"You seem to be under the impression killing me is the worst option on the table. Anyone that goes against Franco? Will spend *days* getting tortured before he finally puts them out of their misery."

The men stared at each other.

"Very well." The Vigilante's words were measured and deliberate, casting a spell of ominous foreboding that hung heavy in the air. "It seems our negotiations have failed."

As Anthony shifted his hip slightly, a palpable tension filled the air, like a coiled snake waiting to strike. Anthony's eyes darted around the space.

"Let me go," Anthony said, his chest heaving quicker than it was before.

The Vigilante tsked. "I might have considered letting you go." His voice was low, each word edged with a simmering rage. "To gather the intel I normally require that proves you killed those two women. But do you want to hear what your fatal mistake was?"

The assailant's eyes snapped to me, to the van's closed hatch, then back to the Vigilante.

"You came after *her*," the Vigilante said.

Silence eclipsed the thunderous clouds.

"Look away, Ms. Payne."

CHAPTER 16
Luna

My eyes widened as blood spurted across the Vigilante's shirt and poured down Anthony's skin, his throat split open with a gash. Anthony's eyes widened through several wet gasps before rolling into the back of his head.

His lifeless body slumped to the van floor.

Instinctively, I inched backward, like the blood was a toxin that could infect me, pressing my body against the van's rear hatch. Nausea swirled in my gut while my eyes were fixed, unable to blink.

I tore my gaze away from Anthony's lifeless body to the Vigilante, who was crouched a couple of feet away, his knife's blade glistening with a sheen of blood. There was something primal about his presence, something that defied easy explanation—a moment of conflicting emotions, I guess.

The Vigilante had just saved my life. And for that, I was immensely grateful. Especially since my death had been scarily close...and he'd also made Anthony answer my questions, and had been my ally in the fight against my would-be killer.

But the Vigilante hadn't merely knocked Anthony out of the way to save me or called the police to turn him in after we got our questions answered. He'd *killed* him. Slit his throat.

Just like he'd slit Dominic's throat.

The image of *Dominic's* neck sliced open like a gory steak, *his* blood pooling beneath *him* while the Vigilante stood there waiting for him to die, crashed into my mind. Reminding me who the Vigilante really was.

Not a protector, but a killer. A ruthless one who'd slaughtered *many* people in this city.

The only thing that I knew for certain was that the Vigilante was lethal. I'd just witnessed a second murder he'd committed, and now he was facing me, holding a knife.

"Stay back!" I shrieked.

"It's good to officially meet you, Ms. Payne," the Vigilante said in his growling whisper of a voice.

"You saw the press conference," I surmised.

"The one where you declared war against me? Yes, I did."

Maybe he wanted to be the one to do the honor of silencing me for good.

I grasped around behind me, trying to find a button that could open the van's hatch from the inside.

"But I knew your name before that," he said.

My fingers trembled. "How?" How did a killer know my name?

"You've helped many guilty go unpunished. Predators who roam the streets and prey on the innocent. Including Mr. Hopkins."

I clenched my jaw. "Dominic was innocent."

He tilted his head slightly. "I'm afraid you're wrong, Ms. Payne. He killed that man."

"The jury said otherwise."

"I have proof."

"In case you forgot, I was his lawyer during the case. I already saw all of the evidence."

"You don't believe me," he said.

"Believe the man who killed my friend? No. I don't."

Was there even a hatch release button back here? Why wouldn't they put some type of lever in the back to open this door in case one finds themselves trapped with a dead body and a killer who was coming after them next? Just past the Vigilante, the front seat beck-oned me with its freedom, but when I calculated my odds of diving over him without his knife severing one of my arteries, my shoulders dropped.

Odds: not good.

"I got my hands on a video of the murder," the Vigilante said. "It was recorded to provide a warning to others of what happens if you don't pay your debts."

"How convenient. And this *supposed* video didn't get submitted as part of the trial against him because…"

Maybe I could break one of the windows back here and dive through it. *Break it with what, Luna?*

"The jury was already out for deliberation when it came into my possession. Too late for it to enter the trial."

"You still should have turned it over." But he couldn't because there was no video.

"My sources would stop supplying me with information if they found out I was working with law enforcement by handing over evidence they provided."

"Which is it?" I asked. "You got it too late, or you would have not turned it over?"

"Both."

"You expect me to believe that bullshit?"

"There are some types of people in this world who aren't willing to talk to cops or lawyers. But they will talk to me. Especially if I offer some"—he slanted his head—"persuasion."

Maybe I could grab the knife out of his hand or reach *my* steak knife, which was lying on the ground behind him. Or maybe I could convince him to set his down for a second.

"Well, if what you say is true, show it to me." I raised my eyebrow.

"Afraid I can't do that."

"Because it doesn't exist."

"The people who gave it to me required assurance it would not be shared with law enforcement or individuals involved with law enforcement. They might be willing to help me, but they have no interest in helping the police or being branded their informant. If they found out I handed it over to you, it would jeopardize my operation."

"Operation. Is that what you call being a serial killer?"

I patted the floor behind my back. Landing on something firm and small.

Is that what I think it is? It is! The dead man's box cutter. The one the Vigilante had knocked out of his hand when he'd lunged at him.

I grabbed it, a rush of hope flooding my limbs.

"Next time, you should vet the clients you take on more thoroughly," the Vigilante lectured. "With a little digging, perhaps you would've realized he was guilty of murder, and you wouldn't have helped him walk free."

He twisted the knife's blade in his hand.

"Everyone deserves their day in court, and it's my job to ensure the scales of justice remain balanced."

"You've helped a lot of guilty people go free, Ms. Payne."

"So, you're here to kill me, then?"

Because I'll fight back, you sick, twisted piece of shit!

"If I wanted to kill you, you'd be dead already."

How dare he say something so vile with a hint of amusement dancing through his words.

"Wow." I gripped the handle of the box cutter tighter. "That'd make a great title for your first Ted Talk."

"I admonish your role in helping guilty people walk free, but you're not guilty of a crime, Ms. Payne."

"And that's your standard, is it? Only killing people who are supposedly guilty?"

"I have a code, Ms. Payne. But you did create a complication."

"*I* created a complication? You should look in the mirror, you stabby piece of shit!"

When he leaned closer, I raised my box cutter. "Stay back, you homicidal dickwad."

His lips, which weren't covered by his mask, tightened. "I just saved you."

"So, you're being a Good Samaritan, then? For all I know, you two worked together." I nodded my chin toward the body.

His lips thinned even more. "You think he and I are the same?"

"You killed Dominic."

"Dominic was a killer."

"He wasn't. But even if he was, you had no right to kill him."

"He had no right to walk free."

"It's not your place to be the judge, jury, and executioner."

"That's where you and I disagree, Ms. Payne. When all other avenues have failed, I won't sit back and hope justice is served. I'll step in and do it myself."

When he leaned forward, I hurled my weapon toward him. But before it could connect, his grip locked around my forearm, halting its momentum.

"Careful, Ms. Payne. I don't want to hurt you."

He turned my palm face up, and despite my yanks, he pulled my fingers back, releasing my grip on the handle.

In the distance, sirens blended into the rumbling thunder.

"You've seen the other reports on the Windy City Vigilante, yes?"

As he tossed the box cutter into the front seat, out of my reach, my eyes stung.

"Has he ever hurt an innocent person?"

I lifted my chin. "Yes. Dominic."

His mouth set into a firm line that looked to be frustrated impatience.

"Maybe you're actually an imposter, posing as the Windy City Vigilante," I added. "Maybe you're really one of Franco's hired men."

"Why would I *save* your life just to turn around and end it?"

"Maybe you're here to abduct me and take me to Franco. Maybe there's a bounty on my head, and you and he"—I nodded toward my assailant—"fought to claim it."

The Vigilante slowly placed his knife into his pocket and held his hands up in surrender. "I'm not going to hurt you, Ms. Payne."

I studied his mask. Half of it cloaked in black, the other half a startling blood red. Its sleek surface looked like it would be cool to the touch while the gray mesh concealed his eyes.

My muscles should *not* relax slightly with his probable lie. But the truth was, most of my anger was nothing more than bravado, hiding my fear of dying, of Dad rotting in prison forever.

"Then what are you doing here?" My words tumbled out, my voice quivering.

The sirens grew louder.

"Protecting you."

"Protecting me?" I choked. "I don't understand…"

"I heard what happened with Franco after I left, how he thinks you have evidence against him."

"How did you hear that?" I demanded.

"I have ears on the street," he said.

"Ears."

"I never meant to put you in Franco's line of fire. Least I can do is watch out for you, Ms. Payne."

I blinked. "You've been watching me?"

"I lost sight of you when you started running through the cars." He looked at Anthony. "I'm sorry for that."

"Well, I don't want your protection."

As the Vigilante's face angled back to me, a strange tension sparked between us—something that I couldn't quite identify. It was as if an unspoken understanding had passed between us, a sense of trust begging to be embraced.

I found myself asking, did I trust him? I got the sense that the Vigilante was sincere with what he was saying, and despite everything that'd just happened, a part of me believed him.

Which was absurd. He'd killed my friend, accused him of a heinous crime, and then slaughtered another man right in front of me.

But he'd also saved me. Literally killed a man to protect me, and I couldn't shake the unsettling feeling that Dominic might have had a more sinister side than I'd realized.

Though the Vigilante's mask concealed his eyes, an unmistakable warmth washed over my skin, as if his hidden gaze enveloped me in an unspoken embrace. What a strange feeling—both unsettling and comforting at the same time, as if we were connected in a way that defied explanation.

As we stared at each other, one thing became crystal clear: I'd be dead if the Vigilante hadn't saved me.

"Who are you?" I tilted my head slightly.

The Vigilante stared at me as the sirens grew so loud, they had to be near the prison now, if not entering the lot.

"I'm sorry for this, Ms. Payne."

And then he jumped over the seat, out the passenger door, and vanished into the tree line that surrounded the parking lot.

CHAPTER 17
The Vigilante

T
hat was too damn close.

Luna Payne could have been killed. When she'd come out of the prison, I'd followed her too far back. I kept my distance so she wouldn't spot me, but that careful decision nearly cost Luna her life. It had taken me too many seconds to get to her.

And don't get me started on that goddamned imbecile Franco Hopkins, thinking Luna had the USB drive to begin with. Dominic's attack was as violent as it was swift. The guy never had the chance for a deathbed confession. Let alone to surrender evidence.

And even if he had, Luna would have turned it over to the cops. Immediately. The woman might exacerbate me by defending assholes for a living, but she wouldn't protect a killer by illegally harboring his evidence.

An unnerving fog clung to me, refusing to let go because the attack at the prison meant Franco had dug into Luna deep enough to find out her old man was in jail. And that she visited him regularly. He positioned a guy here to watch for her and was brazen enough to kill a person outside an armed prison.

Another reason this left me on edge was because, for the first time, I'd killed someone outside of my ritual.

I methodically researched my targets long before they took their last breath.

But I couldn't think about that right now; something far more urgent weighed on my mind. Franco Hopkins was about to find out that one of his underlings had been killed.

A death he might blame Luna for. Him thinking she had evidence was bad enough and my fault.

Even though it was supposed to be my only chance to get to him, it was foolish to take Dominic out in such a public place in the light of day where being discovered was a possibility. My failure put Luna in a precarious position with Franco, a danger that landed directly on my shoulders. The only way to make this right was by ensuring her safety.

I had never used my skills to keep a single person alive before.

But Luna Payne was about to become the exception...

CHAPTER 18
Luna

"Where the hell are you?" Hunter asked.

Maybe this was a bad idea. But I couldn't ask Sean to come pick me up, seeing as how I'd borrowed his van. And my stupid car was broken. An Uber from Joliet to Chicago would cost approximately three billion dollars, and I hadn't brought cash for public transportation, so what was a girl to do?

But why did Hunter sound so hostile?

"Is that how you answer every phone call? Your manners need some TLC."

"You didn't tell me you were leaving."

I rolled my eyes.

"Didn't realize you were under the misconception I'd actually comply with your demand to notify you of my whereabouts. Besides, I thought you were spying on me. Didn't you see me leave?"

"If I could stare at security monitors twenty-four-seven, I would, but my security team works in shifts to keep an eye out for danger. Seems we had a misunderstanding. Not just to notify me of a break-in, but anytime you left."

"So, you *are* invading my privacy by keeping tabs on me."

"Your life might be in danger."

I frowned, looking at the van, hating that he was right. "Yeah, about that. Listen, you want the good news or the bad news first?"

"Luna, so help me, tell me what the hell is going on."

"Bad news, someone, uh..." *Stay away from words like* attacked, almost killed. "Entangled me in a bit of a confrontation."

Silence. I swear, I could *hear* his anger trying to stab my ear through the lack of any sound.

"Good news," I continued, "Franco's minion is dead."

Silence. For two more breaths.

"Franco's guy is dead?"

I expected to hear relief. Instead, it was still anger.

"Problem is, the van I drove here is kind of a...crime scene. So, I'm sort of stuck at Joliet Prison, and I was wondering if..." Ugh, barf tasted better than asking Hunter for help. "Well, I was kind of..."

"Stay there," he growled. "I'm coming to get you."

The line went dead.

Yellow tape now wrapped around the area, and folded numbers lay next to evidence while an officer finished documenting it all, her camera clicking.

Tires screeched nearby, followed by the abrupt sound of a car door slamming. Quick footsteps struck the ground with sharp, heavy thuds, just before Hunter Lockwood appeared on the outskirts of the scene. His gaze swept over the circus of police and crime scene tape until it finally zeroed in on me.

Ignoring the police calling his name, Hunter stormed over to where I stood and scanned me up and down.

With clenched fists.

"Hey, thanks for coming to—"

"Is Luna dismissed?" Hunter asked the detective without letting me finish. Or taking his eyes off me.

The detective raised a brow as he glanced at Hunter, then back at me. "We have your statement. I'll be in touch if we have any follow-up questions."

Hunter grabbed my hand and began tugging me toward his car.

"Hunter…"

He didn't stop or look back at me over his shoulder, just stomped through the parking lot, dragging me like a child. By the time we reached his Aston Martin, my confusion gave way to a fiery rage that burned up my core and wrapped around my neck.

Hunter opened his passenger door and glared at me.

"Get in."

I didn't appreciate the way he was talking to me, his tone growling and angry. I didn't appreciate the way he was looking at me, like his gaze could stab daggers through my eye sockets, and I didn't appreciate his body language, which was possessive and controlling.

And callous.

"Why are you acting like this?" I demanded.

An icy fury frosted through his eyes.

"Get. In."

I yanked my hand away from his, nearly falling over from the effort it took.

"I thought you'd want to know what happened, but maybe I shouldn't have called you."

I took a step around him, but he shot his hand out onto the roof of the car, blocking my path.

"Get in, Luna." His voice boomed through my skin to my bones. I swear to criminy he hadn't blinked in, like…ever.

"In case you forgot, I don't respond well to someone ordering me around."

Hunter stepped closer until I could smell mint gum on his breath, and could see deeper into his eyes than I ever had before.

I hated that when he was this close to me, it disrupted my normal flow of emotions, like hijacking a frequency and changing its channel. I hated that something *other* than anger flashed through me, that my lower belly warmed, curious what he was about to do next.

If he was about to yell at me.

Or kiss me so hard, it'd bruise my lips.

Because honestly, it looked like it could go either way.

The fact that I was wondering if he'd slam me against the car and stroke his hands over my body was psychosis-level concerning. The fact that I kind of wanted it? Made me wonder if I was sane at all.

"Please," he said through gritted teeth, his chest rising closer to mine. "Get in."

Hunter Lockwood should not look sexy to me right now. I shouldn't notice how his normally polished hair looked like he'd been shoving his hand through it repeatedly as he raced to come help me. And I shouldn't feel this sensual energy bouncing between us as Hunter towered over me, commanding me to obey.

Nor should I surrender to him and his orders, and yet I pushed aside my hurt and confusion—making a mental promise to confront him about it—and plopped into the passenger seat.

I was glad I'd buckled my seat belt because once Hunter pulled out onto the road, he shifted his aggression to the gas pedal. Within a couple of minutes, he flew onto the on-ramp and accelerated to ninety-five miles an hour, weaving in and out of traffic.

Outside my window, the asphalt flew beneath our tires, and I clutched my seat belt tightly, but not nearly as tight as Hunter's grip that was strangling the steering wheel.

His silence began to grate on my nerves, especially when it exceeded twenty minutes. Then forty. By the time an hour of silence had passed, anger reclaimed control of *my* steering wheel.

"Look, you're obviously pissed, and I get that it's upsetting that Franco's guy came after me, but what is with the attitude?"

"You're a magnet for danger." Hunter twisted his hands on the wheel. "You know that? You're a danger magnet."

I gripped the sides of my seat. "I appreciate you coming all the way out here and giving me a ride, but you're being mean right now."

"If you wanted to get yourself killed, you should've done it before I grew to give a shit about you."

"That's so sweet. You should put that on a Hallmark card."

"This isn't funny, Luna. Do you have a goddamned death wish?"

"A death wish? I visited my dad."

"*Before* they found Franco and locked him up. And"—Hunter

shoved two fingers into the air—"someone else threatened you if you didn't drop your dad's case, not to mention the conference that might've pissed off the Vigilante." A third finger rose. "Yet you traipse over to Joliet Prison all by yourself."

"My dad was in the infirmary on Friday, and I wanted to check if he was okay."

"Does he know you risked your life to come there?"

I clenched my toes.

His Aston Martin lurched off the expressway.

"Please just take me home," I urged.

But when we got close, Hunter turned down the long, winding driveway of his mansion. *Not* the small one that led to my cottage.

"So, you're going to what, kidnap me, then? Just to be clear."

His chest inflated so much, it looked like it was about to pop.

"Let me ask you something, Luna. As soon as Franco finds out his guy got killed, what do you think his reaction will be?"

I crossed my arms over my chest.

Hunter opened his massive garage door and pulled his car inside. As soon as he threw it into park, I unbuckled my seat belt and jumped out.

"The hell do you think you're going?" He blocked my path.

"Home. Move." I tried to push past him.

"You're really going to make me do this, aren't you?"

"Do what?"

"Last chance," Hunter warned. "Come with me."

"Pass."

I took two steps before Hunter grabbed my wrist and ducked his shoulder beneath my waist. He tossed me into a fireman's grip so quickly, the garage blurred until the ground crystalized beneath his feet.

"Put me down!" I punched his back, but he didn't even give a hint of exertion as he opened the door and brought me into his kitchen.

Where he set me down on the center island's cold marble countertop, standing between my legs and slamming his palms on either side of me, caging me in.

His body pressed against my inner thighs, an intimate touch that sent a jolt of desire to my core. Every nerve in my body seemed to come alive, tingling with an intoxicating mix of longing and passion. The gnawing sensation deepened within me, and the harder I pushed it away, the more intense the hunger grew.

His attire wasn't helping: a pair of cotton pants that hugged his waist in all the right areas and a gray T-shirt that battled with his muscles.

But I forced my mind to hold on to the anger—anger was my only hope at stopping myself from pulling his mouth to mine.

"This is what's going to happen…" Hunter said.

"Let me stop you right there." I pushed my palms against his chest. But it was like trying to shove a wall, and it had the irritating side effect of noticing how deliciously firm his muscles were. "I'm not going anywhere with you."

"I won't allow you to get yourself killed, Luna."

Allow. There was that word again. The guy needed a thesaurus.

And get myself killed? What the heck? Like all this was *my* fault?

Maybe I wasn't handling the situation perfectly. But you know what? Neither was Hunter. He chastised rather than offering comfort. He demanded rather than requesting. What we needed was a playbook for the perfect ways to respond to situations such as this.

All I knew was that I was handling things the best way I could. And what Hunter needed to understand was that I refused to run and hide in fear of Franco or give up my life's purpose by caving to a stranger's demands. I would not hand over control of my life to anyone.

But Hunter just didn't seem to get it, acting like I brought this on myself, as if I deserved it.

And that made a lump grow in my throat.

"You know some people?" My voice quivered. "When they find out someone was almost killed, their reaction is very different. They wrap them in their arms and ask if they're okay. They don't yell at them and try to make them feel like it's their fault."

I hated that tears burned my eyes and broke over my cheeks.

This was humiliating. The whole thing. The almost dying. The not-my-greatest decision of all time to go to the prison alone. The fact that I was scared. Having to call Hunter to come help me.

And most of all, having him look down on me.

Just like everyone had looked down on me and my family my whole life, living in the stain of my dad's supposed crime.

Hunter let out a long breath, his features melting into regret, and gently cupped my cheek. His hand was huge and warm and surprisingly tender as he trailed the pad of his thumb along my skin.

His touch instantly cooled my burning anger, and his eyes locked on to mine, a raw intensity shimmering within them that mirrored my deep longing to feel his arms wrap around me.

"I'm sorry." Hunter's voice was low with a tempo of guilt softening its tone. "For being an asshole."

I wasn't sure what to say. Part of me still wanted to storm out of his kitchen while another part swallowed the thickness lingering in my throat. But at least we were out of the tornado of anger that had taken over us.

Through my haze of tears, I met his gaze. The fever in his eyes burned like a live ember, and as they lowered to my lips, a warm yearning spread through my stomach. His stare trailed back up while his thumb tenderly caressed my cheekbone.

"When I realized someone almost killed you, it...infuriated me." The heat in his voice only added to the simmering tension between us.

His thumb grazed a sultry line along my jaw, sending waves of heat down my spine. "But I misplaced my anger." His eyes searched mine for understanding. "I'm sorry."

An electric current of desire surged around us, whispering over my skin with the echoes of my breaths. The air was thick with passion, ready to ignite at the slightest touch.

Hunter's eyes, now a vivid turquoise in the kitchen light, fixated on my mouth and, charged with a magnetic pull, drew closer to mine.

CHAPTER 19
Luna

I studied his lips as they lowered closer to mine, my heart racing with a mixture of excitement and apprehension as Hunter tilted his head. The heat emanating from his body pulled me to him, and the intoxicating scent of his cologne—rich with a hint of leather and sandalwood, with its blend of warm and spicy notes exuding confidence and masculinity—intensified the allure even more.

But with each beat of desire, my heart also boomed with nervousness, reminding me I hadn't kissed anyone in years for a reason. A reason I struggled to remember as Hunter kept his eyes on my mouth, slowly closing the distance between us.

Until finally, our lips met. The world seemed to stand still as the warmth of his mouth mingled with the taste of him, igniting a fire deep within me, as if a long-dormant volcano had suddenly sprung to life.

Especially when he opened his mouth slightly and delicately licked my lower lip before pushing his tongue into mine.

Oh my word. I wanted to open my mouth wider and pull him to me, my stomach warming with a heat that spread between my legs. I pushed my face closer to his, snaking my fingers through his silky hair. As our kiss deepened and our tongues became greedier, I relished the feeling of him pushing his body harder against my thighs.

He tasted divine, and as I shifted my head more to the side, Hunter cupped my chin, our kiss growing deeper, more desperate, as though he feared losing even a second of our connection.

But that was the whole problem. I didn't want his mouth to ever leave mine. I wanted his kisses to trail down my neck, my chest, and only leave my body temporarily, when he stripped me of my clothes. I wanted to feel him on top of me, feel the weight of his hips press into my thighs as he did more than just kiss my skin.

His hand shifted to cradle the back of my head as he deepened the kiss, our tongues dancing together in a fiery passion.

An unbearable yearning grew in the pit of my stomach as I slid my hands over the warm rivets of his shoulder muscles while our breaths synced with one another. My lower belly burned as I gently nibbled on Hunter's lower lip.

His hand slipped down my back, pulling me closer to him, and I couldn't help but moan with pleasure.

Which incited a groan of his own as our kiss evolved even further —a perfect rhythm of tongues connecting over and over while we greedily pulled at each other, unable to get enough.

An intense desire coursed through me, urging me to give in completely to this man. Surrendering to this kiss, I fell deeper under his spell, unable to resist the pull he had over me. His lips were like a drug, and I craved more of his intoxicating touch.

His hardened abs and chest pressed against my own, sending my back arching, and his growing desire throbbed against my core. Gently, he pressed me forward to lay me down on the countertop.

Which sent my damn heart into alarm.

I pushed against Hunter's chest. "Wait."

Hunter's lips abandoned mine, his eyes devouring every curve of my face as his knuckles trailed under my jaw.

"What's wrong?" he whispered.

I want this too much.

"I..." My eyes burned through the fight raging in my heart—one side wanting this man more than any other man I'd known, the other side more terrified than I'd ever been because of it.

"Tell me." His legs pushed against the inside of my thighs, his mouth still distractingly close to mine.

I swallowed. "I...I don't think this is such a good idea."

Hunter tilted his head slightly, and damn it if that didn't make him look sexier.

"Why?" The word rolled off his tongue, smooth and velvety, making the air around us seem to grow warmer with each syllable.

"We're opponents in the courtroom, and you're also my landlord. Going any further would make our working relationship uncomfortable."

He trailed his thumb along my lower lip.

"I can tell that's not the real reason, Little Leopard."

My stomach fluttered at his pet name, and my chest cheered that he knew me well enough to sense my dishonesty.

I trailed my hands down his chest, attempting not to feel all sorts of sparks, and then I dropped my gaze to the ground, trying to think of how to get out of this without embarrassing the hell out of myself.

Hunter placed his knuckle beneath my chin and lifted it.

"Luna, talk to me."

I bit my lip. "I don't date, not seriously, and I don't want to lead you on."

His mouth curled up on one side. "And you and I would be serious?"

Heat engulfed my chest.

His knuckles brushed softly against my face once more, each touch sending electric charges down my torso and intensifying the heat between my thighs. Every fleeting contact seemed to crumble my carefully built defenses, challenging the resolve that I clung to.

But I had to hold on to my rational reasons. Every second I stayed on this counter, a fog of temptation swirled around me, but the damage it would cause if I surrendered fully was too big to bear. It was like a delicious cocktail that had far too much alcohol in it. Yes, it might be delightful while you were consuming it, but the next day, you would feel like crap.

"Why don't you date seriously?" Hunter asked gently.

I shook my head.

"Luna, if I have any hope of controlling myself around you, you're going to need to give me a damn good reason."

When I twisted my hands on my lap, Hunter released my face and put his hands on mine.

"Tell me you don't want this," he said.

My eyes burned. "That's the problem," I said. "I...can't."

"Because?"

"It's embarrassing."

"Try me."

I didn't want to answer the question, but he needed to realize that this boundary was firm and uncrossable.

"I have a hard time trusting people," I admitted.

Correction: I never trusted people. I never felt safe enough around anyone to do so.

"Because people assume your dad is guilty?"

I shook my head, unable to look him in the eye as I said, "People will claim to be there for you. They may even claim to love you unconditionally. But when push comes to shove, they'll break your heart by turning their back on you and abandoning you when you're most in need of their support."

To put it bluntly, people will betray you.

This time, when he stroked the side of my face with his knuckles, he brushed my skin with a gentle, reassuring warmth rather than the underlying fire.

"Who hurt you, Luna?" A mixture of vengeance and worry pulsed through his words.

My heart's fracture cracked opened slightly, like it always did when these thoughts invaded it.

"Everyone claimed they loved my father, and when he was first arrested, they believed in his innocence. I thought it wouldn't matter how many times my dad was cast as some cold-blooded killer on the news, but I was wrong. Because one by one, they started to drop like flies. It was like a fire burning my home with us inside of it, and instead of helping us put out the flames, some of them doused it with gasoline, giving stories to the media that made him look bad.

"Once my dad was convicted, they all turned their backs on my mom and me. Every single one of them. No one wanted to talk to us anymore. The people that shocked me the most were our family members."

A particularly sharp memory breached my dam and flooded my heart.

"I don't ever want to go to their stupid Thanksgiving dinner again anyway," I cried, the area around my eyes stinging from all the tears I'd shed. "Or Christmas. I don't care if we never see them again!"

I lay in my bed, Mom rubbing my back.

"Luna..." Mom said. "You don't mean that."

"I do mean that!" I sat up, my shoulders shaking. "If they never want to see us again, then fine, I never want to see them again either! Because if they don't love Dad, then I don't love them!"

"This isn't about love."

"Yes, it is!" My voice came out pinched from the snot clogging my nose. "Dad loves them, and he'd never abandon them."

"They're not trying to abandon him."

"But they are! And they want us to abandon him, too!"

"Luna..."

"They said if we visit him, we're not welcome to come over anymore!"

"People have strong convictions," Mom tried to explain gently. "And sometimes, they want to take a stand. I know this is hard to understand when you're nine, but..."

"It's not hard. It's simple. They said they loved him, but now they don't. No one does."

I never realized how cruel people can be. I never wanted to leave my bed. I never wanted to go to school, ride my bike through the neighborhood, or see anyone ever again.

Except my dad.

"Their love was never real," I cried. "I trusted them with my whole heart, Mommy. Everything they claimed was a lie."

I hated that another tear broke free; those people didn't deserve my tears. I bet they didn't even think of us anymore.

"I feel alone because I know I'll never be able to trust anyone again." Trusting meant surrendering to complete vulnerability, and I'd been so vulnerable and out of control for most of my life that I didn't have the strength to endure it again.

It was as if you fell off a horse and crushed every bone in your body, suffering agonizing pain that was so intense, you just wanted to die. After years in the hospital and rehab, your body was a severely weakened version of what it once was—and it would never be the same again. To be brave, you were told to get back up on that horse.

But you vowed to never put yourself through that torture again.

"I know myself, and I'll never be able to fully trust someone," I said.

"Maybe it's worth trying."

The truth was, I wanted Hunter more than I'd ever wanted anyone before, and pushing him away before we even had a chance twisted my insides with barbed wire. But starting something wasn't fair to him. I knew my limitations, how I'd never be capable of fully trusting him, and without trust, a relationship was doomed. He didn't deserve to get hurt by me.

"I tried once, in college." Out of desperation and loneliness, I'd tested the waters by forcing myself to go on dates with a guy and then forcing myself to keep dating him, even though my insides were crawling with mistrust. I thought maybe I could push past it because I was so damn lonely. But I couldn't push past it. Finding out he cheated on me was merely the icing on the cake—my test had failed.

"What did he do to you, Little Leopard?" Hunter asked as his muscles tensed.

The flashback punched me in my gut.

. . .

"It's over!" I grabbed the takeout containers I'd surprised him with because the thought of the two of them having a meal that I bought? Made my skin crawl. I'd suffered enough humiliation, walking in on my boyfriend with another woman, thank you very much.

"Fine," he snapped, following me into his living room, still naked. Still excited from being inside of her. "You're too fucked in the head to have a normal relationship, anyway, what with your psycho dad's DNA."

I refused to show him the lump in my throat had grown tenfold, so I stormed out his front door and slammed it behind me.

When I walked past his unlocked car, I told myself people say terrible things they don't mean when they're in an argument. And that a noble person would keep walking. Leave it there.

Guess I wasn't very noble, because as the first tear broke free, I hid the contents of our meals—two fish entrées—under his seat. A little fuck you bomb, if you will, waiting to explode with the gut-wrenching smell. Not my finest moment. But a girl can only get run over so many times before she lashes out.

"What did he do to you?" Hunter repeated firmer.

I hesitated. "He cheated on me, but that's not the point." Not the one I was trying to make at least.

Hunter's jaw shifted. "He knew you had trust issues before he did that?"

I shrugged in affirmation.

Which made Hunter scrub his jaw so hard that skin cells were probably lost.

"He knew you had a hard time trusting people, and he still cheated on you." His voice dripped with disdain, every word laced with a biting edge.

"If I hadn't written off the red flags as my own issues, I might've seen it coming."

To this, Hunter bit his lip so hard, that it lost its color.

"What's his name?"

I blinked. "Why?"

"Exceedingly curious if the man has any warrants that could use prioritization."

My mouth curled up. "Anyway"—I cleared my throat—"it was proof I can't trust people." Proof I was broken inside, incapable of giving someone else what's required to make a relationship work.

Hunter's gaze morphed from fury toward my ex to a pool of sorrow that seemed to reflect the painful understanding that we could never be more than friends. He was silent for a long time while I grappled with having divulged something so personal to him. I was surprised I had done it, but I was even more surprised that confiding in him felt right.

Hunter eventually stepped back and grabbed the back of his neck.

"You might not be able to trust me," Hunter said. "But I hope you know I'm here for you. Even if it's only as a friend."

A pang sliced through my gut. I'd never had a man care about me like this before, but this expansive hope trying to break free had the power to destroy me. Hunter deserved better, too. Here he was, so generous and caring, willing to settle for whatever pieces I was able to give. When I was too broken to ever let him in.

"A friend sounds great," I said.

He hesitated, then offered a slight, disappointed nod. "Meanwhile" —his voice deepened—"I'd like you to stay here at the house temporarily. Franco sent a guy after you today, and I can't stomach the idea of you being down at that cottage without protection."

The act of violence was a definite escalation, but I didn't trust myself to live in Hunter's mansion without something physical happening between the two of us.

It's funny how a threat to your heart can seem more catastrophic than a threat to your safety.

"The security cameras were a good idea." I nodded. "I'll leave them up, and I'll close my blinds and take precautions. I'll call the detective daily to get an update on Franco's whereabouts, and now that we know he's hunting for a USB drive, I'll ask them to turn over Dominic's place to look for it. But for now, I'm going to stay at my place."

He put his palms up in surrender. "I promise I'll behave myself."

But I couldn't make the same promise. If I stayed here, something would happen between us, and there would be no going back. Everything in my life was so out of control. I needed to hold on to the stability that was at my core. I might not be able to protect myself against everything that was coming at me, but I could at least protect my heart.

I slipped off the center island where our relationship almost transcended into something different.

"I'll be just down the hill," I said.

A frown tugged at the corners of his mouth, his gaze distant for a moment before looking down at me with those sapphires. Judging by the way he was chewing the inside of his cheek, he seemed to want to debate me, but after a moment, he nodded grimly.

"I called the auto repair shop earlier," Hunter said.

Crap. That was on my list, and I forgot.

"Your car needs a new timing belt."

"That doesn't sound so bad." So, what was with his *I'm sorry for your loss* face?

"To repair it, they have to replace damaged pistons, valves, and cylinder heads. Plus, the water pump and tensioner to prevent future issues."

Yikes.

"Total estimate is $2,675."

Damn.

"I'm going to pay it," Hunter insisted.

"No."

"Luna."

"You're not paying for it," I retorted. "And as for the repair, I want to think it over. I might pay that just to have another thing break next month, so I have to decide if I'm going to invest the money trying to limp this thing along or use that money as a down payment on a new car."

"I can buy you—"

"Hunter." I raised my hand up. "I really appreciate the offer, but I'll figure this out on my own."

He stared at me, fidgeting with his fingers for a moment before relenting with a nod.

"As for the incident today," he started, "if anything else happens, you're coming to live here."

CHAPTER 20
Hunter

I never wanted that kiss to end. I wanted to undress her and suck on her breasts and make her my own. But I wasn't just awestruck by her beauty.

Her feisty personality performed a hostile takeover of my thoughts.

I'd heard about Luna Payne long before I'd formally introduced myself to her. Not just her name on the tenant agreement—I'd heard about the rising star in the public defender's office and found myself mesmerized by what people were saying about her. Intelligence was always a turn-on. Hard work was another, but passion?

Passion was something I rarely came across in my career. I found most people seemed to be going through the motions in life, navigating into a career path that fit them best, but when I'd heard that Luna was so passionate about her work that she shaped her entire life around it—even turned down jobs that would pay her far more—well, the pull began.

When I met her, my attraction only intensified. Especially after seeing her in action, impressed with how she commanded the courtroom.

It was impossible to not be enamored by her contradictions. Brave enough to fight off a killer but terrified of a needle poke. I loved how defiantly stubborn and independent she was. Every aspect of her was a perfectly crafted puzzle piece, molded together to shape the most fascinating woman I'd ever met.

And after tasting her mouth? All I wanted to do was taste it again…

I rubbed the back of my neck as I glanced out the window, taking in the sight of my cottage. Everything around me belonged to me, save for that which I wanted most dearly.

"It's almost Shakespearean, isn't it?" I asked Grayson.

He had popped over unannounced again just as Luna left, and we were both currently sipping one of my single malt liquors, watching her walk toward her cottage. Slowly, like the fresh air was helping her nerves.

"How so?"

I sighed heavily. "For the first time, I feel something for a woman. But she has trust issues too big to ever give me a chance."

Grayson took a sip of his drink, the clink of his ice cubes hitting his glass. "So, earn her trust. Fight for it."

I shook my head despairingly. "That's where the Shakespearean part comes in."

She could have told me a million reasons we couldn't try this, but only one had the power to make me step back on my heels: that she might run away.

"People I love tend to leave." Mom and Dad didn't want to leave us, of course, but the footprint of their absence left its mark on my soul all the same. "If she walked away from me…" I shook my head. "She's so terrified of being betrayed that she's one blink away from running. How can I get close to someone who's such a flight risk?"

"It's easy to push people away when you don't have feelings for them, but you already do with her. How can you let that go?"

"She deserves better," I said.

My brother evaluated me. "This is about Dad's murder again, isn't it?"

I said nothing.

"You still blame yourself for it."

I took a sip, the liquid coating my tongue in velvety smoothness, unfurling layers of honeyed malt, quickly followed by a burst of citrus zest and green apples that were dominated with tones of oat and a hint of almond.

"You were a kid when an *armed man* broke into our home. There's nothing you could have done," he insisted. "It's not your fault that Dad was killed."

But he didn't know everything that happened that night. In all these years, I'd been too ashamed to tell him. Still was.

And if Luna found out what I really did the night my dad died, she'd leave me.

The memory of the first time I'd visited my father's grave slammed into my mind—specifically when my mother had given each of us boys a moment alone by his headstone.

My father's name was engraved on the shiny brown granite—the finality of his death slicing my heart open.

"I'm sorry," I choked.

What a tragically inadequate phrase for costing him his life and creating an irreversible void for my family. A weight settled so heavily in my chest, each breath burned, and as I looked over my shoulder at my mom and brothers, I thought, I don't deserve to live with them anymore. Maybe I should run away. Or worse...after what I did, I deserve to have a headstone of my own. *But disappearing would inflict even more pain on my mother.*

"You blame yourself for the killer going free, too," Grayson accused, snapping me out of that memory and back to the present. "Because your description wasn't detailed enough for the sketch artist to find him in photo lineups. So, you hunt him. And you lock up as many bad guys as you can. But hunting Dad's killer won't bring Dad back."

My stomach roiled.

"And by being so fixated on that"—Grayson gestured toward the window—"you're robbing yourself of relationships."

My scotch had tendrils of smoke that twisted and curled around the glass, as if whispering secrets of isolation and betrayal. The ice cubes, once a solid companion to the alcohol, had slowly melted away, leaving the alcohol robbed of its strength and character.

In the depths of the golden liquid, a swirling vortex of hesitation mirrored my soul, reluctant to open up and risk being left behind, alone and empty, once more.

"Not just because you're afraid of being left," Grayson said. "Because you've convinced yourself that you're not worthy of being loved."

The weight of his words pulled at the very fabric of the room, and each second that passed felt like an hour—the distant hum of a clock's ticking was the only evidence that moments were passing at all. I was caught in a whirlpool of introspection, each word from Grayson echoing louder in the caverns of my mind, while the walls seemed to close in around me.

As Luna arrived at her front door, I set my drink down. Opting for a different way to burn off my energy.

"I'm going to get a workout in," I said.

But as I walked away, Grayson asked me one final question.

"If you have feelings for her, how long do you think you'll be able to resist acting on them?"

CHAPTER 21
Luna

"What the hell happened?" Sean demanded.

Sean's sandy-blond hair was longer at the top, styled in a messy but intentional way, while the sides were buzzed short, his huge arm muscles bulging beneath his tight black T-shirt. Six foot four inches tall with a thick build, he commanded attention everywhere he went without even trying.

His piercing brown eyes scanned me from top to bottom, looking for any signs that I was hurt.

"I'm so sorry about your van," I said.

It was the first time I'd been to my cottage since the prison incident.

"Screw the van, Luna." Sean stepped into my space. "I want you to tell me what happened."

So, I did. About the guy at the prison attacking me, thinking Dominic gave me a USB drive. How the Vigilante had killed the guy right in front of me, thus saving my life.

Sean's eyes widened in shock, his face draining of color. Every muscle tensed, his lips parting slightly, as if struggling to find words or maybe to simply breathe amid the overwhelming dread.

He asked a lot of follow-up questions, but eventually—and thank-fully—our conversation began to wind down.

In addition to taking a shower, maybe I would take a nap because this entire situation had drained me.

"You know what I think you should do?" I asked as I walked down the hallway toward my bathroom. "I think you should do a true crime podcast about the Vigilante."

I turned the shower water on so it could warm up.

"No one knows who this guy is or how he's able to carry out all these killings with such stealth. Or how he manages to get his hands on evidence that cops can't seem to obtain."

Sean leaned against the doorframe.

"It would probably be a very popular episode or maybe even a series of episodes. You could explore all the murders, go through the evidence, and try to uncover his identity. You could even have people call in with tips."

Warm water finally trailed over my hand.

"We could even do it together," I added. "Remember that follow-up podcast about my dad's case we did together? We ordered pizza and ended up going two episodes long."

His mouth curled downward. "That was the first time I saw you cry."

I flushed under the weight of his stare but squared my shoulders.

"For, like, a minute." Hello, we were picking at the deepest wound of my life. I was proud tears had only slipped out briefly and even prouder that I managed to shake it off. It was easier to feel lighter sitting with someone who truly believed in my father's innocence. I remember that bond forming quickly because of it and how my guard had crumbled.

"But I also laughed. We *enjoyed* working on that podcast together," I pushed on, trying to sound optimistic. "Think about how much fun it could be to team up on this."

He studied me intently for a moment before responding in a low voice, "We might never uncover the identity of the Vigilante."

"But we might, and it would be exciting to try."

Sean held the back of his neck. "That's not the kind of crimes I cover on my podcast."

I raised my eyebrows. The Vigilante was all over the news. Even right now. A reporter's tone rose in pitch as she talked about the latest attack at the prison.

"I thought you liked to work high-profile cases?"

"Murders. I focus on victims. Not killers."

"Think about what a boost it would be for your show if you cracked the identity of the Vigilante."

When Sean said nothing, something unsettling swirled in my chest —something I couldn't name.

"It was strange that the Vigilante turned up at the prison," I mused.

It bothered me now that I was thinking about it. The Joliet Prison was a long drive from Chicago, and the Vigilante, to my knowledge, had never been spotted outside of the city—his hunting grounds. And while he had said he was trying to watch over me, it was a serious stretch in his radius to go all the way to Joliet.

"How would he know I was there?" I guess he might've researched me and found out I visited my dad regularly, just as Franco had, but that would mean staking out the prison the entire weekend, waiting for me to show.

No one knew I was going to be there at that exact time, except for my dad.

And of course, Sean, whose van I had borrowed.

A flitting thought skated through my mind. A ludicrous thought for many reasons, only one of which was that Sean had no vehicle while I was gone. So, there would be no physical way for him to get to the prison.

Right?

But then how did the Vigilante go to and from his crime scenes, undetected? Surely, someone smart enough to continually evade the police wouldn't be stupid enough to use his own vehicle.

I'd never given much thought to it before. And now that I was studying Sean more closely—who was also the right height and build as the Vigilante—something else was different from when I'd left him this morning.

"Did you just get out of the shower?"

He was wearing a different outfit than when I'd left, and his hair was damp, his body smelling fresh of body wash.

"Yep," he said, tugging at his ear.

"Another one?"

His shower this morning had been so long, I'd run out of hot water.

"I went for a run while you were gone." Sean crossed his arms over his chest.

"I thought you had to record a podcast?" Yet now that I walked back into the living room, all of his equipment, which was temporarily set up there, looked like it had gone untouched.

I was about to press him on it, but my cell phone interrupted with a buzz.

Hunter: An unknown vehicle just pulled into your driveway. Don't open your door under any circumstance. I'm sending security.

My muscles tensed, and a moment later, a pounding knock at the front door made me jump. The door groaned in protest at each strike, as if cracking under the weight of the force lurking just beyond its threshold.

Hunter: Don't move.

My throat ran dry.

"You think it's Franco?" Sean whispered.

Images of what happened in that van flashed through my mind like a horror movie. The blood. The gore. The evil intent in the guy's eyes, and instantly, my body started to quiver.

"I don't know." But I wasn't going to stand here defenseless, so I grabbed a baseball bat from my bedroom. When I returned to the main area, Sean was positioned behind one of my lace drapes, peeking out through the front window as if the semi-sheer curtains could hide him.

Outside, a loud crash preceded a thud. I tightened my grip on the bat, my palms sweating as muffled cursing and scuffling rose in volume until, finally, it stopped.

The silence haunting.

"Get off me, man!" one voice snapped.

"Whoever it is, is detained." Sean walked to the front door.

"Wait!" I snapped.

But he opened it.

On the other side, one man was pinned up against the porch's side wall, his arms restrained behind his back by some humongous man who reminded me of G.I. Joe. Behind him, out of breath and wearing nothing but workout shorts, was Hunter Lockwood.

"Get off me," the pinned man shouted.

"Do you know this guy?" Hunter's eyes narrowed at me.

G.I. Joe reluctantly released his iron-fisted grip and stepped back, allowing me to see who it was.

Standing at six foot four, he had a short black beard wrapped around a square jaw, staring at me with chocolate eyes that lay almost hidden beneath his bushy brows. His dark hair had a sprinkling of silver along the temples with tattoos wrapped around both arms.

"Sort of."

"The hell does *sort of* mean?" Hunter asked.

The bodyguard next to him shifted and looked at Hunter, awaiting orders regarding the captive man's release.

"Let him go," I said.

"Like hell," Hunter snarled, his hired man unrelenting with his vise-like grip.

"This is Rodney. My dad's old cellmate and friend. Rodney, what are you doing here?" I asked.

"Your dad sent me," Rodney grumbled. "Now will you tell your guard dogs to back down?"

"Please let him go."

After a silent exchange between the bodyguard and Hunter, Rodney yanked his wrists free and looked like he wished he wasn't on parole so he could clock that bodyguard right in his jaw.

"Rodney, how do you know where I live?" I flexed my fingers at my side.

He scratched the back of his head. "Your dad gave me your address."

"Why?" I muttered.

"Your dad heard you were attacked."

"How did he hear about it?" I stepped forward.

He raised an eyebrow. "Girl gets attacked in the prison parking lot; you think the entire prison hasn't heard about it within the hour?"

I scowled. Right. "Why'd he send you here?" The words came out sharper than intended, betraying the tension knotting my stomach.

"He demanded I come lay eyes on you and see for myself if you're really okay. He didn't trust you to be honest with him over the phone."

Here my father was, in a cold, unending dungeon, suffering a fate that would shatter the strongest of spirits. Yet, amid his torment, he was worried about *my* safety. It was a testament to a love so profound that even in the darkest abyss, it burned brighter than the sun.

I was fine. Physically at least, and these haunting images of what almost happened, what could have happened, in that van would go away soon. I'd stop reliving that blood seeping from Anthony's skin, seeing it as a crimson reminder that it could have been my own as I lay there, dying.

No one else seemed to notice that my fingers began to tremble, but Hunter glanced at my hands with furrowed brows. He hesitated, perhaps torn between comforting me and wanting to respect the boundaries I'd put up. Which made me want to break them down even more.

After a few seconds, Hunter quietly moved to my side and wrapped his hand around mine in a soothing embrace—a tender moment that enveloped my heart like a warm blanket on a cold winter night. I locked eyes with his, overwhelmed by his kindness and adoration. I'd never had a man look at me like this—capable of making even the most chaotic scenes fade in my periphery.

Even after I'd rejected him, Hunter dropped everything to come over here and make sure I was safe, comforting me in the process.

Unleashing affection like a fog escaping a bottle—impossible to control.

Only this time, I wasn't sure I wanted to…

It took a concerted effort to break my stare with Hunter and clear my throat.

"I'm fine, Rodney. Please tell him not to worry."

Rodney's eyes jumped from me to the three men around me. "Who the hell are these people?"

"How did he make it to her front door?" Hunter glared at his bodyguard, who lifted his chin.

He said, "Sent the alert as soon as I saw him drive up."

Hunter ground his jaw, tightening his grip on my hand.

"They're watching out for me," I assured Rodney.

Rodney regarded the men, then turned his attention back to me.

"I'll be keeping an eye on you, Luna."

CHAPTER 22
Hunter

"What did you find out?" My voice was tight as I settled into the black leather chair behind my desk, squeezing a stress ball as if my life depended on it.

My home office was a grand and impressive space, drenched in natural light from the oversized window that dominated one wall. The room was anchored by a massive mahogany desk, its polished surface gleaming in the sunlight, positioned opposite the window, which offered a stunning view of the surrounding landscape. Most notably the cottage at the end of the road.

I stared at Barry Mansfield, who sat opposite me. He wore that worn leather jacket again, and there was something about the way he carried himself—his confident stride, the slight narrowing of his eyes when faced with a challenge—that hinted at a willingness to bend rules when necessary to get the job done.

Making me wonder…

What methods did he use to get answers that had evaded everyone else?

"Franco's still in the wind, but the good news is, Luna isn't facing this alone. Franco made a mistake, sending that thug after her. Now that someone physically attacked her, police are taking it much more seriously and have ensured that precautionary measures are in place. They're driving past the Lockwood estate on a regular basis, and they'll also be keeping an eye on her office. Plus, cops are actively looking for that USB drive as we speak."

"Good. But we need to keep digging, too. Franco Hopkins isn't banking on someone like you trying to find him."

"I'll give you an update as soon as I have more." Barry nodded. "Now, as for the other matter you asked me to look into." He took an exaggerated breath before asking, "You want the long version or the short version?"

I swallowed hard before responding with a curt, "Short version."

Barry sighed heavily in resignation. "The letter threatening Ms. Payne is untraceable. Whoever sent this knows how to cover their tracks." His eyes tightened when he said this last part.

"So, it's a legitimate threat then," I uttered in a low voice.

He slowly nodded his head in agreement. "It would appear so."

Fuck.

"That said…" Barry's tone soothed around the edges. "I've encountered a lot of death threats in my line of work. But honestly, most of them are never acted on."

"But some are?"

Barry licked his lower lip slowly. "Yes, some are."

My stomach dropped as I racked my brain. What the hell were we up against?

"We need to get to the bottom of Ms. Payne's case and fast." My voice pitched a notch higher. "Someone is out there who knows something about that case, and we need to find out who that someone is."

Barry's eyes held a deep weight as he slowly dipped his chin, the gravity of the moment evident. He had agreed to take on this additional investigation if I funded extra staff to help him with my father's case.

"I'm going to start with the police records, see if anyone else was suspected at the time of the young man's death. If there's any motive behind these threats, it must be from someone with something to lose by Mr. Payne's potential acquittal."

My chest fell in a deep, drawn-out exhale as the burden of this investigation pressed down on me.

"Something still doesn't add up." I squeezed the ball, and spun my chair slightly. "Even if Mr. Payne's conviction were to be overturned, and even if the investigation were to be reopened, and even if they found another suspect, any defense attorney would shout *reasonable doubt* from a rooftop."

Barry nodded thoughtfully, clearly understanding where I was going with this.

"After another man was convicted of a crime, reasonable doubt is a given," I scoffed. "So, if there is a real killer out there, they'd know they had nothing to worry about."

Barry opened his hands. "Maybe they don't know that. You're a prosecutor. It's black and white to you, but maybe the person believes their freedom is in danger."

"Maybe," I drawled. But I didn't believe that. "Any person who is sophisticated enough to send an untraceable letter to a woman who keeps her address private must be smart enough to know a thing or two about the law. That they'd be in no real danger of getting convicted of the crime."

My eyes drifted out the window toward Luna's cottage.

"So, the big question is: what has this person so concerned that he's threatening to kill Luna over it?"

"I'll have my guys keep digging," Barry said. "But if you want my opinion, the more urgent matter right now with regard to her safety is Franco Hopkins. The Payne case will likely drag through the courts slowly, whereas Mr. Hopkins has a critical problem on his hands. Police now know about the USB drive and that it might contain evidence. And they're looking for it. If he's got eyes on the street, he'll know that."

"If Franco's smart, he'll come to the conclusion Luna never had the evidence."

Barry pursed his lips. "Let's hope he's smart."

Meanwhile, I wasn't about to let Luna out of my sight.

Which posed a problem. Tomorrow night, I was hosting an annual gala at my home for a charity I'd founded, and it was too late to cancel it. The people invited were cleared on the guest list months ago, so theoretically, the chances of an uninvited guest slipping through were slim to none.

But anything greater than zero was unacceptable.

Which left me with only two options.

As soon as Barry left, I called Luna and invited myself over tomorrow evening—option number one.

"Wh…just the two of us?"

How delightfully perplexing that the melody of her voice had the power to simmer my boiling rage. If only temporarily. It didn't hurt, hearing her frazzled *oh shit* tone, either. In fact, I found myself smiling.

"Well, three of us, if your…"

"Friend," she retorted, prompting a wry smile from me.

"Your friend Sean will be there."

I hated him. But I hated her being alone even more, and at least the guy was a human shield for her, I guess.

A long pause. Tension in her voice when she said, "I don't think that's such a good idea."

"Give me one good reason."

"How about the possibility you and Sean murder each other?"

I chuckled, looking out the window at the cottage, seeing her gorgeous frame in the window.

"And if I promise not to murder your friend? Can I come over then?"

She began to pace in front of the window, looking down at her feet. "I…think it's best if we stick to more public places."

The tension in her voice made me wonder if it was as hard for her to keep her hands off me, as it would be for me with her.

"And why's that?" I tilted my head.

She looked at me, I think. Hard to tell, this far from her cottage.

"I…I'm trying to maintain the boundaries we put up."

I smiled. "So, you're having a hard time doing that, then?"

"Shut up, Hunter."

I laughed this time. Damn, I couldn't remember the last time anyone made me laugh.

"Well, with everything that has happened, I'm afraid I can't have you out of my sight tomorrow night."

"Why?"

"I'm hosting an event. We could go into the city, I suppose, but my uncle will be furious if I don't make an appearance."

"What kind of event?"

"A gala. For charity."

I left out what charity. No need to give her another reason to say no.

Option two.

"Come with me," I said. "To the gala."

"I'm…not sure about that."

"What's wrong?" I teased. "Worried if you see me in a tux, you won't be able to keep your hands off me?"

She stopped in front of her window. "Arrogant much?"

I chuckled.

"I don't have anything to wear to something like that."

"All you have to do is show up. I'll arrange everything else," I said. "And, Luna?"

She waited.

"For the record, you don't need a dress to look beautiful. You're stunning, no matter what you wear. I'd venture to guess even more stunning wearing nothing at all."

I heard the soft breath before her shaking voice said, "See, this is why it's not a good idea for me to come over."

"I don't want you out of my sight, so either I can come there or you can come here."

She paced faster in front of the window.

"No," she finally said. "Coming here's a bad idea."

I couldn't decide what I loved more: how worried she seemed to be at the two of us being alone together or the fleeting desire in her voice that tempted her to take that plunge.

"Then it's settled. Be here by six."

"I...I'm not sure if—"

"Luna?" I interrupted. "I'm not taking no for an answer."

The smart thing to do, if I had any hope of not falling head over heels for Luna Payne, was to keep a reasonable distance from her. I had money to hire more security, so logically, I didn't need to have her in my eyesight to keep her safe.

But I couldn't stand the thought of being away from her when she was in danger. Having her here would ease my anxiety about her safety, but it created another problem: I no longer trusted myself to behave.

In fact, if I saw her in a gown, I wasn't sure how I would keep my hands to myself.

CHAPTER 23
Luna

I questioned my sanity for agreeing to this.

Not because Hunter had hired a beauty team to come to me in the "safe" confines of his mansion. Having the finest hairstylists, makeup artists, and others was like being Cinderella for a night.

I loved picking out the colors of my makeup—a smoky eye and nude lip—and watching a high-end artist accentuate my face until I looked as gorgeous as a bride on her wedding day. And I didn't know my hair could be this shiny, this elegant, draped over my shoulder. But the dress had to be my favorite with cuts carefully crafted for a woman's curves, making anyone in it feel like a princess.

All of it was enchanting.

The part that had me questioning my sanity was the next part of the agenda—entering a room of rich, powerful people where I'd have to try to act like I wasn't a fish out of water.

The last thing I wanted to do was embarrass Hunter Lockwood in his own home.

CHAPTER 24

Hunter

The night that would become one of my best dreams started off terribly.

I clenched my fists, anxiety winding through my spine with all the people in my great room.

Waiters carried silver trays with bubbling champagne flutes. The violinists were tucked away in the dimly lit corner, their instruments screeching out tunes to a room of deafening indifference, and a roaring fire devoured logs in the fireplace, casting an orange glow across the gowns and tuxedos.

All four of us Lockwood brothers were in attendance—me, Bryson, Jace, and Grayson—all standing in a loose circle.

"I'm surprised you showed," Jace said to Grayson.

"I told you I'd be here," Grayson replied casually.

"No offense, but you commit to lots of things you never show up to," Jace retorted.

Grayson pursed his lips.

"Let me guess." Bryson raised a brow. "You were *traveling*."

Grayson took a sip of his drink. I wondered if Bryson or Jace would continue to question him, but before they had the chance, social obligations intervened, pulling them away and leaving me and Grayson alone.

He studied me. "You look like you're about to go two rounds with Mike Tyson."

"Nice subject change." I adjusted my shirt collar. "I'm not thrilled about people being here tonight."

I told Grayson about Franco's threat and how no amount of security would ever make me feel like she was safe.

"Maybe this was a mistake," I said. "Any one of these guests could be on Franco's payroll."

"How many security guards did you say you hired for tonight?" Grayson asked.

"Thirty."

"Positions?"

Even I didn't know all of their positions. That was the point, my security leader reminded me. Discretion. The ones I knew about were at every single entrance. Perimeter. Drive. Road leading to the drive. And a flock of them around the party, disguised as guests.

My goal was to spend no more than an hour here before I whisked Luna away to the upper floor of my mansion, surrounded by several guards.

I seriously hoped she wouldn't give me grief about that, too— about what I needed to do to keep her safe. The girl was critically dangerous to herself.

"Grayson, Hunter." Uncle Alexander put a hand on my shoulder. "Great turnout, eh?"

My uncle's eyes swept the space, pride straightening his shoulders, undoubtedly because of all the high-profile people in attendance. Politicians. Business leaders. Even a few big-name athletes and celebrities.

"Do you boys remember the first gala I took you to?" Alexander asked.

"Grayson bid on every item in the silent auction," I remembered.

"I thought it was a contest to see who could come up with the right price," Grayson argued. "Besides, I only won *one* thing."

"Mom was so pissed at you."

"We all enjoyed that boat," Grayson grumbled.

"Perhaps we should do this gala more than once a year." Alexander rubbed his chin. "The fundraising committee is estimating twenty percent higher donations this year over last." When he scanned the crowd this time, I assumed he was counting heads.

"I don't see Luna." Uncle Alexander tried to hide his relief, but it was there, lurking beneath his fake surprise.

At this exact moment, Luna was upstairs getting ready, so she was most definitely going to be in attendance, but she'd also make her entrance from the top of the grand staircase. Which would make it very clear she was here as *my* guest.

"It's probably for the best," Alexander said.

He must have seen the irritation on my face.

"It's just the optics," Uncle said. "She's a defense attorney, helping criminals get off."

I glowered at him.

He squared his shoulders. "Having the daughter of a killer at a charity that benefits victims of violent crimes would be a bad look."

"Luna is not responsible for the crimes of anyone else, including her father. Even if he *is* guilty of murder, that's not on her."

Alexander sighed. "Hunter, I'm not trying to be disagreeable. I'm sure she's a very delightful young woman."

"But you think she should be shunned from society because of something her father was accused of."

"Her showing up to this event could leave a stain on the charity. It could be misconstrued by some as being insensitive to the victims of violent crimes."

I couldn't decide which I was angrier about: what my uncle said or the fact he might be right—people might be highly offended if they knew who Luna was and that she was here at tonight's gala.

"If people get upset, donations might decline," Alexander said. "And the victims of violent crimes are going to be the ones to pay the price."

Was I in the wrong here? Was I being a complete asshole, putting Luna's needs above the possible backlash with the charity?

I did not want to hurt the victims of violent crimes; I was the one who founded this charity, for God's sake. Not Alexander. Alexander's interest only sparked when the charity began to hit headlines—a shining light on the good that the Lockwoods were doing after the tragedy that had plagued our family.

But I started this charity to help people. I didn't start it to run it as a PR campaign, to make decisions on what might look good or bad in the press.

And someone—*someone*—in this world needed to prioritize Luna's emotional needs.

Once she'd learned what the gala was for, it had taken a lot of convincing on my part to get her to agree to show up tonight. She was insecure, terrified of what people would think. It was why she avoided a lot of things in life, isolating herself from society and, I suspected, relationships.

And just when she was finally brave enough to come, Alexander was reinforcing that very fear of her not being accepted.

Maybe I couldn't be everything to her.

But maybe I could fulfill one very important purpose in her life: to help give her the confidence to stand tall among those who wanted to tear her down. Because, as I had told Luna before she started getting ready, she deserved to be here just as much as anyone else. And she had nothing to be ashamed of.

Someone needed to send that message to the rest of society, so why not start tonight? And who better to send that message than me?

I was Hunter Lockwood. I'd spent years parading around in social circles, acting aloof—it was what I was known for in the blogs and the online tabloids that would run stories about me. The unapproachable, impenetrable Hunter Lockwood, the serial dater.

Many wondered if I would ever settle down and, if so, what "lucky" woman would land my elusive attention.

I couldn't solve all of Luna's problems, but I was going to make a statement to everyone in this room—of just how much worth Luna

Payne had in this world by linking her arm with mine and showing them she was the queen of this ball.

Grayson cleared his throat loudly, and I followed his gaze to the grand staircase.

Where, at the top, Luna stood in a sparkly red gown that draped around her body like a glitzy ribbon on a package, hugging every perfect inch of her curves in elegance and grace. Her hair was swept over one shoulder, tickling her exposed collarbone and accentuating her eyes.

Which were the center of her look, drawn up with smoky black shadow and eyelashes that would give any teenage boy a wet dream.

She looked like a goddess. I'd never seen anything more beautiful in my life. She deserved to strut around this place like she owned it, yet she looked around with those timid eyes, gazing at the crowd as if worried she didn't belong.

I wanted to take her hand and reassure her this was *exactly* where she belonged—right here, in my home, by my side. In my eyes, this stubborn, infuriating, argumentative woman was perfectly imperfect, and I wouldn't change that in any way.

Alexander sighed in disapproval, but he was polite enough to say nothing more. Maybe he could tell by the way I was staring at Luna that she wouldn't be going anywhere. No matter what.

Unable to break my stare, I moved through the crowd toward the staircase.

"Holy crap." Brody Miller stopped me, slapping my back like we were friends.

I hated Brody Miller. Known for his DUIs that his senator father always helped him get out of, the guy did more drugs than a band on a world tour. Slept with more women, too, and had even fathered two children who he never bothered to meet. He was too busy trying to weasel out of child support, even though the DNA proved he was responsible for them.

The guy was so narcissistically into himself, he never fathomed that I hated his guts, no matter how many times I'd tried to make it clear.

Brody's gaze slid over Luna, lingering a touch too long on her curves, a smirk tugging at the corner of his lips. "I'm going to have to hit that, bro."

A blazing rage ripped through my spine and wrapped around my ribs.

I grabbed Brody's shoulder. Hard.

"If you go anywhere near her"—I smiled—"I'll break your legs."

He laughed. Until he looked in my eyes and realized I was dead serious.

I shoved him off and walked toward Luna, who had yet to spot me.

It wasn't just Brody that upset me. It was the thought of any other man touching her. It banged against my bones so hard, it felt like they'd break under the mere idea of it.

Luna's eyes met mine, and damn if time didn't cease to exist. She held my gaze as I slowly walked up the staircase, one agonizing step at a time.

"Everyone's staring," she whispered, biting her lip.

She was trying to hide it, but nervousness flickered through her eyes as she looked down at the great room. But what she didn't realize was, in the sea of people who filled my house, there was only one that I cared about right now. One that I wished I could have for my own.

"I'm warning you, Luna, if you want to stay just friends, you're going to have to wear a different dress."

CHAPTER 25
Luna

"You look stunning." Hunter's tone was low and seductive.

"You look...devastatingly handsome. I can see what the blogs are so worked up about."

But it was almost like Hunter didn't hear my compliment, lost in a potion of drinking me in.

"Do me a favor and stay close to me tonight."

Of course I would. But...

"Why?"

"You're the most gorgeous woman here, which means every single man will want you."

When he stared at me, something passed between us, my thread of resistance beginning to fray.

"That's not true."

"It is. None of them are good enough for you, and if I see one of them try something with you, I don't trust myself to not break his jaw."

Holy crap. Was it wrong that I found his possessive side sexy as hell?

Hunter was in rare form tonight. His eyes bored into mine until he saw me swallow, smirking at the effect he was having on me.

"No one is going to try something here," I reasoned. This wasn't a frat party.

"Every man in this room wants you right now," he disagreed in a tone laced with jealousy.

When flames heated my cheeks, Hunter's smirk widened, and he leaned in and whispered, "I guarantee they're imagining getting you alone, pulling this dress off of you."

My increasing pool of blood beneath my skin appeared to egg him on even more.

"And pleasuring you until they see what face you make when they bring you to the brink."

My heart throbbed in my chest, and I stammered, "Well, they wouldn't be able to...I've never...I wouldn't know..."

Hunter's gaze flamed with desire, staring at me like the entire party suddenly vanished around us. This time, he leaned in even closer, his hot breath tickling my ear as he whispered, "Luna, so help me, if you tell me you're a virgin, I won't be able to control myself."

"No, I'm not...I...I've been with one man, but..."

"*One?*" His eyes widened with a spark. "But what?" he challenged.

"I...in college, that guy and I...but he never..."

God, this was embarrassing. Verbal diarrhea spewing from my mouth.

"But he never made you come."

Good Lord. Hearing that word out of Hunter's mouth did all sorts of naughty things to my lady parts. Him looking spellbinding in a tux, his hair with a different polish to it, smelling so delicious—sandalwood with a citrus edge—I wanted to bury my nose against his skin. All not helping.

I put my hand over my eyes. "Can we please talk about something else?"

Hunter was silent for several heartbeats, and then he gently pulled my hand away from my face, his gaze so fierce, it cut into my soul. According to the blogs, this guy had more sexual experience than a Hollywood star. His chest rose and fell faster as he looked over my entire body again, pulling his lower lip between his teeth, before finally angling himself closer.

"Luna..." His voice dropped to a sultry whisper, the words rolling off his tongue with a predatory smoothness that made me quiver. "If you wanted to stay platonic, you really shouldn't have told me that."

I swallowed under the ferocity of his stare.

"Because now," he said, the heat of his breath once again tickling my ear, "the only thing I'm going to be able to think about all night is burying my tongue inside of you until you scream my name."

Holy mother of...

A flash of heat radiated down my stomach, between my thighs, imagining him doing just that. Craving it, if I were being honest. And as Hunter stared at me with a flame of need, I wasn't sure I'd be able to resist him if he tried...

"I'll attempt to behave myself tonight." Hunter extended his elbow to me, his eyes glued to my face. "But I can't make any guarantees."

I don't want you to behave...

CHAPTER 26
Hunter

How the hell was I going to get through this damn party? Now I only wanted—could only focus on—one thing: Luna's thighs spread open in front of me.

As a billionaire, I'd been able to acquire almost everything I longed to have.

But being the first man to give her an orgasm? I'd give up my entire fortune for that.

It took a lot of damn effort to recalibrate after that earth-shattering conversation. No way I'd let this evening pass without making a move—see how far she'd let this go—but first, we needed to make our rounds.

They'd be quick—I could guarantee that.

As I held out my elbow, Luna hesitated.

"I'm the daughter of a convicted killer. You're the son of a murder victim. Maybe it would be best if we stayed on opposite sides of the room in front of these people."

I stepped closer. "Luna, even if the whole damn world was against you, there's nowhere I'd rather be than by your side."

I raised my elbow, making it clear I'd wait. I pretended not to notice the shimmering tears threatening to spill over her cheeks when she hesitated for a moment before threading her small arm through mine.

Even through the fabric of my tux, the spark between us crackled to life, as if someone had just lit a fire in my veins. Focusing on the intense sensation of her arm touching mine, I couldn't stop imagining what it would feel like to touch other areas of her body instead.

Or to hear my name roll off her lips as I feasted on her.

After slowly descending the stairs to the crowd of onlookers, I made introductions as we gradually mingled among the guests. Some showed flickers of recognition at the mention of her last name, and some didn't, but all of that faded into the background as my attention became laser-focused on observing Luna.

The way she'd nibble on her lower lip when she was anxious. The way she'd politely laugh at everyone's jokes—even though most of them weren't funny. And the way she'd squeeze my hand when she was ready to end the conversation.

I watched her the entire time, falling deeper into the abyss of unprecedented feelings. And the deeper I fell into her well, the more I wanted to drown in it.

Until finally, I couldn't take it anymore.

"Luna," I said, my voice cracking with restrained urgency, eyes darting to a more secluded spot, "come with me."

CHAPTER 27

Luna

Hunter tried to pull me away, but suddenly, a couple—a spiky-haired woman and a man with a terrible comb-over —intercepted us.

"I don't believe we've ever seen you before," the lady said to me. Was it me? Or was her tone a little snotty? Territorial, even? So many people longed to get Hunter's attention, and I wondered if some people were envious that a stranger to this social circle would be granted it.

"Luna"—Hunter put his hand on my lower back, a gesture that about made my knees buckle—"this is Katherine and Charles Gardner."

"It's nice to meet you."

As small talk ensued, Hunter tried to hide his impatience, but I could tell from the way he shifted his footing that he was eager to get away from them.

Meanwhile, a waiter dressed like he was going to a movie star's wedding came by, holding a silver serving tray so shiny, that the fire's reflection shimmered off of it. The tray held various flatbreads and a bowl of something black.

Which the waiter offered to me first.

"No, thank you," I said.

"You have to try it," Katherine insisted. "The Lockwoods spare no expense with these things."

I didn't want to drip something on this dress, but I didn't want to be rude either.

I wasn't sure what the mystery black dip was, but at least this tray wasn't filled with the giant shrimp going around that people were dipping in red sauce.

Hunter was being a gentleman, letting me go first. The couple was waiting for me, too, watching as I stood up a little straighter—*graceful, Luna*—and delicately picked up a napkin, which was embroidered with the HW logo. Only Hunter would have a logo for his name and have it printed in gold on napkins.

When I took the little hard bread thing and dipped it into the sauce, the lady snickered.

"It's caviar, dear," Katherine said in a condescending tone while I tried to hide my humiliation. "Haven't you ever had caviar?"

The only reason I cared this much about being the butt of her joke was because I didn't want to embarrass Hunter, but he didn't even flinch.

Instead, he looked at me with a warmth and depth to his gaze that made my heart flutter before shooting Katherine an icy glare as he picked up a piece of bread and plunged it into the caviar the same way I had.

"Caviar tastes the same, no matter how it gets on the melba toast, Katherine," Hunter snarled before popping it into his mouth.

Katherine's face fell.

"Come on." Hunter took my hand and again tried to lead me out of the room.

Again, we were intercepted.

This time by the mayor.

"Hunter," he said, "may I have a word with your date?"

I blinked, taken aback. He wanted to talk to *me*? Why? And why alone?

Outwardly, Hunter played the role of the gracious host. "Of

course," he even said. But his patience unraveled when he whispered in my ear, "For the love of all things holy, please make it quick."

I smirked at the notion I was making such a powerful man sweat. I had a good idea why he was trying to pull me away, but if we were intimate, what would that unleash? Hunter used one-night stands as a way of emotionally distancing himself from people. But if I slept with him, it would do the opposite, unraveling something I wouldn't be able to put back.

The problem was, I wanted to be with Hunter—if only for one night—so much that it scared me.

Hunter paused for a moment, lips pressed tightly together. Then, with a final lingering glance, he turned and stepped away.

"Mayor Kepler," I said, shaking the man's hand.

This really was the party full of Chicago's elite.

I wish Sean could have made it to see this. Hunter extended an invitation to him, albeit begrudgingly, in an effort to make me happy. But Sean said he'd rather have a root canal performed by a blind dentist than spend his evening with the likes of Hunter and his friends.

"It's an honor to meet you," I added.

Kepler was in his mid-fifties, and the top of his head sported a glaring bald spot the size of an apple that he attempted to conceal with a comb-over. He had a well-groomed mustache that matched his light-brown hair color and a neatly trimmed beard that added to his distinguished appearance.

"I had no idea you would be here tonight, Ms. Payne," the mayor said, as if this were a pleasant surprise.

But I was still unclear. "I wasn't aware you knew who I was."

"It's not every day someone dares to challenge our city's notorious Vigilante with such composure and eloquence."

"You saw the press conference," I realized.

"Pretty sure half the city of Chicago saw that press conference, if not the subsequent repeats since then. It was quite impressive."

"Perhaps *all* people are finally starting to see the Vigilante for the dangerous criminal he truly is," I speculated.

The mayor smiled warmly at me. "Perhaps they needed someone as graceful as you to show them. I heard you had another encounter with him. That he came to your rescue. Is that true?"

A wave of frustration hit me. "It is."

"Did it change your opinion of him?"

I hated that the mayor wanted to clarify this point with me, and I hated it even more that there was a slight rumbling of disagreement in my heart with how I felt.

I'd replayed that incident in my mind many times, and what was disturbing was that I'd had to *actively* remind myself of the brutality that the Vigilante was capable of. I'd imagined his victims perhaps walking to their cars, just like Dominic had, only to be ambushed and executed. If I didn't focus on that part of the Vigilante, I risked my gratitude toward him for saving my life overshadowing the truth of who he really was.

A monster.

"I'm grateful he stepped in when he did, but I would never stand for someone who murders people," I said.

The mayor's shoulders relaxed.

"I was hoping you were going to say that because I want to propose something to you. As you may know, I'm running for reelection," the mayor started, voice filled with tentative hope. "There are several problems that need to be fixed in this city. Some are harder, like emergency response times."

Emergency response times were an evolving issue in this city, thanks to the increased volume of violence.

"Some are quicker fixes. This Vigilante is making a mockery of our judicial system. What's more, he's a liability. A threat to public safety. It's only a matter of time before he kills an innocent person."

Would he? I wasn't sure about that. He'd killed Dominic, but after what Rinaldi said, I was starting to wonder if Dominic was as clean as I thought. Moreover, I could tell by the mayor's tone that he didn't mean the Vigilante would get it wrong and accidentally target the wrong person. He meant hunting and ending innocent people.

"I've decided my top priority will be to locate and expose this Vigilante, and I'm organizing my campaign around it. As such, I'll be releasing extra funding to pay for overtime and other resources needed to hunt this guy down, but we need to put public pressure on him. The more people that are looking for him, the harder it will be for him to hide."

"You want the media all over this."

"Precisely. Which is where you come in." He motioned to me with his champagne flute. "I would like you to become the face of this initiative."

"Me?"

My stomach began to swirl with unease. I'd done that press conference and thought that part of it was behind me. Now I had Franco to worry about, plus my dad's case, not to mention a looming, anonymous threat hanging over my head.

And then there were my growing feelings for Hunter. Which I was failing at beating down, by the way. Taking on a city initiative was the last thing I had time for.

But the Vigilante had killed my friend, and not getting involved would be a betrayal to Dominic. No matter how clean or unclean he might have been, he didn't deserve to be killed like that.

"What does that entail, sir?" I pressed.

"Practically speaking, a few press conferences. Some speeches to keep this alive in the media, keep people looking for him."

A few speeches. That didn't sound too overwhelming, I guess.

"Why me?" I wondered aloud. "Wouldn't the media pay more attention to someone of your status?"

"I'll be giving speeches as well, of course, but I need someone else up there on that podium alongside me. Telling the story and fighting the fight to give reporters something to talk about."

"I'm honored you thought of me, sir, but wouldn't Hunter be a better fit? He's a prosecutor, and I'm a defense attorney."

"That's the whole point. A prosecutor getting a hard-on to put the Windy City Vigilante behind bars won't make people blink. But people see a defense attorney step up and call for his arrest? They take notice. Your voice is louder because it's unexpected. It's more likely to create a change in public opinion of the Vigilante.

"Plus, the public needs a heroine who has been personally affected by the criminal we're hunting. Someone who lost a longtime friend to him, for example."

As I looked at his glass of champagne, watching the bubbles flee from each other, a surge of anxiety washed over me. People in fancy outfits laughed and smiled all around us, but all I could do was frown at the request to help hunt down the killer that took my friend's life.

Yet had saved mine.

"You've seen him twice, Luna. Be on that stage with me when I declare war against him."

I chewed the inside of my cheek.

"Do you not want the Vigilante captured?" the mayor asked.

"I do."

"Then why the hesitation?"

I sighed. "To be perfectly honest, sir, I'm worried these public speeches and press conferences will require a lot of time." Time needed to dedicate to my father's case. As much as I've advocated for the Vigilante to go down, I didn't want it to come at the expense of my father's freedom.

"I can work around your schedule."

I bit my lip—a gesture the mayor seemed to notice. He shifted his stance, pointing his glass in my direction.

"I hear you're also quite an advocate for justice reform," he said.

"I am," I said.

Did he know about my father? He had to, right? A man at his level surely did his research on anyone he was about to go public with.

"Justice reform has been a longtime passion of mine," the mayor said. "But I've never had the right person to spearhead it. I'm told you have some ideas on the matter, yes?"

I damn near balled up on my tiptoes. "I do."

"I'd like to hear some of your thoughts."

It was possible he was only asking me this to get me to agree to the speeches, but with his sharp gaze, he looked sincere.

My heart came alive with the sensation of being on a stage with the spotlight poised in my direction. Every word I was about to speak was capable of transforming the justice system in this state, and then maybe other states would follow suit, and the entire country would be better for it.

It was probably arrogant to think I could have that big of an impact, but a person can dare to dream, and I was officially standing in front of an individual that had the ability to direct funding and resources to enact real change.

And I was a person with incredible passion. Together, change was absolutely possible.

I went over some of the broader strokes of what I would be looking for in justice reform, the mayor nodding and asking for clarifications along the way.

"Tell you what," the mayor said. "If you help me catch the Vigilante by lending your face and voice to this effort, I will fast-track the initiative for justice reform and name you as the lead."

"You think you can secure the funding for that?" I could donate my time, but without a budget, it would be a pipe dream.

"I do."

I studied his eyes, looking for any hint of insincerity, but saw only determination.

What does a girl say when some of her biggest dreams are coming true? Answer: nothing. She nods and shakes the mayor's hand, solidifying their deal.

And as it turned out, the first person I sought when one of my dreams was coming true...was Hunter Lockwood.

I glanced around the elegant room and spotted him.

As the host of this charity gala, I'd assumed he was tied up in conversation with guests, but he was leaning against the wall, doing nothing but staring at me.

It took a confident man to not insert himself into such a powerful exchange with the mayor, and I admired him even more because of it.

Heck, it turned me on.

His gaze was an electric current, igniting a spark deep within with that same connection I'd had in his kitchen. Even in a room full of people, it felt like we were the only two here. The way he looked at me was a mix of admiration and desire, an unspoken invitation that beckoned me to come closer.

He tilted his head ever so slightly, a playful smirk forming at the corner of his lips, and as his eyes wandered over my figure, a shiver of excitement ran down my spine. He took me in with a deliberate slowness, his gaze lingering on the curve of my hips, the arch of my back, and the contours of my face.

There was a magnetism to his gaze that I couldn't resist, drawing me in. In that moment, I felt like he saw me for who I truly was—a person whose confidence was a mask hiding deep-seated vulnerabilities that had been planted there as a child and rooted in trauma.

And behind that magnetism, a tenderness in his eyes cradled my vulnerabilities like prized possessions, making a warmth expand in my chest, paired with an undeniable pull to know him as intimately as he seemed to know me.

He raised his eyebrow and gave me a sultry wink, my cheeks flushing with a heat that spread between my thighs. I swear, every time his eyes met mine, they smoldered with this raw, undiluted hunger, making the world fade—leaving me breathless and completely enthralled.

And once the mayor finally walked away, Hunter pushed off that wall. With determined steps, he closed the distance between us, his gaze intense, unwavering, and possessive. Every movement exuded a sense of ownership, as if I was already his.

I couldn't take my eyes off him, couldn't catch my breath until he reached me, and when he did, Hunter held his hand out, a silent invitation to escort a lady to another area of the party.

The moment his fingers brushed against mine, I knew I was in trouble. It was a seemingly innocent touch, but it sent a jolt of electricity through my entire core, and any lingering strength to resist the magnetic pull between us crumbled into dust.

"Come here." Hunter gently tugged my hand and began to lead me away from all the people.

"Where are we going?" I asked.

As he pulled me through the kitchen and into the garage, locking the door and quickly shutting off any security cameras in view, Hunter turned to look at me. His eyes, dark and smoldering, held a promise of passion, and I knew in that instant, I was about to let this happen...

CHAPTER 28

Luna

The last time I'd been in this garage was five days ago, right after the prison incident. At the time, I'd been too pissed to notice the details, but this place was pristine. The flooring had some kind of shiny speckled coating that reminded me of marble, and the walls were painted black with blue shelving containing red plastic bins that didn't look like they had an ounce of dust on them.

It didn't even smell like a garage normally would. More like a men's cologne commercial, a musk scent mixed with smoked wood.

Above us, soft lighting illuminated each of Hunter's cars, as if on display on a showroom floor. He had a Jeep. A truck. Some kind of old vintage thing—a Mustang maybe? And of course, his prized Aston Martin, which was parked two feet from where I now stood.

I hadn't even had a chance to turn around when, suddenly, Hunter was behind me, pressing his chest against my back, wrapping his hand around my midsection.

My heart raced uncontrollably as the anticipation surged through my veins, finally culminating in the moment I had longed for.

"I can't stand seeing you in this dress for one more second without touching you."

His touch, like a whisper, grazed my skin, igniting a wildfire of need that threatened to consume me. His fingertips danced along the curve of my shoulder, making my breath hitch as he traced the outline of my collarbone, so light and delicate, it was almost unbearable.

I closed my eyes, savoring the heat of his body against mine. The warmth of his breath caressed the nape of my neck, and a delicious shudder rippled through me as I drowned in the intoxicating scent of his musk cologne.

"Hunter..."

He let his hands roam over my stomach, down the front of my thighs.

My body reacted in ways I had never experienced before, my hips involuntarily pressing back into him.

Making him let out a wanton sigh.

The world around us faded, leaving only the sound of our ragged breaths, the tension building with a crescendo of passion that threatened to overtake us both. Surrendering to him was dangerous, but the fire that burned within me was too powerful to ignore.

Hunter began kissing my shoulder, and my body came to life, paralyzing me with yearning. For all my talk about friendship and pushing against this pull, I couldn't stop thinking about what it would feel like to have Hunter touch me the way he was now. To have his hands caress me the way my body craved.

I knew I should push him away. We had agreed to be just friends for a reason, but that reason became a lot harder to remember when his hands slid up my body and grasped my breasts, causing me to arch my back, wishing there wasn't fabric separating us. I wanted to feel his palm cupping me without any barrier getting in the way.

I couldn't believe this was happening.

The hottest guy I'd ever laid eyes on—with his dark hair and commanding jawline—had his mouth on my neck, my jaw, and was inciting a riot of disagreement for having ever resisted this.

His fingers breached the top of my dress and slid down over my breast. My chest ached at his touch, and when he squeezed me, I groaned.

Slowly, his tongue trailed from my shoulder to my collarbone, leaving behind a frost when his mouth would abandon me.

I tilted my head to give him better access, my breathing quickening as he slid his hands down my thighs and grabbed fistfuls of my gown's fabric.

Inching it up slowly.

I could tell him to stop. I could end it right now, but that would mean never knowing the pleasure of Hunter Lockwood sinking himself deep inside me.

His lips brushed my earlobe as he inched the dress up farther before they lightly ghosted a path back down along my neck. "I want you to scream my name when I make you come."

Oh my word.

I wanted that too. But lacking the experience as proof that I could, I wasn't sure if that was possible.

"I don't want to disappoint you," I said.

He slipped his finger into my panties and growled when he felt how turned on I was for him.

It was hard to focus with his finger slowly trailing between my folds, rubbing me, warming me.

"You could never disappoint me, Little Leopard."

He slipped his finger inside of me, making me groan.

I arched my back even more.

Hunter moaned in response, and he wasted no time, starting to move his finger. It felt so damn good. I had never imagined it could be like this.

"Luna." He bit my earlobe, eliciting a yipe from me.

Without warning, Hunter shoved himself off me, spun me around, and grabbed my neck.

Pressing his mouth to my jaw as he walked me backward, he pulled the fabric of the dress up to my hips, and my back suddenly collided with the front of his Aston Martin.

He hoisted me up, positioning me on the hood, leaving him standing between my legs. It was such an intimate and intoxicating experience, having him pressing against my inner thighs as he claimed my mouth.

I surrendered my tongue to his, wanting it to never leave. It was soft and hard, all at the same time, while Hunter's growing excitement pressed against my thighs.

"I want to immortalize my name across your lips," he whispered over my mouth as he trailed his fingers up the inside of my thigh— every nerve ending coming alive with his soft touch. "I want to be the first man to make you come."

He pressed me down until I was lying flat across the hood.

"I don't want to scratch your car," I said.

"Fuck the car," he growled, tugging my panties down my legs, over my heels, and then placing them inside his breast pocket like a trophy.

Right before pressing my legs open for him.

Out of bashfulness, I tried to close them slightly, but he held my thighs down and locked eyes on to mine with an unyielding intensity —silently warning me to keep them spread wide.

I'd never been this exposed to someone before—my ex had never gone down on me, and this was so much more intimate than I expected. Hunter bit his lip as he looked over my sex and fell to his knees, slipping a finger up and down the folds with a gentle caress. Good Lord, this was better than my wildest dreams. And then he started kissing my inner thigh, starting near my knee and slowly working his way up.

Holy crap.

I knew what he was about to do, and I couldn't believe it. Hunter Lockwood, one of the most powerful men in the world, was on his knees for me, kissing my other calf, moving up my thigh, and steadily making his way to the sweet spot nestled between my legs.

I gasped when he licked near my center. Slowly. Up the side. His tongue was soft and teasing, so close to the spot I wanted it to be. But he tortured me again, licking the other side. Again so close, it was painful.

Just when I thought he was going to finally claim me, he kissed up my side yet again.

"Please, Hunter," I begged.

"Say it," he demanded. "Tell me what you want me to do."

He kissed my inner thigh again, making it clear he wasn't going to do anything until I commanded it.

"Take me. With your mouth."

Finally, he licked up my center, making me gasp in ecstasy.

"You're delicious," he groaned.

His tongue was magic, my center coming alive with need and want. Selfishness and hunger. All it wanted was his tongue, moving, working me. Nothing else in the world existed, except his tongue sweeping across my nub.

He started at my base again and came up slowly.

I leaned my head back, wondering what we looked like right now. Hunter Lockwood fully clothed in his tuxedo—handsome as hell—on his knees, as I lay on the hood of his car with my dress around my waist. Him holding my thighs spread wide—me completely exposed and raw—while he buried his face between my legs, moving up and down the top of my center, then side to side. Groaning with pleasure, I squirmed from the sensations.

He moved his lips to the top, circling the apex of my sex, pressing his face deeper into me, while I began to writhe under the euphoria of his tongue.

"Look at me, Little Leopard," he demanded.

I looked down at the hungry, determined eyes staring back at me. "I want to hear you scream my name," he reminded me, his voice deep and firm.

His mouth returned to me, swirling and sucking until a wave began to climb through my lower belly. Hunter's blue eyes met mine, and a desperate moan escaped me. His focus then shifted back to the feast served up before him.

He licked me harder, making my eyes roll back in my head.

"My name," he demanded. "Only mine."

Then he began swirling again.

I couldn't stop my hips from rocking, making him groan as I grew closer and closer. I couldn't believe this was about to happen, climaxing with him.

"Don't stop," I begged. The wave was growing and growing, a warmth radiating from the apex between my thighs, up my stomach, to my chest. "Please don't stop."

He knew the right pressure points, the right rhythm. The right everything as he circled my center over and over and I grew closer and closer.

And then...

The wave crashed over the shore, so hard, I arched my back and grabbed Hunter's hair.

"Hunter..."

He growled, pressing harder into me, drawing out its ripples that continued to roll on and on and on, each one making me jerk with pleasure with every lash of his expert tongue.

The waves started to slow, but he kept working every last ounce of ecstasy from it.

"Hunter..." I whispered, out of breath.

Spent on the hood.

Hunter stood and leaned over me. His mouth, covered in my essence, was only inches from my own as he stared down into my eyes.

I thought he was done, assumed he'd want to have sex with me now, but instead, he dipped his finger back inside of me, watching my mouth fall open, my head tilt back.

"I'm not finished with you, Luna. Not even close."

And then he got back onto his knees.

"Let's see how many times I can make you come."

With his finger pumping inside me, he met my center with his talented tongue once more.

CHAPTER 29
Hunter

This knot that had bound my soul since the age of nine was starting to unwind, and it scared the hell out of me. I wanted to take Luna as my own, fully and completely, right there on the hood of my car. I'd been the first man to make her come, and I couldn't get enough.

She'd screamed my name six times, her legs quivering from fatigue as she lay breathless, but I wanted to make her scream my name every night, have her pull my hair as she drowned me in her pleasure.

Which was when I knew something had shifted. Sex for me had always been just sex. But with Luna, it was different.

As I'd looked at her, lying with her dress hitched up, I knew that once I took her without reservation, there'd be no going back.

The problem: I had no idea if what happened tonight changed anything on Luna's part.

Did she want more than just a friendship? Would she be open to considering it? Because as much as I hated handing my heart over to someone who could easily destroy it, my heart was taking on a mind of its own. Reaching for her.

We'd need to talk about this. But not tonight. Not when I needed to keep her safe. If I scared her off, she might move out of that cottage, might wander off into danger, just to get away from the man who breached her boundaries.

I couldn't let that happen.

I needed to keep my feelings to myself.

And hope I could control this knot—its rope stretching for Luna, longing to tie her to me.

CHAPTER 30
Luna

I stood at the podium, scanning the rows of expectant faces—reporters with their cameras and notepads at the ready, eager to capture my words. The murmurs of anticipation from the audience filled my ears as the scent of the mayor's aftershave lingered near the microphone.

I was dressed in a maroon-and-black pantsuit, my hair pulled back into a tight ponytail, trying to keep my voice calm with an air of urgency.

The mayor stood to my right, his hands clasped after giving his spiel.

As I prepared to speak, I tried to focus on my next words instead of replaying that night on Hunter's car—a fantasy that had gained permanent prominence, playing in my head over these last three days. In particular, Hunter slowly gliding the flat of his tongue up my center, my thighs around his head as he looked at me.

We hadn't slept together, which had shocked me at the time. But looking back on it, it shouldn't have surprised me. The moment Hunter found out I'd never climaxed with a man, all he wanted to do was pleasure me.

Which he did. Repeatedly, until I could barely stand.

I wasn't sure what this meant for our relationship. Nothing had happened since, and I wondered if Hunter was feeling the same thing I was: that my walls were crumbling down, my heart unlocking from its cage.

"Ladies and gentlemen," I began, reading my prearranged speech, forcing the romantic thoughts from my mind, "as many of you are no doubt aware, our city has been plagued by a dangerous vigilante. This person, who remains at large, has been causing chaos and destruction throughout the city, killing people in cold blood."

I paused for a moment, letting my words sink in—the eyes of the reporters and cameras fixed on me.

"I know that you may feel a sense of security and protection from this individual, believing that he is keeping your communities safe because he targets people who have allegedly committed crimes. However, as a society, we must abide by the law and not take justice into our own hands."

I'd be lying if I said my feelings toward the Vigilante hadn't been confusing, but the law was black and white and someone's personal feelings shouldn't come into play with it. The Vigilante had no legal authority to carry out his brand of justice; therefore, I needed to push my own bias aside in favor of the law.

"The Windy City Vigilante may have started out with good intentions, but who is to say that he won't cross a line and become a danger to you all? What happens when his moral compass becomes more twisted and he starts to come after lower-level criminals? Or people innocent of any crimes?

"I'm calling on the citizens of this city to be on alert. To watch for any suspicious activity and report it immediately to the authorities. We must hold those who break the law accountable, and we cannot allow this Vigilante to continue to act outside the bounds of our justice system.

"It's time the Windy City Vigilante is caught and put behind bars."

Out there somewhere, the Vigilante might be watching me declare war.

CHAPTER 31
Luna

"So, you found nothing?" I asked Detective Rinaldi after wrapping up the press conference.

We stood in the corner of the room as folks began to disband. She'd been one of the people up there with us, and I couldn't let her leave without pressing her again about the Franco situation.

"Dominic's apartment is clean," she said.

"He must have given the USB drive to someone," I said.

We continued discussing Franco for a few minutes, but when nothing meaningful came of it, my shoulders dropped in defeat.

"We aren't giving up," she assured. But it was hard to hold on to hope because of how much she had on her plate. Finding the evidence Dominic supposedly gave me, locating Franco Hopkins. Not to mention...

"How is the hunt for the Vigilante going?" I asked.

She clenched her jaw, and a hint of irritation crossed her face. "Not as fast as we'd hoped."

"Do you think the press conference will help?"

"Too early to say. The first press conference drummed up a lot of leads but nothing with legs yet."

"That sounds incredibly frustrating."

"He's good at hiding, but we'll find him," she declared, her voice unwavering.

"What kind of person could be behind this?" I mused aloud.

To this, Rinaldi let out a deep breath. "There are several theories going around, but it's difficult because the Vigilante's victims don't seem to have commonalities. They differ in age, ethnicity, occupation, and income level. There doesn't seem to be any correlation or connection between them."

"Except they have all allegedly committed crimes." I bit my lip.

The detective nodded, her face drawn in a grim expression. "Some victims were accused and acquitted. Some were never even suspected in the crimes the Vigilante *claims* the victim committed."

"Has anyone looked into those alleged crimes?"

"We have a team set up that's looking deeper at them now," she said, her eyes darting around the room. "When this all first started, the department prioritized resources to finding the Vigilante, not investigating accusations he made against his victims. But now, we're starting to dive deeper into those allegations to look for any clues that might lead us to his identity."

I wondered what it would dig up. Had *all* his victims been accused of murder? Or other crimes, too? And how would he know about them? Was he privy to jailhouse snitches? A cop himself with access to arrest records? Or someone with an obsession with unsolved cases?

Unsolved cases...

Where the assailant was never brought to justice.

My gut swirled, something tightening in my chest.

It was a crazy thought, a fleeting one. Yes, Sean's income was based on unsolved cases, and, yes, he'd become a savvy detective in his own right, getting access to information most others didn't. It was what set his podcast apart and made it so successful. He had a knack for getting people to talk to him in a way they'd never talk to the police. Perhaps providing him with information about suspects that had never come out to the public.

No. Just because the Vigilante was the same height and weight as Sean, it didn't prove anything. I had been friends with Sean for years.

And, yes, he worked odd hours, but he wasn't a violent person. In fact, I didn't know any violent people.

"What's your gut telling you?" I asked. "What type of person do you think is doing this?"

To that, she pinched the bridge of her nose. "Unfortunately, there isn't a typical profile for a vigilante we can leverage because the motivations and backgrounds of these individuals vary widely. However, we have some possible common traits that could be in play."

"Such as?" I pressed.

"The most obvious, of course, is this particular vigilante's perceived injustice, for which he wants to exact his own brand of retribution. Other vigilantes have expressed a severe need for control, attempting to take charge of their environment and situations through vigilantism as their way of asserting that control."

"Kind of like rapists?" Many people think rape is only about sex, but often, it was about control. Domination.

Rinaldi nodded. "Some have a lack of faith in the justice system. They believe the legal system is corrupt, or biased, or inept in providing adequate justice and, therefore, must take matters into their own hands."

I thought back to the reason Sean was drawn to true crime in the first place. Back in high school, his girlfriend had gone missing, but despite an all-out search, the police weren't able to save her in time. It was what propelled his involvement with true crime, and tragically, it also left a festering wound beneath the surface.

He definitely thought the police had dropped the ball, and he had a disdain for our slow and imperfect justice system—because once her killer was finally caught, it turned out the guy should never have been out on the streets to begin with. He was out on bail for attacking another woman at the time.

A point of contention earlier in our friendship. It took him some time to see my intention in being a criminal defense attorney was not to get criminals off; it was to protect innocent people accused of crimes they didn't commit and ensure proper processes were followed for those that didn't.

But if Sean was the Vigilante, why would his attacks have started suddenly two years ago? What would have been the driving motive then? Or now, for that matter?

I mean, yes, in his career as a podcaster, he'd seen plenty of criminals walk free due to a lack of evidence or some other judicial problem, but if I were making that argument, so had Hunter Lockwood.

His family had been the victim of a killing that had gone unsolved.

But Hunter didn't see the legal system as corrupt or inadequate—he'd dedicated his life to it. And while, in his eyes, some criminals got off, he worked every day to put others away. He played a huge part in the justice system, in holding people accountable for their crimes.

Further, Hunter was three inches shorter than the Vigilante and twenty pounds lighter. And to my knowledge, he had never displayed any violent tendencies.

Plus, Hunter would have nothing to gain by murdering people in the city. Along with his role as a prosecutor, Hunter Lockwood had the power and the influence to leverage his connections to bring criminals to justice. If he had any information relating to a crime where the perpetrator got away scot-free, he could work with law enforcement to bring about charges. He didn't need to don a mask and prowl the streets of Chicago, slitting throats.

Nor would he risk everything to do it.

Neither would Sean.

Plus, the Vigilante had said it was nice to officially meet me. I had met Hunter Lockwood by that point, and Sean had been in my life for years. The only person fitting the Vigilante's profile—who I had not officially met at that point—was my dad's old cellmate and friend, Rodney Murphy.

He had a perceived injustice with the legal system, and he'd gotten out of prison right around the time the Windy City Vigilante took to the streets and made his infamous actions known.

"And, of course," Rinaldi continued, "one of the most common traits we see in vigilantes is a tendency toward violence. They typically have a history of violent behavior, and vigilantism provides an outlet for that aggression."

"You think it's someone with a record then?"

She shrugged. "Depends on whether they ever got caught before. My guess is this guy has been escalating for years. You don't lose your virginity to murder. You start out smaller. Maybe beatings or something like that. Chances are, this guy has been a violent person his entire life, and now, that violence has escalated."

While I didn't know Rodney's full criminal history, I recalled my dad once telling me that Rodney got into a brutal fight with another inmate.

It would seem *all* these boxes were checking.

"There is one terrible rumor circulating that needs to be squashed." Her voice was soft and hesitant.

"What's that?"

When she spoke, her words came out in a stuttered, stilted flow, and her eyes darted around the room as if worried someone might overhear.

"Whoever started the rumor is probably just someone working for the mayor's opponent," she reasoned. "The very idea that a mayor would orchestrate these vigilante attacks just so that he could come swooping in and rescue the city from a dangerous criminal on the loose is absolutely ludicrous."

"The hell?"

"Like I said, ludicrous."

It was absolutely ludicrous, not even worth talking about further. When she let out a barely audible sigh of exasperation as she shifted her weight, I could tell she didn't give any weight to the preposterous accusation, but rather, she was annoyed, protective of the mayor, who was actively working to take this Vigilante down.

My mind circled back to the more tangible information we had been talking about.

"But to your knowledge, he's only targeted people accused of heinous crimes," I said.

"To our knowledge, yes, but…there's no telling what he may do if he gets backed into a corner."

CHAPTER 32
Luna

When one was protected by a bodyguard, how would someone get her alone?

Answer: they'd create a diversion.

In this case, a man who tried to steal my purse, only to be taken down by my bodyguard, who shouted at me to get back inside my office building and lock the goddamned door.

I should have considered how strange it was—that a person would be stupid enough to target a woman who wasn't alone—because as soon as I ran past the small space between my office building and the structure next door, a hand shot out and grabbed my wrist.

Another smothered my scream as a figure pulled me into a dark alley.

The smell of leather mixed with the musty scent of the concrete passage while the sound of dripping water echoed with the distant sounds of car engines on a nearby road. Mingling with my ragged breaths through my nose.

"Don't scream." The deep voice sounded like sandpaper scraping over gravel. "I'm not going to hurt you, Ms. Payne. I have something to tell you, and then you can be on your way."

I jerked away from his touch. Taking several steps back and

clenching my fists, I glared at his red-and-black mask. Realization consuming me with anger.

"It was you," I accused. "You had that guy try to mug me."

"That man mugs lots of people," the Vigilante said, stepping between me and the alley's entrance. In case I got any bright ideas to try to run, I guess. "I might have given him a tip that you had a large stack of cash in your purse. The rest is on him."

"He could have killed me!" I snapped.

"I always vet my prospects, Ms. Payne."

"What does that mean?"

"The man is a thief, but he's not violent. I would never put you in danger, Ms. Payne."

"Says the guy who yanked me into an alley. What do you want?"

He taunted me by taking a step closer, a smug smirk pulling at his lips, the only part of his face not covered.

I didn't appreciate him scaring me like this, making my heart spasm with vulnerability. I mean, what the hell? No woman liked to be dragged into a dark alley at night, and it pissed me off he'd had the audacity to do this.

"I saw your press conference yesterday," he said, as if expecting a reaction from me.

"Interesting. I didn't realize sewers had television screens."

His smirk faded, and he stepped forward again, his steps certain and slow.

I bet he wanted me to back up, wanted me to show my fear, but I swallowed it down. Because screw him.

"You keep forgetting that I saved your life, Ms. Payne."

"While I appreciate you saving me, you keep forgetting that you ended two dozen others. You're a serial killer."

"Is that really how you see me?"

Yes. No. I don't know.

Ugh! I told myself I would *not* acknowledge this confusion anymore. This guy wasn't just a ruthless killer; he was a manipulator, toying with my emotions to try to lure me to his dark side of thinking. This was proof of that, and I hated him for it.

Angling my chin up slightly, I challenged him with, "You still haven't told me what it is you want."

"I can't have what I want, Ms. Payne."

"Do you enjoy speaking in riddles?"

His lips tugged up devilishly. "Do you enjoy solving them?"

If he thought I'd stand here and wait around for him to get to his point—or accomplish his next act of violence—he had another thing coming.

I dug around in my purse—the one the mugging guy failed to steal—hunting for the small aerosol container that contained poisonous gas for his eyeballs. I could only hope my mace would penetrate that mesh screen that covered his arrogant eyes.

I whipped out my trusty mace, holding it with both hands as far away from me as possible, my finger close to the trigger.

"Back off!" I shouted.

He grinned before retorting, "You really think mace can stop me?"

"Even devils have eyeballs."

It might not stop him, but it should slow him down while I ran, and I needed every advantage I could get if I had any hope of escaping.

Escaping was the smart thing to do. Not hesitate with curiosity, wondering why he'd dragged me here. For all I knew, he'd had a change of heart and wasn't here just to talk.

He might have given me a pass for that first press conference, which had been a knee-jerk reaction to the murder that took place at the courthouse, but the second press conference was a declaration of war.

He took another step closer—now only six feet away.

I shook my hand, one last warning, as if he couldn't see the mace threatening his eyesight.

But the arrogant bastard disregarded it and advanced even closer.

My fingers fumbled to press down on the trigger, and a stream of white mist shot forward toward his face.

But in a flash, the canister was yanked from my grip, and thick-gloved hands pressed my shoulders against the wall.

"Word of advice, Ms. Payne. Never pull a weapon on someone far more seasoned than you are at using them. You'll only get yourself hurt."

I thrust my knee up toward his crotch, hoping I could kick high enough to compensate for his height difference, but he twisted away with ease, pressing his hip bone into my stomach, pinning me.

With only hands to defend myself, I shoved him as hard as I could, but I might as well have shoved a concrete barrier. My flailing hand grasped for something to hit, aiming for his face, but he caught my wrist mid-swing and clamped it firmly against the cold wall. He seized my other hand next, imprisoning it with the same dominating ease.

His hands were like unyielding iron bands, the strength in them highlighting his raw, masculine power. His broad shoulders dwarfed my smaller frame, amplifying the frantic rhythm of my heart as I realized he had me completely at his mercy.

"Let me go, or I'll scream."

He lifted his lips to one side. "The fact you haven't already proves you're curious enough to want to hear what I came to say," he murmured, his words woven with an intoxicating blend of dominance and allure.

"Let me go," I repeated.

His tongue slid leisurely across his lower lip. It caught the faint light in the alley, transforming it into a glistening ruby—the sight of which sent a strange wave of heat through me.

The moment stretched, tension building in the air around us, until he finally loosened his grip. His retreat was graceful, the calculated movement of a predator backing away, but not entirely relenting.

"What do you want?" I asked.

His reply was a low, husky whisper that seemed to wrap around me like an embrace. "I'd like you to stop publicly telling the city to come after me."

"Talk to Mayor Kepler—it's his initiative."

"The city's listening to you, Ms. Payne. He knows it, and you know it."

So, the press conferences had him worried.

Interesting.

"I'm afraid I can't do that, so you'll either have to let me leave this alley or hurt an innocent person—allegedly for the first time."

In a calm yet threatening tone, he replied, "I don't hurt innocent people, Ms. Payne."

"He says as he's holding an innocent woman against her will."

He smirked.

"You're scared," I accused, jutting my chin out. "This is the first time you've thought that there might actually be repercussions for your actions, isn't it?"

He clenched his teeth.

"Having half of the city ready to catch my every misstep will prove to be a nuisance in my day-to-day business."

"You poor thing. Maybe there's a vigilante support group out there somewhere."

"Quite the mouth on you." He flashed a mischievous smirk.

"This is really about your ego, isn't it? It must suck, having the city turn on you."

His mouth tightened. "Not all of them, Ms. Payne."

I cocked an eyebrow.

"Me? I was never on your side," I lied matter-of-factly. "And I never will be."

"I only kill bad men. Men who have hurt others, who have committed heinous crimes."

I scoffed. "Taking the law into your own hands is unforgivable. We have a justice system for a reason."

Screaming was too risky—it might provoke the Vigilante to attack me, but maybe I could keep him talking until my bodyguard came looking for me.

Which should be anytime now.

The Vigilante leaned forward. "And what about when that justice system fails? When criminals slip through its cracks, when they walk free because of loopholes or technicalities? What then? Do we just sit back and wait for them to hurt again? Do we let them continue to terrorize innocent people?"

The Vigilante reached into his pocket, pulled out a photo and held it in front of my face.

Based on its resolution, it looked to be a still shot of a video. A photo of Dominic killing the man he'd been found not guilty of murdering.

My stomach rolled. I studied the picture for a moment, trying to convince myself it was doctored. Photoshopped. Made up. But it appeared to confirm what my sixth sense had been telling me ever since that fateful day in the prison parking lot—that maybe I hadn't known Dominic at all.

The Vigilante allowed me to stare at the picture in disbelief for several seconds before putting it back in his pocket and pulling out another.

"This man," he said, "was responsible for the murder of a nineteen-year-old college girl who was majoring in nursing. He was acquitted on a technicality, and the victim's family was left without justice. Do you honestly believe that he deserved to walk free?"

I studied the photo of a man walking through an intersection—a shot with a telephoto lens, by the looks of it.

"No," I admitted quietly. "He didn't."

The Vigilante nodded and shoved the photo back into his pocket.

"That's all I'm asking you to understand," he said. "And," he added, "to call off the dogs."

But no matter how convincing his argument was, I could not get behind his methods. And it offended me that he thought holding me against my will like this, shoving the crime scene photos in my face, would fundamentally change my point of view.

"I agree men like that don't deserve to walk free," I said. "But murder is still murder, regardless of how you justify it."

The Vigilante's mouth tightened.

"Do you think I should have let Anthony live? So he could have killed you?"

Guilt etched at my insides. How disturbing to feel grateful he'd killed someone.

I didn't want to tell him that this entire encounter had again rattled me—a defender of those accused of crimes, finding myself relating to this masked madman who took the law into his own hands. I didn't want to tell him that it appeared we had something in common—a burning desire to see justice served. Or how being confused about my feelings fueled some of my animosity toward him. Because our methods were very different, and despite his righteous intentions, no one was above the law.

"You should turn yourself in."

"I won't be doing that, Ms. Payne."

"And I won't stop helping them hunt you down." My tone was resolute and unwavering.

He seemed to consider this, and I worried that maybe he *would* choose to hurt an innocent person. If he did, the woman declaring war against him would be at the top of that list.

I hid the erratic destabilization of my heartbeat, surprised when his lips curled into a smile.

"You like hunting me, don't you, Ms. Payne?"

I glared at him and spat out each word with contempt. "Your ego is the one that needs to be cut down."

Another smirk from him.

When I turned slightly, the Vigilante's body went rigid, and his head cocked. I followed what I presumed to be his line of sight and noticed that the light's reflection was making my white scar shine. The one on my inner elbow from all those years ago. It was faint, usually unnoticeable unless certain types of light hit it at just the right angle.

The Vigilante stalked forward and made me gasp when he wrapped his gloved hand around my elbow and raised it up for a closer inspection.

"What is this from?" he demanded.

I tried to pull my arm back, but his head tilted back up, like he was looking at me in the eyes now.

"It looks like a cut from a blade." His voice pulsed with anger. "Who did this to you?"

"Why do you care?"

"Answer my question. Now."

I yanked my arm back. "It's not from a blade."

"Then what's it from?"

"I cut it inside a dumpster, okay?" Why was I even answering his question? Curiosity maybe? And why the hell did he seem so…pissed about it? Was he worried there was some copycat Vigilante hurting women? It was an old scar—anyone could see that.

"Inside a dumpster," he said. "Elaborate."

I blinked. "Why?"

"Just answer me."

I swallowed, beyond confused.

"It's from my senior year of high school. The quarterback joined the other kids in bullying me and decided to up the ante. Threw me into the dumpster behind the school, and I got cut on a glass bottle inside."

"He hurt you?" he growled.

"It was a long time ago."

"What's his name?"

"Why?"

"Because I'm going to beat him mercilessly until he begs for his life."

What in the actual hell?

"He doesn't fit your code; he isn't a killer."

"Never said I'd end his life."

My heart accelerated with a fresh wave of confusion. Rescuing me from being murdered was one thing. Enacting revenge against some douche from my high school days was another.

"I'm not going to give you his name."

He pulled his lip between his teeth. "Luna Payne. Senior year. Won't be difficult to find the name of your school, and each football team has only one quarterback."

"What the hell are you talking about?" I asked with a shaky breath.

"Luna?" My bodyguard's voice sounded through the night.

I stared at the Vigilante, whose words sent ripples of confusion through me. Was he truly longing to avenge my honor? The very notion of it made no sense, but beneath my disorienting emotions, a steady beat of caution throbbed in my mind. Reminding me that I was cornered in an alley with a confessed serial killer.

Be smart, Luna. Don't fall for his...manipulation, or whatever this might be.

"I'm over here!" I shouted. "In the alley!"

The corners of the Vigilante's mouth rose higher. "You know I rather enjoy this cat-and-mouse game we have going on here."

Anger shot to the front of my emotional line. "That makes one of us."

"Well"—he took a step back—"I do hope you'll consider what we discussed about justice, Ms. Payne."

"Luna?" My bodyguard's voice appeared at the entrance to the alley. I made the mistake of looking over at him, and in that moment, the Vigilante ran to the other end of the passageway. Vanishing in the shadows before I'd had the chance to stop him.

"Who the hell was that?" my bodyguard asked, his hand on his gun, watching the Vigilante disappear.

"A guy that could've ended me after his diversion," I said, fear sharp in my tone.

"Diversion?"

"Where's the mugger?" I asked.

My bodyguard tightened his jaw, his voice tight as he said, "Detained. Police are on the way, but we can't wait for them. We need to leave. Now."

"Why?"

He took a beat, and his tone dropped. "There's been a break-in."

CHAPTER 33
Luna

"How did he get past the security system?" Hunter demanded. Still wearing his custom-tailored suit with a bright red tie from his day at work, he paced my trashed living room while Sean leaned against my dining room wall, watching security guards, Detective Rinaldi, and other police officers sift for clues.

My once-cozy cottage now looked like a battlefield. The drawers and cupboards in the kitchen were open, dishes and silverware scattered across the countertops like casualties of war. I had already been in my bedroom, where my pearl-white nightstand, which always held books for easy reading when I turned out the lights, had been ransacked. Its wooden drawers hung open, and the ones in my bathroom lay strewn across the floor, their contents thrown across the porcelain tile.

Hunter shoved a hand through his hair as he glared at his lead security officer, who stood with his arms crossed over his chest. It was the G.I. Joe look-alike with buzzed hair, a square jaw, and bicep muscles that could probably bust a human skull just by clenching. I'd learned his name was Adam, but based on his appearance, I would have expected it to be more like The Crusher or something.

"He broke a window," Adam said.

"I don't mean to sound ungrateful." I was trying not to take my anger out on the wrong people, but Hunter had filled me in on the alarm tied to the security cameras. "But I thought the security system had some sort of a trigger to it, so that if anybody broke in, it would signal an alarm, and police would rush to my cottage."

"It does. And we arrived on site within fifty-three seconds of the alert, but the perpetrator was already gone. We set up a perimeter to search for him, and we immediately mobilized local authorities."

The cottage was no more than a thousand square feet, so it wouldn't take more than fifty seconds to do this level of trashing here. And *trashing* wasn't the right word. It was clear they were looking for something, going through as many drawers and cabinets as they could before running out of time.

"Well, it's a really good thing she wasn't home when it happened. It'd have taken a few *seconds* to kill her!" Hunter shouted.

"Hunter..." I couldn't blame him for being angry. I was, too, on so many levels, but Adam was on our side here.

"It's fifty-three seconds too late," Adam agreed. "Unfortunately, no security team, unless they are positioned *inside* the premises, can respond here in less than fifty seconds. Which is why we've always recommended that Ms. Payne not stay here alone."

I didn't bother arguing that I wasn't alone, that Sean had been staying with me. Thank God he'd been on a jog, or something might have happened to him—all because he'd stayed here to try to keep me safe.

"Even a security system has its limitations."

Hunter exchanged a brief glance with me, and I remembered the desperation in his voice that day in his kitchen when he begged me to stay at his house. I couldn't let myself feel guilty about that now, though.

"You should've seen them coming!" Hunter demanded. "Do you know how much money I pay you guys? With one objective—to keep her safe."

The security guard's jaw looked so tight, I wondered if he was cracking his teeth in irritation.

"We have cameras positioned on every road leading up to these buildings," Hunter continued.

"The perpetrator didn't come in from a road, sir. He must've come in through the woods."

"So, he's a professional."

"That's my guess, yes."

Rinaldi studied the broken dining room window.

"This was Franco," I said to Detective Rinaldi. "Wasn't it?"

Her eyes softened, brimming with empathy. "We've turned Dominic's apartment upside down, looking for that USB drive. Twice. It's possible he gave it to somebody else for safekeeping. Or that it never existed in the first place. It's possible Dominic was claiming he had evidence over Franco when he really didn't. He might've just been saying that to try to keep himself alive."

"And where are we at with finding Franco?" I didn't mean for my voice to sound so tense, and I doubted the detective appreciated the glare coming from Hunter.

"We'll get him," Rinaldi said.

"He's escalating and getting more desperate," Sean said. "First, he sent a thug in that prison parking lot. Now, he took a big risk to break into her home, and he still doesn't have what he needs. Desperate people do desperate things, so there's no telling what he'll do next..."

CHAPTER 34

Luna

"Would you slow down?" I was basically being dragged up the slight hill, for crying out loud.

The sprawling lawn extended as far as my eye could see, peppered with trees that stretched up toward the sky, filtering the moonlight that joined the landscape fixtures to lightly illuminate the space. Hunter's front lawn was pristine, perfectly manicured and in control, unlike the frazzled state he was in.

"Let her go!" Sean demanded.

But Hunter entwined his fingers with mine and continued pulling me toward his mansion.

I could have fought him the whole way, but I had to be realistic. After the detective left, he'd taken me by surprise when he grabbed my hand and pulled me out the front door. His strength was impossible to match, and yanking my hand away would only make things worse.

The better scenario was to let him calm down first.

Plus, deep down, a strange thrill ignited at his fierce determination to protect me. His decisive grasp warmed my chest and spread heat to my lower belly that I didn't want to fight against.

Sean didn't find anything sexy about this, though.

After countless demands that Hunter release my hand, Sean broke into a sprint, headed directly for Hunter, ready to shove him, but Hunter's guard, Adam, intercepted and slammed Sean to the ground.

So hard, Sean moaned.

"Oh my God! You're hurting him. Let him go!" I snapped.

Adam's stare bored into me, then Hunter, his brow furrowing as he evidently waited for his boss's approval. He eventually tore away from Sean and shuffled back a step, his fists clenched at his sides.

I offered my hand to help Sean stand up.

"Come on, Luna. You can stay at my place," Sean said, averting his gaze from Hunter's icy stare.

"Over my dead body," Hunter bellowed, the cords of his neck taut. "You were staying with her at the cottage, but you still let that," Hunter said, pointing at the dwelling, "happen."

"I *let* it happen? Screw you, man."

"Where were you?" Hunter demanded.

"Hunter..." I cautioned.

"Jogging, not that it's any of your business."

Hunter stepped forward. "You should have been here. Making sure she was safe."

"So, this is my fault now?"

"It's no one's fault," I said, stepping between them.

"And where were you?" Sean demanded.

"Prosecuting lowlifes."

"This is *your* property. *Your* security system and team," Sean said. "You want someone to blame here, look at yourself in the mirror."

"Franco's the one to blame," I said. "And arguing with each other isn't solving anything."

"You're staying with me," Sean said.

"Not a chance," Hunter spat through gritted teeth.

"She's not your possession." Sean pointed his finger toward Hunter.

"You think I would put her life in your incompetent hands?"

"Hunter..."

"The hell did you just say to me?" Sean stepped forward but was brought to an abrupt halt by the bodyguard's strong hand on his chest.

"You really think you can take me down?" Hunter asked.

Sean was taller and bigger, so the odds had to be stacked in his favor.

"You're too much of a chicken to let me try. You hide behind your bodyguards, so you never get your hands dirty."

This time, Hunter was the one to launch, but thankfully, Adam stopped him and pushed him back.

"Enough!" I faced my longtime friend.

"Sean," I said, "you live an hour outside the city, two hours during rush hour. And between the two of us, we have zero vehicles, so that won't work." I'd decided not to repair the Kia. In speaking with the repair shop, the thing was dying a slow death. Searching for a new car was on my never-ending to-do list. Point was, right now we didn't have a vehicle between us.

"I think it would be best…if you left for the night," I added.

Sean looked at me with a menacing glare that made my hairs stand on end. His expression was intense and intimidating, but I could also sense something else deep in his gaze—a hint of rejection.

I hated that I felt like I was choosing sides, because if that were the case, Sean had been my friend for years. He was the person who had been loyal to me, and if I could reasonably stay with him for a while, I would in a heartbeat.

But logistically, his place would not work. And truthfully, I didn't feel safe, going to a hotel. Not with Franco out there.

Plus, it was just for the night. Tomorrow, I could reevaluate where I'd stay—and for how long—after the shock of this all wore off and I had a good night's sleep.

I felt like I was letting Sean down somehow, but in fairness, I couldn't afford to worry about my safety when I needed to stay focused on my dad's case, so after a moment, I walked up to Sean and gave him a quick hug.

"I'm so sorry about all of this." I held him against me, ignoring the stares of the bodyguard and Hunter. "I'll call you tomorrow, okay?"

I pulled back and looked at Sean. His shoulders slumped, his gaze distant and hollow—every ounce of vibrancy seemingly drained. I was grateful he chose not to argue further about this, grateful he agreed to go to his place for the night and cool off, regrouping tomorrow when we could figure out our next steps.

"Please be careful," Sean said to me, eyeing Hunter. "Money can't solve everything, Luna, and you're in some serious danger."

Sean's eyes locked with mine for several more seconds before he trudged off toward the cottage.

"Wait," I said. "How will you get home?" Could I convince Hunter's driver to take him?

"I'll call a ride." When Sean answered without looking back at me, my stomach twisted, and I clenched my fists.

I waited until he was out of earshot before I crossed my arms and drilled Hunter.

"You can't be angry at Sean. It's not his fault," I snarled.

Hunter took an angry step forward, and my heart raced, but I forced myself to hold his gaze.

"I'm angry because some asshole had the nerve to come onto my property and threaten the only thing I care about."

The only thing I care about.

The words echoed in my head like a lullaby, and his eyes bored into mine, dark and unwavering, as if each syllable had been carved from his very soul. Before I had the time to process his declaration, he grabbed my hand and tugged me further along our path.

"Come on."

My heart throbbed with a chaotic storm of emotion as Hunter pulled me toward his estate. There was a rush of passion from his unwavering defense of me; shame for hurting Sean's feelings; fear, though I hated to admit it, as I was forced to accept that a madman had escalated into breaking into the very place I called home; and fury over the unfairness of it all.

"Call your men," Hunter barked to his bodyguard. "I want this place surrounded. You got it?"

Adam nodded and pulled his cell out of his pocket as Hunter hauled me into his kitchen.

"Maria, you can take the night off," Hunter said.

Her worried gaze darted between Hunter and me before she took off her apron and scurried out the door.

"You're staying here until further notice," Hunter declared.

Okay, protectiveness—sexy. Bossiness to the level of telling me *until further notice*—not so much. If he kept this up, he'd get a taste of what women of the twenty-first century were capable of when provoked. Namely, the female species didn't hold back from thrusting her knee into the male's crotch.

Especially since he was now pulling me through the kitchen by my hand.

"Hunter, stop."

Through the great room.

"You need to calm down," I said.

Up the staircase, down a long corridor of white paneled doors, and into what I presumed was a guest bedroom.

A chandelier cast a gentle, soft glow over a plush bed in the center —which was layered with white linens and matching pillows in various hues of gray and ivory. The walls were painted in a shade of blush, and the room was decorated with antique furniture that added a touch of elegance to the space.

Floor-to-ceiling windows overlooked the mansion's lush garden. Outside, leaves rustled in the moonlight—a tranquil and peaceful setting that should have relaxed me.

But the look in Hunter's eyes was wilder than I'd ever seen.

"I'm hiring you an army of bodyguards. And you're staying here," he commanded, clenching his fists so tight at his sides, that his knuckles whitened.

Part of my heart bloomed, realizing he'd escorted me to a guest room rather than his bedroom, perhaps in an effort to respect my boundaries.

"You need to calm down."

"After what just happened, you think I'll calm down? You could have been home when he broke in." His voice filled the room like thunderous clouds as each word carried immense rage. He stepped toward me, closing the already-tight space between us, his eyes burning with anger and desire.

"But I wasn't," I managed.

"You could've been killed," he muttered through clenched teeth.

"They broke in during business hours when they knew I'd be at work." I wasn't trying to defend the guy—I just wanted Hunter to settle down.

He clutched my chin, and despite the gentleness of his touch, it caused me to gasp. His anger transformed into something else— something more passionate—as he moved so close, that our noses almost touched. His chest heaving with a blend of vengeance and lust.

"Hunter..."

"Let me make this abundantly clear." His hot breath danced across my lips. "You will *allow* me to protect you."

His eyes were blazing with an unexpected, intense desire, sending a flood of warmth through my body.

Because I sensed that behind his anger, desperation and fear pulsed through every cell of his body. He had already lost two people he cared deeply for and had been powerless to stop it. And now, he was not about to sit back and allow anything to happen to someone else. Not on his watch.

His fierce protection made my skin tingle and ignited a fire in my lower belly.

Ever since that night on the hood of his car, I hadn't been able to stop thinking about our encounter—the way his hands explored my body, the heat of his breath on my skin, the smell of his cologne, his mouth pleasuring me. But mostly, how the rest of the world simply faded away, how nothing else mattered, except the two of us in that moment.

Even after he left my side, his presence lingered on my skin like a ghost that I didn't want to shake off. It all had a captivating effect on me, leaving me thirsty for more.

I wanted to be completely consumed by him. I fantasized about feeling his weight on top of me as he filled me with his passion.

And now I felt like he could read my soul, see the desire that brewed inside of me, begging to be claimed by him in a way that no one else ever could match.

He let go of my chin and took a step back, yanking at the knot of his tie.

With a fierce determination in his eyes, he loosened it, his gaze never leaving mine. And then, with one swift motion, he yanked it off and hurled it to the ground—leaving me breathless and yearning for more.

The fire in my belly became an inferno as I watched him slide off his tailored jacket, revealing the tight fit of his linen shirt clinging to his muscular frame. He began to unbutton it angrily as he stared at me with a raw sexual tension that flirted with fury.

"You will allow me to keep you safe," Hunter growled.

My life had been full of disappointment and heartbreak for as long as I could recall. I felt like I was walking in the dark with no one to guide me or be my anchor amid a never-ending storm. Then, suddenly, Hunter appeared out of nowhere, standing up to all the dangers that threatened me, without any expectations or demand for recognition. In the midst of despair, it was as though a light had been switched on in the darkness of my life, illuminating a path forward, bringing hope and possibility back into view. Every fiber of my being was drawn to him, and I couldn't stop this growing sense of gratitude, admiration, and something else...

Trust.

I was beginning to trust Hunter Lockwood.

He tossed his shirt to the ground, unzipped his pants, and threw them to the side.

And then, wearing nothing but a pair of dark gray boxer briefs that strained against his desire, Hunter stalked forward...

CHAPTER 35

Luna

My heart pounded in my chest, my breath coming in short, ragged pants.

Hunter grabbed my lower back, pulled me toward him, and crashed his lips to mine with a passion that was both violent and tender.

Everything else in the world faded to black, and all that mattered was the taste of his lips and the pressure of his body against mine.

Hunter grabbed my shirt and ripped it open, the buttons bouncing along the ground with little dings.

I gasped. I'd never had someone rip my clothing before. The tiny part of my brain that worried about how much this shirt had cost me was silenced by the desire that engulfed me from his eagerness to get me naked.

Hunter broke the kiss so he could tear the fabric away from my body while I stood paralyzed by a mixture of yearning and shock—thrilled and eager to find out what he planned to do next.

My skin was on alert, begging to be touched by him.

He kept me locked in his sapphire gaze as he reached behind me and unlatched my bra, my breasts falling free. Hunter's eyes dilated at the sight before him, and he reached out and grabbed both of my breasts. Squeezing them with a pleasuring bite of pain.

My nipples hardened at the contact, and my mouth watered as Hunter devoured my body with his gaze, scanning down my stomach, my thighs. A playground waiting for him to take his anger out onto.

With my chest bare and exposed, he unzipped my skirt and let it fall to the floor. Next, he grabbed my panties and ripped them off, too, with a merciless intensity that made me shudder in the best possible way.

The raw sexual energy between us was palpable as he pressed himself against me, his breath hot against my lips, lingering above my own. It was as if we were two wild animals caught up in a frenzy of desire, unable to control the primal urge that was driving us both to the brink of ecstasy.

Keeping his eyes locked on mine, he pressed the palm of his hand against my stomach, sliding it lower and lower until his fingers dipped between my folds.

I opened my mouth in pleasure, the bundle of nerves alive beneath his warm touch.

"You'll scream my name, Little Leopard." His finger breached my entrance to the knuckle. I spread my legs slightly wider, silently begging for him to go deeper, because this was torture—so close to what I wanted that it was almost painful. "Louder than you did on the hood of my car."

It was an order, one I'd gladly obey.

Hunter thrust his finger all the way inside of me, making me topple forward slightly from the intense ecstasy. He caught me with his other hand and righted me, then palmed my breast as he pulled his finger out slightly and—never breaking angry eye contact with me— thrust it deeper inside of me again.

"You will do as I say." He curved his finger to hit the magic spot of pixie dust inside my body, making my head tip back, mouth gaping. "You've had to do everything on your own for far too long." He curved his finger even more as he pumped his finger in and out and then

moved his thumb on the external bundle of nerves. "You will relin-
quish that control and allow me to keep you safe."

He added a second finger to his rhythm, groaning as he looked
down at me.

"You're so tight," he said.

My thighs began to quiver around his hand, a wave starting to
build.

"Not yet," Hunter demanded as he removed his fingers and pulled
his boxer briefs down, revealing his massive size. I stared at it, my
heart fluttering with nerves that it might not fit. "You'll scream my
name when I'm deep inside of you, Little Leopard."

I wanted that more than breathing right now. If an orgasm felt that
good with his tongue on me, I couldn't even imagine what it would
feel like wrapped around him.

This. This was the making of fantasies...

His angry lips wrestled with mine again, and when he clutched my
breast, a lightning bolt jolted deep inside of me in this storm of pleasure. His kiss grew deeper and more passionate as I greedily devoured
it all, hungering for everything that I knew would happen next.

Hunter grabbed my hips and spun me around, pressing my back
until my chest pressed onto the bed.

I could imagine how this looked—me standing, bent at the waist
with his hand against my shoulder blades, my right cheek pressing
into the comforter, while I was completely exposed. I twisted my head
slightly, my thighs heating even more at the sight of him standing
behind me—his eyes burning, his tongue tracing his lower lip as he
lined himself up at my entrance.

"Tell me you're on the pill." His voice was both commanding and
desperate.

"I am," I said, grateful for the cramps that had provoked my doctor
to prescribe them.

"You will allow me to protect you." He pushed himself inside of me
a couple of inches.

I groaned, my body stretching around him with a bite that came
from my inexperience and his massive size.

"Damn, you're so tight."

He pushed forward slowly, allowing my body to consume another inch of him, waiting until my quivering subsided before pushing forward another inch. With each press of his body, he stretched me open one glorious inch at a time, sliding deeper and deeper inside of me as we both moaned.

When I looked over my shoulder again, I could tell by the hunger in his eyes and the firm grasp of my hips that he wanted to take off into a sprint. Claim me. Hard and fast, take out his anger. But he was generous enough to give me the time to take him in, unhurriedly at first, so it didn't hurt as much.

"You feel so good," he groaned, and then, with one last push, he sank all the way inside of me.

We both shuddered, and I clung to the bedspread as harshly as his fingers dug into my hips, relishing the sensation of being wrapped around him—filled by him, his hips pressed against my ass. I loved how he stood there for a moment, letting my body quiver with him fully buried inside me. Before he pulled out slightly and thrust back in.

We both let out another sharp breath before Hunter drew back and then pushed in again. Slowly. Testing me, waiting for my body to spread around him.

"Damn, Little Leopard," he growled, pulling out and pushing in again—harder this time. "You feel so damn good."

My flesh grasped his, pulling him into me with a greedy desperation. He pulled back slightly and then drove deep again. Again and again, he filled and emptied me, until I was silently begging for mercy—mercy to never have this end.

As an orgasm began to build, burning in my lower belly.

Of all the ways I had fantasized about Hunter and me finally having sex, I had never imagined this. There was something feral and protective about our union that brought the ecstasy to a whole new level.

Passion boiling over as he grabbed my hips so hard, I'd probably have bruises on them tomorrow.

Marking me as his own.

I turned my neck and peered into Hunter's eyes. His burning gaze seared into me, intensifying the blazing heat of our passion. His movements became more deliberate, his thrusts plunging me further into an abyss of pleasure.

Hunter felt so damn good, like his body was made for mine, and then he made my heart still by putting one of his hands on the bed while his other reached between my legs and found that sweet spot of ecstasy.

Making it clear he remembered my words—that I'd never climaxed with another man before him. Hunter had already made me tremble with his tongue, but this time, he intended to bring me over the edge with him inside of me.

I moaned as he swirled his finger around the apex of my sex.

"I want you to scream my name," he reminded me over my lips, his breath hot and exhilarating as he found a perfect rhythm.

A swelling wave of heat grew between my thighs.

"Hunter…"

He growled and pounded into me even deeper. Harder.

Which was beyond sensual.

The wave rose so high, I was terrified of losing it, creating pressure in my chest that made it difficult to breathe.

He changed his angle slightly from behind, hitting that bundle of nerves deep inside. My eyes rolled back as Hunter continued massaging the sensitive bud of flesh between my thighs, driving me to the brink.

"Hunter…" I moaned, grabbing fistfuls of the bedding as I began to break over the edge.

"Scream my name."

I crashed—completely, violently—shuddering as a tsunami of pleasure radiated from every cell in my body.

"Hunter!"

I cried out from the most powerful orgasm I'd ever had in my entire life, my walls tightening around him as he continued moving his body with mine. Through the waves of my climax, I quivered and moaned, my thighs trembling.

He drove harder, and my core tightened with each passionate thrust, pushing my body to its limits, as I completely lost myself in the sensations cascading through me.

After I crested the peak of euphoria, I looked back over my shoulder and found Hunter's possessive gaze watching me intently, clenching his teeth, as he witnessed my world shattering around him —my pleasure derived only from *his* touch. It was undeniable how deeply he desired to possess me, to be the first man who ever made me come undone like this.

And I loved it.

As the last pant of pleasure left my lips, Hunter's grip on my hips tightened, and he drove himself into me with a force that sent shock waves through my body. He quivered behind me as his own climax reached its peak, his gaze locked on mine in a moment of pure bliss.

CHAPTER 36

Luna

I woke up with a sense of contentment that I couldn't quite put my finger on. And then I remembered last night, how Hunter and I had finally given in and had sex for the first time.

I blushed at the memory and smiled, feeling a deep sense of connection to him that I had never felt before.

As if reading my mind, Hunter entered the room, wearing nothing but a pair of black cotton pants, and leaned down to kiss me gently on the forehead.

"Good morning," he said, his gaze filled with tenderness.

His beauty was breathtaking with piercing eyes that sparkled with intrigue, set beneath perfectly arched dark eyebrows. A tousled head of raven-black hair added allure, making him even more irresistible when it fell into an artfully messy style.

"Good morning."

I pulled the covers up to my chest. We had never made it out of the guest bedroom last night, surrendering to the exhaustion right here in each other's arms.

As the sun rose slowly over the horizon, its warm rays filtered through the sheer curtains of the bedroom, casting a soft glow on everything it touched. The gentle light enveloped the room in a tender embrace, as if the room itself was infused with a sense of love and intimacy that the two of us shared.

"I have a surprise for you," Hunter said, offering me his hand. "Come with me."

"I don't have anything to wear. You tore everything, except my skirt."

A mischievous gleam flickered through his eyes. He walked over to a dresser, opened the drawer, and pulled out a T-shirt.

"You keep clothes in here?" I asked.

"Occasionally, one of my brothers would have too much to drink at one of our events and wouldn't drive home. So, I threw a few T-shirts in here."

Hunter tossed the T-shirt onto the bed and put his hands into his pockets, watching me slide it over my body.

"Perhaps we should forget the surprise and have a repeat of last night."

I smiled as I stood up, the T-shirt coming down to my mid-thigh. "But I want to see the surprise."

Hunter offered his hand to me—a gesture that spoke volumes, even more than our spicy night. Sex could have been a momentary release of passion, fueled by anger and fear stemming from what might have happened. But this...he was offering his hand to me *after* the storm, when he was altogether calm and collected.

I placed my hand in his, that same spark igniting that I'd had last night when he touched me. Maybe even more so now, as he guided me down the hallway.

I digested everything around us—the black-and-white photos of Chicago hanging on the walls, the hardwood flooring cool beneath my feet—and when we passed by a bathroom, I halted.

"You have a whirlpool tub?" I asked. Which was a stupid question. Of course his mansion would have a whirlpool tub. Probably more than one.

"You like baths?" Hunter asked, as if every little detail about me was profoundly interesting to him.

"Growing up, the apartment we lived in had one bathroom with only a shower. Then I lived in the college dorms, a small apartment after that, and now the cottage. Which also has just a single shower and no bathtub. But one time, when I was a teenager, we stayed in a hotel room that actually had a garden tub. When I soaked in it, the whole world just vanished around me. Like there was no room for my problems."

Hunter's Adam's apple rose and fell. It seemed to take him a moment to collect himself, clear his throat, and nod his chin toward the staircase.

"Come on."

Upon entering the kitchen, I was greeted by a magnificent array of mouthwatering food blanketing the entire center island. A vibrant display of colors and scents beckoned to be tasted. Golden-brown plates of pancakes, waffles, and French toast sat invitingly, accompanied by crispy hash browns. The deep reds of ripe strawberries vied for attention against the rich blues of plump blueberries, and amid this enticing medley, the aroma of sweet, velvety maple syrup wafted through the air, making my mouth water.

"Are you hosting a breakfast?" I asked, suddenly worried a flood of people were about to walk in on me, wearing nothing but a T-shirt.

Hunter squeezed my hand.

"This is for you, Luna. I didn't know what you liked, so I had Maria make a little of everything."

As I stood there, taking in the scene before my eyes, a wave of emotions washed over me. My heart swelled with gratitude, and a warmth spread through my chest, but behind it, a hint of guilt seeped in.

Did I deserve all of this?

"You made this for me?" I asked.

"If I had, even the strawberries would be burned," Hunter said.

I grinned. "It's stunning. Can I thank Maria?"

"She's giving us privacy. There's something I need to talk to you about."

I didn't like the serious tone in his voice or this feeling of dread that our euphoric bubble might soon pop.

Hunter poured two cups of coffee from a silver shiny thing before he kissed my forehead.

"Make a plate. Meet me in the dining room."

The back of my eyes burned slightly because it scared me, realizing how much I wanted this. Waking up with Hunter, getting to spend breakfast with him—just the two of us.

I never really thought much about what I might be missing when I had shut myself off from the prospect of relationships before. Even when I became friends with Sean, our friendship didn't fill me in a way that changed me forever.

But now I *was* changing forever. It was like exposing yourself to a level of happiness you never imagined existed, and now you knew that no matter what happened from this point forward, you would never be the same.

I forced the unwelcome emotions down my throat with a swallow, and then I quickly made myself a plate of eggs, pancakes, blueberries, and sausage patties, before padding with my bare feet along the cool hardwood floors to the dining room.

Where I was struck by the beauty of its decor. The color scheme was dominated by white and gray with a few accents of silver that added a touch of elegance to the space. The chairs stood tall and imposing—their gray upholstery adding to the sense of formality and severity in the room—while the centerpiece of the table was a large, ornate silver bowl filled with white roses, their delicate petals seeming almost out of place in the stern environment.

The walls were adorned with minimalist art pieces, their monochromatic color scheme adding to the sense of coldness and control in the space. It was a room that spoke of power and authority, a space designed for strategic meetings and calculated conversations.

No doubt what this one was about to be, based on the tense look in Hunter's eyes as he sat at the head of the table. Still shirtless with sexy bedhead but brimming with that domineering control he always had.

I stared at the different chairs, wondering where I was supposed to sit. *Should I sit across from him, which was twenty feet away? Next to him?*

Sensing my trepidation, Hunter smiled and pulled the chair out closest to him.

I ambled over and sat down, worried I'd scratch his table or spill something on the decadent furniture.

"Do you ever get used to the grandness of it all?" I asked as he sat back down.

"What was your dining room, like growing up?" he asked, taking a sip of coffee, his eyebrows raised in a display of curiosity.

"We had a folding table and chairs in our kitchenette."

He set his mug down and leaned back in his chair, studying me. "What was that like?"

I shrugged. "It was hard to care about the type of table we had when someone was missing from it for every meal. I mostly just stared at Dad's empty seat."

He nodded slowly, empathy etched in his eyes.

"You've probably hosted a lot of dinners at this table," I surmised, wanting the tone to lighten a bit. I looked around at the seats, wondering. "Who's the most powerful person who's been here?"

Hunter considered this for a moment. "The vice president."

"Of the United States?" I choked.

He nodded.

"Geez. The most powerful person who ever sat at ours was the neighborhood electrician. She gave us a discount, so Mom thanked her by inviting her to stay for food."

Mom. Gosh, I never really allowed myself the space to realize how much I missed her.

I forced the unexpected emotion away and picked up my fork, taking the first bite of my eggs.

Oh my word. Maria was an artist.

Hunter cleared his throat. "I don't want you living alone until Franco Hopkins is caught." His tone was warm but firm.

I took a deep breath. "I'm going to need a whole pot of coffee for this conversation."

Hunter placed the second mug of coffee in front of me, waiting for me to drink from it before he continued.

"We can't take any chances. I've called the detective and offered the services of my private investigator. He's the best in the country, and if anyone can flush out Franco Hopkins, it's him. But it won't be easy. Franco is a smart criminal who knows how to cover his tracks."

I set down my coffee. "You don't think the detectives will find him."

"We need to find him as fast as possible. He sent someone to break into your cottage. Maybe even did it himself, and now that he hasn't found what he's looking for, we have no idea what his next move will be."

I couldn't argue with that; I needed to take more precautions. Just to be safe.

But there was one thing that concerned me about all of this. With my growing feelings for Hunter, how would I discern what Hunter *wanted* to do for me versus what he felt *required* to do for me to keep me safe? I knew he had feelings for me, and last night had catapulted our relationship into a new direction. But this would be confusing. What if he started to lose interest in me, but I was oblivious to his shift in feelings because of all his noble, protective gestures?

In the grand scheme of things, this wasn't something I should be worried about. But now that he had activated my heart, a rope wrapped around it and tightened.

"I liked staying here last night," I said.

Hunter sat back in his chair and folded his hands on his lap. "But?"

"Maybe I should find somewhere else to stay until this all blows over."

A mixture of hurt and offense washed over his face. "Why's that?"

I took a sip of coffee, willing it to give me the courage, to be honest.

"Because I really like this, Hunter. I don't want to screw up what's happening between us over Franco Hopkins."

A slow smile stretched across Hunter's face.

"I really like this too," he said, holding my eyes. "And I'm not going to allow Franco Hopkins or anything else to interfere with this." He motioned with his finger between the two of us.

Relief unwound the rope in my chest, especially when Hunter

leaned forward and gripped my hand.

"Stay," he said.

I wasn't sure what to do. Should I protest and insist I stay else-where until this whole Franco situation was finally put to rest? But how long would it take? And why did I have to deprive myself of something that made me so happy in the meantime? Why would I let the psycho bully Franco take this from me, too?

After a moment, I nodded. "Okay."

Hunter's smile widened, but only briefly, before he sat back in his chair and brought his coffee mug to his lips, taking a long sip while he watched me eat my breakfast.

"There's something else," he said.

He cleared his throat and set his mug down. "I should have told you this before, but my private investigator looked into that letter that was sent to you. The one threatening you about your dad's case."

"Looked into it how?"

"He tried to identify the source of the letter, but whoever sent it was sophisticated enough to leave no trail. He thinks the letter was a legitimate threat, Luna."

"I assumed it was," I said.

"If the letter is legitimate, someone wants you to stop pushing for your father to get released."

"That will never happen."

He pursed his lips and met my determined gaze with an even, steady one of his own.

"Franco had someone break into the cottage last night, so he's the more urgent threat we need to focus on. But in the meantime, I've asked my private investigator to examine your dad's case. To see if there were any other suspects or anyone that sticks out that might get nervous if the case is reopened."

A mixture of emotions crashed through my chest. Fear was first and foremost—fear that Hunter, through his PI, was about to open the hood and look around my father's case. It was rattling, to say the least. Hunter was a trained prosecutor. What if he uncovered something incriminating that convinced him of my father's guilt?

Could I be with someone that didn't believe in my father's innocence?

The thought infected my mind and heart, making me realize how much it mattered to me that Hunter believed my father was innocent. Hunter seeing my father as a ruthless killer instead of the loving dad that he was would be a betrayal of the worst kind. One that would break my heart and one that I would likely never recover from.

I had to swallow my anxiety. I was getting ahead of myself, and we had enough on our plate without my emotional freak-out.

I should focus on the hopeful side of Hunter having his PI look into this. If this private investigator was half as good as Hunter claimed, maybe he would find the evidence that others had missed, proving my father's innocence. Maybe he would even find the real killer.

"I want to be there when he tells you what he finds," I said.

Hunter studied me before eventually nodding. "Fair enough."

I thought that was the end of the conversation, but when I took another bite of the eggs, Hunter said, "One last thing."

I blinked.

"I'd like you to sleep in my bedroom from now on."

Eggs lodged in my throat. I had to take a large swig of coffee to chase them down.

I wanted to sleep in his bedroom, too. But this was all moving so fast. Two weeks ago, I never thought I would be in a relationship. Now, here I was, having all these feelings for Hunter Lockwood.

And while we would undoubtedly continue to sleep together for however long I was staying at his mansion, moving into his bedroom was symbolic to me. So much of our relationship had been forced upon us, and I wanted to control some parts of it.

Notably, the decision to move into his bedroom.

If I ever made that move, I wanted it to be the next step in our relationship. Not a more convenient location for us to sleep, given the circumstances.

"I'd like that, too, but for now, I'd feel more comfortable sleeping in the guest room."

Hunter's face fell slightly.

"With you," I added.

I loved the way the hurt evaporated from his face and the edges of his lips curled into a smile.

"You've been independent for so long; it must be hard to let that go."

Damn, this man could read me.

He took the last sip of his coffee and stood up, leaning on the table with one hand so his face dangled inches from my own.

"I have one more surprise for you. Finish your breakfast and then meet me in the hallway upstairs."

Hunter brushed my lips with his before walking out of the dining room and climbing the grand staircase of his estate.

I downed my food in a hurry, excited to race upstairs and, hopefully, have a repeat of last night. In fact, I only ate half my breakfast—because I didn't want to be full, if that was his surprise—before putting my dishes in the sink and walking back upstairs into the hallway.

Where Hunter Lockwood stood, his hands in his cotton pockets, smiling at me beneath that messy head of hair of his.

He looked stunning, his sculpted physique on full display with no shirt. His broad shoulders and chiseled chest commanded attention, each defined muscle effortlessly showcasing his strength, as the sunlight from a nearby window danced across his skin, casting shadows that accentuated the contours of his well-built body.

His powerful biceps and triceps were reminiscent of a Greek statue, their firmness and symmetry a testament to the discipline it took to achieve such a physique. Equally taut and toned were the muscles on his chest and rippling abdomen. A perfectly etched six-pack, each abdominal muscle stood out, creating a mesmerizing pattern that spoke of both power and endurance.

He waited until I walked up to him before he cupped my cheek, stroking my skin with the pad of his thumb, and stared into my eyes. Warmth radiated from his touch, through my skin, and into my bones.

"I can't make all your problems in life go away," Hunter said. "No matter how much I want to. But maybe I can make them disappear for a little while."

Hunter stepped away and opened the door, revealing the same bathroom I had walked past earlier. Only now, pink rose petals scattered around the room, along with a few candles.

As I approached the large whirlpool bathtub, the sight before me was truly enchanting. The jets were on, creating a soothing hum that reverberated through the room, the calming scent of lavender filling my senses.

The tub was filled with steaming water, and bubbles were frothing at the top, like clouds floating in a serene sky, inviting me to sink in and enjoy the luxurious experience.

"The motor will keep the water heated for as long as you like," Hunter said.

This was the part of Hunter I wasn't sure I'd ever get used to. To others, he was an iron-strong control freak, but with me, he bent his metal and shaped it around me. Listening to my every word, wanting to not only protect me physically, but also emotionally.

My eyes stung slightly, and it took me a second to turn around.

I peeled the T-shirt from my body and savored the way his eyes darkened as it glided over my exposed breasts, as if it were taking every ounce of willpower to not grab me and make me his own again.

But he managed to stay in place, watching me settle into the tub.

My body sank into the warm water, the jets massaging my skin, soothing my muscles, and easing my tension. The sensation was divine, and I let out a contented sigh.

As I closed my eyes and leaned back, I was surrounded by a world of relaxation and indulgence. The warm water, the bubbles, and the soothing jets, all combined to create a moment of peace.

A moment that lasted for over an hour before Hunter knocked on the door and then opened it.

"Luna?"

I looked over my shoulder, taken aback by the fire in his eyes as he gazed at my nude body lying in a sea of bubbles.

He cleared his throat and said, "You have a visitor."

CHAPTER 37

Hunter

I have this hypothesis. That your heart can only be shattered so many times before it turns to stone and can never come back to life. How many times was too many? My guess? Three. My heart had been shattered when my dad died and again after the death of my mother, so if I gave it wholeheartedly to Luna, what if it broke again?

There would be no coming back from it, I bet.

I wanted her completely. I wanted to satisfy her every desire, her every dream and goal in life. I wanted to hold her hand and fight by her side.

And I had this deep-seated intuition that if I did not allow myself to be with her, I would never try again with anyone else.

But after extending the invitation at breakfast for her to stay in my room—an invitation she'd declined—I'd started to worry.

What if this bliss didn't last? What if she'd take a knife to my heart?

Just as everyone in Luna's life had left her, I was secretly terrified of the same thing—of plunging into the deep end with her, only to have her reject me.

After all, I wasn't the warmest or most compassionate person. One might argue that, up until now, my demeanor had been cold and detached, emotions locked away tight. But that was by design. I kept everyone at a distance for a reason.

Opening yourself up to people made you vulnerable. You hand your fragile heart over to others and silently pray that they won't destroy it.

The man I loved most in this world left me suddenly, without warning. The catastrophic scar was still deep and raw when my mother died of cancer.

Letting myself get close to someone again was terrifying.

I stared out the window at Luna walking the grounds with the guy whose jaw I wanted to crack. Sean. The only thing that kept me from punching him in his mouth when he showed up here today was that he was Luna's friend. She cared about him, and if I broke his jaw, she'd probably get pissed.

So, I'd let him in. Let him take her on a walk around my grounds as I stood here, alone, wondering...

If Luna left me one day...what would I do?

CHAPTER 38
Luna

"I am so sorry about last night," I said, wearing one of the outfits Hunter's guard kindly retrieved from my cottage.

With a bodyguard in tow, Sean and I slowly wandered the sprawling Lockwood estate with its emerald lawns, a rainbow of flowers, and perfectly pruned trees.

The property stretched as far as the eye could see, a lavish oasis overlooking the vast blue waters of Lake Michigan.

We stopped at the edge of the cliff, where the world seemed to pause for a moment, as I closed my eyes and let the sun's gentle caress wash over me, the heat seeping into my bones and driving away the chill that had settled there. A comforting embrace in the otherwise dark chapter of my life. The scent of freshly cut grass and blooming flowers filled the air, and as I listened to the distant lapping of waves against the rocky shoreline and birds singing songs that sounded like whispers of hope, I couldn't help but marvel at the serenity that seemed to envelop the estate.

"Forget last night," Sean said. "I just want to make sure you're okay."

But I could tell there was something more he'd come to say. Sean had traveled by Metra, bus, and Uber to get here, like a ridiculous public transportation triathlon. A ninety-minute journey that could have been avoided by simply calling to check on me.

"I didn't mean to offend you," I said.

"You didn't offend me, but I've been your friend for years, Luna. I thought you'd *want* to stay with me instead of the Addams family's long-lost cousin."

"Addams family?" I arched a brow.

Sean looked up. "The dude lives in a creepy mansion."

"It's not creepy. And there would be no realistic way for me to travel into the city every day to work. Plus, I don't know how long this is going to take."

"So, you're staying with Dracula indefinitely, then."

I wondered if Hunter was standing by one of the many windows, watching us right now, joined by his uncle and his brother Grayson, who'd arrived shortly after Sean.

"*Indefinitely* is a strong word," I said.

"I take it, that's a yes."

"He's a nice guy," I said.

"If you say so," Sean muttered, his tone dripping with sarcasm.

I couldn't help but smile.

"You like Hunter, don't you?" Sean accused.

When my cheeks burned, Sean's gaze settled on them, a frown creasing his brow.

"You like him a lot."

I did. God, I liked him so much, it scared me.

"He's...different from I thought," I hedged.

Sean scrubbed his jaw, looked up at the mansion that towered over us, and then shoved his hands into his pockets. He paused, his gaze dropping to the ground as he chewed the inside of his cheek, and then, after a prolonged silence, he lifted his eyes, a newfound determination shining within.

"I don't like him for you, Luna. He's not good enough for you."

That's what this was about. He'd sensed my feelings for Hunter and wanted to come rescue me from emotional peril.

"The guy is wrong on so many levels. He's nothing but an arrogant, rich philanderer, who's never photographed with the same woman twice. He was born into a world of wealth and privilege with a team of people doing whatever he orders them to, so he's used to getting his way, always."

Sean looked up at the mansion with disdain, like its monstrosity was an eyesore to the pristine landscaping around us.

"I won't sit back and let you get hurt, Luna. You've been through too much."

The concerned gaze of my friend made doubt swirl through my heart like unwelcome smoke.

"Hunter's a good guy," I assured. "He's trying to protect me, too."

Sean stared at me, shaking his head. "There's nothing I can say to make you dislike him, is there?"

"He's going above and beyond," I said. "He's even having his private investigator delve into Franco."

Sean grabbed the back of his neck, as if reeling from failing to convince me to see Hunter in a different light. But it was clear the most urgent issue to him was safeguarding me from Hopkins. He could continue trying to convince me to leave Hunter another day.

"I've started researching Franco myself, too," Sean said. "I have contacts in the true crime world that can help me flush out people willing to talk to me. People who won't talk to law enforcement or even private investigators."

I didn't like this one bit. Franco was dangerous. Look at the guy that had attacked me in the prison—I didn't want Sean to get caught in the crosshairs.

"I don't want you to get hurt," I said.

"I don't want *you* to get hurt."

His past had to be haunting him right now, making him terrified history was about to repeat itself with the murder of his high school girlfriend. I wished I could take away his fears. Obsessing over a man who was trying to hunt me down couldn't be healthy for him, not with his heartbreaking past.

"Look, instead of poking around dangerous criminals, why don't we work together to try to uncover the identity of the Windy City Vigilante?"

As soon as the words left my mouth, I regretted them. With everything going on, I hadn't fully processed what the Vigilante had told me.

"So, you still want to take the Vigilante down."

Still.

That one word crawled over my skin and dug into my stomach. Why would Sean think my point of view on the Vigilante had changed? I hadn't told him about my encounter with the Vigilante yesterday, and I certainly never expressed my confused feelings about it.

The only other person who would suspect my feelings toward the Vigilante might have changed would be the Vigilante himself.

"Why wouldn't I?" I asked.

Sean shrugged. "You said he saved you in that prison parking lot."

Yeah. That had to be all he meant. Right? That perhaps my gratefulness toward his rescue had cooled my flaming hot rage for him.

Because there was no way Sean could be the Windy City Vigilante.

Right?

CHAPTER 39
The Vigilante

My target didn't see me hiding in the shadows of the alley, stalking him. He was oblivious, making his way toward his car with his gaze fixed on his cell phone's screen—the glow the only illumination in the blackened night.

People didn't realize that every moment their eyes were glued to their cell phones, they weren't sweeping their surroundings for dangers lurking. Like me.

It had been trickier getting to the high school quarterback who'd left Luna with a scar. He'd been on his guard, though it was only because he'd been worried about getting caught cheating on his pregnant wife. Her pregnancy gave me the added encouragement to leave him with just a beating. A bloody face and a million questions, but a heartbeat all the same.

This guy, on the other hand, wouldn't be so lucky. He was one of Franco Hopkins's right-hand men—the closest to my real target I had come thus far.

But I would find Franco soon enough. I would make sure of it.

I clutched the dampened cloth in my hand, my muscles nearly trembling with the anticipation of what I was about to do, and as I got closer, a fire began to burn in my chest.

My target loomed ahead, his silhouette shrouded in the darkness of the night. At just under six feet tall, he was pudgy around the middle, which would make it harder to carry him. But not impossible.

Satisfaction surged at the sight of him. Finally, I'd be carving my knife into his body, draining every ounce of his blood for information.

I glanced around the space, my senses heightened by the tension that hung heavy in the air. In the distance, the metallic screech of the "L" train only added to the sense of chaos and danger that seemed to permeate every inch of this desolate alley.

Even if he turned around, he probably wouldn't see me. Knocking the two light bulbs out with my fist saw to that, plunging the passage into darkness.

My heart raced as every nerve in my body ignited with excitement, adrenaline surging through my veins, the way it always did in anticipation of a kill.

In a flash, I sprinted toward him, my senses heightened by the thrill of the hunt—the guy too oblivious to sense the impending doom until it came crashing into him.

I shoved the cloth tightly to his face, smothering his nose and mouth with the fabric soaked in the fast-acting drug. While my other arm wrapped around his chest from behind.

He struggled for a few moments, thrashing about in a futile attempt to free himself from my grasp, but it was no use. Within seconds, he was unconscious, his body slumping to the ground with a thud.

I stood over him, my body pulsing, knowing this was only the beginning.

Normally, I didn't take people to my underground bunker. There was no need; the job was usually done with one slash to their throat, but not this time.

This time, the stakes were too high. I needed information from him, and I wasn't about to let him slip through my fingers, so last night, I'd prepared a space where I could extract the answers I needed without any interruptions.

The guy was heavy, like a sack full of stones. I grunted as I heaved him up and slung him over my shoulder, walking through the dark alley until I reached my awaiting vehicle—a glossy black Lexus LS 500h, capable of high speeds with a quiet motor, complete with tinted windows. I threw him in the back seat as quickly as possible, knowing I only had a few minutes to get him to my bunker before he would wake up.

In the depths of a chamber hidden underground, stone walls encased a space filled with shadows and dread. The air was laced with a sinister aura, as if it could whisper the secret of my crimes.

It was here, in this very room, that I kept evidence that I was the Windy City Vigilante: a collection of weapons—mostly knives that could never be traced back to me. A lone computer and printer, where I could research crimes anonymously and pin that research to a board mounted to the far wall. It was here where I could unleash the darkest part of my soul and pick my next target.

Like this guy, who now sat bound to a battered, wooden chair that creaked and groaned under his weight—his face etched with terror.

The room's dim light—cast by battery-operated bulbs strung haphazardly around the room—accentuated the darkness that permeated the space. A lingering scent of damp earth and musty air assaulted my nostrils.

A sense of unease invaded my bones because this was unfamiliar territory for me—I was used to working in the shadows, taking down my targets quickly and quietly.

But this time, everything was different.

A sense of foreboding lingered at the risk that someone might find out he was here. I'd considered other locations to take him, but this was the only place in the city where I could extract answers without risking interruption or capture by police.

Besides, I reminded myself, it was underground. No one knew about this place, and no one would even know how to find it.

"Who the fuck are you?" the guy demanded.

Despite the cool temperature down here, sweat shone across his forehead, and his breathing cut through the silence with his trembles of fear.

He was a rather ugly man with tiny eyes buried in an oval face and two giant nostrils.

I wondered how many women had to stare at those giant holes while he raped them and then killed them when they fought back.

"Who I am doesn't matter," I said. "What matters is who *you* are."

"Look, I don't know who you think I am, but—"

"I know exactly who you are."

The man swallowed, his Adam's apple bobbing down his throat.

"You're Lonnie Whig. One of Franco Hopkins's right-hand men. Unlike Franco, though, you're a little easier to find because you're a rapist who got sloppy."

And a killer. Don't forget the killer part.

He had the nerve to glare at me. That's the thing about assholes— even when they're completely screwed, they never turn off the A-hole switch. It's like a mantra or something.

"See, the thing is, you counted on the women you raped and let live to be too scared to go to the police. Especially since you choose working girls as your victims. But the thing about working girls is that they always have each other's backs, which means they warn each other about johns that get violent. So, while they might not have enough courage to go to the police, they know when one of their own was last seen with you before turning up, rotting in the dumpster a few hours later. Especially when it starts to become a pattern. And that, Lonnie, is when they're willing to open up to me."

"What the hell do you want?" he snarled, a feral glint in his eyes.

"You're going to tell me everything that I want to know." My voice was cold.

"Why would I do that?" His eyes cast around the space, looking at the weapons. "You're just going to kill me, anyway."

Maybe he was fishing. Looking for reassurance that his fate hadn't already been sealed.

"This will be the last free choice you have on this earth," I said. "Do you want to have a civil conversation and die a swift death? Or do you want to spend your last hours on earth getting slowly tortured?"

I gestured toward the wall behind him, filled with instruments of pain. Ice picks, saws, and screwdrivers all glistened under the light.

Torturing him would create a massive complication. The longer I stayed down here, the more likely someone would notice I was missing, risking exposure. I hoped he'd just tell me what I needed to know so I could get on with this.

He looked at the tools, appearing to calculate his next move, before he looked back at me with gritted teeth and asked, "What do you want to know?"

I smiled. This was going better than expected.

"Tell me where Franco Hopkins is."

The exhale this guy released reeked of bacteria, like he collected it with the same enthusiasm as a baseball card collector. As if his victims hadn't suffered enough, they'd had to endure his putrid breath.

"I don't know where he's at these days," the guy said.

A surge of adrenaline coursed through my veins as I finally got a whiff this guy might talk. It pissed me off to no end, how infuriatingly difficult it was proving to be to find Franco Hopkins. I'd never hunted for someone who'd spent the last several years overseas, lacking people here who could help narrow his position.

"Don't lie to me, Lonnie. Tell me where he is," I ordered calmly.

The guy licked his teeth.

"You don't have to worry about Franco torturing you," I said. "I assure you your fate with me will be much worse if you do not cooperate."

Lonnie's lips thinned. "He moves to a new location every few days," Lonnie said.

"Where is he now?"

"I don't know where he is until he tells me. His location is on a need-to-know basis."

"Where was his last location?"

He hesitated. "Club Eighty-One, but he's long gone, man."

"How often do you see him?"

"As often as he needs something from me. He calls me from a different burner each time."

Shit.

"How often does he need something from you?"

"Depends."

"Will he be needing something from you soon?"

To this, the guy went cold. "No. And even if he did, I'd never lead you to him, man. I ain't walking into that."

I measured the resolve in his eyes. This A-hole wouldn't budge on this point, and damn it if that didn't create a complication.

I pulled the knife from its sheath and glared at him.

"Franco's been obsessed with intel he thinks Dominic had. He won't let it go. Why?"

"Threatens his freedom."

"There's more to it than that." That much was obvious with his relentless and incessant pursuit.

No response.

"He thinks Dominic gave this intel to someone, but if he did, the only way Franco would assume he hasn't been arrested is if law enforcement was sitting on it. Why would Franco think law enforcement would do that?" My tone wasn't a question; it was a demand.

No response.

I punched him in the head to remind him who was in charge of this conversation.

Have to say, the moan he tried to stifle gave me crazy good satisfaction.

"Allow me to remind you, you don't have to worry about Franco killing you, Lonnie. You're not walking out of here alive. So, you can either tell me the information that I want to know, or I will make your death so brutal and painful, you'll wish you were never born."

It had been my experience that some of the most violent criminals in this country were also the biggest cowards. How easy it was for them to dish out death, but when death was pointed at them? They'd nearly piss themselves.

Being tortured? To hell with that.

But who knew? Maybe Lonnie was stronger than all of the other killers I had come across. Maybe he would be loyal to Franco, even though Franco would never do the same for Lonnie.

The question was: how far did Lonnie's loyalty stretch? Was he really willing to be tortured to death?

"Okay, okay, fine..." Lonnie said in surrender. "I'll tell you whatever it is you want to know."

I refrained from grinning.

"I want to know what information he thinks Dominic leaked and why Franco's gone to these lengths to stop it from coming out."

Lonnie licked his lips, hesitating, a clear battle of indecision playing across his face as he looked down, remaining silent for several seconds before clearing his throat.

"Franco has been building a drug empire in Europe for the past few years. But the goal was always to bring it to the United States."

"Talk faster." I had to dispose of his body, and the clock was ticking.

The guy glared at me before continuing.

"Franco's expecting the arrival of his first big shipment here in the States."

"When?"

"I don't know. Soon. Point is, everything he's worked for over the last several years is about to come to a head."

"And this is the information he thinks Dominic had on him."

"Franco wanted a family member to help him run the organization here. And even though Dominic wasn't as strong as Franco, Franco seemed to think he could whip Dominic into shape. So, he brought Dominic into the fold and told him everything."

"Risky move on his part," I said.

"Franco thought he could trust blood."

But I could see the offense in Lonnie's eyes; he thought Franco should have leaned on Lonnie. Not Dominic.

"When Dominic pushed back on killing that guy, Franco made the rules clear. It was Dominic's life or the man's—who'd screwed him out of money. Dominic still didn't want to go through with it—tried to get out of it—but Franco sent someone to babysit him until it was done. *And* Dominic's mother. Dominic went through with it, but that's when he finally drew the line and told Franco he was out—he didn't want to be part of his enterprise. Which was a big slap in the face to Franco."

"He threatened to kill Dominic."

And I bet Lonnie wouldn't have minded that one bit. Even criminals got jealous.

"But then Dominic claimed he had evidence against Franco, and it would come out if anything ever happened to him," Lonnie said.

"So, Franco *wasn't* going to kill Dominic over it?"

"He was. If Dominic was found guilty, there was going to be a hit right there in the county jail that night. But Dominic was found not guilty, so Franco was going to drive him somewhere and take care of *the situation*—permanently." He eyed me up and down. "Heard you got to Dominic first."

How unfortunate I'd killed someone who was already a dead man walking. This was like washing your car and then having it downpour.

Not to mention, I picked the wrong family member to dispose of first—that was for damn sure. Franco Hopkins was a time bomb waiting to explode.

If Dominic knew what, when, and where this shipment was going to arrive, police could intercept everything and destroy Franco's organization before he got it off the ground in this country. Plus, they might even be able to trace it overseas and take that organization down, too.

"Franco has people he's accountable to overseas?" I surmised.

He nodded.

When what was probably millions of dollars on the line, if you screw it up, you don't have to worry about going to prison. You'd be killed before that ever happened.

No wonder Franco Hopkins had been such a loose cannon. He had to make sure the evidence Dominic had threatened him with never got into the wrong hands. Everything was on the line for Franco: his new organization, his old organization, his freedom, and his life.

That's why Luna was in so much danger.

"Final question," I said. "When does Franco plan to kill Luna Payne?"

The guy's brows furrowed slightly. "The lawyer chick?"

I waited.

Lonnie's face softened into a smug smirk of arrogance, his voice taunting.

"That's what this is about? Some stupid bitch?"

"When?" I needed a timeline to make sure I wasn't roaming the streets of the city in pursuit of Franco while he was actually on the other side of Chicago, slaughtering Luna Payne.

"If that's all you care about, you're fucked." His eyes lit up as he leaned in, savoring each word.

I brought the blade of my knife to his jugular, pressing in until a drop of blood pricked near an overgrown black hair on his skin.

"Start explaining. Now."

He looked up at me, his smile widening, as if he had just won this battle.

"Franco put a bounty on her head yesterday. A half-dozen hit men in the city are out, hunting for her right now."

Every muscle in my body tightened in fury.

"When they find her, they won't kill her quickly. They've been ordered to torture her until she's begging for death. Maybe even have a little *fun* with her first. I know I would," he taunted.

"You're lying." Franco might be psychotic enough to eliminate any possible threat to his freedom, but there was no reason to take it to the level this guy was claiming. He was just trying to get under my skin, his last act of defiance before losing his life.

"Franco has a drug empire on the line. He'll do whatever it takes to find out what kind of exposure he has."

My heart beat against my ribs in anger.

"She has bodyguards," I growled.

The fear in the room shifted like a disease, spreading from him, infecting me.

"You don't know Franco's hit men very well, do you?" he goaded.

"Tell me how to stop it."

"You can't. Only person that can is Franco himself. That girl has been marked for death, and there's nothing you can do about it."

I pressed my knife harder into his neck at an angle to inflict as much pain as I could without actually ending his life.

"There will be no one to pay those hit men if I cut the head off the snake," I snarled.

And then I shoved my hand over his mouth, raised the knife, and plunged it into his chest, savoring the muffled screams of my captive, the soft echoes of his cries reverberating off the stone walls.

My relief from killing him was short-lived, because if what this dirtbag was saying was true, then Luna Payne was in a lot more danger than I realized.

It had been bad enough that her life was in peril, but hearing that she'd likely be tortured and raped took it to a whole new level. It was my fault she'd stumbled onto Dominic's death, and I wasn't going to let her suffer such a horrific fate.

Which could come at any moment, because out there, right now, an army of hit men were sprinting in a deadly race to see who could get to her first.

CHAPTER 40
The Vigilante

ow easy will it be to kill Luna Payne?
It wasn't the question I had come here to answer, but now that I was staring at her office building, noting her security detail, my muscles tensed with concern.

It was evident to anyone who watched that the bodyguard was top-notch with the way his eyes constantly swept for danger and how he stayed close to Luna as she exited the car and made her way through the double doors. How he followed her inside, positioned just outside her office to vet anyone that would come in or out.

But even top-notch security had its limitations. I mean, even presidents of the United States and other countries had been shot in the past despite a swarm of the highest-ranking security around them.

How easily *could* her protective detail be breached? How safe was Luna? Only once I had that answer would I move on to my original reason for coming here…

I briefly considered the different scenarios for getting close to her. Trying to get a meeting with her by posing as a client would not work, not with the attire and mask the Vigilante wore. And I was not about to let her, or anyone, see my face.

Too risky.

Another scenario. If she exited the building to go to a coffee shop or restaurant—and so help me, I'd punch her bodyguard in his windpipe if he let that happen—I could follow them. But since she knew better than to do that, I certainly wouldn't bank on it.

I sighed, realizing I knew exactly what option that left me with.

Luna Payne was not going to like this one bit.

CHAPTER 41
Luna

I t felt great to be back at work, back in a structured routine that required my mind to focus on anything other than the chaos going on in my life. I needed this, I realized. This sense of normalcy in the midst of a hurricane.

"I have to use the ladies' room," I said to my bodyguard for the second time today, whose presence was equal parts stifling and comforting.

Like last time, he nodded in reply.

Like last time, he followed me, maintaining three steps behind as I walked down the long hallway toward the women's restroom that everyone on this floor of the building had access to.

And, like last time, he stepped into the bathroom with me, looking into each stall. Only this time, one of the stalls was closed, and when he knocked, a woman emerged, looking frustrated to pieces.

It's not every day a burly man invades the privacy of a women's restroom.

"Excuse me, ma'am," was all he said, watching her scurry away without even washing her hands.

"I'll be outside," he added to me.

Then he walked out the door, where I knew he'd be positioned, preventing anyone from entering. I needed to hurry. I hated that nobody was allowed to use the restroom here until I was done.

Before I turned around, though, something slammed into my back, and something else pressed against my lips, muffling my scream, spinning me so my body was now situated away from the only escape.

"I'm going to need you to be quiet, Ms. Payne." The man's breath heated my ear.

I know that voice. That sandpaper voice that was hiding the real one beneath it.

"Will you promise not to scream?"

I nodded, knowing it was the only way he would release me from his irritatingly strong grip.

He let me go slowly. My heartbeat accelerated as I turned around and stared directly into the mesh-covered eyes of the Vigilante's mask.

The last time I'd seen the Windy City Vigilante was four days ago, when he'd shown me crime scene photos, trying to convince me to drop the manhunt against him. A deliberation that had echoed around in my head since, but I hadn't gone to the mayor on his behalf, nor had I quit the team hunting him. Maybe he heard as much from his ears on the street and had finally lost his patience with me.

The stall where the woman had run from—that's where he must have been hiding, and based on the frightened look on that woman's face, she hadn't been hiding with him willingly.

What if he was here to make me pay for not heeding his *request?*

I tried to run past him, but the Vigilante was like a predator, locked in on every movement of his prey. In a flash, he blocked my path with his gigantic body, causing me to bounce off the expanse of his chest and abs, rocking me on my heels.

Scream, Luna.

No. Not yet. If he's here to enact vengeance against you for not convincing Mayor Kepler to stop his hunt, the Vigilante will slit your throat, and there will be nothing the bodyguard can do to save you.

Get away from him. Wait for enough distance between the two of you, then you can scream.

"How did you get in here?" I asked, taking a step back.

He reached over and turned on the faucet, all the way up, drowning out conversation to anyone who would be listening.

"Getting in wasn't difficult, Ms. Payne. Being patient enough to wait for you to show up was the hard part."

"You held a poor, defenseless woman against her will."

He shrugged. "I knew if your bodyguard was decent, he would sweep the room before letting you inside. I needed someone in that stall."

"She might tell my bodyguard you're in here," I realized, hope taking flight in my chest.

"If she did, he'd have busted in here already."

The hope came crashing down, but I tried to keep it alive, taking another step back. "Then she's probably calling the cops right now."

"Most likely."

Which meant he'd have only four or five minutes before the place was surrounded.

But I'd scream or run long before then. I just had to wait for the perfect moment.

I glanced at the door again, my gaze lingering on the possible escape route, my heart pounding with the urge to flee.

"If you run," he warned, his voice a smoky whisper that made my throat run dry, "I'll catch you."

The promise in his words held a seductive edge that made my breath catch, and his posture seemed to darken with anticipation, as if he were intrigued by the prospect of the chase, of capturing me in his arms.

For a moment, neither of us moved, and time seemed to stand still as we silently stared at each other.

"Why are you here?" I demanded.

"To warn you," the Vigilante said. "I had a chat with one of Franco's men last night. It seems he's hired some people to find you. And kill you."

Oh God.

"You can't be out in the open like this, Ms. Payne. It's dangerous."

He took a step forward, his movements deliberate and predatory, perhaps trying to intimidate me.

I hated that it was working. That I remembered the wound on Dominic's neck, the blood pouring from that man's body in the prison parking lot after the Vigilante had effortlessly killed him.

And now here I was. Alone with him.

When he advanced toward me, each of his steps echoing in the small space, I retreated. His towering frame was a blend of power and intimidation—an unwelcome reminder of the danger I was in.

Based on the slight angle to his head, he assessed me up and down, amusement flickering on his lips as if enjoying the nervousness he was causing.

"Are you afraid of me?" he growled in that grainy voice of his that was a blend of allure and danger.

No matter what he claimed his intentions were for trapping me like this, I was a hostage to a confessed killer. Any man capable of doing what the Vigilante did had to be psychologically unstable. And dangerously unpredictable.

"The whole city is afraid of you." I continued to step backward.

He matched my steps, moving forward with the grace and precision of a predator closing in on its prey.

I glanced at the door, wondering what the odds were of me getting out of here, or at least alerting my guard before it was too late.

His mesh-covered gaze appeared to follow mine, a silent promise of a game of cat and mouse playing out in the curl of his lips—like an acknowledgment of the unspoken challenge.

"I've killed fifty-three men."

I about choked on my tongue. *Fifty-three?* The news media had the body count way low.

My back hit the wall, and I suppressed a gasp. He stepped forward again, his body perilously close to mine, and rested a palm against the wall, near the side of my face. The heat of his hand seemed to radiate toward my skin.

"But I've never savored killing a man as much as I'll savor draining the blood from the person who ordered your death." His low, sensual voice danced along my nerves like a dangerous caress, stirring a flurry of emotions I couldn't fully comprehend.

I swallowed, blood surging through my veins with the rush of adrenaline. His face was closer to mine than I wanted, his hand capable of reaching up and strangling me in an instant if I made the wrong move.

And yet...that comment. It activated a sixth sense begging to be heard, telling me I wasn't in any danger. That he was, in fact, here to protect me.

"The woman in the stall," I said, trying to keep my voice steady. "If she'd resisted you. If you were backed into a corner, would you kill an innocent person if it was your only way out?"

He didn't answer, his silence thickening the air with a tension that seemed to wrap around him like a fog.

"I've never used my skills to keep someone alive before," he mused, his voice a dark and tantalizing whisper. "This is...new territory for me."

"I don't need your protection," I said, defiance momentarily drowning out my alarm. "In case you didn't notice, I have security now."

"And yet here I am," he said. "Talking to you alone. Don't let having a bodyguard give you a false sense of security," he continued. "It only takes a moment to get to someone, Ms. Payne."

My heart rate spiked at his words, and I shifted uncomfortably.

His lips curled up into a ghost of a smile. "You have my protection whether you appreciate it or not. And if anyone hurts you, I'll slit their throat." The promise in his voice was as chilling as it was decisive, making my blood pump faster through my body.

I was ashamed of feeling a flush of adoration for this man, but maybe it was only human. When someone would be willing to go to extreme measures to keep you safe, to enact vengeance should anyone hurt you, it was hard to *not* experience a wave of gratitude for that.

"But Franco? He won't be given the mercy of dying quickly," he continued, his voice dripping with dark intent. "There are six places you can stab someone that results in death rapidly. You can rest assured I'll avoid all six of those locations when I get my hands on him, Ms. Payne."

"I don't want you to kill Franco. I want him turned into authorities, to face a trial of his peers."

To this, the Vigilante looked amused, the edges of his mouth lifting, adding an air of ominous foreboding to the fog snaking between us.

"I will never stop hunting him, Ms. Payne. And I'll never stop protecting you."

Protecting me. The phrase ripped through my heart, sending its beat into a rhythm of confusion.

It seemed unconscionable to be grateful to this man who was out there, trying to keep me safe. Maybe it was just a survival thing—hoping if it came down to it, if Franco slipped past all other defenses, he might be intercepted by someone as capable of violence as he was.

In the distance, sirens began to wail.

"They're coming for you."

"Most likely, yes."

"Which gives you no more than a minute or two to escape before they arrive."

"Plenty of time."

"But there's only one way out of here." I nodded to the ladies' room door. "And on the other side of it is my bodyguard." Whom the woman must have run past so fast from terror, she hadn't alerted him. "You'll never make it past him. So, what's your plan?"

He leaned closer, the heat from his skin igniting a thousand tiny fires within me.

I couldn't decide which fire it was, though. Anger at him for having cornered me here? Or a sick appreciation that this man was working so hard to protect me?

"I have a plan, Ms. Payne. I'm afraid you won't like it very much. And I apologize in advance for what I'm about to do to you."

His lips curled into a friendly ghost of a smile, and when they did, some sort of recognition flickered.

One I couldn't place.

"Why do I get the feeling I know you?" I asked.

He stilled.

"Because I get the sense that I do," I pressed.

His mouth tightened. "You would be well advised to not try to guess my identity, Ms. Payne."

"So, that's a yes? I do know you?"

He dropped his arm from the side of my head and stared at me for another moment before clearing his throat.

"Inform your bodyguard that I walked in the front door of this building and checked in under a pseudonym. I got you alone in here, while he didn't check on you once. And, Ms. Payne?"

I waited.

"I *am* sorry about what I have to do next."

In a flash, the Vigilante spun me around and put his hand over my mouth, muffling my cries as his other arm clenched around my stomach and lifted me a foot from the ground. Despite my kicking and thrashing, he pulled me to the door and released his grip over my mouth long enough to swing it open.

To his credit, my bodyguard acted swiftly. It took him a second for his widened eyes to take in the scene before him and to launch forward, but the Vigilante was expecting it, shoving me off of him and into the chest of my security detail.

My bodyguard caught me, wrapping his arms around me as the Vigilante fled faster than an Olympic sprinter.

"Are you okay?" my bodyguard asked.

"Yes."

He looked like he wanted to run after the Vigilante, but doing so meant leaving me alone, exposed and vulnerable, should this be a ruse to lure the bodyguard away.

As sirens wailed in the distance, the Vigilante vanished into the city.

Leaving me with more questions than ever.

CHAPTER 42
Luna

D o I know you?

The thought echoed through my mind, haunting me, eating at me like a cancerous growth devouring everything in its path. Because the more I thought about it, the more I sensed that the Vigilante was somebody I knew. Why else would he be so intent on protecting me?

"You're fired," Hunter snapped.

We were standing in his great room, where Hunter had angrily intercepted me and my bodyguard after we'd come home. I knew seeing Hunter for the first time since he'd heard about the bathroom incident would be hard, but he looked even more frazzled than I'd expected.

His suit normally made him look controlled and calm, but he'd undone the top three buttons and yanked his tie down several inches, so it hung like a green noose around his neck. And he was pacing, glaring at the bodyguard like he was seriously considering punching him.

"Hunter," I cautioned.

Hunter's furious gaze pulled away from my bodyguard and slammed onto me.

"You could have been killed," Hunter growled.

"I could've screamed," I said, trying to give the bodyguard some credit. "I was trying to bide my time for the cops—"

"You should never have wound up in a room alone with anyone." Hunter glowered at the bodyguard one last time. "Get out of my house."

I offered the bodyguard a silent apology before he quietly ambled away.

"Don't you think you should give him one more chance?" I asked.

"I won't forgive *any* mistakes when it comes to your safety, Luna."

I didn't have it in me to debate the bodyguard's situation any further; I'd tried to reason with Hunter for the last ten minutes, and I could tell it was a lost cause.

Plus, I had bigger things on my mind right now. Namely, who was the Vigilante?

After what happened in the bathroom, I couldn't shake the feeling that the truth of his identity was lurking just beneath the surface, taunting me, daring me to uncover who he really was. Nor could I shake the feeling that I did, in fact, know him. I mean, the guy had threatened to beat up a high school bully of mine, for crying out loud.

And if I did know him, that meant my already-fractured foundation might get rocked once more.

While I hadn't let anyone fully into my heart since the betrayals in my past, the truth was, I *had* let some people in—albeit in small doses. I trusted my father's friend, Rodney, believed he had a good heart, and was, in fact, innocent of his charges. I trusted that he was the person he'd claimed to be to my father and that he wouldn't break his heart like all the other people in his life. Rodney knew what my father had been through. Surely, he wouldn't foster a friendship if, behind the scenes, he was a killer.

I trusted Sean a lot more than I'd understood until this moment. He was the first real friend I'd had since I was a kid, and I'd bled my heart out to him about my father's case and the heartbreak it had caused. The whole time I'd been exposing my vulnerability, was he weaving a web of lies, meticulously designed to fool me?

And then there was Hunter. I hadn't known him as long as I knew Sean, but my connection to him was profound. Was it possible that beneath the calm, caring man who was trying to protect me lurked a monster that slaughtered people in cold blood? A killer hiding behind the camouflage of an attorney sworn to uphold the law?

Or was there someone else in my life that I needed to consider? Was someone in my past that I had once trusted responsible for all the death and carnage?

The thought was chilling.

It reminded me of something my father had said to me when I was little.

"I don't like that story," I said. "I hate it."

Daddy closed the book and regarded me with a sigh.

"Little Red Riding Hood should have known he was the wolf. If she knew he was the wolf, she wouldn't have gotten eaten."

I laid my head on my fuzzy pink pillow, and snuggled up against Daddy's side. Daddy was always so warm. The musk scent of his aftershave had faded during the long day, but it still lingered on his neck with the hopeful promise of a new morning.

"I know, honey. But it has a good message."

"That out there somewhere, there's always a wolf waiting to eat us?"

"That we need to be careful, because people aren't always who they seem."

People aren't always who they seem.

My eyes blurred with tears.

"People think you're the wolf," I said.

I hated it when Daddy looked sad like this. He sighed as he swiped a tear from his cheek. "We told you not to watch the news."

"Mr. Mike was your best friend," I said. "He made you sound like a bad guy."

Daddy stroked my arm.

"The truth will prevail, honey. Don't you worry, okay? Everything is going to be okay."

. . .

Of course, it hadn't turned out okay then, and now, my instincts screamed that someone in my life might not be who they claimed to be.

My fear begged me to bury my head in the sand, warning me my heart couldn't handle any more damage. But I refused to live in the shadows of doubt, haunted by fear.

The time had come to face the truth—because it was no longer a question of *if* I wanted to know the truth. I needed to learn the identity of the Windy City Vigilante and to determine whether the trust I had so painstakingly started to build was destined to crumble under the weight of betrayal.

If it did, the ramifications would be irreversible. I'd never feel safe enough to allow anyone in my life again, not even mere acquaintances.

Anger radiated off of Hunter.

If he was the Vigilante, why would he risk getting caught today to warn me of impending danger? He could have told me himself, could have simply beefed up security.

Unless…unless he'd acquired that intel about Franco acting as the Vigilante and thus had to pass along the warning in disguise.

"I'm getting you the head of my security team," Hunter said.

I pressed my finger against my temple.

"This isn't up for debate," he snarled.

"It's not that. It's just…this whole thing rattled me." But not in the way Hunter probably assumed.

I mean, here I was, wondering what the chances were that *Hunter* was the *Vigilante*, for God's sake.

Until I uncovered the Vigilante's true identity, I wouldn't be able to look at anyone without suspicion, would I? The trust I was working so hard to finally build would be on pause, wouldn't it?

Hunter's lips pressed firmly together as he came closer, the fury in his eyes intensifying. His hand shot up suddenly, cupping my jaw with a fierceness that made my breath catch in my throat.

"You're not leaving this house until Franco's caught," Hunter declared.

"The Vigilante could have been lying," I said, testing him to see what his reaction would be. "For all we know, there are no hit men out there."

"That's not a chance I'm willing to take," Hunter said.

Which didn't help. That could be a response, no matter who Hunter really was.

"We have no idea how long that will take," I said.

"I don't care."

"Well, I do. The police have been looking for him for two weeks—this could drag on for months. Maybe even longer."

"You can't leave this house, Luna. It's not safe. Give us some time. This is new intel, so the cops will put more people on it."

I evaluated him, unwilling to admit that I was scared. Being scared made me feel like I was letting the bad guys win, but I needed to be reasonable here. So did he.

"Fine," I said. "I'll reschedule every case on my calendar for the next week and hide out here. If they haven't caught Franco by then, I'll happily accept a *sharp* increase in security until they do."

Hunter didn't like this compromise. That was clear in the veins pulsing through his neck, but luckily, before he could argue this further, his cell phone rang.

When he pulled it out of his pocket and glanced at the screen, his lips turned down.

"Barry's waiting for me in my office," Hunter said. "Have Maria make you whatever you want for dinner."

He kissed my forehead before answering his phone and turning around.

"Grayson. I can't talk right now," Hunter said as he ambled out of the great room and down the lower-level hallway.

Leaving the upstairs completely empty...

The staircase stretched in front of me, my throat running dry at this sudden opportunity.

I couldn't pass this up.

I just hoped I wouldn't get caught...

CHAPTER 43
Hunter

"Candidly, I don't understand why you're giving me pushback," I said with restrained anger. "You were already investigating Franco."

"While working your father's case in parallel. You're asking me to allocate *all* resources to this."

"Until Franco's caught, yes."

Barry scratched the side of his temple.

My home office was usually a place of peace and order, but now it was tense and ominous, like a storm brewing on the horizon. The leather armchair looked like it was trying to swallow Barry as he sat in it while the window cast shadows that flickered across his face.

"With respect, sir," Barry started, "I was hired to investigate your father's murder. I've extended patience thus far, but you didn't hire me to chase after Franco Hopkins. Something like that is…"

Below his pay grade. That's what he was about to say.

I clenched my jaw and looked him steadily in the eye.

"Franco Hopkins represents an active threat against Luna. Her life is in danger. Is that not more important?"

"I have the names of several other private investigators that can take over the case of Franco Hopkins."

"I need you, Barry," I argued. "And I still don't understand your pushback. I've retained your services and am paying you top dollar. What difference does it make what I ask you to do?"

"I take pride in the types of cases I work, Mr. Lockwood. The unsolved murder of the patriarch of the Lockwood empire is something that sent shivers through the law enforcement community. It's a significant case for private investigators. Understanding who killed this powerful man and why is something that sparked my interest years ago, and that's the case I agreed to take on. Not Franco Hopkins. I have other jobs lined up, waiting for me once I've completed this one."

My voice grew desperate. "I'll double your pay."

He shook his head slowly. "It's not about the money, Mr. Lockwood."

I leaned forward in my chair, elbows on the mahogany desk. "Name your price. I'll make it worth your while."

His eyes shifted away from mine, but the words were firm. "The Chicago Police—"

"Are working a multitude of cases, this being only one of them. I need someone who wakes up every single day and has a team of people working this twenty-four hours a day, seven days a week until we locate Franco. I need somebody who is highly skilled at finding people and information that others cannot. And that person is you, Barry. So, tell me this. What is it going to take for you to work this case?"

Barry ran a frustrated hand across his jaw. I wondered if he was considering walking away, but if he did that, he would lose the opportunity to work on my father's unsolved murder case. And might spend the rest of his career regretting it.

People like Barry got off on the hunt, the thrill of the mystery solved. And the thrill of being the one to solve that mystery.

"I still want you to work on my father's case," I said. "That will not change, I assure you. But I will not be able to focus on anything so long as Luna is in danger."

Barry let out a deep, exasperated sigh. His gaze dropped to the ground, and he remained quiet for what felt like an eternity. Eventually, his eyes met mine, wrapped in contemplation.

"What's your plan once you find him?" Barry asked.

"Turn him over to the police. Have him arrested for threatening Luna and breaking into her cottage."

Barry stared at me.

"You could hire a team of people to help you with this," I said. "And I will fund that additional team for two years after our work together has concluded. Think about all the cases you could take on over the next couple of years with that extra help."

More mysteries to solve. No matter how much he denied it, money like that didn't come around every day.

Barry's fingers moved in slow, circular motions as he massaged his temples, his eyes closed in concentration.

I leaned back in my seat as silence stretched between us, heavy and palpable.

Finally, he opened his eyes, his gaze intense, before offering a slight nod.

My body dropped in relief. Finally a break.

I stood up and set off to find Luna.

To tell her the good news.

CHAPTER 44

Luna

Geez. I was overwhelmed by the sheer scale of Hunter's closet, not to mention the rich finish on the white shelves, built-in cabinets, and drawers. Meticulously arranged clothing, shoes, and accessories wrapped around a room larger than my entire cottage—complete with its own center island with a white-and-gray marble counter, where expensive-looking colognes were on display.

The smell of fine leather wafted through the air from a collection of exquisite Italian shoes that sat on the shelves along the far wall—each shelf with custom light. All held in the perfect temperature and humidity, thanks to the hum of the climate control system.

It was staggering. How could I look through the entire thing for clues fast enough?

And what was I looking for exactly? A confession note that said, *Dear diary, I'm secretly the Windy City Vigilante because I enjoy killing people, and I have an affinity for slitting throats?*

Ugh!

I quickly raced through his clothing first, looking for anything that resembled the Vigilante's black outfit, mask, and combat boots.

But there was nothing.

The Vigilante wouldn't be stupid enough to keep his suit in his own closet, though. Still, I rifled through the drawers, into the nooks behind his clothes, searching for a quick-change bag of some kind.

But there was nothing.

And the more I looked, the more I realized none of these clothes would even fit the Vigilante; he was bigger than Hunter. By three inches and twenty pounds, minimum.

The shoes were all the wrong size, too—far too small by three or four sizes, in fact. But I already knew all of this, so why had I questioned it?

Even if he was the right size, he was a prosecutor working all day on the other end of town. He wouldn't have the time to play Vigilante and hold a woman hostage. Not to mention, he'd have no reason to come check on me in the first place.

I lived with him right now, so Hunter could see firsthand how I was doing. There was also no need to go through the trouble of warning me about Franco the way he did.

And you know what? There was a legitimate reason I was struggling to trust Hunter, and it had nothing to do with the Vigilante. It had to do with my trust issues in general, worried he'd let me down, just like everyone else had done in the past.

That's what this was really about, wasn't it? This was me panicking, because up until now, I hadn't let myself get this close to anyone —this trusting of anyone—not even Sean. I was letting Hunter all the way into my heart, and clearly, my subconscious was so terrified that this would all crumble around me that my mind was coming up with possible scenarios of how it could come crashing down.

I was falling in love with him, I realized.

That's why I felt so scared.

That's why I was acting irrationally.

Hunter was *not* the Vigilante.

I sighed, relieved, but also frustrated with this itch I needed scratched. That left two suspects—both of which were the right height and weight and both had motives. Rodney was wrongfully imprisoned and burned by the justice system. Sean, whose girlfriend had been murdered, was a true crime podcaster who focused on horrific crimes where no one was ever prosecuted. He'd have the right equipment and detective skills to find the types of victims the Vigilante targeted.

But it couldn't be Sean. I couldn't handle it if it were him—I cared about Sean and trusted him.

No matter who it was, though, I had a defining choice to make.

Despite the Vigilante's desire to keep me safe, I couldn't let a personal relationship cloud rational judgment. I wasn't on board with allowing a serial killer to continue his reign of carnage, even in the name of justice. I couldn't let his spell blind me to his crimes.

If I believed in justice, there was only one thing to do.

Before I could chicken out or allow any doubts to enter my mind as to how to proceed, I pulled out my phone and drafted an email.

Mayor Kepler,

I'd like to meet with you in person regarding the Windy City Vigilante. I am starting to suspect he might be someone I know, and I'd like to discuss the appropriate steps to vet this. And how to protect the integrity of your search if I'm correct.

Sincerely,

Luna Payne

I pushed Send, shivering at the Pandora's box I just opened, but I couldn't sit here and panic for long. I was snooping, and I didn't want to get caught.

I shut off the lights in Hunter's closet, and exited his bedroom...

And bounced off his hard, muscular chest.

Hunter righted me by holding my upper arms, and then his suspicious eyes glanced past my shoulder.

"Were you in my room?"

Be honest. Tell him you were snooping and why. Tell him that you think the Vigilante might be someone you know.

No. Don't tell him. He's already panicked enough about Franco. Don't freak him out even more by telling him someone in your life might be a serial killer.

"I was looking for you." I smiled.

CHAPTER 45
Luna

Hunter was sprawled out on the couch, his shirtless torso illuminated by the fire's crackling glow as he typed away on his phone.

This was our last night before Hunter and I returned to work after taking off a few days together. Over the past week, I'd managed to get a lot of work done off-site. Between video calls and Hunter retrieving some case files from my office, my home confinement here proved to be less of a problem than I thought. And it was nice, not only living in a bubble with Hunter, but also seeing Hunter's brother Grayson and his uncle Alexander again, who'd stopped by for dinner one night.

That bubble was bursting though, because tomorrow, I needed to be in court. After that, I had a meeting with Mayor Kepler about my email—something I tried not to think about, since it gave me anxiety.

As I entered the room, my heart raced when his gaze traveled up my body, lingering on the curves that failed to hide beneath my tight spaghetti-strap tank top and skimpy boy shorts. His eyes burned into mine as I sat down next to him and grabbed the book I'd been reading off the side table.

I ran my finger across the spine, pretending to focus on it rather than the magnetic pull between us.

"If you want to read that book in peace, you need to change, Little Leopard," he growled.

I couldn't suppress my smirk, flattered that something as simple as a choice of clothing had the power to dominate him.

"This outfit is comfortable," I said.

Hunter's gaze was heavy and smoldering, like a bed of coal ready to burst into flames. The atmosphere in the room crackled with electricity as the flames ate another log in the fireplace.

And oh, how I was glad he'd sent his staff home for the day, leaving us all alone. Because right now, all I wanted was to be engulfed by him. Hunter had the power to make me forget all the problems lurking beyond his front door.

"Last warning. Change your outfit, or you won't read any pages tonight."

He pushed his hand against a growing bulge in his pants.

I looked at him, deadpan. And opened the book with a smirk.

That was all he needed.

With a throaty growl, Hunter threw his phone to the ground and grabbed my neck, pulling my mouth to his. Sliding his tongue along my upper lip, demanding I open up for him.

His kiss seared through me like a wildfire, setting off sparks from every nerve ending in my body that begged for more.

I gladly obliged, groaning when he slipped his tongue past my swollen lips. This man kissed like a king, like he'd studied it as a doctorate program. Heat blazed down my throat, shocking me between my thighs.

As Hunter continued kissing me, I reached over and rubbed the bulge in his pants, savoring the growl that escaped him. He shoved his hand through my hair and twisted until bites of pain prickled my scalp as I rubbed him up and down.

It felt empowering, knowing I had such an influence over such a strong, commanding man—his moans of helpless surrender captivating and thrilling.

"Get on your knees for me."

My heart pounded wildly in response to his command, my legs quivering with anticipation at the thought of him towering over me as I knelt before him.

I complied, Hunter standing from the couch and taking a position perpendicular to the fireplace as I snaked my fingers around his waistband.

I stared directly into his eyes as I began to tug his pants down, watching his pupils dilate as his erection was freed from the confines of the fabric.

Tossing his pants to the side, his impressive tool made my core pulse at the thought of it stretching inside of me.

Our eyes locked when I grasped it in one hand, exploring it tentatively with the other—savoring the way Hunter's breath hitched as I did so. He reached down to stroke my cheek before running his fingers through my hair and gathering it into his fist.

My mouth salivated in anticipation. I wrapped my fingers around his base and licked seductively around the crown, pushing my saliva down the shaft, teasing him as I worked my way back up.

Then I leaned down and took him into my mouth as far as I could, watching Hunter's head fall back in barely contained ecstasy. I worked my way back up, adding my hand to the base, wetting it with my saliva so I could stroke the part that my mouth couldn't accommodate.

I moved gently yet firmly, the vibrations of his delight rumbling in my throat. His hand pushed me closer to him, and his stare drilled through me.

I swirled my tongue around the tip again while he dragged himself out of my mouth and then plunged back in again, pushing deeper with each forceful thrust. His breaths became labored, and he groaned with unrestrained desire.

"Suck on it," he demanded in an animalistic growl, pushing himself back inside my mouth.

I gladly obeyed, hollowing my cheeks and falling into a rhythm.

Hunter's hips jerked from time to time in involuntary spasms—silent affirmations I was bringing him closer to the edge.

"Don't move," he commanded, his hands grabbing both sides of my head. He held me firmly in place as he bucked his hips, thrusting deeper than ever before. I could only moan as he filled my mouth, pushing so deep into the back of my throat, that I nearly choked while shock waves of thrill pulsed through my body.

My eyes watered from the sensation, but I loved every second of his dominance while my submission allowed him to lose control. I loved that he was using my body for his satisfaction, the way he'd used his tongue to satisfy me on the roof of his car.

"Your mouth feels so good."

I looked back up at him, watching his curled lips as he snapped his hips forcefully, moving in and out, faster and faster. Hunter Lockwood kept his gaze pinned to mine—a mixture of sexual hunger and something undefinable passing through them. His eyes were piercing, his affection coursing through my veins.

In that moment, I felt like he could see every piece of me, and I knew I was more than enough for him.

My mouth moved up and down his length with purpose, and I knew he was close with the tightening of his thighs.

"If you don't want me to finish in your mouth, you need to pull away now," Hunter warned.

But I didn't pull away. I watched Hunter's body shudder and quake as he roared my name, and warmth cascaded down my throat.

As soon as the last tremble subsided, Hunter pulled me to my feet and kissed me, his swollen lips hard against mine as he tugged the tank top over my head while guiding me backward. Was he taking me upstairs? It would take forever to get there, and the heat between my legs couldn't bear such a long wait.

But he didn't guide me up the grand staircase. Rather, Hunter sat on the fourth step and pulled my mouth to his.

He left a trail of kisses down my neck, to my chest, lingering on my breasts before taking a nipple into his mouth. My body arched as a wave of pleasure shot through me, and I threaded my fingers through his soft hair, watching him suck on the hardened peak. His hand squeezed my other breast firmly as he teased and caressed my aching nipple, sending waves of warmth crashing throughout my body.

He kissed my breasts hungrily, tenderly stroking my fevered skin and fanning the burning flame of desire between us as he slowly inched my shorts down and off.

Standing before him bare, my body trembled with passion. His gaze was intense as he ran his hand from my breast to my stomach before finally making his way to my center. One finger expertly slipping between my moist folds.

I gasped at the touch.

"You're so wet for me," Hunter rumbled, and then he slipped his middle finger into my entrance. Slowly at first, only to the knuckle, as he watched my mouth fall open before delving deeper inside me.

With his other hand, he pulled the back of my knee and guided my leg up, until my foot perched on the third step, my center exposed and vulnerable to him. His gaze was transfixed by the sight of his finger sliding in and out, curling to hit that hidden bundle of nerves.

It felt so damn good, I began to quiver.

Hunter moved his finger along the length of me, each stroke a little slower than the last, until far too soon, he pulled his hand away.

He laid his head back on the stairs and drew me closer to him.

At first, I didn't know what he was doing, because he was positioning my hips too high to align with his shaft.

"Put one knee here," he demanded, pulling my right knee down on the step a foot from his ear. "And the other here." He guided my left knee to the step below his head, so my center lined up with his face.

"Now lower yourself to my mouth, Little Leopard." His voice was thick with desire.

"I...I don't want to hurt you."

His eyes snapped to mine, smoldering. "Don't make me tell you twice," he warned impatiently, like a starving man with a freshly prepared meal in front of him.

I did as he said, gasping when he welcomed my center with his tongue, his possessive grip on my hips keeping me in place like a helpless offering.

I grabbed the railing for support as he licked the sides of my center slowly, base to tip, one side at a time. Teasing me as the heat between my legs became unbearable.

Every caress that didn't hit the bundle of nerves was sweet, agonizing torture. But he continued his tantalizing pattern of almost-theres until finally, he flattened his tongue and licked up my center to that sweet spot between my legs.

I moaned, grabbing his hair as his tongue circled the apex of my sex, lightly at first. Around and around until it grew in intensity.

He stared up at me, adoration mixed with yearning, radiating from his gorgeous eyes.

I wished I could get a bird's-eye view of this—Hunter sprawled out naked on his stairs, holding my thighs, as I sat on the face of one of the most powerful men in this country.

His tongue flicked, delighting every nerve ending, my walls tightening with desire as he drank me in, savoring my every drop like a precious elixir.

He slowed his tempo, making my wave build slowly, painfully making me wait for it, knowing the release would be a thousand times better for it.

My inner walls clenched at the sight of him beneath me, his tongue flicking out from my sex, our eyes locked on each other in an ultimate connection.

My hips began to move slightly, inciting a groan that rumbled from his throat against the sensitive tissue. Quickening my pace, my mouth fell open wider as his tongue swirled around me, and he began to suck, coaxing ripples in the depths of my core. I speared my fingers through his hair, guiding him exactly where I wanted him to be.

Every inch of my body throbbed with need. I shuddered, eagerly grinding myself against his tongue while he expertly teased every sensitive nerve.

My walls clenched harder against the tsunami of ecstasy building, about to break over.

"Don't stop," I whimpered.

Provoking Hunter to growl and squeeze my breasts as his tongue gained momentum. Circling me. Sucking on me.

The man was a magician with his tongue. If he were mine, I'd beg for this to be on the menu every single night.

I was so close now, and as he squeezed my nipples and kept his blue eyes locked on mine, I grabbed the back of his neck, grinding harder against his tongue.

The guy knew exactly how to work my body, but holding him there, riding out the release, made it so much better.

A tingling sensation traveled through my body until a crash of pleasure erupted through my core.

"Hunter!" I pulled his face harder against me, surrendering to him completely.

He let out a low, guttural growl as my hips bucked. His strong hands gripped my thighs and forced them down, pinning me to his face—his burning tongue swirling around my center, every lick like lightning igniting my flesh.

He licked and swirled against me, riding every last wave of my orgasm, as I continued to shutter and moan his name.

With the last quiver subsiding, I looked down at Hunter, and my heart trembled. His strong body beneath me, his eyes locked with mine, a wave of emotion washed over me as the realization sank in harder than it had before.

"I'm falling in love with you," I professed.

Hunter carefully studied my face. Had I crossed the line by saying it? Scared him away, even? What if he didn't feel the same way? I mean, love was an extraordinarily strong word. I knew he cared for me greatly, cared for me more than anyone else in my life seemed to, but love denotes a powerful emotion that could certainly complicate things between us.

Especially for someone like him, who'd had his heart broken by losing his parents.

Hunter pushed me off of him, scooted me to the side, and stood up.

My heart sank.

I just screwed everything up, didn't I?

Suddenly, though, his reason for standing up became clear when he grabbed ahold of my waist and hoisted me up so my legs wrapped around his torso. He carried me back to the great room and laid me down on the rug in front of his fireplace. The heat of it warmed the left side of my body when he positioned himself over me.

He lined himself up between my legs and leaned his lips down to hover over mine as he stared into my eyes.

"Tell me that again," he growled.

My heart danced with joy, and I wrapped my fingers through his hair, making sure his blue eyes were securely clasped on to mine as I uttered the words that would forever transform our relationship.

"I'm falling in love with you," I whispered.

In one swift motion, Hunter plunged inside of me and consumed my mouth with his own as he began to slowly move his hips. Delicately, not angry this time.

I moaned and arched my back, inciting a growl from Hunter's throat as he pulled back and looked down at me once more.

"I've already fallen, Luna," he said, moving his hips steadily, methodically. He rolled his lower body, swirling over that sweet spot of nerves as he held my gaze, letting our words settle into our souls.

I grabbed the back of his neck and pulled his mouth to mine.

The backs of my eyes stung, realizing this was what true love felt like. Like everything. All-consuming. Happiness, strength, and vulnerability, all mingled together in a heavenly way.

I wasn't just falling for him, either. I'd already fallen, too. I loved this man with my whole soul.

Hunter really began to move, watching my face as he hit all the right spots, watching me come undone beneath him over and over again. His hands roamed over my body, his mouth exploring my breasts as he slowed himself down—I suspected to keep himself from crashing over the edge sooner than he wanted.

Even the slow weight of his hips pressed against mine couldn't stop the tsunami of pleasure that kept crashing around him repeatedly.

We made love three times before finally surrendering to exhaustion, wrapped in each other's arms on the floor of the great room.

CHAPTER 46

Luna

"What's it like? Living in a mansion?"

Beneath my ear, Hunter's heart beat in a perfect rhythm. We were lying nude on the rug, the fireplace dwindling after hours of lovemaking. The logs kept spitting, like they were just as exhausted as we were, and the smell of sex blended with the smoky scent of the wood.

"You've been staying here," he said with a hint of amusement, trailing his fingers down my bare back.

"Yeah, but, to me, it feels like a temporary getaway. What's it like, having so much living space?"

Hunter seemed to consider this. "The bigger the place, the more rooms that are empty. The bigger the reminder that you're alone."

I traced my fingernails along his chest. "Why do you live here if it makes you sad?"

Drawing in a long inhale, Hunter's rising chest lifted my head before he slowly released a deep, resounding breath.

"This is the only tangible connection to my father I have left. I kept everything the same in this house for the longest time, but then, during a particularly dark period of my life, I had a massive renovation done. I convinced myself that if this place looked different, all the memories of him would hurt less, because they wouldn't smack me in the face every time I turned around."

"Why were you going through a dark period?" I asked.

Hunter trailed his fingers up and down my back three times as he stared pensively at the grand room ceiling.

"My whole life has been one long, dark period, Luna." The sadness in his tone made my stomach wrench in empathy. "It's just that sometimes, the dark is so oppressive, you can't see anything past it."

My throat swelled at the despair lurking beneath the surface, hiding, but always there to take him down.

When I first met Hunter, I thought he had everything together. His wealth, his looks, blogs tripping over themselves to try to get his attention. So did the ladies and anyone else who thirsted for him or for his wealth or power, for that matter. It never crossed my mind that inside, he might be hurting just as badly as I had been. Maybe even more so.

"But I suppose," Hunter continued, "that particular time in my life was especially hard, because I had a private investigator come back after a six-month investigation with absolutely no more information on my father's killer."

Oh gosh, I knew exactly what it felt like to hit dead end after dead end with my father's case, too. It was a brutal torture to keep pushing, because the only way to keep pushing was to keep hope alive, no matter how many times it nearly perished.

"I felt hopeless that I would ever get to the bottom of what really happened to my father," Hunter continued, "and I was trapped in this house with his memories haunting me everywhere I looked. Just like my brothers had warned me could happen when I insisted on buying our home after Mom died. I thought about selling this place, but I couldn't bring myself to do it. I just wanted to hurt less. So, I settled for a renovation."

I trailed my finger along his abs.

"Did it help? Did the renovation make you feel better?"

"No."

The poor guy.

"In all these years, there's only been one thing that stopped the pain, Luna."

He tilted my chin up, so he was looking directly into my eyes, his blue gems seeming to pierce my soul.

"You," he said.

I blinked back tears, my heart fluttering, splintering, and reforming, all in the space of a second. His words echoed in the hollow compartments of my mind, reverberating sentiments I'd only dreamed of hearing.

For the first time, I truly felt seen, adored, and cherished. And I felt more than just special to another soul—I felt indispensable and irreplaceable.

"I know this all seems sudden," he continued. "It's crazy how quickly feelings can develop in such a short amount of time, but it doesn't diminish how I feel about you."

I nodded. "I feel the same way." Shocked at how quickly things could change.

"For as long as I can remember, the only thing that has inhabited my heart has been pain. But you've managed to push that pain aside and fill my heart with…joy instead. Because of you, I don't feel that constant ache anymore, Luna."

I wanted to store those words in my bones to be released at steady beats throughout the rest of my life.

"Falling in love with you has made me realize something," he said. "I've spent my entire life convinced that the only thing that will make me feel whole is finding my father's killer. But even if I find the guy who murdered my dad, nothing will bring my father back. That's what I've been chasing."

"You shouldn't give up the hunt," I said.

"I won't. I'll still work to find him, but not for the same reasons as before. Now, it's about closure. And getting justice for my father. But as for making me feel complete, *you* make me feel whole, Luna. Only you."

My heart quivered against his soft words that wrapped my chest in a comforting embrace.

I was honored that he was again sharing such deep professions with me that I suspected, based on the pain in his voice, he never shared with anyone, and it gave me the courage to keep digging, because I wanted to learn every fragment of his soul and piece it together in my heart's puzzle.

"What was it like for you," I whispered, "losing him?"

Hunter was silent for long enough that a log completely split open and cracked with a loud pop.

"You would think that me witnessing my father's murder," Hunter started, "would allow me to skip the denial stage of grief. The one where you keep questioning if they're really gone. But grief is a complicated beast, I guess.

"Because for a while, every night when I was lying in bed, I would stare at my bedroom door, expecting him to walk through it and tuck me in as usual. We'd talk about my day, like we always did, and he'd ask me about my day's high and low points. Both, he'd always say, were opportunities to learn and grow."

From the brief pause in Hunter's voice, I could discern the faint, strained sound of him swallowing hard.

"Three months before my dad died, he'd given me a journal as a birthday present. So, after he died, when he was no longer here to tuck me in at night, I would write to him about my day in it, describing the high and low points. It was hard to find a high point, because I was just drowning in sadness, and I had lost all hope...

"But I wanted to keep our tradition alive, so I'd force myself to find one thing, no matter how small it might be. Like maybe I spotted one of Dad's favorite trees—a weeping willow. The low point each day was always the same—that he wasn't there with me to see it."

My eyes stung. I remembered all those times as a kid, wishing my dad were with me to see special things too. Or even mundane things, for that matter.

"I would end each entry the same, telling him that I loved him, that I missed him, and that I would give anything to have just one more hug from him."

Hugs. We place so much value on material possessions, but many of us just wish to hold someone we lost.

"After he died"—Hunter's voice cracked slightly—"I couldn't stop thinking about the days leading up to his death and how much I took his presence for granted, assuming that I could see him whenever I wanted. Like in the mornings, when my dad would be sitting at the table, having his coffee. I'd gotten this PlayStation for my birthday, and I was always playing some stupid game, tuning him out instead of acknowledging him."

Hunter shook his head.

"I'd give anything to go back and treasure that time with him. I wish I had known those were going to be the last mornings I'd ever have with him. I wish I'd talked to him, hugged him, and just...savored those last ordinary moments instead of playing that stupid game and barely answering him when he tried to talk to me. Because they turned out to be the most precious moments of my life. And I wasted them."

My eyes brimmed with tears, and I held on to him tighter, wishing I could take some of his pain and put it on my heart to ease his suffering.

Hunter kissed me, and once again, everything shifted between us, because he was being so raw and honest with me, giving me a glimpse into his most complicated emotions. I felt honored and privileged that he was sharing something so deeply personal with me.

When he eventually pulled back his kiss, he stroked my cheek with his fingers.

"I want you to move in here permanently," he said, taking me off guard. "I want you to be *mine*, Little Leopard. Only *mine*."

I smiled.

"Move in with me."

I couldn't believe that his proposition of living together didn't freak me out. Yes, I loved Hunter, but moving our relationship to the next level was a big deal, one that left me vulnerable.

"You don't want to move in," he surmised, based on the hesitation reflected in my features.

"No, it's not that. It's just…I guess the fear of getting hurt is still there, even when you're with someone you trust."

Hunter's eyebrows furrowed into pain. "And you think I'll hurt you."

There were many ways in which to hurt someone. And not fully supporting me in my quest to exonerate my dad topped the list.

"I believe in my father's innocence, but you may not, and as I go through these court dates with him and I continue to research his case, I can't handle it if you betray me the way everybody else did when he was found guilty. I can't handle one more person betraying me like that, Hunter. Especially you."

In his eyes, there was a blend of compassion and empathy, as if Hunter wished he could protect me from the painful memories of my past.

"I'm scared too," Hunter admitted. "That once you see how broken I am, you'll walk away from me."

I had already seen some broken parts of him. The possessive part who literally carried me into his kitchen after getting attacked at the prison. The man who'd put up cameras around my property against my will. I knew Hunter might have some boundaries we'd have to work on, but that was what love was about, wasn't it? Loving someone despite their flaws?

"I won't leave you," I said.

Something flashed through his eyes, and he broke his gaze with mine as despair cascaded through his features—despair that made my heart wrench.

"Luna, I have something to tell you."

My heart spasmed in fear as my mind raced for clues to what it might be. Hunter Lockwood had a reputation for being a playboy. Had he been dating another woman on the side?

Or far worse, when he'd been looking into my dad's case, had he found some pretty damning evidence?

"Mr. Lockwood?" Maria called out from the kitchen.

Holy crap. I jumped up before Maria could see my nakedness, but Hunter was more subdued with his movements, slow, even. I charged up the stairs and into the guest bedroom, where I waited for him to arrive a few seconds later. Still completely nude, still with that somber look on his face.

"What is it?" I asked, my heart firmly lodged in my throat again.

He swallowed. "We need to leave in a few minutes for work. Let's have dinner tonight, and we can discuss a few things."

"Just tell me now," I pleaded.

He cleared his throat. Looked down. "This isn't something I want to rush, Luna. I'm sorry. I shouldn't have said anything until after work."

The morning sun streamed through the windows, reflected on the clock's screen. Crap. I had a court case starting soon.

It scared me that in a few hours, he might say something that had the power to change everything.

CHAPTER 47

Luna

"I don't know. That's all he said." My driver pulled onto Lakeshore Drive, the city skyline appearing taller.

My driver's eyes tightened when looking in the rearview mirror, but I thought nothing of it.

"Listen, ninety percent of the reason I hate this guy is because he's not good enough for you," Sean said.

"And the other ten percent?"

"What's not to hate about a billionaire who drives a car the rest of us only dream of?"

I smiled.

I felt like a traitor answering Sean's phone call when I had suspected he might be the Vigilante. Especially since the more I thought about it, the less likely it seemed.

In fact, now that I was no longer panicking about it, I didn't think anyone in my life was the Vigilante. What the hell was I thinking, sending that email to the mayor, telling him I suspected the Vigilante was someone I knew? I could've just triggered an investigation that would put an innocent person behind bars, someone that I cared about.

I, of all people, should have known better after what happened with my dad. I'd been reckless, putting the people I cared about in danger of becoming another innocent person charged with a crime they didn't commit. When I met with Mayor Kepler later today, I needed to backpedal.

Fast.

And hope to the Lord it would work. Because out of all the people that they might home in on, my dad's friend and old cellmate, Rodney, was most at risk of being targeted by an investigation. He was a convicted felon with a grudge, who had been released from prison shortly before the attacks started.

The chances of him being wrongfully suspected were high.

And I was ashamed of myself for putting him, or anyone else, in that position.

"So, as much as it pains me to say this," Sean said, bringing me back to the conversation at hand, "is it possible you're freaking out because of your trust issues?"

"You didn't see the look on his face. I think whatever he's about to tell me is going to be something very bad."

"You're scared he's going to let you down," Sean surmised.

"I'm scared of getting my heart broken."

I heard Sean's drawn-out sigh.

"Do you have any idea what it could be?" he asked.

My stomach clenched. The truth was, I did have a gut feeling. But I couldn't say it out loud: that Hunter had his private investigator looking into my dad's case and might have come back with something damning. Something that might even prove my father's guilt.

It was unfathomable that my father might actually be guilty.

My whole world as I knew it would be rewritten. Hunter knew I'd never be able to cope with it, and he probably knew it had the power to bring down our relationship before it even started. That was why he wasn't going to rush the conversation.

But that couldn't be it. It'd be too painful.

I glanced at the three bodyguards in my sedan—the driver, the one in the passenger seat, and one back here with me. I turned away from them all and covered my hand over my mouth as I whispered into the phone.

"Maybe he's fathered a dozen secret babies."

Sean chuckled.

"Luna, this guy has been in the spotlight since he was a kid. News organizations, bloggers…everybody under the sun has researched this guy—even private investigators trying to help reporters unearth a scandalous story to help sell papers. And in the process, any hidden skeletons have been dug up and are probably already in online articles."

That's right. I sat up straighter.

"You researched H…" I cleared my throat. "When you were looking into the…" Lockwood case. "So, you read about him. What were some of the things that came out?"

"Luna…"

"Just tell me."

Sean sighed. "The problem with some of these reporters is that you can't always sift through what's fact from fiction. I mean, they get a lead on a possible story, and they run it with a caveat. Even if it's not true."

"And some of those stories were?" I pressed.

"Anything from allegations of him being a playboy, to having secret children, to knowingly putting innocent people behind bars." My gut clenched. "One article even shared a wild accusation made against Hunter stemming from when he was a kid. The family's lawyers sued for defamation over it."

"What claim?"

"It was bullshit. It came from some former housekeeper who lost her job after Hunter's dad was murdered and they downsized the staff. She claims she overheard some kind of confession that Hunter made."

"A confession."

"It was ridiculous. Police even checked out the woman's claim before it was ultimately dismissed. And the family won the defamation suit."

I turned my head toward the window, whispering into the phone again.

"So, tell me what this so-called confession was if it was so ridiculous. Even if it's not true, as his girlfriend, it would help me understand what he's been through and what he's been accused of."

"Luna..."

"You know I'm not going to believe accusations just because someone made them. So, just tell me, what was it?"

Sean hesitated, and after a few seconds, he said, "There was a rumor that he was the one who killed his dad."

"He was nine."

"Exactly. He wouldn't have the physical strength to take down a man of that size, which is why it was beyond ridiculous. My point is, no one has uncovered anything earth-shattering about this guy that proved to be true, even after all that investigating. So, as much as I hate the dude, don't let fear be the reason you break up with him. Break up with him because he's a dickwad."

I rolled my eyes.

"You know what this is actually about, don't you?"

"Do tell," I said.

"The hard part about trusting someone completely is that it opens you up to potential heartbreak. Again, don't get me wrong. I would love nothing more than for you to leave his ass in the wind, but life is going to deal you a million reasons to start doubting people. And if you do that, you'll wind up miserable."

I sighed. He was right.

I watched as we turned toward Michigan Avenue, all the pedestrians walking along happily, like they were going to have the best day of their lives. Not spend it worrying about what bombshell their boyfriend was about to drop.

"Thanks, Sean."

His voice turned playful. "Let's say, hypothetically, he's going to tell you he's totally broke. Wouldn't that be a tragedy?"

I smirked. "Okay. I'm almost to the office, so I should probably let you go."

"All that being said, if he does break your heart, I'll end him."

I rolled my eyes again. "Do you want to have lunch today?"

My offer slipped out before I could think. It's funny how you go your whole life not worrying that Franco Hopkins or one of his paid goons is about to jump out from around the corner and cut you in half with a hatchet.

"I can't," Sean said. "I'm actually out of town."

"Really?"

"Duty calls."

How strange. I swore I could hear the "L" train—with its highly distinguishable metal grating noise—grinding in his background. In fact, I did hear it.

Which meant Sean wasn't out of town; he was in Chicago.

Why would Sean lie about his whereabouts?

I was about to challenge him on it, but he said, "Talk to you later, Luna," and hung up before I had the chance.

Unsettled, my eyes drifted back to the driver, who was still staring in the rearview mirror.

"We're being followed," he said in a tense voice.

CHAPTER 48
Luna

In the early morning hours, downtown Chicago was transformed into a tranquil sanctuary, the recently risen sun casting a soft orange glow over the towering skyscrapers—its light kissing the reflective glass of the sixty-story buildings that defined the skyline. The smell of freshly made coffee wafted through the air as local cafés began brewing their first pots, infusing the atmosphere with warmth and comfort.

Echoes of car engines and the metallic screech of the "L" train served as a reminder that soon, the metropolis would be overflowing with people. But at this hour, only the early risers peppered the streets and sidewalks with cars and pedestrians. In these quiet, serene moments, the city exuded an air of calmness.

Until now, that was.

"Four cars back," the driver, Leo, said. "Audi A8. Black. Tinted windows. No plate."

I glanced behind us. Our black sedan rumbled through the skyscrapers as if it were carving a path through a tunnel of steel and glass. We had been driving leisurely, but now, the engine groaned, and my back pressed against the seat with the force of the increased speed.

"I'll call it in," Carl, the front-seat passenger, said.

While he did that, Leo changed lanes, watching in the rearview mirror for what the other vehicle would do next. I quickly glanced out the back window and saw that the black Audi changed lanes, too.

My heart accelerated, and my mouth ran dry, but I was fine. I was safe, protected in the car with three bodyguards—bodyguards that I was suddenly incredibly grateful for.

"We can't take her to the office. Plan B," Leo said.

"What's plan B?" I asked.

Leo changed lanes again, swerving to the right so quickly that my body jerked. My back pressed harder into the seat as the engine revved even higher, vibrating the leather with its acceleration.

I couldn't stop my eyes from glancing back again, like looking at a bad car accident. As we'd increased our speed to double the posted limit, so had the black car following us.

While Carl called the Audi's pursuit into Hunter's private security team, I searched around the vehicle for any kind of weapon. Surely, it wouldn't come to that. In the unlikely event the Audi caught up to us *and* intended to attack, all three bodyguards were armed, and they were highly trained in protecting people from assailants.

The pins and needles shooting through my fingers didn't seem to agree, though.

Our engine ground even louder as our driver swerved left and then right, cars and trucks flying past us, merely inches from my window. All the while, the black Audi gained on us, following our maneuvers with ease, as if we were in the middle of a video game and they were highly skilled at this course.

There was absolutely no doubt they were following us. And there was no doubt, based on the reckless driving, that if they caught us, they weren't just here to talk.

The streets of Chicago became an unintended racetrack as we navigated the city's concrete labyrinth. The buildings that lined the roads flashed by in a blur, like abstract paintings in shades of gray and beige. The iconic architecture of the city—soaring skyscrapers and historic facades—created a terrifying backdrop for our chase.

The seat belt cut into my shoulder and chest, a constant reminder of the dangerous speeds we were traveling. My ears filled with the symphony of the city—the cacophony of honking horns, the faint screech of tires against asphalt, and the ever-present hum of the wind as it whistled past our windows. The sound of the engine was a powerful, guttural growl that resonated deep within me, vibrating my bones.

"Police headquarters is on Michigan," Leo said to Gabriel—the bodyguard sitting to my left. "Call ahead and tell them we're coming. Have police ready, and armed. Carl, text Red, let him know the plan."

These guards were smart. They were going to use this chase to their advantage and lead these guys into a trap. An army of police officers waiting to take them down the minute we turned into the parking lot.

And at this speed, we'd be there in no time.

Now, I could only hope that the Audi wouldn't give up chase.

But my relief was short-lived, because to keep the Audi at a safe distance behind us, we had to keep increasing our speed. First forty miles an hour. Then fifty. Then sixty. Downtown Chicago streets were not set up for these kinds of speeds. Even in the lighter morning traffic, there were still too many cars on the roads to support it with no shoulders to leverage. Instead, massive buildings encased us from all sides. Not to mention, there were lights and crosswalks.

Crosswalks peppered with pedestrians—including mothers holding the hands of their small children, who could be out having breakfast before the start of school.

We might not make it to Chicago Police Headquarters. Not without killing someone first.

The piercing sound of screeching tires pinched my eardrums every time the vehicle swerved and dodged through the traffic.

A block ahead of us, a traffic light turned from green to yellow, warning it would be red before we arrived.

"Red light!" I shouted.

But Leo gunned the engine. I held on to the seat, my fingers digging into the leather. With my heart racing, I watched in horror as a young mother holding her son's hand stepped closer to the cross-walk, oblivious to the danger approaching.

"Stop!" I screamed.

But Leo continued to dart around vehicles and plunged through that crosswalk and through that intersection, narrowly missing the mother and child. I turned around in a panic, but thankfully, the mother had yanked her little boy back, terror filling her eyes, as the Audi mirrored our movements, nearly hitting them.

"This is too dangerous!" I snapped. "We're going to kill someone!"

"Police are ready," Gabriel said to Leo, ignoring my pleas.

I refused to let this trail of devastation infect the city and endanger the people in it. These innocent bystanders didn't deserve to lose their lives just to try to save mine.

"Slow down," I begged.

But suddenly, a new danger appeared before us.

Construction. Orange cones sectioned off the street ahead of us, a construction worker standing in front of a dump truck with a sign that said *Stop*. It was one of those construction setups where only one lane of traffic could go in and out at a time, but right now, both lanes needed to stop.

Because behind the man, a blue-and-white cement truck was lurching through the intersection—currently blocking more than half of it and closing the distance to block it all. It might as well have been a brick wall in front of us, because with buildings on both sides and a wall of traffic to our left, there was nowhere to turn around.

"Hold on," Leo snarled.

He did not slow down. The construction worker started waving his hands, but when he realized we weren't going to slow or stop, he jumped out of the way and onto the sidewalk just in the nick of time. Our sedan jerked to the left, around the dump truck, and careened through the intersection so close to the still-advancing cement truck that our right-side mirror clipped off with a pop.

Behind us, the Audi tried to follow our path, but they were two seconds too late. The cement truck was blocking the intersection now; there was no way around it.

I swear, my heart had never beaten so fast in my life.

"That was too close," Leo finally said, *finally* slowing down. He kept his eyes trained on the rearview and left-side mirrors, looking for any hint of that Audi.

"No shit," Carl agreed. "When do you think they made us?"

"I don't know. But I don't think they randomly saw us on the streets of the city," Leo said.

"You think they followed us from Lockwood's estate?" Carl asked.

Leo was silent for a minute, as if mentally retracing our steps. We had left the estate from the sanctuary of the garage, and surely, we would have noticed any vehicles in the long driveway to the road. Theoretically, we would've noticed someone parked along that road, too. But somehow, they'd found us, and I agreed with the driver: I didn't think they randomly found us in downtown Chicago.

"If they were following us all the way from Mr. Lockwood's place, why wouldn't they have intercepted us sooner?" Carl asked, his voice tight with worry.

"I don't know. Maybe they assumed we could outrun them on the highway."

"So, why not intercept us on the side streets near the Lockwood estate? Be a lot easier to pull it off there than on the streets of the city."

Leo licked his lips. "It's possible they'd seen how heavily secured the Lockwood estate was. Might assume an army of guards would come after them there, but here, it would just be us."

"What does your gut say?"

To this, Leo looked even more conflicted, scrubbing his jaw.

"Call a possible threat in against Lockwood himself."

"You think they're going after him too?"

"If they want Ms. Payne and any information she might have—and they know that she's been staying at the Lockwood estate instead of the cottage—they might be interested to find out if she shared any of that information with Mr. Lockwood."

Oh my God. "You think Hunter's in danger?"

Leo looked at me through the rearview mirror. "Don't worry, Ms.

Payne. It's just a precaution. You're safe now, and we'll be taking you—"

The pop of a gunshot and high-pitched cracking of glass preceded the high-pitched squeal of our tires, just as the driver jerked and then dropped his hands from the wheel.

At that moment, time seemed to slow down to an almost standstill, my brain slowly registering the gruesome scene before me. The dashboard was splattered with blood, red drops dripping down the navigation screen as Leo's head hung unnaturally to the side, his eye nothing more than a gory hole of blood and flesh.

The car accelerated, Leo's foot evidently pressing harder against the gas pedal, as if his body had jerked when he'd been shot and then remained in that tense position. With the engine revving up higher, our sedan began to careen to the left.

"Shit!" Carl grabbed the steering wheel and tried to pull us back into our lane.

"Kick his leg off the gas!" Gabriel said.

"I can climb over." I had the best angle, diagonal from the driver. I could climb over the center console, and since I was the smallest person in the car, I had the best chance of wiggling between him and the dashboard to kick his foot off the gas and press mine to the brake. But just as I grabbed my seat belt's buckle, Gabriel placed his hand over mine.

"Keep your seat belt on."

"I can't get his foot off!" Carl screamed.

The metallic beast careened wildly through the urban maze of towering skyscrapers—the cityscape blurring into a dizzying whirl of high-rises as our car sped toward its inevitable catastrophe. At the intersection, a traffic light blinked its futile warning. Horns blared from other vehicles, their drivers slamming on their brakes in a desperate attempt to avoid the speeding missile.

Carl's knuckles were white as he tried to control the car, but the car swerved violently from one lane to another, narrowly avoiding pedestrians who dived out of its path.

With each near miss, the car continued its rampage, forcing

onlookers to scatter, their screams drowned out by the deafening roar of the engine. Teetering on the precipice of disaster, my throat clenched as I tightened my seat belt, bracing for impact as the car lunged into a busy intersection.

With one final, horrifying swerve, a guttural crunch sent my body into my seat belt like a bullet, and then aftershocks of bent metal and shattering glass mingled with gravity pulling my body in different directions.

It took me a few moments to get my bearings, immense pressure flooding my head as I dangled upside down in the wreckage. My ear was squealing a high-pitched note, broken glass scattered around me. Gabriel groaned to my left, reaching for his ankle holster, but Carl wasn't so lucky. He lay half inside and half outside the vehicle, his body having burst through the windshield upon impact, his head wedged between the hood and the asphalt.

His skull reminded me of a broken egg that had fallen from its bird's nest at the top of a tree—its goopy insides spilling out onto the pavement.

Shock consumed me, but I needed to snap out of it quickly if I had any chance to live. I couldn't allow myself the seconds to assess this shock or ascertain my injuries.

Because walking toward us through the echoes of screams and car horns was a man holding a semiautomatic rifle. He was dressed in camouflage, as if entering a battle in the middle of a forest instead of an urban city of steel.

Gabriel grunted as his gun finally broke free from its holster.

I grabbed my seat belt and clicked the button, thumping to the roof of the vehicle. Shock was a good thing, masking pain with adrenaline.

The camouflaged man was only thirty feet away and closing, and behind him were two more men. Also holding guns.

People around the intersection ran with screams while in here, I quickly gauged my best shot at survival. I needed to run, but I also needed a weapon, and just in case I failed to escape, I needed my phone.

I glanced around, spotting it on the roof of the car, which was now the floor. I stretched my arm toward it, groaning and extending my fingers until my nail caught the lip of the case and pulled. Once. Twice. The third time, it shifted within my reach, so I grabbed it—a quick *thank God* ringing in my head—and shoved my cell phone into my pants to hide it.

Gabriel started firing off shots out of his smashed open window with a *pop-pop-pop-pop*.

With bullets exploding around me, a flood of relief filled me when I spotted Leo's ankle dangling within reach. I shifted closer, pulled up his pant leg over the holster, and unstrapped the gun—grabbing it tightly.

I risked a quick glance and noted the camouflaged man was now only ten feet away. And with one final pop, he nailed Gabriel in the forehead.

A shocked gasp escaped me as he went limp, but I couldn't let myself slow down. I began crawling through the open window on the opposite side of the man, groaning as shards of glass dug into my elbows.

But I wasn't fast enough. Two hands grabbed my upper arms and wrenched me from the confines of the twisted metal, throwing me onto my back.

I aimed my gun at his crotch and pulled the trigger.

But to my horror, the gun merely clicked.

My eyes widened as his tightened, and then the camo man kicked the gun out of my hands and slapped me across the face before grabbing my arms and yanking me to my feet.

The man's bald head gleamed in the morning light, his muscles so massive, they had to have been formed with a generous dose of steroids. A pulsating network of veins wrapped around his tattooed neck, slithering like serpents wanting to escape his body.

"Trying to shoot me was an unwise move, you stupid bitch." Another slap. "I'm going to take my time with you for that."

My stomach sank.

He began pulling me toward his vehicle, but if he thought he'd take me without a fight, he was wrong. I leaned down and bit his hand, but that only made him squeeze my arms so harshly, that I worried the bones were about to snap, making my eyes burn with tears. I glanced around at the handful of pedestrians fleeing from the massacre, but none of them had weapons or were willing to go up against three armed men who had left at least three dead bodies in their wake.

I began kicking him, flailing, thrashing.

"Fine, you stupid bitch. We'll do it the hard way."

He shoved me to the ground and then raised his gun, slamming the butt of it against my skull.

Making everything go black.

CHAPTER 49
Hunter

"What the fuck do you mean, she's missing?" I stood in my ADA office, clenching the phone so hard, I swear the screen was about to crack.

"I got a call from Carl that they were being chased by a black Audi," Red explained.

Mac "Red" O'Sullivan had been with me for years. Always impeccably dressed in a suit, complete with a discreet earpiece and concealed weapon, he had a muscular build and fiery red hair.

"Follow-up text said they were heading to Chicago Police Headquarters on Michigan Avenue. They planned to lure the Audi there, but they never made it. And now, all three men aren't answering their phones."

I grabbed two fistfuls of his shirt and slammed the redhead of bad news against the wall, my voice simmering with fury as I asked, "Where the fuck is she?"

Red's face began to turn crimson from the pressure I was putting on his chest, even though he could take me down with ease.

He was highly skilled in various forms of martial arts and hand-to-hand combat with a black belt in Krav Maga and a proficient knowledge of Brazilian jiujitsu.

His background in the military made him an effective strategist when it came to assessing potential threats and planning contingencies.

But he'd screwed up this time. Massively.

The plan hadn't worked—three armed bodyguards. Driven from our garage to the front door of work, Luna flanked by two of the men while a third provided extra cover. One would remain by the building's entrance to assess every single person coming into that building, one would be stationed outside her office door, and one positioned inside.

He swallowed hard, his voice strained as he spoke.

"I pinged Luna's phone," he gasped. "Hers is on the move."

I loosened my grip around his shirt slightly.

"Luna still has her phone?"

"Appears so, sir."

How did she manage that?

Because she's smart as hell, Hunter. She wouldn't let herself get taken without a way to call for help.

With a frustrated growl, I pushed off him and shoved a hand through my hair as the rage inside me mixed with an icy terror.

"Where the hell are they taking her?"

And what were they going to do to her once they got there?

CHAPTER 50
Luna

Pain smashing into my cheekbone pulled me from the abyss of darkness. It took me a moment to stretch my eyelids open, a light blinding them as a blurry figure in front of me crystallized into a solid form.

"Wake up, bitch," he said.

My gaze traveled from his black shoes and slacks up to his black button-down shirt before staring into the eyes of Franco Hopkins. Smirking, sucking on a toothpick between his teeth.

Several more seconds dragged on while memories flooded back of being chased through the streets of Chicago, crashing, and my bodyguards losing their lives simply for trying to keep me safe.

All so Franco Hopkins could abduct me and what, kill me?

No.

If he wanted to kill me, he would have done that at the crash scene.

The question was, how long did I have until he did kill me? And how could I get myself out of this?

A lone metal chair pressed against my back, creaking slightly as my gaze swept through the vast expanse of what seemed to be an abandoned warehouse. The air was heavy with the pungent scent of damp wood and rusted metal, subtly mixed with the lingering odor of mold and mildew. The echo of water dripping from a leaky roof reverberated throughout the space, creating an eerie and unsettling soundtrack.

A pair of harsh, incandescent lamps pierced the thick darkness, casting long, distorted shadows on the concrete floor. The intense light rays revealed the faint traces of dust particles floating in the air, creating an almost-surreal backdrop to whatever Franco and his men intended to do here.

Three mysterious male figures stood in front of that light, their postures exuding an air of menace and authority. It took a moment for my eyes to adjust to the lighting, to recognize them as the men who had relentlessly pursued us through the city streets.

They stood with rifles draped across their front while my arms were wrenched behind my back, bound by what felt like duct tape.

"Luna Payne," Franco said.

God, what I wouldn't give to shove that toothpick into his eyeball. In fact, all I wanted to do was slap that look off his face and knee him in his groin for killing those bodyguards, for the hell he'd put me through. But I couldn't. Even if I wasn't tied up, I needed to be smart here.

It was four armed men against me. In a big-ass warehouse with nowhere to run and hide from flying bullets.

And even if by some miracle I made it out of this room, I had no idea how many other guards might be positioned outside, let alone where this warehouse was located. I didn't even know how long I had been unconscious. Had I been here for minutes? Days?

I was most likely screwed. But so help me, I would keep fighting with every cell of my being.

No matter how doomed it might be.

Even if that fight was purely psychological—playing nice to try to negotiate a release.

"What do you want?" I asked.

Franco smirked, and pulled that gross toothpick out from between his lips.

"You and I are going to have a little chat."

"I don't have the USB drive." It was seriously hard to keep the tone of my voice calm.

"Yeah, here's the thing, sweetheart…I don't believe you. Dominic told me that he gave you information that can be used against my organization."

I tried to hide the clenching of my jaw. This guy was either the dumbest or most paranoid guy to walk the planet. My guess was a combo of both.

Keep your cool, Luna. Dad needs you to stay alive. Otherwise, he'll be trapped in prison for the rest of his life.

You can do this. You persuade people for a living, and you can persuade this guy that you are not a threat to him. You can persuade him to let you go.

"He was bluffing," I managed.

"And why would he do that?"

"He thought you were going to kill him. He probably thought it would make you hesitate, and he was right."

"Dominic was not that smart," Franco said.

"I have no information about you from Dominic or anyone else."

Franco slowly paced, like a predator watching the meal he was about to consume.

"Who else did Dominic talk to?" Franco asked.

That's the information he really wants—who all knows? If he thinks I'm the only person with information against him, he'll just kill me to protect himself. But even if I lie and say Dominic was talking to others, he'll probably kill me anyway. And then he might go kill anyone else he suspects.

My mind raced for a scenario that could save my life while protecting innocents.

And suddenly, a possibility came to me.

A daring one, but it was the only card I had.

"Fine," I said, quickly layering on details to my story to make it more compelling. "Dominic told me everything. And he did give me a USB drive. That USB drive has information on it that will put you in prison for life. But Dominic also warned me how dangerous you were, so I created an insurance package for myself. If something ever happens to me, or if I disappear, multiple copies of the USB drive will be delivered to law enforcement officers all over the city."

Franco put the toothpick back between his teeth and spun it, as if its every rotation was a lie detector test. And then a slow smile spread across his lips.

"You're a terrible liar," he said.

I swallowed. "I'm not lying."

"You don't have any evidence, do you?"

Translation: I had nothing keeping me alive anymore.

Nothing physical, anyway, but based on the look in his eyes, he must have thought I still had information. Because I could tell he was far from done.

"Just let me go," I said.

"No can do."

My throat was a desert.

Think, Luna. Think of something else to say to him. Denying it didn't work. Pretending I did have information that could hurt him didn't work.

I straightened my spine and tried to hide the fear in my tone.

"Release me now," I said sternly. "And I will tell the police my abductors wore masks, and I don't know who they are." *Keep your eyes steady; don't let him see the lie on your face.* "This is a onetime offer," I said.

He had the audacity to look at me with pity. But his pity was laced with a psychotic thrill gleaming in his eyes, as if whatever was about to happen, he looked forward to it.

"Unfortunately for you, I'm not the only one who put a bounty on your head."

Wait, what? "What are you talking about?"

"Now"—he motioned to me with that toothpick—"I believe that you don't have the USB drive. If you did, it should have turned up by now, and if the police had it, I'd have gotten wind of it at least. If not been arrested. But I don't believe that Dominic didn't tell you anything about me or my organization that could help in a future prosecution. You probably told others and helped them build a case."

I wanted to circle back on that whole *someone else put a bounty on my head* thing. But persuading people was about giving them what they wanted—or at least giving them the illusion that they were getting what they wanted—and what Franco wanted was to vet how much had been leaked about his criminal activities.

Plus, he was probably lying. I mean, honestly, no one else would put a bounty on my head. A prosecutor maybe. Even a judge. But not someone *defending* criminals.

Trying to reason with a psychopath was proving exceedingly difficult.

"Dominic didn't tell me anything," I said, and more to myself than to him, I added, "He didn't deserve to die."

"The Vigilante saved me the effort, but Dom was a dead man walking." Franco cracked his neck. "Dominic never had the balls to be part of my business in the first place. Dominic had always been a pussy. Only reason he got involved with dealing drugs was because he needed money for his mom's medical bills, but you don't just walk away after dealing thirty grand in heroin. He's an idiot for thinking he could."

Or a man so desperate, he wasn't thinking straight when he first signed on.

The fact that Franco was talking this much was a bad sign; high-ranking criminals didn't talk unless they thought it'd have no repercussions. Like if the person they were spilling this all to would soon be dead, for example.

"But I never wanted to walk away. I embraced this shit. I love every second of it. Moving drugs under the noses of law enforcement," he said, like doing so made him smarter than them. "Moving up from small to big, from dealing to distribution. Making sure people remember who the boss is and what happens when they step out of line."

So, he enjoys hurting people, then.

"But Dominic? Only reason he killed that guy was because if he didn't, he'd have been killed himself. I'm the one that's always had the balls to be in this organization, not him. Dominic wanted out, but there was no getting out. He figured the only way was by taking me down, and he knew that if he ever had a shot, it was now or never."

"Why now?" I asked.

Franco looked annoyed. "You know why."

I didn't. That was the whole problem. But based on the nervousness in his eyes, Franco must have been particularly vulnerable to being arrested. Maybe even getting killed himself if he screwed up.

He stepped forward and positioned a knife just under my chin.

"I don't let nobody interfere with my organization. So, let's try this again. And this time, every lie will have a punishment."

My stomach clenched with nausea. Plan A didn't work. Plan B didn't work.

Now, there was a knife to my throat.

It was time for plan C.

CHAPTER 51

Hunter

I stormed into my house, slamming the door to the garage behind me, and I rushed through the kitchen, where Maria froze and stared at me with wide eyes.

"Please take the rest of the day off, Maria," I said. "Tell everyone to leave."

I walked into the great room, and as I jogged up the stairs, two at a time, Maria's frame ambled out of the kitchen.

"Mr. Lockwood, is everything okay?"

"I hope it will be, Maria."

I didn't know how this was all going to go down, but if I had any hope of rescuing Luna, I needed everyone out of my damn way.

And if I failed her? If I got to her too late?

I'd light the world on fire and burn it to the ground.

CHAPTER 52
Luna

"If I knew anything, you'd have been arrested already," I said.

"You think I'm that stupid? I know why they haven't arrested me."

I waited.

"They catch the shipment, I go away for life, and they confiscate it all. Get some other players, too. So, you're going to tell me what information Dominic told you and what you told the police, so I know which ports are compromised with a possible sting."

Ports. Shipments. Something was coming into this country.

Something that must be too big for Franco to stop. Franco might be a big man in his criminal enterprise, but even Franco was accountable to others. And those individuals likely yielded more power and delivered swift, lethal consequences. They wouldn't take too kindly to encountering major complications with this massive shipment—of what I could only assume was narcotics or weapons—especially if they believed they'd been double-crossed. Hence, Franco had a lot riding on this shipment.

I didn't know that I believed in miracles. It was a hard thing to grasp on to when everything in our family had gone so horribly wrong, but right now, I began to second-guess that. Because semi-lodged in a cut on the top of my forearm was a tiny shard of glass, no bigger than a pea. One I could reach, thanks to my wrists being crossed in an X behind me.

Whether it became lodged there during the car accident or when I was subsequently dragged out of that car, I didn't know, but it became a beacon of hope in this otherwise bleak situation.

The little shard was my key to survival.

"How many?" Franco asked.

"How many what?"

"Ports! How many fucking ports, exactly?"

I needed to say something that would make him leave for a moment—or at the very least, turn his back to me so I could free my arms. I opened my mouth and rolled the dice on an answer.

"All of them are compromised," I claimed.

Franco stared at me, and looked at the three men behind him, as if weighing my words. Did he believe me? I wasn't sure, but he and his three goons walked off to the side and had some sort of huddle.

"Call Diego," Franco said. "Ask him if he sees any signs of surveillance. I'm going to make a call, too."

While Franco and one other guy moved farther away to make the calls, the other two guys began talking in hushed whispers while also texting from their phones. Not the ideal distraction, but it would have to do.

Hopefully, they'd be preoccupied long enough for me to free myself.

Determination coursed through my veins as I began to widen my wrists, trying to loosen them a bit so it would make it easier to saw my way through them, but no matter which way I moved, I couldn't seem to make any progress.

My eyes stung, the frustration and desperation of my situation intensifying. The helplessness of holding the key to my freedom yet being unable to unlock the shackles that bound me was agony, mocking my every attempt to escape.

But even in the face of despair, I couldn't give up. I had to find a way to free myself and escape this nightmare.

It took a concerted effort to twist my fingers at the right angle, but I managed to grab hold of the jagged piece in my upper forearm, trying not to wince as the sharp edges dug into the skin between my finger and thumb.

Despite the pain, I squeezed it even harder because, covered in blood, the thing could slip through my grasp in a split second.

Now, a new challenge. I had the shard of glass between my finger and thumb, but reaching the duct tape was incredibly difficult. And once I did, I couldn't stop the shard of glass from also scraping against my skin. But I had no other choice.

I began scraping what was probably a centimeter of the tape. It stung, and the tape was stubborn, glued to my skin, but the great news was how minimally my body was moving. Franco and his army—still making their calls and texts to vet the problem with the ports—seemed none the wiser as to what was happening behind my back.

The first split of duct tape made my heart swell with hope. As I predicted, it loosened the tape just enough to work on the next millimeter. Again, the glass scraped against my wrist, my skin stinging, and burning, the tool on the precipice of being dropped.

It was strange how life and death had come down to this little pea-sized sliver of glass.

When I got halfway through cutting the duct tape, it actually tore a little bit. Creating a split-second sound of fabric spearing open.

Franco stopped speaking to whoever was on the phone and swiveled his head to me. I tried to hide the destabilization of my breathing, knowing if he looked closer, he would see what I had done. Since I wasn't even free yet, I wouldn't be able to defend myself against his vengeful blows.

His stare was a guillotine dangling from a frail string, but I managed to shift and grunt slightly, as if trying to get more comfortable, in hopes of convincing him that this was the sound he'd heard. His gaze remained on me for one second.

Two seconds.

Three seconds.

But finally, he looked away and resumed talking to whoever was on the other end of that phone.

It afforded me the last few seconds I needed to cut through my bindings. Though the duct tape was cut, there were still pieces of it fashioned to my left wrist, and I had to slowly pull them from my skin.

But once I did, my wrists separated.

I shot out of the chair and sprinted behind me, to my left. The warehouse was dark and impossible to see the best escape route until I caught sight of an illuminated Exit sign hanging above a doorway forty feet from me.

"The fuck!" one of the men shouted.

"Don't shoot her yet," Franco barked.

I never considered myself a particularly good runner, but holy shit, it was amazing what wonders adrenaline could do in a life-threatening situation. Footsteps pummeled behind me, but based on the sound, I was closer to the door than they were to me. And now, I was almost home free.

Oxygen pumped in and out of my lungs so rapidly, it burned, and my thighs were on fire.

I opened the metal door and escaped the main area of the warehouse, slamming the door behind me as I ran down a long hallway toward another Exit sign. I could only pray that this exit would lead me outside, because this hallway offered no place to hide.

The Exit sign was only seventy-five feet ahead, but it felt like a thousand.

Behind me, a metallic groan, followed by footsteps, emerged, followed by rising voices of men shouting at each other.

Fifty feet from the exit, I pushed myself harder, running faster.

I risked a quick glance over my shoulder and noted the men barreling toward me, but once I made it outside, I could scream, I could call 911, I could run toward a road if there was one nearby.

So, I ran even faster.

My God, I'm going to make it.

They weren't going to catch me in time. The door was only thirty feet away now, then twenty.

Closing the final distance, I reached my arm up toward its handle so I could shove it open without hesitation.

But suddenly, a figure blocked the door.

He'd come from what I could only assume was a different exit path from the warehouse.

I stopped in my tracks, nearly falling to the ground from the momentum. I quickly glanced around for another escape route or for someplace to hide, but there was nothing.

I was sandwiched between my captors.

Who had just herded their prey.

"That was a very stupid thing to do, you bitch," the man in front of me said just before he cracked me over the head with his gun.

CHAPTER 53
Hunter

Red's number flashed on my screen as I walked toward my bedroom.

"Tell me you have something," I snapped.

"Her phone stopped moving. I'm sending you the location now. I'll send guards there, but you're closer, sir."

Coordinates flashed on my screen.

"I'm on my way," I said.

"I can also notify the police."

"I'll do that," I said, ending the call.

In a race to save Luna, I'd take all the help I could get, but I needed to time that carefully. I needed the ability to get into that building with no police stopping me, because I wasn't going to be careful—I was going to do whatever was necessary to stop Franco from ending my only reason for existing.

My love is in the arms of a violent, sadistic enemy. What is she going through right now? What are they doing to her?

I stormed into my bedroom, into my closet, and pressed against the shelving unit on the far end that opened on hidden hinges.

The one my own staff was unaware of. Hell, even the contractors who helped me remodel this place two years ago were ignorant of its purpose; I made sure of it with a careful string of nondisclosure agreements, combined with carefully peppered use of contractors working on individual aspects of this job so no one had enough information to even think of what it might mean.

Imperative groundwork to protect my anonymity.

The covert door opened with a bounce, and I walked through it into the hidden secondary closet that sat behind it, knowing that if I didn't get to Luna in time, I would spend every waking moment of my life hunting every single man who had anything to do with her abduction. And I would torture them slowly for weeks at a time until they begged me for fucking mercy.

Only then would I unleash the most excruciating method to kill someone and finally stop their heart.

I flipped a switch, and incandescent lights bathed the secret space that no one knew about in a golden radiance.

It was in here, in this second closet, that I kept my second skin, if you will—the black shirts, black pants, and the vests that added twenty-two pounds of girth to my frame. Vests I'd had custom-made to be light, resemble the exact muscles of a torso, and were, of course, bulletproof. The boots were custom-made, too, from overseas—taking my size ten foot and encasing it in a size-fourteen combat style with lifts to add to my height. All of which were counter forensic measures I'd deployed from day one to protect my identity.

After all, it wasn't just me that I was protecting should I ever get caught; it was my entire family.

The Lockwood name, the company, and its thousands of employees could be at risk.

It was the fractured remains of my family's hearts that needed the most protection—hearts that might shatter if they found out who I really was.

But I couldn't think about that shit right now.

I suited up faster than I ever had before, my heart pounding out of my damn chest.

In the farthest corner of the closet, past rows of deceptive armor, another nondescript door called to me, its mundane wooden appearance disguising the secrets it guarded. When I opened it, I was greeted by the scent of damp earth, and a cool metallic kiss met my hand from the spiral staircase leading below.

Normally, excitement charged through me when I jogged down the steps to the basement that sat beneath this aging mansion and navigated the shadowy tunnel to my weapons room—the same room where I'd interrogated Franco's man.

But this time, rage smothered my emotions as I threw a handful of knives and a gun into a black backpack and tossed it over one shoulder. I clenched my fists as I hurried down the smaller hallway that branched off this weapons room—the one that led to my underground garage, hiding the vehicle that I used to slip in and out of the city, undetected. The garage was not attached to the main driveway, of course. Rather, it spit out onto the other end of the estate, behind the blanket of trees, where anyone coming across it would presume the gravel road belonged to an old outhouse on this property.

In one fluid motion, I tossed the backpack into the vehicle's passenger seat, its interior lighting up in response. I slid behind the wheel and awakened the engine, its low growl resonating with my own brewing storm.

Luna didn't know what I was truly capable of. The news reports had only disclosed partial facts to the public—they hadn't disclosed the gory details of the particularly gruesome killings committed by the Windy City Vigilante. But she was about to find out the truth.

That I had two sides to me.

The man.

And the villain.

CHAPTER 54
Luna

When I woke up this time, I was in the same chair, but now each ankle was individually duct-taped to its legs, and my arms were yanked behind my back, my wrists bound so many times that my fingers were already going numb. One of the men stood in front of me with the tape still in his hand, watching me—waiting for any sign I'd breach his work, I guess.

A warm trail of liquid dripped down my temple as my eyes once again adjusted to the light. Franco stood to the side of the duct-tape man, raising a cell phone.

"Nice try, hiding this," he said, holding it up to my face to unlock it. He spent a minute scrolling around my apps, I presumed, before handing it off to one of his guys. "Go through her messages, her emails, too, if you can. Just to be safe. Look for *any* information that could compromise us."

Then Franco walked back over to me and snarled, "You're lying to me. My men see no concrete signs of a targeted sting operation at the ports."

"I told you, I don't know anything!"

"And I told you, I don't believe you. We've seen increased police presence at two ports, but it's inconsistent. I need to know if that's a coincidence or if we need to shut them down. Shutting them down is a problem, one I can't create unless I'm certain it's compromised."

"I. Don't. Know. Anything."

Franco stepped closer.

"Want to know what I think?" His tone was cool and hauntingly calm. "That you believe I'll eventually swallow your bullshit story that you don't know anything and I'll let you leave here. And by keeping your mouth shut, you'll get to see us all busted." He leaned down so his face was inches from my own. "But that's not going to happen."

He tapped my cheek, making me recoil from his vile touch.

"And I've run out of patience. So, you're going to give me the information I want. If you don't, Rafe here will offer you a little incentive."

Franco motioned toward a blanket on the ground, which contained all sorts of scary paraphernalia. The blanket wasn't there before. How long had I been unconscious, affording them the time to set this all up?

At first, my eyes settled onto the pliers, bolt cutters, axe, and a variety of other torture devices intended to pry information out of me that I didn't have. But they quickly slid right past those and focused on the roll of duct tape, a tightly wrapped role of plastic sheathing, and just past the light, a shovel.

My stomach roiled.

"Now, this can go the easy way," Franco said, as if my entire world hadn't just imploded around me. "Or the hard way."

The white-hot rage that had been boiling inside my body now simmered in despair.

If they planned to torture me for information I didn't have, how long would that torture go on?

It took considerable effort to hold back the burning in my eyes. I refused to show them weakness by crying in front of them.

"Did Dominic give you port names?" Franco said with irritation.

"I told you"—the strength had left my voice—"I don't know anything. You could spend however long you want torturing me, or you can accept the truth now."

Franco stopped in front of one of the lights, his body transforming into an ominous silhouette.

A few quick tugs of my arms and ankles confirmed I was tied down so tightly, I was royally screwed with no hope of escape.

And with no information to barter with, I couldn't talk my way out of this, either.

"Rafe." Franco nodded with his chin toward one of the men.

My spine straightened as I watched the bald-headed man set his gun down on the cement and amble over to me.

Fear was a funny emotion. Normally, it might make me cower, but this time, a volcanic explosion of anger burst through every cell of my body. They might do horrible things to me, but I would not give them the satisfaction of seeing me scared.

I met his angry gaze as he raised his giant palm in the air and slapped me across my cheekbone so hard, I could taste blood.

I yelped and jerked at my hands and my ankles so harshly, that the muscles in my shoulders and legs threatened to tear.

The four men laughed at me—their chuckles echoing through the empty warehouse like an infestation.

"You'd better start talking, bitch," Rafe said.

"You can hit me a thousand times, but it won't change the fact that I don't know anything!"

"A thousand, huh?" Palm Slapper said. "Let's see, shall we?"

He slapped me across my other cheekbone, which exploded in a stinging pain, radiating down my sore body.

It was like my body was finally waking up from a fog, now aware of the aches and pains from having been in a car accident.

"One." He smirked.

Slap. This one hit me so hard, that my neck jerked to the side.

"Two."

"You motherfucker!"

Slap. This one split my lip open, the pain stinging as a drop of blood trailed down my chin.

"Three."

"Screw you," I said.

"You'd be wise to show some respect," Franco chimed in.

"I don't have any evidence against them. Trust me, if I did?" I leaned forward. "I would've handed it over to the district attorney and gotten a bowl of popcorn to watch your ass get arrested."

"The ADA," Franco said in a taunting tone. "Now we're getting somewhere. You've been fucking him, yeah?"

My stomach plunged.

"What information did you share with him?"

I wanted to slap that smirk right off of Franco's face.

"Leave Hunter out of this. He has nothing to do with any of this."

"I'll be the judge of that. Besides, that piece of shit deserves what's coming to him. Hunter Lockwood put some of my colleagues behind bars. It'll serve as a warning to everyone else what happens when you put people like us in some jail cell like we're animals."

You are animals.

I might not be able to save myself from his horrors, but I needed to protect Hunter from suffering this same fate.

"Leave him alone. I'll do anything you want if you just leave him alone."

Franco squatted before me, his thin, nasty mouth grinning, as he slid his fingers up my leg, coming dangerously close to the space between my thighs.

"Anything?"

I swallowed the bile that launched into my esophagus as he squeezed my thigh.

"Don't worry, princess. I'll be taking a piece of that, too," he said.

The other men shifted their stance, two of them rubbing their crotches, and with a dread sinking into my bones, I suspected they'd all take what they wanted from me.

CHAPTER 55
Luna

"You'd better start talking," Franco said.

He gripped my throat so tightly, that I couldn't breathe, much less speak, and my windpipe threatened to crack under the weight. Pressure mounted in my head while the solace of unconsciousness crept into my mind. I reached for it, surrendering to it, willing it to take me, because anything was better than what he was doing to me.

Like last time, he let me go just before the sweet bliss of blackness offered me my escape.

He motioned for one of his minions to hit me. Again.

This time, a punch in the stomach with such force that what was left of my breath escaped me once more. My muscles tightened involuntarily, pressing against my diaphragm and constricting my flow of oxygen in addition to making me nauseous.

It took me a few moments to regain my breath. Through my sweaty hair, I slowly lifted my gaze to the man standing before me.

"I told you…" I said through the taste of blood in my mouth. I was panting from the pain, but I tried to hide the fact that my body was starting to break down. "Dominic didn't tell me anything."

Franco used a small blade to clean the filth from under his nails, standing casually, as if having his men hit me repeatedly hadn't been enough.

Then, he walked over to me and pressed the blade against the skin of my neck, digging in just deep enough to make it sting. A shallow cut, nothing deep.

Yet.

"That's not what Dominic said."

"How many times do I have to tell you this? He lied."

"He said you two knew each other. Quite well."

"When we were *kids*. I hadn't seen him for years."

Why did Dominic have to use me as leverage against his psychopathic cousin?

My anger toward him quickly dissipated in pity, though. How desperate and alone he must've felt under the threat of his cousin closing in on him.

But while he might've felt desperate, giving my name to this violent guy was beyond negligent. He knew what his cousin was capable of, and yet he still threw me to the wolves in order to protect himself. The betrayal cut deep, and the pain of it burned the back of my eyes.

It was stupid to feel hurt. Dominic was most likely a murderer, but he was the last person in my life who hadn't let me down.

No, that wasn't true. My father had never let me down. And neither had Hunter.

But I had let Hunter down. I had put myself in danger by insisting on going to work, giving Franco's men the opportunity to abduct me. And now, if I didn't come up with something soon, I would lose my life because of it.

Sentencing my father to serve out the rest of his life in prison. And sentencing Hunter to fall into the abyss of emotional torment. Only to be killed by Franco himself.

My worry instantly halted as Franco drove the small blade into my arm forcefully, causing my muscles to feel like they were tearing in slow motion. The pain was so intense, I couldn't help but scream.

But that wasn't enough for Franco. No amount of my suffering was enough for him, so with the blade still in my flesh, he began to gradually twist the handle.

"Please stop," I cried.

Dammit, Luna! Begging this man? Sobbing so hard, tears are marching down your cheeks?

I'm only human, I internally whispered to the furious side of my thoughts.

Deep down, I knew begging wouldn't save me. Nothing would. Franco had hunted me down and then murdered my bodyguards in cold blood. Now, he took immense pleasure in torturing me, with no desire to stop.

Ironic, how afraid I was of dying in that car chase. And now I wish I could go back in time.

And unbuckle my seat belt right before the impact.

CHAPTER 56
Hunter

In the heart of the desolate industrial wasteland, a massive, decaying warehouse loomed like a titan, its shadow swallowing the surrounding area in darkness. The once-vibrant paint on its exterior had long since been stripped away by time and neglect, leaving behind a skeleton of rusted metal and crumbling concrete.

Tall, overgrown weeds and thistles wrapped themselves around a corroded chain-link fence that was adorned with warning signs—a futile barrier against those who'd breach this warehouse's boundaries.

It was in there that Luna's cell phone was omitting its signal.

I had been careful, arriving in the parking lot, watching for any sign of exterior guards as I parked my vehicle near a corner.

Normally, I would've parked farther away. But I would not waste any time getting to Luna.

I checked my cell phone one more time to ensure her signal had not moved before jogging to the closest door.

Locked. Shit.

I couldn't risk trying to shoot it open, not without tipping my hand that I was here.

Twelve feet away, another metal door was also locked.

Damn it.

I could use my lock kit if it became necessary, but I typically targeted my victims on the streets of the city, and my lock-picking skills needed some work.

Could I do it? Sure. But it would take a lot longer than I wanted it to, and Luna might be inside right now, having God knows what being done to her. I needed to hurry.

I ran another thirty feet until I found another door.

This one was ajar.

I grabbed my Smith & Wesson and slowly opened the door.

The thing groaned like it was trying to shout a warning to everyone inside, alerting them to my presence. I stilled for a moment, listening for any sounds of footsteps. But I was met with only silence.

I had no idea what I was walking into. How many men might be positioned throughout this warehouse, standing guard.

I started walking down the hallway, staring down the barrel of my gun. In any of these doorways, a man could be waiting for me, ready to strike. And while my vest was bulletproof, my head was unprotected. If I got ambushed and died, I wouldn't be able to rescue Luna.

The narrow, disquieting hallway stretched out before me like the throat of a monstrous beast, threatening to swallow me whole before I could even locate her. The air was stale and suffocating, saturated with the faint, acrid odor of mold and dampness that clung to the decaying walls.

Overhead, a single fluorescent light flickered with an ominous, hypnotic pulse that seemed to taunt me—its buzz the only sound in the otherwise silent hallway.

Each hesitant footstep upon the warped, splintered floorboards seemed to echo, betraying my presence to the men who had taken Luna here.

I continued to advance slowly, but there were so many little rooms, such a big space, how would I ever find her?

I swung my weapon to my right, entering a small room that appeared to have once been a supply room. Now, beer cans blanketed the floor as if local teenagers had found this place and used it as a party spot. No Luna. No men.

I returned to the hallway and advanced another twenty feet. This time, the door to my left was closed. As I turned the knob with my left hand, holding the gun with my right, I wondered who was waiting on the other side. I wondered if they could hear the doorknob twisting and if they were lining up their shot right now.

I swung the door open quickly, intending to bash them in the face with it.

Another empty room. No men, no Luna.

What if she wasn't here? What if someone had tossed Luna's cell phone here and taken her somewhere else? Or what if her cell phone was being used as bait to lure me into a trap?

What if they knew my identity and knew that I would track her down?

But this was my only lead on where Luna might be, and time was running out.

I stepped out of the room—back into the hallway—and advanced another forty feet until the hallway split into three different directions.

I could continue going forward or turn either left or right. I looked down at each of the hallways with an impatient nervousness. There were too many doors, too many rooms. Sweeping every one of them would take too long. I needed to get to Luna now.

I considered calling her phone, seeing if I could hear it ring, but what if I did that and it put her in further danger?

Just when an oppressive weight pressed down on my chest, fearful that it might take me too long to find her, a distant sound broke through the hallway to my left.

Luna screaming.

CHAPTER 57
Luna

I had always prided myself on never giving up hope. After all, hope was the only thing I had to hold on to as I fought the injustice waged against my father.

But right now, hope felt like a distant memory—water evaporating into a fog that I couldn't grasp on to. Floating away from me, leaving only sorrow.

I wish I could warn Hunter that these men were coming for him next. I wish I had never gotten involved with him—if I hadn't, maybe Franco would have left him alone.

But now, Hunter might face the same fate as me.

I wasn't sure how long they'd been hurting me. Correction: *torturing* me. It could be hours, or it could be minutes. When every single breath that you took was laced with pain, fear, and hopelessness, time stretched on like an eternity.

The only thing that existed at this moment was the pain radiating everywhere. Sharp pains. Dull pains. In my arms, and all over my body, but none of them were damaging enough to end my suffering.

It's tragic how many ways your body can be hurt without it becoming life-threatening.

Franco let go of the small knife that he had been twisting in my arm and finally stepped back. He nodded to one of his accomplices, who walked over to the array of instruments strewn across the blanket on the ground.

The man squatted down as his fingers traced over the pliers, then a hammer, then the screwdriver, until finally, he settled on a rope.

A giant rope that was so long, I'd assumed it was to tie up the tarp after they'd wrapped up my dead body. Instead, he glanced around at the beams twenty feet above our heads, stood up, and hurled the end of it up into the air. It missed its target and thudded to the ground.

My heart found a way to beat even faster in my chest, knowing what he must be getting ready to do.

And as he finally strung the rope as he wished, looping it into the shape he wanted.

All I could think was, *At least it's almost over.*

Just as Franco stabbed my arm again.

CHAPTER 58

Hunter

Racing down the dimly lit hallway, I could barely hear my heartbeat reverberating in my ears, because the deafening screams of Luna tore through the air—each guttural cry for help slicing through my soul.

My mind raced with the fear that I might not make it in time to save her.

The sound of my footsteps seemed to echo in the confined space, amplifying my desperation as I pushed myself to run faster, sweat lacing my forehead beneath the suffocating mask.

I could not let her die; I would not allow myself to fail her.

With each of her cries, images of what the men might be doing to her flashed in my mind, fueling my fury—a cyclone of rage and helplessness brewing within.

I clenched my teeth.

So help me, I'd make them pay for every single tear she had shed, for every scream that had escaped her lips.

As I neared the farthest door, the screams intensified, and so did the pace of my heart.

I'd have only one chance to save her. One chance to storm into this room, assess how many men I needed to take out, and end every single one of them before they could get to me.

If someone took me out with a bullet, Luna would be done for.

My veins coursed with adrenaline as I prepared to confront her tormentors.

I would do whatever it took to save the love of my life and make those responsible suffer for their actions.

No matter the cost, I would be her protector, her avenger, her salvation.

With a deep breath, I pushed the door open as silently as possible, glancing into the largest room I had come across yet.

CHAPTER 59
Hunter

Three armed men—one scrolling through a cell phone—stood twenty feet behind a man who was clearly the leader—a man that was most likely Franco Hopkins, though I couldn't be sure without getting closer.

My stomach retched at the sight of the love of my life tied to a chair. Her arms twisted behind her back, a man standing near her side.

But my pride took a back seat to my rage, because her cheek was flaming red, her lip was busted open, and bruises were forming on her upper arms—bruises in the shape of handprints from where massive hands had grabbed her. Not to mention the blood dripping from her forearm, and the man on her side holding a knife.

Worse, one of the men was tying a noose at the end of a rope that was hanging from one of the overhead beams.

Rage blurred my vision, and I clenched my teeth so hard, that something cracked in my jaw.

I quickly assessed the situation, noting different avenues of possible escape routes that might lead Luna out of this warehouse—picking the one I'd tell her to use while I went about the business of slaughtering these men.

And then I took light steps closer.

These guys probably left the warehouse lights off because it was supposed to be vacant, and they didn't want to attract attention outside, but the darkness allowed me to slip into the shadows two dozen feet without being seen.

It was here, on the border of light and darkness, that I stopped.

I could probably shoot one of them in the head, maybe two, before the third fired back. And Franco probably had a gun on him, in addition to the knife he was holding, so he could fire, too. But what if they didn't shoot me? What if they shot Luna instead?

I needed to be smart. I needed to gain control of these men, and the best way to do that was to take on the leader.

I launched myself full speed across the room toward the guy I could now see was, in fact, Franco. With each step, my muscles tensed, and my breath quickened.

In what seemed to be slow motion, Franco turned toward the sound of my steps, his eyes widening just before I slammed into him, knocking the knife from his hand.

It clanked loudly on the gritty, cement floor while the henchmen around him scrambled and pointed their rifles toward me.

But it was too late. I had Franco's neck tucked into my elbow, my gun pointed at his temple.

"Set your guns down," I commanded.

The guy who'd been holding a cell phone had already tossed it to the ground, holding his firearm with both hands now.

"Fuck that, shoot him," Franco said with a strained voice, trying to yank out of my hold. "And then shoot her."

"You know who I am, yes?" I asked the guys.

I could tell they did through the fear in their eyes.

"You *try* to shoot me?" I aimed the barrel at them. "You'll be dead before the bullet leaves your gun. And if you shoot her?"

Keeping Franco's neck in the stranglehold of my elbow and using his body as a human shield, I pointed my gun at Dead Man Number One's crotch.

"I'll blow your dick off and then shove it down your throat."

"Shoot him!" Franco threw an elbow back, but that was the other lovely benefit of this custom vest; it absorbed the energy of the blow, so I barely felt it.

The men exchanged glances before having the smarts to slowly lay down their rifles.

"Now move over there," I said, pointing to a space far away from their guns but close enough to me where I still could—*and would*—end their lives.

CHAPTER 60
Luna

The Windy City Vigilante pistol-whipped each man until they were incapacitated enough for his liking, I suppose. Franco took the worst of it, now groaning on the floor, half conscious. The Vigilante looked down at the moaning piles of garbage before eventually walking over and squatting in front of me.

He kept his masked face at an angle where he kept eyes on the enemies should they be stupid enough to make a move.

"Are you okay?" He brought his hand up to my cheek.

With my voice trapped beneath a rock of fear and shock, all I was able to do was nod.

One of my assailants jumped up to his feet and started running. The Vigilante twisted slightly, so calm and steady with his movements that his demeanor alone had to be terrifying to them.

The Vigilante raised his weapon and shot with ease—nailing a bullet in the guy's calf.

The guy screamed as he went down on his belly and began to army crawl.

But the Vigilante's posture seemed completely unalarmed by it. It was like he knew he had complete control over the situation and that none of them would escape his wrath.

That's when he appeared to notice the array of torture instruments nearby—his lips tightening to bare his teeth. It took him a moment to snap out of what seemed to be a debilitating case of rage before he moved behind me and trailed his finger down my hand.

"Who taped your wrists?" His voice was so cool, it was chilling.

I wasn't sure why it mattered, but the entire scene seemed to be on pause until I answered his question. He wasn't moving, and the men were staring at us, one still army-crawling away.

"I don't know who taped me up the first time, but the second time—"

"What do you mean, the *first* time?" the Vigilante asked, a glint of rage pulsing through his words as he moved in front of me.

"When I woke up here, I was already taped up. I managed to cut through the tape and attempted to escape but..."

It didn't work.

"They dragged you back in."

"Yes."

Silence.

"Who taped you the second time?"

Unsure what else to do, I nodded my chin toward the man army-crawling away.

The Vigilante walked over to the blanket and looked over the torture devices like a kid salivating over the different flavors of ice cream offered, trying to decide which one he wanted most. He chose the axe.

And then he began walking toward the man. Slowly.

The incandescent glow of the lighting behind the Vigilante cast his strong form into a looming silhouette and glistened off the axe's metal blade as he dragged it along the floor behind him.

The grating, high-pitched screech of the axe scraping against the cement floor reverberated through the warehouse, each chilling metallic rasp puncturing the eerie silence. Its rhythmic drag was like a sinister metronome, filling the air with an unsettling dread, as the man tried to crawl away from the Vigilante faster, who hunted him with an eerily tranquil demeanor.

When the Vigilante reached his target, his form became an outline, a nocturnal echo in the dark no longer in front of the portable lights.

"Please, please!" The man rolled onto his back and put his palm up. "This wasn't my idea. I was just following orders!"

"Funny thing." The Vigilante dragged out every word. "You probably could've gone through the rest of your life hurting more people and breathing the oxygen meant for the rest of us. But then you hurt *her.*"

The Vigilante raised the axe with both hands, and though the guy screamed, "Please, no!" he slammed it to the ground with a grating clash of metal against stone—the sound ringing through the air like a ruthless chime.

The man's severed arm rolled away from him as blood squirted out from his shoulder, and he howled like the dying animal he was.

Shock clenched my heart. I don't know what I expected, but that certainly was not it. I had to clamp my eyes shut, but I couldn't shield myself from the horror playing out. The man's piercing screams hurt my eardrums, and I began to tremble as I heard another loud clank of the axe hitting stone.

I waited several seconds before opening my eyes. The Vigilante had cut off both of the man's arms, but he didn't end his life quickly.

"What did *he* do to you?" the Vigilante asked, nodding his chin toward one of the other henchmen.

I shook my head. I wasn't participating in this.

The Vigilante seemed to stare at me for a minute before looking down at the ground. "Very well," he said. "I'll have to use my imagination."

I didn't want to see this. I appreciated the Vigilante rescuing me, and I hated these men with my whole soul, but I didn't want to see or hear them being tortured.

"Let me go," I pleaded.

The Vigilante seemed to regard me.

"You deserve to see them suffer after what they did to you, Luna."

Luna. Not Ms. Payne. He had never called me by my first name before.

I tried not to watch the torture inflicted on the other men, but it was like witnessing a car accident, unable to look away completely. When I heard a scream, I would risk a peek from my eye and see something horrific. Blood. Missing fingers. Men's terrified faces as they watched their colleagues getting tortured, making a failing attempt to get away. Only to suffer the same fate of cracking bones and torn flesh themselves.

Eventually, their tortured screams slowly diminished into moans and then silence.

I opened my eyes again, noting that Franco Hopkins—who was still lying on the ground, growing more conscious—was the only one left alive.

CHAPTER 61
Hunter

I walked back over to Luna and finally unbound her. Should've done it right away, in hindsight, but what can I say? Rage had a way of taking over.

As soon as she was free, Luna shot up out of her chair. She stumbled slightly, breathing heavily, but groaned through the pain as she shuffled to Franco. Pounding her fists on his ribs while she let out this hybrid of a scream and a cry.

If Franco hadn't been pistol-whipped so many times, he might've fought back, but instead, I let the beauty beat the shit out of the beast for a bit.

It was mesmerizing, to see her rage. It did something to me, made me wonder if she and I were more alike than I realized, but the moment of amusement collapsed when she fell into a sob.

He would lose a limb for that sob.

In the distance, sirens began to screech through the air.

Making her look up with furrowed brows.

"How did they know I was here?" she asked.

"I called them." On the way, just in case I was killed when I went in.

Her eyes widened, mouth slightly agape, as she appeared to process what she'd just heard.

While the sirens were good news for her, for me, it meant I needed to hurry.

I spotted her cell phone lying on the ground, and grateful it hadn't broken when the guy had tossed it down, I handed it to her. She took her cell hesitantly, in shock, I guess.

"I need you to run, Luna. Go through that door." That exit led to the front parking lot, where the police cars would most likely park.

She looked hesitant, looking between me and Franco.

"I'll hold him for the police," I lied with a smile. "But you need to run. If I lose control of him, he could come after you."

Her eyes widened.

"Run, Luna."

She appeared to contemplate her decision, but after suffering the trauma of being kidnapped and tortured, Luna—holding her bleeding arm against her body—shuffled out the door, just like I told her.

Leaving me smiling.

Luna was safe.

And as a bonus, I had Franco Hopkins in my possession.

I felt like a kid on a twisted Christmas morning.

But the sirens were too close. A mile or two away, best guess.

Which was a huge problem.

Franco Hopkins didn't deserve to die a quick death. After what he did to Luna, there was no way he would get off with a bullet to the brain or a slash to his jugular.

Luna's injuries would require transport to the hospital—an overnight stay, most likely. A few hours, minimum.

Giving me time to make this motherfucker pay. And I was going to enjoy every second of it.

I needed to get him out of here—now. Not ideal. But when it came to vengeance against the man who tried to kill the woman I loved? I was willing to make an exception.

I hoisted the guy up over my shoulder, walking toward the back of the warehouse. Where my car was waiting.

CHAPTER 62

Luna

"You didn't find them?" I asked, my heart plummeting to my feet.

The scene before me was nothing short of chaotic. Police cars, their lights blazing, were strewn haphazardly around the perimeter while morgue vehicles parked ominously nearby—their presence a grim reminder of the day's events.

Events that had left me in shock, I think. My mind raced to recount what had happened inside that cold, unassuming building while EMTs finished bandaging my arm up with butterfly tape and gauze and prepared to take me to the hospital.

"Not yet," Detective Rinaldi replied in a comforting tone. She was wearing her hair in a bun, but a few strands had escaped, like this case was getting to her, too. "We found the bodies of the other men."

"Franco and the Vigilante...they're both missing?" My unease grew into an all-out alarm.

Rinaldi's eyes softened, a sadness creeping into their depths, like she worried each revelation had the power to make me break in half. Because it very much did.

"We should head to the hospital now," an EMT said.

"We have officers conducting a second search." Rinaldi held up a finger to the EMT, silently asking him to give us a minute. He stepped out of the ambulance and made his way to the front. "It's a big warehouse, Luna, with lots of places to hide."

"Yeah, but the Vigilante and Franco were both in that main room when I escaped. They were both alive." I mean, of course it crossed my mind that the Vigilante might've been gearing up to kill Franco, but evidently, that wasn't the case.

What if Franco escaped? Worse, what if he'd killed the Vigilante?

Worse? Why did that word come into my mind?

Because he saved your life. Again. And I didn't want him to die.

Yet, I was also disturbed. He didn't just kill those men. He tortured them. He cut off a man's arms with an axe, for God's sake.

And even more horrifying, he looked like he *enjoyed* it.

The Vigilante wasn't just a killer. He was…something far more tormented than I'd realized.

"It's possible the Vigilante heard the sirens and took off," the detective said calmly.

"Then where is Franco?"

"He may be hiding somewhere in that warehouse. Or he might have gotten away on foot. We're bringing a canine team out here, and we're setting up a search perimeter now."

"But Franco had a head start to that search. What if he got away?"

"Luna…"

"Franco threatened Hunter Lockwood! And now Franco's missing!"

"I hate to state the obvious here, but it's possible the Vigilante killed Franco somewhere in that warehouse and we just haven't found his body yet."

But that didn't make any sense. The Vigilante had Franco right in front of him. With cops closing in, he wouldn't have taken the time to drag Franco to some other area of that warehouse. He could've sliced his throat in a matter of seconds and then fled. If he'd acted quickly, it would be entirely possible that the Vigilante had slipped away before this place was surrounded.

The more likely scenario was that he'd fled to save himself from arrest, likely believing Franco was too injured to simply run off and that police would undoubtedly nab him.

But then Franco must have somehow managed to get away.

"Hunter's in danger," I repeated. "He's not answering my calls or texts. Something is wrong!"

"Officers have already been dispatched to his office and the court-house; trust me, we're looking for him."

"But he wasn't there?"

My mind raced, wondering where Franco might attack Hunter.

"In speaking with his colleagues, it sounds like Hunter left work early. We have an officer en route to the Lockwood estate right now."

"One officer? That's not enough!"

"Luna." The patience in her tone was waning. "You need to trust us. We've got this."

"When you get to his house, you'll go inside, right?"

"If the officer sees enough evidence to determine probable cause, such as a break-in or signs that indicate Hunter is in there with his life in active danger, of course."

"If?" I snapped. "They need to bust down the door!"

"Without any signs of a break-in or any obvious danger, we can't barge into people's houses without a warrant. You know that."

"I'm staying there, and I give you permission to enter."

"It's not your home, but, Luna," she said, placing her hand on mine, "we'll track him down, okay?"

Not fast enough, they wouldn't.

Maybe Franco had a getaway vehicle with people who had picked him up.

Hunter had security cameras, I assured myself. And a security team that included bodyguards who could probably race to his mansion in plenty of time to save him. Plus, a police officer would show up shortly and knock on Hunter's door.

But none of that erased my fears, seeing as how Franco had gotten to me when I was just as heavily guarded. Franco was smart, and he would probably know the Lockwood estate was armed with security.

He would find a way in.

In fact, he might already be there.

When the police filled me in on the location of this warehouse, I learned it was only a fifteen-minute drive from the Lockwood estate.

I couldn't sit here in the back of an ambulance or in some emergency room while Hunter was in danger. I needed to go to him. I needed to see that he was okay with my own eyes.

"Take me home," I demanded.

"Luna, you need to go to a hospital. You probably have a concussion, and you need stitches in your arm."

"That cut is butterflied with tape." So it wasn't bleeding profusely.

"You need to get checked out by a doctor for any other injuries you might have—"

But I was no longer listening. I had jumped off the back of the ambulance—against the screaming arguments of pain rippling through my body—and started running.

"Luna!"

Rinaldi's voice was as loud as my aching body, which also screamed at me to stop.

Rationally, my rushing to Hunter's house served no purpose. But my heart disagreed. It was cracking open in my chest and bleeding in fear that, right now, Hunter was a sitting duck.

Maybe already tied to a chair of his own, getting tortured, while we just sat here and wondered.

Screw wondering.

I pulled up my rideshare app on my phone and ordered a car. ETA: two minutes.

Was Hunter safe? Was he still alive? A suffocating dread washed over me, and tears blurred my vision as I trembled, staring at the time on my phone, willing it to slow down.

He had to emerge from this unscathed. He had to.

When the Uber finally arrived, I jumped inside and begged him to hurry as he drove me to Hunter's mansion.

CHAPTER 63
Hunter

S hit.

What was a cop car doing, parked out in front of my home? A brief panic flooded my system, making me wonder if, somehow, I had left evidence at the scene of the warehouse that divulged my identity.

I couldn't imagine what that evidence would be, though. Even if they had cameras, this car had no plates, and I wasn't stupid enough to register it in my name. As a prosecutor, you learn a thing or two about criminal evasion.

Was I being followed? I thought I had gotten out of the warehouse safely, and had peeled out of the parking lot just before the police piled into the other side of it. But maybe I was wrong. Maybe someone spotted me and followed my car. Maybe they figured out the direction I was heading and sent an officer ahead.

I watched from a distance—from the concealed driveway behind these pine trees—as a cop emerged from his vehicle. Slowly.

You don't get out of your car like a sloth if you're here to arrest the most wanted fugitive in the state. And you don't come here alone.

While it was possible other vehicles were hidden around the

perimeter, I didn't see any sign of them, and this guy ambling toward my front door didn't look like any kind of decoy.

A loud bang from my trunk snapped my attention back to my vehicle and the new complication in the situation.

Franco was awake. Pounding and screaming in the back.

I should turn around. Drive somewhere remote, slit Franco's throat, and be done with it. Dragging him into the hidden garage and tunnel and down into my secret bunker would be a very stupid idea if there was a cop outside, sniffing around.

I put the car in reverse and turned around to look over my shoulder.

But images of Luna's bruised and battered body flooded my mind, and when I imagined all the things those men did to inflict those injuries, along with the terror she'd experienced, a rage boiled through my blood.

I hesitated. Squeezed the steering wheel so hard, I wondered if the leather might rip, and then I threw the car back into drive. I kept it slow, so the engine made as little noise as possible as it inched its way toward my hidden underground garage.

I glanced through the trees at the officer, noting he was approaching my front door. His left shoulder to me, there was over a hundred feet and a wall of pines separating him from my car.

My garage door, which had been hidden on a slant along a hill, opened with a hum. It was top of the line, designed to be discreet, but I still worried that the police officer might hear it.

I parked the car, closed the garage door, and acted quickly.

I opened the trunk, pleased when one punch knocked Franco back into a state of unconsciousness. Adrenaline helped chuck him over my shoulder, walk through the door on the far end, and hustle down the corridor that led to my weapons room.

Once in there, I secured Franco rapidly, wrapping him in duct tape and slapping some over his mouth in case he woke up. With my heart pounding, I panted as I pulled out my phone.

When I did, a bunch of missed calls and texts from Luna lined my screen, begging me to tell her that I was okay. Evidently, soon-to-be-dead Franco Hopkins had threatened me when he'd held her hostage.

The guy would pay for that, but he'd have to wait.

I opened the live feeds from my home surveillance system, clicking on the one over my front door.

Only one cop still. His hands were on his hips, and he was staring at my front door. I could ignore him, but the look on his face told me that might be a mistake. He looked determined.

If he heard or saw anything that gave him probable cause, worst case, he might enter my residence.

I couldn't let that happen.

I knew what I needed to do.

CHAPTER 64

Hunter

"Officer?" I offered with a surprised tone, as if this was the first instance I had seen him. "What can I do for you?"

I ran a towel through my wet hair, as if opening the door, wearing only pants, my chest glistening with water, hadn't confirmed my alibi enough that my delayed response was because I had been in the shower.

Downstairs, in the basement chamber that was a mere one hundred feet from my main residence—connected by a tunnel— Franco Hopkins might be waking up at this very moment. And though I had confined him the best I could, he felt like a ticking time bomb down there.

I needed this cop to go away. Now.

"Sorry to bother you, Mr. Lockwood."

"Hunter." I smiled. "And it's no bother at all."

Get away, dude. Now.

The cop hitched a thumb over his shoulder. "Dispatch has been trying to locate you."

I raised my eyebrows. "Really? Why?"

"They're worried you might be in danger."

"Ah." I allowed a hint of amusement to dance through my tone on purpose as I half-rolled my eyes. "If people had to check on us every time some asshole ran his mouth, the city would have no police left for the citizens, am I right?"

The guy smirked, my comment's arrow hitting the bull's-eye of its target: stroking his pride. Putting us together on the same team, subject to the same heated comments that sometimes spewed from the venomous mouths of the people I prosecuted and the people he slapped cuffs on.

Judging by the relaxing of his shoulders, it also succeeded in its primary purpose: to put him at ease.

"I was sent here to check on you and make sure you're safe."

I opened my arms. "Safe and sound. I appreciate you stopping by."

He nodded toward his vehicle, which was parked right out front.

"I'll be just outside if you need me."

"That's not necessary," I assured with a smile.

"It sounds like a *direct* threat was made against you," he explained.

"Well"—I motioned toward the security cameras positioned along my front—"I assure you, I have all the protection I need. My security team is watching me and every angle of this house right now." Except for the purposeful dead spot in the lenses, where I dragged my unconscious victim downstairs.

But I digress. If you could please go away, I'd like to get back to torturing the man.

This was akin to starving and smelling the most delicious meal wafting through the air while someone stood here gabbing away, preventing you from eating.

The police officer hesitated. He looked around again, over his shoulder, along the expanse of my lawn, until the radio fashioned to the officer's shoulder crackled to life.

"Attention all units in the area. We have a domestic violence disturbance on Elm Street. Suspect is armed and dangerous. Officers requested to respond with caution and prioritize the safety of all involved parties."

"Elm Street." I glanced at the officer, feigning concern. "That's just four blocks from here."

How convenient. It was almost as if *someone* had planted that 911 call as a decoy—before stripping out of my clothes and dousing my hair and chest in sink water.

A momentary conflict flickered across the guy's face, but he knew the priority here. There was a victim out there in imminent danger, and I was standing here perfectly safe, in an armed fortress, with my own team of high-end security.

"I'll call you if I see anything suspicious," I assured.

The cop hesitated for one more moment before looking at my cameras and backing away as he said his goodbyes.

I shut the door, locked it, and watched him drive away on my phone. Before smirking and walking toward the basement stairs.

I'd call the hospital soon to find out how long I had to make Franco Hopkins pay. Would Luna spend the entire night? Or just a few hours?

The night. Let it be the entire night. A few hours wouldn't be nearly enough for what I was about to do to Franco.

Then again, what if that cop came back once he realized the call was a fake? What if he came back with reinforcements? Franco's threat against my life was proving to be a disappointing snag.

I needed to hurry. I hated that I needed to rush, but I'd at least make the asshole die a painful death.

I took off running, up my stairs, through my closet, down the spiral staircase.

And down the long tunnel toward my prey.

CHAPTER 65
Luna

"Thank you," I said.

I hopped out of the car, wincing when my arm swung the door shut, and ran to the front door, grateful I still had my keys. Hunter had given me a set when I essentially moved in here.

I glanced up at the security monitor, wondering if his team was on the other end of that lens, watching me right now. Or was Hunter calling them, screaming he was in danger somewhere else?

Because the scary reality was, if Franco went after Hunter, he would probably take him someplace remote, just like he had taken me to that warehouse. The prospect had haunted me the entire drive here, and I wished I knew where Franco might take Hunter, where else to look.

But desperate and terrified, I proceeded with my original plan to check his house first. After that, I would go to the cottage, and after that, I would head to his office and look for him there myself, because maybe Franco had taken him to a different room in that building. After that, I wasn't sure where I'd look.

Hopefully, he'd turn up before then.

With my body screaming in pain, from both the car accident and all the blows I had sustained from Franco and his men, I walked through the front door and quickly punched in the security code, like Hunter had told me to do when I first stayed here.

I didn't want his security team to rush over here unless we needed them; Hunter might be out there in danger somewhere, so his team needed to be armed and ready to rush to his aid. If the danger was here, I'd activate the alarm with one button.

As soon as I stepped into the great room, my heart sank. I don't know what I expected to find, but there was no trace of Hunter.

No trace of his staff, though, either. Which was weird. I mean yeah, Hunter sometimes sent his staff home, particularly when he and I were having a romantic night, but why weren't they here now?

No sound of footsteps or any indication of life inside these walls.

"Hello?" I called out. "Hunter?"

No response.

My cell phone buzzed with a call.

"Hello?"

"You shouldn't have left the scene." It was Detective Rinaldi's irritated voice.

"No one understands how much danger Hunter might be in."

"Where are you?"

"I just got to his house."

"Luna, we need to finish your statement and take you to a hospital. You could have a concussion, and if something happens to you? All due respect, you're basically the mayor's pet right now, so if anything goes sideways because you left, it could blow back on me."

"All due respect, I don't care about careers right now. I'm not going to the hospital until we find Hunter, so instead of arguing with me about it, help me find him."

She sighed. I doubted she would normally put this much effort into any person who fled a scene, but I was part of the law enforcement community. And we try to protect our own.

Speaking of which.

"You told me a cop was sent to check on Hunter, so why is there no cop here?"

"I...I don't know. Maybe the officer dispatched hasn't arrived yet."

"I took an Uber *without* blue and red lights and beat a cop here?" *I don't think so.*

"I don't know. I'll find out what's going on. Meanwhile, do *not* go inside."

"Too late."

She let out a seriously irritated breath. I bet more frazzled pieces of her bun were evacuating the pins on her head.

"I'm sending another car now," she said. "Leave the house."

"How long will that take?"

"A few minutes at most."

Even though the house was silent, for all I knew, Franco had already come and left, and Hunter might be lying somewhere in here, bleeding out.

I was not about to let him die, not if he was within my grasp by staying.

"I'm going to search the house, so you'd better tell your cop to hurry."

CHAPTER 66

Hunter

I thought I knew rage, but oh, how wrong I was.

This room's stone walls would provide optimal sound to echo his screams, and the musty scent of damp rock would soon be overshadowed by the iron scent of his blood. The cold air underground would be a welcome relief to my body's heat once I got started. Right now, that air drifted over my skin with the icy promise of his demise.

As I stared at the asshole before me, it was as though my fire of anger became so hot, it could incinerate everything in its path.

And, yes, I would incinerate him.

This man deserved a fate worse than death after what he did to Luna.

I clenched my fists and looked over his body, trying to decide how I would begin. I would break every single bone in his body, one by one. I would avoid all major arteries so he wouldn't bleed out too quickly, and I would have to space his pain out so he wouldn't die from shock.

He laid hands on Luna. For that, he'd lose both of his.

He said vile things to her. For that, he'd lose his tongue.

And then...then the real fun would begin. Between breaking each bone—snapping them with my bare hands or a hammer—I'd cut pieces of his flesh off. Inch by inch.

I'd start with sensitive areas, and if he lost consciousness, I would bring him back so I could continue.

Whatever remnants of control I'd had were obliterated. The desire to be cautious was wiped out, too.

The only thing that existed now was me and my villain, staring at the devil himself.

I'm going to enjoy every second of what I'm about to do.

CHAPTER 67

Hunter

"Wake up, you piece of shit."

When I ripped the duct tape off his mouth, Franco Hopkins opened his swollen eyes. It took a few seconds of blinking before his gaze apparently came into focus, his eyes widening in shock.

Yeah, how does it feel, you asshole? Having someone abduct you like you did Luna.

Did he recognize me? Remember me from the trial? Because I was no longer wearing my Vigilante mask. I'd tucked it with my other uniform, if you will, in the far corner behind him.

There was no need to be concerned about him figuring out my identity; he would never live to reveal my secret. And as an added bonus, he'd get to see the pleasure on my face from extracting my own brand of justice as he died a slow, painful death.

Franco's gaze darted around the room, stilling when he saw all the weapons along the far wall.

This son of a bitch thought he had it all figured out with a team of men that hunted Luna down with the intent to slaughter her. He thought he could torture her for information she did not have, but oh, how the tables had turned; he wasn't the predator.

He was the prey.

"*You're* the Vigilante!" Franco spat, undoubtedly remembering it was the Vigilante who'd saved Luna. And now here I stood.

I smiled.

"The fuck do you want?" Franco spat.

I leaned down, so close, that my nose almost touched his. "You proved harder to track down than most of my targets. Color me surprised."

"What are you talking about?"

"You hide," I said, pointing my finger against his forehead. "But I'm better at hide-and-seek than you are."

Look how confused he looks.

"Let me go, you psycho!" he snapped.

I tsked. "Now what fun would that be?" I motioned to the wall of weapons. "We haven't even started yet."

He tried to hide the fear in his eyes, but it delightfully bulged out as he glanced from my toys back to me.

"You're that prosecutor," he realized.

"The speed of your recognition skills needs significant improvement."

Terror crept along his face, and damn if that wasn't as gorgeous as the sun.

"The Windy City Vigilante is a *prosecutor?*" His eyes widened slightly, and his expression tightened into creases of concern. "I won't tell anyone what you did," he said. "Just let me go."

"Tell me, did you let Luna go when she begged for that very same thing?"

I had to clench my fist. The thought of how terrified she must have been was making it damn hard to keep my focus.

His breathing quickened.

"Had you *ever* planned to let her go?" I taunted.

"Absolutely."

"A, that's a lie. And B, even if it wasn't? Your fate was sealed the moment you started to hunt her."

He swallowed.

"And once you took her to that warehouse and started to torture her, well...there went any chance of you dying a quick, painless death."

Interesting. I didn't know a live person could turn that pale. I wonder what other surprises I'll learn about the human body tonight.

"You picked the wrong woman to try to kill. When I'm done with you, the coroner will have to use dental records to identify you."

CHAPTER 68
Luna

I walked into the kitchen, seeing nothing out of order. I did the same in the dining room, and I slowly made my way up the grand staircase.

"Hello?" I called out.

I couldn't put my finger on it, but a sense of dread weighed heavily upon me, as though an invisible, malignant force lurked just out of reach. The atmosphere around me seemed to thicken with each breath, my instincts screaming in protest, urging me to flee.

What if Hunter was already dead?

What if his killer was still in the house, hiding?

Franco wouldn't have had enough time to get here and kill Hunter already, would he? If he did, he would have set off security alarms, and the entire security team would be here right now.

Right?

So, why did I have such an ominous, foreboding warning as I began to search upstairs?

CHAPTER 69

Hunter

"So many tools, so little time. But you know what?" I said as I walked away from my wall of weapons and stood in front of Franco.

"Sometimes, nothing is as satisfying as using your bare hands."

I cracked my fist against his face. My adrenaline soared through my body, and the villain inside me pulsed through my veins like a live wire. I brought my hand back and cracked him again, watching the blood spew from his lip to his shoulder.

Franco glared at me and then spat.

The crimson drops glistened on my chest.

"Well, look at that," I said with a smile. "The first splat of blood on me. Do you know how much blood the human body holds?"

Franco's eyes darted around the room, presumably searching for an escape.

"One and a half gallons," I said. "It'll be interesting to see how slowly I can drain it all from you. Don't want you to go dying on me too quick."

"I have money," Franco said angrily.

I laughed. "You realize you just said that to a billionaire."

He gritted his teeth. "What do you want then?"

"Thought I was clear," I said in a patronizing tone. "I want to make you suffer. But I can't very well go cracking you with my fist repeatedly. That will leave swollen, split knuckles that I won't be able to explain."

I was speaking like a person mulling over the right ingredients for a recipe, thinking it through out loud. Wanting to watch him squirm, torture him mentally. Just as much as physically.

I walked back to my wall of weapons and made a show of trying to choose just the right one. Sadly, I hadn't bought any of these weapons with the intention of torture—if I had, I'd have added much more effective ones than these—but I'd have to make it work.

I did have some interesting options, though. Ones I had purchased for very different reasons, but they could come in handy nonetheless.

For example, I had a medical cauterizing unit. I had purchased it in case I had ever gotten hurt during an attack and couldn't go to the emergency room with an injury the cops knew the Windy City Vigilante had sustained.

Happy to say, I hadn't needed it.

Now, I looked forward to popping its cherry on Franco. I could cut and stop the bleeding at least a few times in the shortened time frame I had to play with.

I smiled as I grabbed it, then set it next to his chair, offering him a wink.

This is much more fun than I thought.

Who knew I'd been missing out on this with all my other victims?

"You'll never get away with this," Franco said. "If you kill me, the police will find my DNA here."

"Well, let's start spreading it around, shall we?"

I pulled a hunter's knife from the wall. Might as well start off with my favorite weapon.

Franco mumbled a string of insults at me, but I couldn't hear them. I was too fixated on his flesh, deciding where to cut first.

I had once read that the abdomen was a very painful place to be shot or stabbed. It was too high of a risk, though. Too many organs I could hit, which would end this before I even got started.

I grabbed the knife and plunged it behind his kneecap, twisting the blade through his screams, until I heard a tendon pop.

CHAPTER 70
Luna

Was that a scream?

It was so muffled, and sounded so far away, that I couldn't be sure it wasn't my imagination. I was standing in the guest bedroom on the top floor of Hunter's mansion, but I swore I just heard a scream. Or was it an animal outside?

The woods surrounding the mansion often had coyotes howling at night.

But it sounded human.

Or was my imagination running wild, twisting everything into a terrifying possibility?

I stood completely still, halting my footsteps so as not to make a sound, and I waited, listening to see if I could hear it again.

CHAPTER 71

Hunter

Franco groaned. He had a mixture of anger, desperation, and fear, all blending together into a smoothie of death.

I stabbed him in his other knee, twisting the blade until I heard another pop.

My therapist once told me to write out my emotions. If only I could tell her that slicing tendons felt far better.

This time, Franco groaned and thrashed around in his chair, as if his anger alone might hold the key to unlock his freedom.

"Here's what I'm thinking," I said. "I'm thinking I start from the bottom and work my way up."

I pushed the blade of the knife beneath the skin of his thigh, choosing an angle one might do if they were trying to skin a fish.

The sound of Franco's screams was enchanting.

If only I could set my ringtone to it.

"Nah," I decided. "I think I'll just go for wherever the spirit takes me."

I twisted the knife before sliding it out of his thigh, tearing a six-inch gash in his leg.

I'd cauterize it in a minute—I wanted him conscious for that, too, but I'd give myself one other thing to cauterize before that happened.

I grabbed his ear and tugged it away from his skull.

"Don't," Franco whined. "Please, man."

My knife tore through the flesh and cartilage with ease, and in one swipe, Franco Hopkins no longer had a left ear.

He screamed, of course, but I tossed his ear to the floor with a splat and walked to the other side. Grabbing his right ear this time.

CHAPTER 72
Luna

T hose were definitely human screams. While muffled and distant, those piercing cries almost sounded like they came from somewhere *inside* this house.

Adrenaline made my fingers tremble as I raced to think of my next move. The smart option would be to run outside and wait for the police to arrive, who were already on their way.

But what if those screams belonged to Hunter?

I redialed the last incoming number from my phone.

"Luna?"

"I hear screaming," I said. "From inside the mansion."

"Luna, get the hell out of there," Detective Rinaldi snapped.

"Tell the cops they have probable cause. To come in armed."

"Luna!"

"Tell them to hurry."

And then I hung up.

I needed to get to one of the security panels, and set off the alarm so Hunter's team would also descend. They had made it to the cottage in fifty seconds, so chances were, they would arrive here faster than the police.

I stepped out into the hallway and looked right, toward the long corridor that would eventually lead to the grand staircase, which would lead to the great room, and then the front foyer. Security panel number one.

Option two, Hunter said he kept another panel in his master bedroom. Which was much closer to the spot where I was currently standing.

With my body aching in protest, I took off running and charged into his bedroom with my heart lodged in my throat, but I didn't see a security panel.

Where was it?

I ran into the master bathroom and flipped on the lights. No panel.

What the hell?

Frustrated, I ran into the master bedroom again and glanced around.

I thought he said he had a second panel in here, but maybe I heard wrong. Was it in a different room? In the hallway maybe? I didn't have time to hunt; I needed to run downstairs, activate the security panel on the first floor, and then look for Hunter.

But just as I was about to leave the bedroom, another scream echoed through the mansion.

Only...this one sounded closer. It sounded like it was coming from behind me.

I turned around, but the only thing behind me was the master closet.

With slow steps, I advanced toward it. It didn't sound close enough to be *inside* the closet, but I was still afraid to surprise a bad guy all the same.

I entered the closet and looked around, but nothing was out of place. There didn't appear to be any kind of scuffle or a break-in of any kind.

So, where the hell had that sound come from?

Another scream ripped through the air, and this time, I could hear exactly which direction it was coming from. The far wall of the closet. I stepped closer to it, confused. Something about it seemed off, though I couldn't put my finger on it. Not at first, at least.

But as I studied it, I realized the shelving unit to the right was out of alignment.

It's a door.

The last time I'd been in here, I hadn't noticed it because everything had been in order and this door was camouflaged to look like a shelf.

Why would someone hide a door like this?

And why is it ajar?

I quickly glanced around the closet one more time and picked up the largest cologne bottle in Hunter's collection to use as a weapon to defend myself. Then, very slowly, I pulled the door open.

CHAPTER 73

Hunter

"There has to be something else you want," Franco pleaded. "You want me to give you evidence that can put some criminals away? I'll get that for you. We can work this out, man."

I never pegged Franco as a crier. Interesting.

"What do you think hurts more? A knife? Or a handsaw?" I wondered aloud, staring at my board of toys. "I'm thinking a saw," I said, picking it up. "Although I don't really know for sure. Maybe you can compare. Tell me."

His bloody lips tightened.

"You'll rot in prison for the rest of your life!" Franco's words came out in a rush as I brought the blade to the back of his ankle. He tried to thrash around, to knock me out of alignment, but I had his legs firmly taped to the chair. His torso, his arms bound behind his back, just as he had done to Luna.

"I don't know how much blood this will draw," I mused. "But I do know that you can't run once I cut your Achilles heel."

"Wait!" His voice cracked into tears. "That chick you rescued—I'm not the only one after her."

"I know that, you piece of shit. But once you're dead, I'll hang what's left of your body in public sight, so your army of hit men knows they won't get paid. Hit men don't work for free."

"That's not what I mean! Some dude hired me to take her out."

I smirked. "It's pathetic, the lies people come up with to try to save themselves. You've been threatening Luna because of evidence you thought Dominic had. Not because some unnamed guy hired you to do it. Next time you want to change your story, try coming up with something more believable."

"I'm not lying! I *was* trying to find Luna and what evidence she had against me. But then this dude showed up when he learned I was trying to go after her."

"How convenient."

"The dude was, like, really upset about a case she was reopening or something. He said he couldn't allow that to happen, so he gave me money to make *sure* I took her out, because he didn't think some letter did the trick."

Letter...

"That's why I put the bounty on her head—I'd share the guy's money with whoever got to her first. I was gonna..."

Based on the widening of his eyes, he was about to say he was going to kill her anyway, so why not take the payout? But clearly, he realized that saying this to a man who was torturing him for hurting said woman was an unwise move.

"Anyway, I figured, you know, we have mutual interests or whatever, so I took his money. But if you kill me? That dude is still out there. And if he knows how to get in touch with people like me, he'll just hire other people to do the job.

"So, if you want to take the head of the snake off? You got the wrong snake."

I ground my teeth. I didn't want to believe him—what were the odds someone else was still out there, hunting Luna?

Who was I kidding? Luna was a murder magnet. The odds were very fucking high.

Still, Franco could be trying to play me.

But how did Franco know about the threatening letter sent to

Luna? The one my PI couldn't track its source. The one who wanted her father's case dropped. Outside of the police, there were only three people who knew about that letter: me, Luna, and Barry.

Franco Hopkins was going to start talking. Fast.

I'd find out if he was lying, and if he wasn't, I'd get to the bottom of who sent that letter and find out why they were prepared to kill Luna just to end her quest to reopen her father's case.

CHAPTER 74

Luna

Inside the room that was hidden within Hunter's main closet was another closet of sorts, and just as strangely, located on the far side of that wall, was another concealed door. Also ajar.

The heavy wooden panel creaked open, revealing a desolate space where a smattering of dust particles swirled lazily in the meager light. An unsettling chill raised goose bumps on my skin as I grabbed the cold iron banister of a spiral staircase that corkscrewed downward into an abyss of blackness.

A slight amber glow at the bottom revealed the steps went roughly three stories down.

The quietness hanging heavy in the air was not the tranquil silence of peaceful solitude; it was the eerie hush of a crypt, where rumbles of distant voices once again echoed up the chamber.

I couldn't make out what they were saying, but there were two different voices for sure.

With needles stabbing my veins from adrenaline, I clutched the cologne bottle and started walking down the steps as quietly as possible. Trying to conceal my presence from the guy who was hurting Hunter.

CHAPTER 75

Hunter

I drew my blade to his jugular this time.

"You'd better start talking."

Franco's chest heaved up and down as he stared at me, likely calculating his next move.

"If I tell you, you let me go."

Not a chance. "Sure."

He gritted his teeth. "You're lying."

"What's the man's name?"

"I'm not saying a word until *after* you let me go."

Well, this was a damn pickle, now wasn't it? I guess I would have to torture Franco Hopkins slower than I intended; the dude already had two torn ACLs and two missing ears. Apparently, that wasn't motivation enough.

"Name." I pointed the blade to his throat.

He tilted his face to give me better access. "Go ahead. I die? So does the information that could save her."

CHAPTER 76

Luna

M y hand would not stop shaking. But just as I reached the last step, the men's voices suddenly became much clearer. They were coming from the end of a tunnel that sat at the base of the staircase.

The faint amber glow of lamps struggled against the repressive gloom, their light dancing off the rough stone walls and floor. The chilly air was heavy with the scent of damp, saturated earth, a grimy aroma that clung to my nostrils and made me shiver.

My heart pounded a frantic rhythm in my chest as I tiptoed carefully, making sure my footsteps were as silent as a mouse's whisper. I clutched my makeshift weapon tighter, the cold perspiration on my palms making the grip slippery as I walked ever so slowly through the ominous corridor, fully prepared to take on whoever was hurting my boyfriend.

I would save Hunter or die trying.

I kept walking through my panic, kept allowing the voices to grow louder, as a light grew brighter, the closer I got. The tunnel had to be a hundred feet long—an eternity when walking as quickly as possible, yet having to go slow enough to stay silent.

I rounded the corner and froze.

The scene before me was far more horrific and shocking than I could've imagined. I couldn't wrap my head around what I was witnessing, because the picture before my eyes was so warped and twisted and unreal that my mind struggled to process it.

A man was sitting in a chair, bloodied. His ears were missing, blood seeping down his neck, while another man stood over him with a knife to his throat.

But the positions were wrong.

The person in the chair was Franco Hopkins. And the man holding the knife was Hunter.

Franco must've come here and attacked Hunter, and Hunter fought back and gained the upper hand. Taping Franco to the chair and retaliating against him.

But just when the faintest whisper of relief escaped my lungs, my gaze roamed around the room, and a fresh wave of dread crept into my blood.

This room…it was far from ordinary.

Nestled in the depths of a concealed basement, attached to the main mansion, hidden in the shadows from the rest of the world, this stone room was carved into the earth with the purpose of being obscured. Along the far wall, an unnerving array of weapons and knives had been meticulously arranged.

The same type of knives the Windy City Vigilante used.

And there, discarded on the cold, unforgiving floor—in the far corner behind Franco—was the Vigilante's unmistakable garb. The black shirt, the distinctive mask, the combat boots—all silently screaming the truth upon which I had stumbled.

Within mere moments, my eyes darted around the room again, unveiling each clue like a deck of cards—one laid down on top of the other—until the evidence proved to be as sickening as it was indisputable.

I was standing in the lair of the most dangerous person in the country.

The Windy City Vigilante, previously shrouded in enigma, stood within the space, clothed in his customary black pants. Yet his chest lay bare, and his face—now unmasked—was clearly exposed, visible to me for the first time.

As realization dawned upon me with an ominous and suffocating intensity, my heart shattered into a million pieces.

His blue eyes suddenly locked on mine, a mixture of shock and anger radiating through them, as he held a knife dripping with fresh blood.

"Hunter?" My voice, a fragile whisper, betrayed the depths of my heartbreak.

The shock sent a tremor through my entire body, faltering my grip on the weapon I had been clutching so desperately, causing it to slip from my trembling fingers. It tumbled to the floor, shattering into fragments that mirrored my own fractured heart.

The impact was jarring, the sound of splintering glass reverberating through the room, sounding like a scream in the silence, and with it, an intense musk scent overpowered the smell of damp earth.

The suspense hung thick in the air, each moment stretched out like an eternity, as I struggled to reconcile the truth with the person standing before me. The emotional storm raging within me threatened to consume me, casting an oppressive darkness over everything I thought I knew.

Hunter was the Windy City Vigilante.

He had ruthlessly hunted down and killed all those men. He had taken Dominic's life. Hunter was a serial killer, a monstrous being who brutally slit his victims' throats.

As shocking as this was, another chilling thought seared its way into my consciousness: I had unwittingly stumbled upon the identity of a killer who had always maintained his anonymity—presumably by ensuring that anyone who discovered his secret had not lived to tell the tale.

The terrifying realization threatened to crush me beneath its weight, and the icy tendrils of fear wound their way around my heart, squeezing tighter with each passing second.

Beneath the man who had showered me with love lived a merciless killer who now stalked toward me.

Bloody knife in hand, he said...

"You shouldn't have come down here."

Thank you for reading SECRET VENDETTA! Don't miss the heart-stopping, jaw-dropping conclusion of Hunter and Luna's story. **One-click SILENT VENDETTA now.**

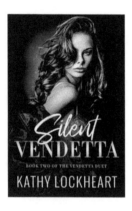

LUNA

I just uncovered the secret identity of the Vigilante. Now, he holds me prisoner in his vault of vengeance. And nothing is as it seems.

Bound in this abyss of secrets and darkness, I ache for Hunter's warmth and light. And vow to reclaim my freedom.

But how does one escape......being the obsession of a killer?

VIGILANTE

The monster inside of me always hungered for death. But it became unhinged when men stole her from me. I savored torturing them, ending their lives with my serrated blade of justice.

I long for her to see the crimson on my hands as a stain of honor, and to convince myself I'm worthy of something other than her disgust.

But what if she doesn't embrace my darkness? What if she becomes its most tragic casualty?

One-click SILENT VENDETTA now!

Don't miss my stand-alone Enemies-to-Lovers Romance, **FATAL CURE**, which has the same touch-her-and-perish vibes.

I had no idea that the criminal kingpin I've been hunting, the one I vowed to make pay for decimating my family, is the man I've fallen in love with...

Dillon has a lot of enemies that would hurt anyone he cares about if he makes a mistake. And falling in love with a DEA agent? Is as big as they get.

Now, we're a target of the world's most dangerous criminals. Our only hope to survive is to work together. But time is running out...

⭐⭐⭐⭐⭐ *"One of the BEST books I've EVER read!"*

One-click FATAL CURE now!

Finally, I'd love for you to join my VIP TEAM! Sign up here: https://kathylockheart.com/join-my-vip-team/

Acknowledgments

First, **I'd like to thank you, the reader.** You have a ton of options when it comes to books, your time is incredibly precious, and you gave *me* a chance. From the bottom of my heart, THANK YOU. Readers mean the world to me, and I'd love to connect with you! Please find my social media links at www.KathyLockheart.com.

Thank you to Susan Staudinger. Your developmental and content editing, combining with our amazing virtual sessions made this book far better than it ever would have been without you.

To Amy and Kristen, my formal beta readers. Thank you for helping make this story even better.

To Valentine and the entire staff at Valentine PR! It's been a dream to become one of your clients, and this book wouldn't be what it is without you. Thank you!

Thank you to my husband for showing me the beauty of true love and being my biggest cheerleader. Thank you to my children for giving me a love I didn't know existed until you were born and for inspiring me to be the best *me* I can be. Always go after your dreams.

To my family for enveloping me with love, encouraging me, and embracing my idea to become a writer.

To my friends, for your never-ending support.

To my editor Jovana, your attention to details polished this story and made it the best it could be! To my cover artists, Hang Le, and Sherri with Wild Love Designs, for bringing such beauty to this novel!

To all the authors who came before me—your success paves the road for new writers to do what they love. Thank you.

~ Kathy

Let's connect!

The easiest way to connect with me is to go to my website, www. KathyLockheart.com, and find my social media links. I interact with readers, so don't be surprised if you see me reply to your post or invite you to join a reader team!

Xoxo

Kathy

a amazon.com/Kathy-Lockheart/e/B08XY5F2XG
BB bookbub.com/profile/kathy-lockheart
f facebook.com/KathyLockheartAuthor
d tiktok.com/@kathylockheart_author
o instagram.com/kathy_lockheart
y twitter.com/Kathy_Lockheart
p pinterest.com/kathylockheart

Milton Keynes UK
Ingram Content Group UK Ltd.
UKHW010856211223
434780UK00005B/315